THE GOVERNOR'S LADIES

THE GOVERNOR'S LADIES

Deryn Lake

LARGE PRINT
Oxford

First published in Great Britain 2005
by
Allison & Busby Ltd.

Published in Large Print 2007 by ISIS Publishing Ltd.,
7 Centremead, Osney Mead, Oxford OX2 0ES
by arrangement with
Allison & Busby Ltd.

British Library Cataloguing in Publication Data
Lake, Deryn
    The governor's ladies. – Large print ed.
    1. Governors – Massachusetts – Fiction
    2. Women slaves – Massachusetts – Fiction
    3. Boston (Mass.) – History – Revolution,
    1775–1783 – Fiction
    4. Historical fiction
    5. Large type books
    I. Title
    823.9'14 [F]

ISBN 978–0–7531–7782–2 (hb)
ISBN 978–0–7531–7783–9 (pb)

Printed and bound in Great Britain by
T. J. International Ltd., Padstow, Cornwall

For Mark Dunton — star archivist,
and for Judy Flower — star astrologer.

Acknowledgements

As always a great many people to thank, the first of which must be Nancy Richard from the Boston Historical Society, who was so warm and friendly and gave me access to many fascinating documents, all of which I photocopied and brought back to England. Secondly were the staff of the Massachusetts Historical Society, in whose building I discovered the Indian weathervane that once used to stand on the cupola of Province House. Thirdly comes Mark Dunton who accompanied me to Boston and was, as ever, his usual charming, cheery self. Finally I must thank my editor, David Shelley, who went through the book with a fine toothcomb, and my agent, Vanessa Holt. Lastly comes Anastasia Hackett, wherever she might be now, who gave me the original idea. I hope this book is worthy of them.

Prologue

April 18th, 1775

He sat in the dimness, not a candle lit in the room, watching the moon rise through the window; at last putting an end to that terrible and frantic day. The moonlight made a path to his feet and he noticed, almost absent-mindedly, that it was reflecting in the silver buckles of his best shoes. Why, he found himself thinking, had he bothered to put them on? Why, on this night of all nights, when the future of the country that he loved so well lay in the most almighty jeopardy, had he bothered to change from his sensible boots and don his fancy footwear. But he was aware of the answer without thinking further. It was because he was to see her within the hour, risking her future to get the information he so desperately needed. For she would know the final details, that much he was certain of. She would be able to provide the missing part of the jigsaw.

He pictured her as he sat in the moonshine, turning his feet this way and that so that his buckles reflected a million diamond shafts. Saw in his mind's eye her dark hair, full of light despite its midnight shade, the luminous, almost transparent, quality of her skin. Above all, though, he pictured her eyes: their dreamy dark amber in which a man could lose himself and

drown. These were the reasons why he, the most practical yet visionary of men, had changed his clothes. Because, in her presence, he must always attempt to look his best.

Shaking his head at his own vulnerability, Dr. Joseph Warren stood up and crossed to gaze at himself in the gilt-edged overmantel mirror, an elegant piece given to him at the time of his wedding to his frail young bride, only a few sad years ago. The glass was full of moonlight, dazzling him, but still a grey image of himself gazed back. He looked a little mad, Joseph thought, light blue eyes staring and tie wig askew. He straightened it, fingered his cravat like an anxious suitor, then went to sit down again, still as a statue in the shadows, thinking of the momentous times that lay ahead and the part in them that it was his destiny to play.

He had risen early, as had many others of that nervous town's inhabitants, but this day he had not worked, cancelling patients so that his appointment book had become empty, and he had been free to use his office as a clearing house for information. There he had received messages and rumours of such an alarming nature that, at noon, he had gone to the harbour to take a look for himself. He had strolled there with nonchalance in his very gait, not wishing to draw attention to the fact that he was out and about. For his was a well-known face, that of a marked troublemaker, of that most dangerous of things, an intellectual free thinker.

At the waterfront there had been a great deal to observe. It seemed to Joseph, watching closely, that the

British must have been active all morning long, though the word British was a misnomer as far as he was concerned. *He* was British, as were all the people of Massachusetts. It was the troops sent from London, even the Governor himself, who were the interlopers.

Leaning on a mooring bollard, his hat shielding his face, Joseph had stared out over the water. Moored in the harbour were the towering warships HMS *Somerset* and HMS *Boyne*. From them, distinctly audible on the flirty April breeze, came the thin whistle of boatswains' pipes, while sailors bustled about the longboats moored beneath the great ships' mighty salt-stained sterns. If ever there had been a scene of preparation, Joseph thought, this was indeed it. The Regulars were getting ready for some kind of action. The question was, what exactly?

He had shifted position slightly, his light blue gaze taking in the Long Wharf. A great many Redcoat officers were striding about and the observer noticed that a knot of them had gathered on the far end, the part of the jetty that extended right out into the water of Massachusetts Bay. Dr. Joseph Warren smiled ironically. It was the one place in town where they would be totally out of earshot, away from those damned inquisitive Yankees, as the Regulars thought of them. The very fact that the officers had chosen to meet there indicated quite clearly that a game of enormous magnitude was afoot. Grim-faced, the physician had turned and walked slowly homeward.

As the day progressed, the town of Boston had reached boiling point. During the afternoon sailors had come

ashore, ostensibly to run errands, but in reality to visit the taverns and the whores. Their careless talk only confirmed what the inhabitants had already guessed: that the boats had been ordered to stand by in readiness. Joseph, sitting in his office, had received nothing but visits and messages from fellow members of the Long Room Club, the secret society which flourished as an inner wheel of the Whig movement in Boston. But not only they had called. Ordinary folk, knowing his position as a declared revolutionary, had come to see him, expressing their alarm and agitation. The hostile preparations taking place had sent a frisson of fear throughout the entire township.

Finally, Paul Revere, the silversmith and avowed patriot, had come through the door, his broad, stocky frame momentarily blotting out the light before he had hurled himself into a chair. He had regarded Warren from beneath the high arched brows which gave him a permanently quizzical expression.

"What are they up to?" he had said briefly.

"They are clearly going on the offensive," Joseph had answered, stating the obvious.

"Yes. But where, how, and what for?"

"God alone knows that."

Revere had barked a laugh. "God and your highly placed informant, no doubt."

"Even they might not know."

The silversmith had shaken his dark head. "They? There's only one God and one spy close to the high command. Are you referring to both of them?"

"Of course not."

"In other words your choice of the plural noun is an attempt not to reveal whether your informant is male or female."

"This is old ground, Paul. You know I am sworn to silence. You won't prise it out of me."

"Not even in circumstances as grim as these?"

"Not now, not ever. It is a trust I will never betray. Now leave the subject alone, I beg you. It is a secret that will go with me to the grave."

Even saying the words made him shiver suddenly.

The fleshy face of Joseph's visitor broke into a broad grin. "Have it your own way. But let me say this much. You must meet with your spy, whoever he might be. It is essential that we know what is going on."

The doctor had nodded solemnly. "I realise that."

"Have you sent a message already?"

"No, I hesitate on the brink. They would be putting themselves in such grave danger."

Revere had sprung lightly to his feet, moving swiftly for a man growing heavy. "You make it sound as if it is the Governor himself."

"Perhaps it is," Joseph answered and laughed without any humour at all.

After Paul Revere had left, the physician had finally made his decision. He must arrange to meet her. In the present uncertainty it was imperative he use every means at his disposal to discover the plans of the enemy. Reluctant though he was to place her in such peril, he had no option. Slowly and deliberately, as if he

were tolling a funeral knell, the doctor had rung the bell on his desk.

His Negro slave, Jacob, had answered almost immediately, his dark face so intent that Joseph wondered whether the servant had guessed already why he had been called.

"You want me, master?"

"Yes. Jake, you must go to the lady. You know who I mean, don't you?"

"Yes, master."

"Make your way to the tradesman's entrance and give this note to her maid. Say it must be placed in the lady's hand and hers alone; tell the maid those are your orders or you will be whipped."

"Yes, master."

As he had been speaking, the doctor had been writing, putting the address of a well-known glove maker at the top of the paper, together with the date, April 18, 1775. The message had been short and simple.

"Your gloves are now ready for your approval, and we would appreciate that you call at our shop at nine-thirty or thereabouts."

They had worked out this simple code between them long ago, half jestingly deciding on the wording that would bring her to him when the need was sufficiently desperate. Joseph had always hoped that he would never be forced to use it, having made the mistake of falling madly in love with the spy to whom he attached the greatest importance of all. But now the situation

was too critical, the tension in Boston too overpowering, for him to hesitate longer. With a sigh, the doctor handed the slave the sealed piece of paper.

"You're to run, Jacob. Go like the wind. But be calm when you get there. Don't draw attention to yourself."

Jake rolled his large dark eyes. "Should I put on my livery, master?"

"No. Go as you are. If anyone asks where you have come from, you work for Quincy the glove maker. Do you understand?"

The Negro nodded. "Yes, master."

Then he had left, his long-limbed body moving as swiftly as only one of his ancestry could. Watching him disappear down the street, Joseph had prayed that the message would get through, that nothing would stop the slave in his tracks. There were Regulars and sailors everywhere, but why should a fast-moving black man attract particular attention? Unless fate were going to play a cruel trick on them all.

By the time Jacob returned, breathless and in a sorry state, the doctor had changed his clothes and washed himself. Then he sat in his chair and watched his buckles wink and gleam in the path of moonlight until the black man, gasping but triumphant, had come to his room.

"Well?" Joseph had said shortly.

"Yes, I done well, master. I delivered the letter into the maid's hands, directly so."

"And?"

"And nothin', master. I turned round and come away."

It had been too much to hope that she would answer immediately, but still Joseph experienced a slight thrill of disappointment.

Jacob looked at the floor. "Did you want me to wait, Sir?"

The doctor shook his head and stood up. "No, Jake, you did right to leave and not hang around. Go to the kitchen and have your supper. I'm going out now."

"Very good, master."

With the slave gone, the doctor took one last look round his room in case he never saw it again, then putting on his hat and cloak he left swiftly, hurrying through the dark streets of Boston, aware of the atmosphere of danger which accompanied his every step.

The stables were dark, the only illumination being two candles in tin holders which stood at either end beneath the windows, throwing a meagre light. He had crept through the hedge at the back of the house's outbuildings, terrified lest he should be spotted in the bright moonlight. But nobody had challenged him, even though at the main entrance to the building two soldiers, formally dressed, paraded night and day. But for all that Joseph hung back, waiting a good few moments in the shadow of the coach house, until he cautiously approached the stables and, slipping back the huge wooden latch, entered.

Immediately the smell of horseflesh assailed his nostrils, that and the stamp and whinny of beasts as

they settled for the night. Muttering softly under his breath, Joseph entered the loose box that contained the mount of the Governor's wife. She was a mettlesome black mare who banged her feet on the ground as he went in, but he continued to talk soothingly and eventually she quietened and went back to munching softly.

Then two things happened simultaneously. He heard the heavy latch rise, then quietly be placed back, and the heady scent of hyacinths suddenly filled the air. She had come to him.

"Here," he called, his voice scarcely above a whisper.

There was a movement, a rustling, as she quietly traversed the distance between them, and then her cloaked figure appeared in the entrance.

"You've come," he said in wonderment, then drew her into the shadows to stand beside him.

She glanced round swiftly. "You mustn't stay long. The place is crawling with soldiers."

Her great amber eyes were staring at him so earnestly that for a few moments he was rendered absolutely speechless.

"Besides I might be missed. I'm supposed to be getting ready for bed," she added.

The doctor recovered himself slightly, gasping, "You have put yourself in the gravest danger. How can I thank you?"

"By telling me what you want to know," she said, then suddenly smiled. "That came out more abruptly than I meant. Forgive me."

"No, you're right. The Regulars are on the move, aren't they? Where are they going?"

She leant towards him, her perfume filling the air between them, then suddenly she froze. The latch on the stable door had lifted once more. Pulling him downwards she and the doctor crouched side by side in the shadows, not saying a word.

Somebody unknown had entered the stables and was walking slowly from loose box to loose box, peering inside each one. The same somebody was also whistling tunelessly and very softly to himself.

She laid a finger over her lips to indicate absolute silence. Joseph became terribly aware that she was just inches away from him and found himself considering the link between danger and the heightening of sexual tension. However, she remained totally unaware of his thoughts and stayed quiet, listening to the stranger's movements. A mouse scuttled in the darkness, only a few inches from where they lay hidden.

"Who's there?" called a voice.

It was a stable lad, that much was obvious from his tone, and Joseph felt her give an inaudible sigh of relief. But for all that she pulled him into the deepest shadows and not a moment too soon. A lanthorn flashed in the loosebox doorway, and the intruder was upon them.

"Who's there?" he said again.

With one final concealing push at the doctor she stepped into the lanthorn light.

"Good evening, Dick," she said.

The boy jumped so violently that he almost dropped his light. "Oh, it's you, Madam," he stuttered. "I wasn't expecting you to be here."

"I came to look at my mare. I think she was a little off colour today. In fact I'm going to sit with her for a half hour."

Dick regained courage. "Oh, there's no need for that, Madam. That's my job. I'll see to her."

She smiled beautifully. "No, though I do thank you for the offer. You finish your rounds, and I'll just stay here a while. I'll be perfectly all right."

"Are you sure, Madam? It's no trouble to me."

"I'm certain of it. Animals are just like people, you know. When they are not well they like to have their own close at hand."

Dick bowed stubbily. "Very well, Madam. Goodnight."

"Goodnight."

He moved away, rather slowly Joseph thought, and after what seemed like an eternity they heard him raise the stable latch and go out. The physician stepped out of the shadows.

"I can't stay here any longer," she whispered. "He might raise the alarm. Listen, the march is tonight. They're going to Concord to burn the ammunition stores, and Lexington to arrest Adams and Hancock."

"Are they travelling by land or by sea?"

"Sea."

He cupped her face in his hands. "The warnings will go out this very night. We'll be waiting for them, never fear."

She smiled faintly but her gorgeous eyes were dark and troubled.

"I beg you to feel no guilt," Joseph added.

The spy he loved shook her head. "I'm afraid you have asked the impossible. I shall bear this burden till the day I die."

"Let me shoulder the responsibility. Blame me for forcing your hand."

His informant shook her head. "I'm sorry, Joseph, that excuse won't do."

"What can I say?" he answered helplessly.

Then all propriety, all decorousness, all standards of good behaviour and etiquette, flew out of the window in one brief and wonderful moment. Bending his head, Joseph Warren did what he had been wanting to do all day. He kissed her full on the lips, his intense love for her heightened to breaking point by the crisis in which they found themselves.

Just for a fraction of a second she melted against him, then she drew back, not in disgust or anger, but because she must.

"Goodbye, Joseph," she whispered.

"Have I offended you?"

"You could never do that. Now hurry. There's much to be done this night."

"It shall be as you say," he answered solemnly, and bowed to her before slipping out into the dangerous darkness and taking what action he must to start the great struggle for independence.

12

PART ONE — MARGARET

CHAPTER
ONE

Christmas, 1756

It had not been an easy journey. The stage coach had departed on its three day trip to New York in reasonably good weather, but by the time the horses had negotiated the horse ferry, situated at the most southerly point of Manhattan Island, it had started to snow. Thomas Gage, a moderately tall man who had not enjoyed the cramped conditions in which he travelled, made this an excuse to rise to his feet. Apologising to a small, nervous lady into whose virginal lap he had almost fallen as the coach jolted over the track leading from the docks, he stuck his head out of the window and announced cheerfully, "It'll be a blizzard soon. I've seen this kind of weather before."

His friend and travelling companion, Robert Hunter Morris, looked up from the two-day-old newspaper he was studying. "The eternal optimist as ever," he replied drily, smiling to himself at the extreme Englishness of Tom's accent, which contrasted so vividly with his own Philadelphian tones.

Tom sat down again, carefully avoiding the spinster, who was now regarding him with something of an uneasy interest, her gaze wandering over his well-cut military uniform and the highly trained body it clothed.

Gage, feeling her eyes upon him, gave a bow from the waist which made her grow pale, purse her lips and look rapidly away. Robert grinned more than ever and announced to the assembled company, "Just ignore my friend. He's an eccentric Englishman."

Most of the other occupants of the coach's interior — for further unfortunate passengers were travelling on the roof — nodded at this and even smiled a little. After all, it was Christmas, and the year was 1756. Though there were murmured complaints about the Parliament and King George II who tried to rule them from London, the colonists were pleased in the main with the way their new and exciting country was developing.

A merchant returning to his home in New York eyed Tom reflectively. "My father hailed from England. Where were you born?"

"In Sussex. Was he also?"

"No, in Devon. Is that close by?"

"I'm afraid not," Tom answered, straight-faced.

"Ah."

The merchant relapsed into silence, then a voice spoke from the corner. "Are you by any chance Colonel Thomas Gage, Sir?"

"That's correct," Tom answered, peering in the direction of a bundle wrapped in a black cloak that had joined them at the last coaching stop and so far on this leg of the journey had not revealed whether it was even conscious. "Have we met?"

"No, Sir," the bundle replied, "but I too am English. Rupert Germain. You were at Westminster with my

16

brother, Lord George. He has a sketch of you at home."
The bundle stretched and revealed itself as a pale
young man with no wig and over-long fair hair.

"My dear friend," said Tom, giving another bow from
his cramped position, "I'm delighted to meet you.
George and I were close friends."

"So he told me. A small world, is it not?" Rupert
answered, returning the salutation.

"Very. So what are you doing making your way to
New York City?"

"I have friends there and am to spend Christmas
with them. I've just come down from Oxford and
thought I'd try to make my way in the Colonies.
Younger son and all that."

"Have you considered the army?"

"I have considered and rejected. I'm far too puny for
any such venture."

"Let us speak of it another time," Tom answered.
"Where will you be staying?"

"With some cousins of mine, name of O'Rourke. The
Irish side of the family. And you?"

"With my cousins, the Peacocks," put in Robert. "We
shall probably run into you. Everyone knows everyone
in New York's small community."

"If they have money," said the merchant, sombrely.

"That's certainly true," added his wife. "But the poor
know one another as well. They have a strong sense of
fellowship."

"We're all colonists, Mam. Rich and poor alike," the
spinster said meekly.

"Well voiced, Madam," Robert answered. "I'd like to think that the American territories are breeding a nation of equals."

"I doubt there could ever be such a thing," said Tom thoughtfully.

"You're a cynic," replied his friend.

"Not at all, just a realist."

They lapsed into silence, watching the dense swirl of snowflakes. The carriage had left the docks behind it and was currently making its way up Broad Street when it suddenly lurched to a stop at the corner of Mill Street, dominated by a huge mill. The spinster stood up, looking apologetic.

"By prior arrangement," she announced to the assembled company. "I live here with my brother. We were both born in this house," she added with a touch of pride.

Tom lowered the window and putting his arm through, opened the door. "Allow me to escort you, Madam."

"I'll carry your luggage," said Rupert Germain, rising to his feet.

She looked almost girlish. "How nice to be attended by two English gentlemen."

"A pleasure," answered Tom, and jumping down into the snowstorm, lifted her out of the coach, placing her on her feet and escorting her to her door before bowing and returning to his seat.

Some twenty minutes later the coach had reached its final destination and was depositing its passengers at

the coaching inn in Broad Way. A small black carriage was drawn up outside its doors awaiting Rupert Germain, and a slightly larger, grander equipage for the other two men. The merchant and his wife, who clearly lived very close by, were met by a bevy of black slaves who hoisted their luggage onto their backs and set off through the snow. The passengers who had travelled on the roof staggered into the hostelry in a body to warm themselves before proceeding to their final destinations.

Rupert, looking very pale and slender in the white surroundings, shivered in the depths of his dark cloak.

"Gentlemen, farewell. No doubt we shall meet again."

"No doubt," said Robert Hunter Morris. "I take it you have been invited to the Van Cortlandts' Christmas Eve Assembly? The whole of town seems to be going."

"My cousins wrote to me that my name was on the guest list."

"Then we shall see you there."

"I look forward to it." Rupert turned to Tom Gage and bowed very low. "It has been a pleasure to meet you, Colonel. George speaks of you often and with great affection. Your servant, Sir."

With that he climbed into the waiting carriage and was gone, waving a pale hand which he rapidly withdrew because of the freezing conditions.

"A bit of a lily, that one," said Robert, watching him depart.

"Probably, but likeable for all that."

"I've nothing against them as long as they leave me alone."

19

"Now you sound like my father," said Tom, and chuckled. "When you've been in the army as long as I have, you learn to accept everyone. If you fight and pee alongside 'em, you've very little choice in the matter."

"I might add that in my experience being the head man also brings you in touch with humanity in all its glory."

"I thought you didn't want that mentioned, that you were travelling incognito."

"So I am," answered the handsome and brilliant Governor of Pennsylvania as he stepped into the coach that awaited them.

Though New York City was very far from large, it had several fine buildings to its credit; a city hall, a library and the beautiful Trinity Church being amongst the most imposing. At the other end of the scale to these gracious structures lay the darker side of the new developments; the public slave market where human beings were auctioned off like so many cowering cattle. Thomas, like many others of his time, was ambivalent about the slave trade, considering it part of normal living. However, he at least treated black people with a gruff politeness, addressing them by their names, that is if he had made the effort to discover what they were called.

But tonight, Christmas Eve, nothing could have been farther from his thoughts as he settled back in the coach, once again in the company of Robert Hunter Morris, this time heading for the Van Cortlandts' vast estate which lay close to the Hudson River.

He was in an odd mood, half homesick, half longing to put the past behind him. Two years earlier, in the autumn of 1754, he had sailed for England's American Colonies with his regiment, their purpose to fight the French who had started sniping once more at British forces scouting in the interior. But he had left behind more than his country of birth when the ship slipped out of harbour. Tom Gage had been convinced that he also left in England his heart, buried in the grave of his fragile, enchanting mistress, who had been snatched from his arms by a tragic and untimely death.

Yet, it seemed to him, and he acknowledged the fact with a certain reluctance, that, at last, time, the great healer, was at work. For Tom had started noticing women again, indeed was ready, though even to admit it to himself seemed disloyal, for a love affair. Sexual needs were, of course, catered for by the host of women, some of considerable rank and fortune, who followed the army wherever it went. Yet these feelings were different. The Colonel was ready to be swept off his feet and fall in love once more.

"You're very quiet," said the Governor of Pennsylvania with such a knowing air that Tom thought for one disconcerting moment that he must have spoken his thoughts out loud.

"I'm sorry. I was preoccupied."

"Well, come back to earth. We'll soon be there, and you will be one of the main attractions. There's nothing like an English aristocrat to boost a hostess's guest list."

"Oh, come now. I'm hardly that."

"Your brother is a Viscount, and these rich Dutch settlers adore a representative of the old British order."

"Now you're making me nervous."

"You? The most elegant man in the army? And don't pretend you don't know it."

Robert's flat Philadelphian tones were starting to make the Colonel smile even without the content of his words.

"My dear chap, you are overdoing it."

The Governor pealed with mirth and slapped his thigh. "Say that to them, just like that, they'll love it. Your accent is preposterously wonderful."

"Are you laughing at me?"

"Of course I am. You're so delightfully old school."

"That young man in the coach was the same."

"He'll be as big a draw as yourself, mark my words. Now brace up and straighten that amazing red uniform of yours. There are going to be some beautiful women there tonight."

Despite himself, Tom felt his interest quicken. "Oh?" he said nonchalantly.

The Governor grinned. "Believe me, the wealthy Dutch spend a fortune on their daughters: gowns, friseurs, jewels, everything. Even the ugly ones contrive to look lovely."

"All this in order to marry more money I take it?"

"That or an English title."

Tom chuckled in the darkness of the coach's interior. "Then I'll hardly qualify."

"Nonsense. You are very well connected."

"If you say so," answered the Colonel, pleased despite himself.

They had left Manhattan or New York Island — that long, thin, streak of a place — by way of the King's Bridge, a stout wooden construction built near Blue Bell Head, on the island's most northerly tip. Now they plunged through forests, making their way along the valley beside Tetards Hill, to where, close to a place called Younker, lay the Van Cortlandts' mighty estate. Turning in through the biggest set of gates he had ever seen, Tom reckoned they travelled another four miles before the house came into view.

It was enormous, a great pillared spread almost twice the size of Firle Place. In fact, the Colonel found himself gaping like a child at the sheer enormity of the building.

"Impressed?" asked Hunter Morris.

"Very much so," Tom answered. "These people must be as rich as Croesus."

"Oh, they are," his companion answered seriously.

Within, the house was equally grand; suites of rooms leading on all sides from a central entrance hall of vast proportions. At the end of this hall rose a magnificent staircase which branched into two at the top. And there, bedecked and bedazzling, stood the family, graciously receiving their guests. Somewhat over-awed, Thomas Gage joined the queue of people slowly ascending the stairs, Robert Hunter Morris beside him.

"My dear Governor," gushed a woman standing just in front of them. "What a pleasure to see you again. What brings you to New York, pray?"

"I'm here for the festivities, Ma'am. And yourself?"

"Likewise. We came in from Philadelphia last week. We're staying with our cousins, the Schuylers."

Thinking that rather like the English aristocracy all the colonists seemed to be related, Tom bowed and introduced himself.

"Thomas Gage, at your service, Madam."

She regarded him appreciatively for a moment before dropping a polite curtsey. "Mrs. Van Heffler, Mr. Gage. Allow me to present my husband."

Mr. Van Heffler bowed and made a gruff noise of greeting. He had very short legs and looked rather like a little fat dog begging. To make his appearance even odder, his face was disproportionately large and heavily dewlapped. Small, suspicious eyes gazed over his pudding cheeks, while his jowls swung, occasionally slapping one another as he moved.

"Sarvant, Sah," he said.

Tom bowed. "How dee do, Sir."

His Englishness clearly amused someone other than the Governor, who stood smiling at this exchange, for from behind the Colonel came a muffled giggle. Unable to resist seeing who it was, Tom wheeled round, then quite literally stopped in his tracks. For the girl he was looking at was neither pretty nor even comely, she was ravishingly beautiful and knew it. Large eyes, the deep rich colour of fine cognac, were slanting at him

quite deliberately, while the toss of her midnight hair was surely so that he might see its sheen and quality.

"Miss Kemble, I do declare," said Governor Morris.

"Good evening, Sir," she answered, and Tom thought he had never seen a more desirable mouth, with its full lower lip and lovely curving smile. "You know my brother Stephen?"

Stephen Kemble, who was young and enthusiastic and brimming with good manners, bowed politely. "Governor, so delighted. It's been an age since we met."

He affected an English accent which didn't quite come off and, at which, his sister laughed all the more. She looked directly at Tom and dropped the slightest curtsey. "I don't believe I've had the pleasure."

Robert assumed a disconcerted expression. "How remiss of me. Miss Kemble, may I present a friend from England, Colonel Thomas Gage."

This time she gave him a proper curtsey. "An honour, Colonel."

"Tom," the Governor continued, "allow me to introduce Miss Margaret Kemble."

He couldn't get his words out, stuttered over them in fact. "Miss Kemble, I am truly delighted to make your acquaintance."

"And I yours, Sir."

The exquisite creature was flirting with him, no doubt about it. Involuntarily, Tom straightened the high-necked cravat he wore with his dress uniform and cleared his throat.

She must have noticed for the slanting eyes glimmered with amusement. "How long have you been in the Colonies, Colonel?"

"Two years, Madam."

"And do you like it here?"

"The countryside is magnificent."

"But . . . ?"

"I dislike the type of warfare that we are forced to conduct."

"But you are a soldier. Surely fighting of whatever kind is your profession."

"It is a profession I have never relished," Tom answered, and momentarily turned away, seeing again, all too vividly, the violent and bloody carnage of the field at Culloden. It was a memory he would carry with him to the grave, he felt certain, and the very thought twisted his guts.

Her hand was briefly on his arm. "Have I annoyed you, Sir."

"I would prefer not to speak of combat, Miss Kemble. Tonight is a night for enjoyment, after all."

Margaret looked very slightly shamefaced, and Tom thought that even wearing that expression he had never set eyes on anyone so gorgeous. "Of course. Do you forgive me?" she said.

This was his moment. "I do. Provided you partner me for at least one dance."

"It will be my pleasure," she answered, then whirled on her brother, tweaking a lock of his blond hair, tucking it beneath his wig, and telling him to present himself well to their cousins, the Van Cortlandts.

"I declare that you've made an impression," said Robert, as the two men turned away.

Tom looked impassive but secretly found it hard to continue polite conversation with his friend as the queue moved upward and, upon reaching the top of the stairs, he was introduced with great formality by the Governor of Pennsylvania, who knew everyone and was known by all, to that most formidable lady of society, Mrs. Van Cortlandt. She regarded the new arrival from beneath her magnificent feathered headdress, recently sent from a milliner in London, the Colonel had no doubt.

"Colonel Gage, your reputation precedes you,"

He bowed. "Surely not, Madam."

"But indeed. I have heard it said that you are a true gentleman, even on the battlefield."

"Nobody is a gentleman on the battlefield," Tom answered seriously.

Mrs. Van Cortlandt chose to ignore this and merely smiled as the Colonel and the Governor continued down the receiving line of husband and children to where champagne, all the way from France, was being served. Behind him, Tom could hear Miss Kemble's delightful American voice as she greeted her cousin with much affection.

"Why, Margaret, you're quite the belle of fashion. What an exquisite gown. Does it come from England?" Mrs. Van Cortlandt was saying.

"No, my dear. I believe in patronising our own dressmakers. It was made for me at home in Brunswick."

So she came from New Jersey, the Colonel thought, and turned to have another glance at her. She was staring straight at him with that clear, frank gaze of hers and there was a marvellous moment of challenge as to which one would be the first to look away. She won, and it was Tom who turned back to Robert, feeling the colour creep up his neck as if he were eighteen not twenty years older than that. But the Governor of Philadelphia, handsome and sought after by the ladies, with whom he could do almost anything, was already circulating, and it was up to the Colonel to follow suit and present himself to the cream of New York society, hoping that they would accept him for what he was, a professional English soldier stationed in one of Britain's colonies.

The Assembly was wonderfully organised. There was dancing for those who enjoyed it and cards for those who did not; there was food and wine in abundance; there were musicians and singers. On a more homely note, Yuletide customs from both Holland and England were being observed, and a yule log had been brought in from the Van Cortlandts' estate and lit with a fragment of last year's log. Tom, already exhilarated by his meeting with Margaret Kemble, drank bumpers of champagne and felt merry as a maypole. So much so that he was emboldened when the music struck up an English air, "Would You Have a Young Virgin", a longways dance for sets of three couples, to go to Margaret's side, give his very best bow, and beg the pleasure of her company as a partner, despite the fact that several young men were there ahead of him.

She cast her eyes round the company with marked effect. "Why, gentlemen, I can hardly refuse a British officer, now can I?"

There were some mutterings, but Miss Kemble took no notice and put her hand into that of the Colonel so that he might lead her into the ballroom.

"That was rather impolite of you," she said, smiling.

"I'm sorry. Put it down to my rough army ways."

"You are not used to social occasions, then?"

He looked at her suspiciously. "Are you teasing me?"

"Of course I am," Margaret answered as they formed a set with two other couples. "I suspect that, as an Englishman of ancient lineage, you have been to more routs and assemblies than the rest of us put together."

"And that is where, my dear young lady," said Tom, bowing as the music began, "you would be totally wrong. School to army, been there ever since."

The dance started in earnest, and they whirled back and forth, joining one another in the centre. "All work and no play? Dear me!"

Her teeth were lovely, Tom thought, even though she was mocking him mercilessly, smiling as she did so.

"Well, there have been a few memorable moments."

"Such as?"

"Oh, breakfasts at Tunbridge Wells . . ." The Colonel wrinkled his nose. "Oh Lud, those revolting waters. Dinners in Paris. Suppers in Dublin. A little gambling at White's. The odd appearance at court. Will that do?"

"Reasonably. What about Mrs. Gage? Does she enjoy socialising?"

Memories of his frail mistress, as enchanting as Margaret, though in so very different a way, flooded back to torment Tom.

"There is no Mrs. Gage," he answered and was horrified by the bitterness of his tone.

They were separated by the dance sequence at that moment but throughout the next few steps the Colonel was more than aware of her open gaze directed straight at him. Yet it wasn't until the dance was over and they were awaiting the next that Margaret spoke.

"You looked terrible when I asked you that, Colonel Gage. Your wife is dead, isn't she?"

He was longing to put his hands on her shoulders as he answered her but good manners did not allow. Instead Tom raised her fingers to his lips and swiftly kissed them.

"There never has been a Mrs. Gage, Miss Kemble. But it's true that I was once very much in love and that she, my sweetheart, did die."

With the candour which Tom had come across time and again amongst the colonists, Margaret asked, "Was she your mistress? I can somehow imagine you having one."

He was astounded. "Why?"

"Because you're dashing and gallant and also typically English and tight-lipped. People like that always have mistresses."

He didn't know whether to laugh or cry, or, indeed, to take offence. Instead he just gaped at her, open-mouthed.

Once again, Miss Kemble creased her face into a contrite expression. "I've been too forthright, haven't I? You must blame it on my mixed blood, Sir. I'll have you know I'm one-quarter English, one-quarter Greek, one-quarter Dutch and one-quarter French. On which quarter should we blame my lack of good manners?"

"The French," said Tom, without hesitation.

She roared with laughter, fresh as a breeze and just as noisy. "I guess you must be sick of fighting them."

"You could say that."

She took his hand and led him to join another set. "Come on, it's "Green Stockings". Will you partner me?"

"Only if you promise that I might call on you tomorrow. Where are you staying?"

"With the De Lanceys. Yet more cousins. And tomorrow is Christmas Day."

"Then the day after?"

Margaret Kemble shook her dark head. "I am in their hands, Colonel. I can make no independent arrangements while I am a house guest."

The music started, and Tom took the opportunity to hold her tightly for a moment. "At least allow me to leave my card."

"Now that," she said, her eyes shining into his, "is something over which I have no control."

It seemed to him, as he finally climbed into his coach, Robert Hunter Morris close on his heels, that he had danced and talked and laughed more this night than he had for years. He also felt more excited, more alive, just

as if the sun had come out on some Arctic waste and breathed the first breath of spring into it.

"You're drunk," said the Governor, who could consume quarts of alcohol and show no sign of it whatsoever.

"Yes, I am," answered Tom wildly.

"With champagne — or with Margaret Kemble?"

"Both. But mostly with her. Oh, Robert, if you regard me as any kind of friend at all, arrange for me to see her again."

"We shall call on the De Lanceys before the holidays are over."

"I said I'd take my card on Boxing Day."

"Then do so, Tom. I will accompany you and make quite sure we receive an invitation to dine."

"Is there any sphere into which your influence does not spread?"

The young and attractive Governor spread his hands. "Very few, I must confess."

The horses were stamping, and they would have set off there and then had it not been for a voice calling, "Colonel Gage, a moment, Sir, if you please." A second later a face appeared at the carriage window. It was Rupert Germain, his pale skin somewhat flushed from the exertion of running.

"My dear Colonel," he panted, "forgive me. I found no opportunity to converse with you tonight and thought I should pay my respects before you leave."

"Step inside," said Robert, opening the coach door. "You'll freeze out there, my dear chap."

"Gladly," answered Rupert, and a second later he had hauled his slight frame into the carriage's interior. In the dim light thrown by the reflection of the moonlight on snow, he certainly looked effeminate, almost girlish.

"Did you enjoy the Assembly?" Tom enquired politely.

"Very much, Sir, but actually I didn't want to see you about that."

"Oh?"

"No, Sir. It was something you said when we were travelling to New York that I wanted to discuss."

"Which was?"

"You asked me if I had thought of joining the army, and I replied that I considered myself too puny."

"Yes, I remember."

"Well, do you think that is really true, Colonel?"

It was said with a fervent earnestness that made Tom feel slightly uncomfortable. He considered his answer carefully.

"There is room for everyone in the army, my friend. Brains are required equally with brawn."

"And if I were to join might there be an opportunity of entering your regiment?"

The Colonel was silent, thinking. "I have another idea," he said eventually. "It has long been in my mind to raise a regiment of my own. A fast, light band of men trained in irregular warfare. The sort of rapidly moving troop that would be ideally suited to the fighting conditions we have here in the Colonies."

"Which are?"

"Warfare in the woods, Lord Rupert. Nothing like any of us has ever been used to before."

"But how could I help with this?"

"If you are interested, you could assist by drawing up the plans for such an enterprise, remaining here in New York while you do so. As soon as Christmas is over, I am going with the 44th to Oswego on the shores of Lake Ontario and will have little time to work on it."

"Do I take it, Colonel Gage, that you would wish me to remain a civilian while I do this?" Rupert asked, as if the Colonel's word was law.

Tom permitted himself a laugh. "Yes, indeed. Until I see what aptitude you have for planning I would suggest that you act unofficially."

"Are you going to pay him?" asked Robert, going straight to the heart of the matter.

"If Lord Rupert is suited to the task, then I most certainly would do so."

The young man got to his feet. "Gentlemen, I take my leave of you. This is the most exciting night of my life. I shall call on you very shortly." He bowed, then wrung Tom's hand. "Thank you, Sir. I shall never forget your goodness in giving me a job on so brief an acquaintanceship. The compliments of the season to you both." He almost fell out of the carriage in his enthusiasm.

The Colonel and the Governor looked at one another, then burst out laughing.

"He's taken quite a shine to you," said Robert.

"Oh, for heaven's sake."

"He has. I know the signs. You've got a life-long admirer there, provided you don't spurn him too cruelly."

"Well I'm certainly not going to encourage him."

"I know what you mean, but treat him gently, my dear Tom. He's a sensitive soul."

"Can we talk about something else, please?"

"Margaret Kemble for example?"

"Yes," said Colonel Gage. "Yes, yes, yes. Let's talk about the most beautiful girl in the world."

"Isn't that rather overdoing it?"

"Yes, no, I don't know. I haven't met them all. But of those I have, Miss Kemble certainly leads the field."

"You are drunk and besotted," stated Robert Hunter Morris firmly. "Now, let's drive on before you follow her coach and make a complete fool of yourself."

"A turn in the parkland before dusk would be delightful," said the Governor of Pennsylvania, and flashed a dark eye in the direction of his fellow guest who was doing his level best to join in the dinner table conversation and stop staring at the belle of New Jersey, exquisite in an exciting shade of red, as was the Colonel himself. In fact he couldn't help but wonder whether she had chosen her hooped satin gown to complement his scarlet uniform, although he eventually discounted the idea as wishful thinking.

With an effort Tom Gage pulled himself together. "I would love to see your gardens, Mrs. De Lancey."

"Well then you shall, my dear Colonel, though I don't hold them to be as imposing as those of Firle Place."

"Firle is very fine, of course. I count myself lucky to have been born there. But the most beautiful of our seats is Highmeadow."

Mrs. De Lancey's eyebrows rose slightly. "Excuse my ignorance, Colonel Gage, but where exactly is that?"

"Near Staunton in Gloucestershire. To the south, in fact from my boyhood bedroom window, there is a simply glorious view of Staunton's church rising above thousands of acres of woodland. I used to sit and look at it for hours."

"You appreciate beauty?" asked his hostess archly.

Robert Hunter Morris coughed and Margaret shot Tom a brilliant glance.

"Very much so," he answered, keeping his face straight and his eyes to the front. "Of course, your house is superb, Madam. Wherever one looks there is an aspect pleasing to the eye."

"How kind of you to say so. Now, ladies, let us retire and leave the gentlemen to their port."

Everything was done just as it would be in the great houses of England, Tom thought. Indeed, it was at moments like these that he missed his homeland the least. It was only when hacking his way through dense woodland, menaced by savages and the sniping French, that he longed to be away from the Colonies and somewhere a little more civilised. Yet there was nothing civilised about fighting, wherever it took place. The torturing vision of Culloden and its vicious aftermath, when the Duke of Cumberland had earned his nickname of 'Butcher' and decimated an entire population, returned to sicken him, and it was with

only the mightiest effort that Tom got a grip on himself and realised that the ladies were leaving the table and that he was required to stand.

"We shall tour some of the grounds in a half hour," Mrs. De Lancey announced as she, Margaret and several other elegant young females — daughters and yet more cousins, Tom presumed — swept through the doorway with much swishing of skirts.

This day, just as dusk was falling, Gage and Hunter Morris had set forth in their coach once more. They had left New York Island by means of Dightnans Bridge from which a road led off to the right going directly to West Chester County. This was the territory of the powerful Colonel James De Lancey, sheriff of the county and a senior member of the all-embracing clan. He was a Loyalist to his very bones and would have dealt with any insurrection against the King by raising a private army and charging out with it. Thomas, looking closely at him, wondered how old he was but found it almost impossible to put an age on him. He could have been anything between thirty and fifty, he thought. Colonel De Lancey, who was passing the port to his left, felt himself being regarded and looked up.

"I drink to you, Colonel Gage. I am proud to have a British officer within these walls."

"Thank you, Sir. I feel privileged to be here."

"Consider this as your second home. Call on us at any time."

Thinking that time was the one thing he was going to be desperately short of, Tom smiled and raised his

glass. The conversation started to drift to people that he didn't know and the Colonel assumed an attentive expression, but allowed his attention to wander, considering Lord Rupert Germain and whether he had made a mistake in giving him the task of preparing details for the formation of Gage's chasseurs, as the Colonel liked to think of his groundbreaking new regiment. Perhaps it had been foolish to entrust such a task to a young civilian, yet there was something about Rupert which gave the impression of a sharp, incisive brain behind the foppish, somewhat languid exterior. But Tom's thoughts did not dwell too long on this subject, turning instead to the powerful thrall in which Miss Kemble already held him. Looking out of the window, the Colonel dreamed.

"Well, gentlemen," said Mrs. De Lancey.

Half an hour had passed. It was time to walk in the snow-covered grounds and breathe in the freezing air. Tom only hoped that Miss Kemble would take the opportunity to draw close to him as they traversed the frost-filled paths.

The males rose to their feet and made their way to the entrance hall where the slaves waited, bearing cloaks and greatcoats. None of the black people spoke nor did they make eye contact with those they were helping, clearly trained by their masters not to do so. Tom, who considered himself as something of an egalitarian, taught by years in the army to mix with all sorts, thanked the lanky Negro who was putting his cloak about his shoulders but only received a frightened glance for doing so. Thinking to himself what a strange

anomaly the Colonies were, so young and hopeful, so bursting with life yet so primitive in certain ways, the Colonel stepped out into the coldness of the winter gardens.

The ladies were already there, muffled in fur-lined cloaks, looking demure; that is with the exception of Margaret Kemble who was clearly longing to stride out and was stamping about like an impatient racehorse. Thomas looked at her, mentally shaking his head, thinking it would need a strong hand to rein in such a mettlesome creature and wondering whether he was up to the task. Then immediately following that thought came the notion that she might already be spoken for, that some strong-minded New Jersey landowner might already be laying his own plans to tame the Brunswick belle. Not liking this at all, the Colonel approached her.

"Miss Kemble, may I accompany you?"

The cool eyes, which in this pale landscape had taken on the colour of topaz, regarded him with amusement. "You're very formal, Colonel."

"My English upbringing. You must forgive me."

"Do I detect a hint of irony in that? Are you suggesting that we Yankees are too free and easy?"

"How could I do so churlish a thing?"

They had fallen into step together and were walking somewhat behind the main party, who were charging ahead making complimentary noises about the stark beauty of Mrs. De Lancey's winter fountains, frozen and glittering.

Margaret looked up at him, a tall girl but still only as high as Tom's shoulder. "Colonel, I find you hard to fathom."

He was genuinely surprised. "Why, for heaven's sake?"

"You are so correct, so old school. My mixed blood rebels against it."

He was amused, yet irritated, a strange array of emotions. Catching her by the arm to bring her to a standstill, Tom Gage said, "I've enough Irish in me to make me as wild as you are. It's simply that I've learned to control it."

"Is that good for you, controlling your emotions to the point of rigidity?"

"Good for me or bad for me, it is how I am. An army man, disciplined I suppose. You obviously consider too much so."

"And does that worry you, what I think?"

The Colonel still had hold of her arm and now he tightened his grip. "It would worry me very much indeed."

"Why is that?"

"Because even after so short an acquaintance, I hold you in the highest regard."

She took a step nearer to him. "Do you, Colonel Gage?"

Tom ran his eyes rapidly over the landscape, a soldier's trick if ever there was one. There was no-one in sight, the other walkers having disappeared into a frost-filled arbour.

"Stop teasing me, Miss Kemble."

40

"Why? It gives me pleasure."

"And does this give you pleasure, too?"

And he kissed her, swift and deep, before she had time to utter another word.

She drew back from him. "Gracious me, Colonel. Wasn't that rather indecorous."

Tom Gage shook his head. "No, my dear young lady, it was absolutely delightful. Wasn't it?"

The beautiful eyes gleamed with unexpressed thoughts. "May I write to a lonely soldier when he is posted away from home?"

"If that soldier is myself, then most certainly."

Removing herself from his grip, Margaret ran ahead, then turned to look at him. "Will you be gone long?"

"I'm not sure."

"It had better not be too lengthy a posting. After all, who will I have to make me laugh when you're not here?"

And with that she hurried on to join the others.

CHAPTER
TWO

August, 1757

The silence in the forest was almost audible. Other than for the breathing of the halted men, panting slightly, glad to have come to a stop, there was nothing. Not a bird sang, not a twig cracked, the quiet was enormous.

Gage held up his hand, put a finger to his lips, then beckoned his second-in-command to his side. Moving as softly as he could, Henry Gladwin eased his way to where his superior stood. Gage mouthed the word "look", and parted the branches so that Gladwin could get a reasonable view of the fort that lay ahead of them. The Major stared, then, equally quietly, allowed the foliage to drop back to its original position.

"What do you think?" whispered the Colonel.

Major Gladwin put his lips to his companion's ear. "Looks horribly deserted to me, Sir."

"And me," Gage murmured back. "I can't see a human soul."

"Is it a trap?"

"If it is, it means we're too late."

The two men stared at each other momentarily, then Gage turned to his troop of soldiers and beckoned them on, again raising his finger to his lips. As quietly

42

as they could, the forty proceeded forward through the dense woodland.

The nearer they drew to the fort, the more there came a sense of unreality, as if they were looking at a paper cut-out rather than a large timber structure. Total silence engulfed the place; nothing moved. It seemed to the approaching soldiers as if the building had long since been deserted. Yet this could hardly be the case. The siege of Fort William Henry had started barely two weeks earlier, but of the besiegers and the besieged there was no sign whatsoever,

For the second time, Gage drew his party to a halt and turned to the Major.

"Well?"

"It could be a ploy, Sir. Perhaps we're meant to walk in."

"Um." Tom Gage deliberated. "On the other hand, we can't hang around in the woods for too long. Let's send in a scout." He turned, whispering, "Calico Joel, can you get the measure of the place for us?"

"Why not?" said a voice with a marked French accent, right behind the Colonel and so close to him that it made him jump. He turned to look at the scout with a slight smile.

"I wish you wouldn't creep up on people like that. It's unnerving."

The half-breed grinned. Part Indian, part French, Calico Joel stood unusually tall for one of his mixed ancestry. His mother had been French and his father a Cherokee warrior, who had abducted her from a wagon train while still a child in a calico dress. His eyes were

deep set, brown and hawkish, his features a mixture of two nations, yet with something of his mother's delicacy in them. But it was his long hair, waist length and black as night, today worn loose though he often plaited it, that the English found amusing. That and his peculiar garb. For Calico Joel wore an old pair of army breeches, together with a strange type of waistcoat made from fur which exposed his chest, even in winter. His hat, though, was the crowning glory. A tricorne, stolen from a dead British colonel, it had a tattered bow on one cock and a Cherokee emblem to ward off evil spirits on the other. This, together with a scarlet feather draped nattily over the crown, completed the ensemble.

"You want me to search, *mon Colonel?*" he said now.

"Go and have a look at the fort. Tell us what's happening."

"*Oui, certainement,*" Calico Joel answered and, turning, vanished into the undergrowth without another word.

Major Gladwin stared after him. "Do you trust that fellow?"

"With my life," said Gage simply, and put an end to any further discussion.

Twenty minutes later the scout returned, his face expressionless. "They're gone," he said briefly.

"What do you mean?" asked the Colonel.

"Just that. The fort is empty of the living. I did not go in, but there is no trap."

"You're sure?"

"Sure," Calico Joel replied, spat upon the ground, and vanished once more.

The Colonel allowed himself the luxury of a laugh. "Well, we may as well find out." He turned to his troop, some of whom had snatched the moment and were sitting down. "Come on, men. Muskets at the ready. We're entering the fort."

There was a general scramble as they came to order, and then the slow advance to Fort William Henry began. Meanwhile the Indian scout loped ahead, hiding himself amongst the trees so cleverly that occasionally he disappeared from view entirely. Eventually, though, the protection of the forest came to an end, and they reached the clearing in which the fort had been built, the shores of Lake George clearly visible behind it, appearing nearer because of the heat of the day. Gage turned to his men once more.

"Advance. On the double!" and unsheathing his sword, he ran across the clearing and in through the double wooden doors, which hung open, listlessly responding to what breeze there was.

It was an eerie sensation, Tom thought as he ran. In normal circumstances there would have been the cry of the soldiers on duty as he approached the gates. But today the only sound was the slight echo of his voice as he crossed the empty clearing and made his way into the unguarded fort. Silently, Calico Joel appeared at his side.

"There's death here," he said briefly.

"What do you mean?"

"That the only men left here are dead."

"How do you know?"

For answer the scout gave a slight shrug but said nothing further, and it was left to Gage to walk silently across the fort's parade ground and enter into the main building itself. Then he heard it. A faint buzzing sound. He turned to Calico Joel.

"What's that?"

"The flies have got here before us."

Even as he said the words, the first faint smell began to assail Tom's nostrils. He clapped a handkerchief to his nose and said, "Oh my God," to Gladwin, who had followed him in.

"Where's it coming from?"

"Somewhere within. I'll go and look. Order the men to keep close watch, will you."

The Major left the room briefly, and Tom turned to the scout. "Lead the way. You know how I hate this."

Calico Joel smiled. "You hate war, *mon Colonel*. You have always hated it."

It was true, Tom thought, as he followed the scout through room after room until eventually they came to what had once been Colonel George Munro's office.

There were papers everywhere; on the floor, on the desk, on the chairs. All scattered with wild abandon and no thought of order. But it was not to the documents that Gage's eyes were drawn, but rather to the heap of bodies, thrown into the centre of the room with careless cynicism. As he took in the full horror of the scene, Tom felt his guts heave and fought to control them. For there were brains and blood everywhere. The men had been scalped, every one.

Beside Tom Gage's foot, so close that he had almost trodden on him, lay a young soldier, his features hacked to bits for good measure, nothing much remaining above the shoulders except an oozing gelatinous mess. The Colonel drew in his breath and struggled to master his feeling of utter revulsion, seeing again the field at Culloden and that sea of kilted corpses, many bearing hideous mutilations.

Calico Joel looked down impassively. "So the Frenchman couldn't control his Indian allies," was all he said.

"Is that what this is?"

"*Absolument*. Montcalm had to allow them some liberties, so he let them scalp their enemies."

Gage made a bitter sound. "Enemies! Why, this poor thing . . ." He indicated the soldier lying at his feet. ". . . could have been no more than eighteen years old."

Calico Joel shrugged. "What difference does age make?"

It was pointless even discussing the situation with him, and Gage did not try, instead calling out to Gladwin, who had come into the room and was standing horror-struck, "Arrange for these wretched creatures to be buried straight away. They're starting to decompose."

The Major, pale, answered, "Yes, Sir," and left rather swiftly.

"We'd better search the rest of the building," Gage said to the scout.

Calico Joel, unmoved by the sight he had just seen, merely nodded.

As they left to continue the search, Major Gladwin came in with several of the harder soldiers, handkerchiefs over their noses, and set about the task of removing the bodies, unceremoniously grabbing hold of legs and dragging the dead out.

"There may be more," Gage warned over his shoulder.

"Let's hope they didn't die like this lot."

But they had. In other rooms there were other bodies, some of them killed while they slept in their bunks. All in all it was a tragic case of ritual slaughter, the ferocity of which Gage did not fully comprehend, seeming savage beyond belief. Yet it was the Indian way to take a scalp as a trophy, and the French and the Indians were now allies against the British.

Eventually his search was done, and he reeled out into the open air, taking in great breaths as he did so. Wiping the sweat from his brow, Tom Gage closed his eyes momentarily.

"It was a vile attack, Sir," said Major Gladwin, close to his elbow.

Tom looked at him. "You have to hand it to Montcalm. He must have taken the fort with great force."

"Yes, I think one could safely say that," the Major replied bitterly.

Gage pulled a wry face but made no reply and, laden with thought, the two men, having ordered that all the bodies should be removed and buried as an urgent priority, made their way to the shores of Lake George.

It was calm as a pond and full of golden light where the sun skimmed and dipped its surface. After the ugliness he had just witnessed, Colonel Gage simply stared, not looking at his companion, not looking at anything, except the vast expanse of water that lay before him. The sky was clear blue, reflecting in the lake, so that it looked bright as hyacinths and smelled almost as good.

"Beautiful," the Colonel said to himself.

Major Gladwin nodded, sitting on the stump of a tree that had been felled to build the fort they had just left. His eyes closed as he basked in the sun, escaping momentarily the horrors of war.

Tom Gage wandered a few paces, seeing again the young soldier who had died so savagely. Then, quite deliberately, he thought of Margaret Kemble, forcing visions of the dead men away. He hadn't set eyes on her since that last time, a time early in January when she had left for New Jersey, to this. But she had written regularly, and he had corresponded with her, though he doubted that some of his letters had reached her. He wondered now whether she would feel the same about him, whether her interest had been dimmed by the passing of time. As for himself, he no longer knew what he felt, whether he was fond of her or not. In fact, at this precise moment, blunted by what he had just experienced, he no longer cared. Thoughts of his dead mistress returned to haunt him, and he considered, at that moment, that he might be better remaining a bachelor.

He must have made some faint gesture because Major Gilbey said, "Are you all right, Sir?"

Tom turned to look at him, resting his eyes away from the glittering lake. "Yes. No. To be honest with you, I dislike the sight of death. Always have. A weakness in a soldier I dare say."

"I didn't relish it either. It was particularly savage. But that is the Indian way I suppose."

"Yes, the Indian way." Gage sighed. "We'd best be getting back. Check that the burials are going satisfactorily."

"You'll have to say a few words over the graves, Sir."

"Yes, I'll say something," Tom answered bitterly, as they trudged back in the direction of the fort.

CHAPTER
THREE

Christmas, 1757

The invitation was totally unexpected. It came from
Peter Kemble himself, head of the Kemble family, and
merely said that if Colonel Gage were at a loose end
this Christmas he would be more than welcome as a
house guest. Of his beautiful daughter, Margaret, there
was absolutely no mention, rather the letter talked
about Stephen Kemble who had been commissioned as
an ensign in Gage's regiment. It was he, apparently,
who had suggested the whole idea. That is, if the
Colonel were free and willing to accept.

At first Tom had been intrigued, then, the more the
idea grew on him, he became full of a restless energy, a
wish to see Margaret again and satisfy his curiosity as
to his feelings for her.

Meanwhile, however, there was much to be done. He
had been in New York for two days and had in his
hands the long-awaited documents, delivered to him
that very morning by Lord Rupert Germain. And what
a triumph they were. Gage had not been wrong about
the effeminate young man having a sharp and incisive
brain. There, on paper, was the master plan for the
formation of Gage's chasseurs. Under the heading The
First Definitely Light-Armed Regiment in the British
Army, Germain had laid it all out.

Gage would be responsible for enlisting five hundred men, consisting of sergeants and corporals from the Regulars and the Colonel's own choice of officers, together with the tank and field who would come from America. No Frenchmen and no deserters would be accepted, and the troops were to be "active, young and healthy and strong, free from all ruptures, sprains or any bodily ailment whatever". In return, Gage would raise and clothe the regiment, provided the government gave him £3,500, the price of his existing commission. For, if the plan was approved, he was to be promoted from Lieutenant Colonel to full Colonel.

As he read through the document, prepared with such intricacy and cleverness, Tom went back in his mind to that Christmas — exactly a year ago — when he had first met Margaret Kemble and Rupert Germain. Had it been as Robert Hunter Morris predicted? Had Rupert fallen in love with him? It would appear from the paper in his hand that perhaps it had been so. But, much more importantly, what were Margaret Kemble's thoughts? Her letters had been full of news and vitality but non-committal, almost to the point of indifference.

Gage sighed. The older he got — and he was now thirty-eight, having just celebrated his birthday — the less he found he knew, especially about women. Could it be that he was still in love with his fragile mistress, he wondered? Or had the passion that Margaret aroused in him been deeper than just a passing fancy?

He got up and took a turn round the room, looking out of the window of the private house where he was

quartered. He could see horses and trees and a carriage which passed slowly by. With a sudden determination, Tom Gage went to his desk, put down the precious papers he still carried in his hand, and picked up his pen. 'Dear Mr. Kemble,' he started, 'What a Great Pleasure it would Be to Spend Christmas with You and Your Family . . . ' Then he laid down the pen again and allowed a slow smile to light his rather tense features as he remembered.

"It's a good plan, Gage," said the Earl of Loudon, his Scottish accent quite pronounced, as it often was when he was tired. "A very good plan indeed."

He looked up over his spectacles at the man sitting on the opposite side of the desk. "I've a mind to give it my full support."

Tom longed to say, 'Why don't you then,' but maintained a dignified silence, allowing himself no more than a deprecating movement.

Loudon studied the document again. "Five hundred men, you say?"

"Yes, Sir."

"And you think that will be sufficient?" Loudon was clearly fatigued because his Scottish burr was becoming more and more pronounced.

"I think that is the maximum I will be able to find, realistically speaking."

"I see." There was a long pause while the commander-in-chief studied the document assiduously. Finally, though, he looked up. "I believe I am prepared to back this."

53

Gage controlled his joy, meanwhile sending a prayer of thanks to Rupert Germain. "I would esteem that a great honour, Sir."

Loudon allowed himself the luxury of a wintery smile. "Furthermore, Colonel Gage, I am prepared to lend you £2,600 from army funds, provided, of course, that you repay this amount when our superiors in London give their blessing to the scheme."

Gage leapt out of his chair. "My God, Sir, this is splendid."

Loudon shrank away slightly. "There is no need to thank me. It is an excellent plan and one which merits support." He cleared his throat indicating that the interview was at an end. "That will be all, Colonel. I shall get my secretary to draw up the necessary papers. Good day to you."

"Good day, Sir," said Gage, bowing stiffly before he saluted. Then he turned and left the room. But once outside he executed a series of dance steps, quite rapidly and to himself, then coloured as he realised that a pair of eyes were looking at him most curiously.

A rather wizened soldier leaned forward from his hiding hole behind a desk and spoke in a whisper. "I take it you won the day, Sir."

"Yes, yes indeed," Tom answered gruffly, bowed once more and went out, wondering what he could possibly have looked like, dancing fantastically and alone.

Rather unexpectedly, a slight figure detached itself from beside a small black coach which was parked in the street outside and hurried in the direction of Tom

Gage, who had already set off at a brisk pace for his lodgings.

"Colonel, wait," called a voice, and Thomas turned to see Rupert Germain, thinner than ever and pale as a cloud, coming towards him.

"I just had to find out what happened," the younger man said by way of explanation. "What did Lord Loudon think? I mean, did he agree to the suggestions or not?"

Gage gave him a broad grin. "I'll say he did. He's even offered to lend me money to fund the entire enterprise. In other words the whole thing was a great success, thanks in no small measure to yourself."

Rupert turned away, his blue eyes filling with sudden tears, and no gesture could have said more. "I'm so glad," he muttered.

Gage hesitated. Normally he would have clapped Germain on the shoulder and thanked him for all his work but now, suddenly, he felt embarrassed.

"My dear fellow," he said hesitantly, "please don't upset yourself. It really was your good effort that helped enormously."

Lord Rupert brushed his sleeve across his eyes and turned back to face Colonel Gage. "Well, what next, Sir?"

"Next I suggest that we repair to a tavern and I buy you a well-earned drink."

"I will accept your kind offer but may I suggest we go by carriage. There's a bitter wind blowing, and I'm afraid that I suffer with the cold."

It was on the tip of Gage's tongue to say that Lord Rupert ought to get some more flesh on his bones, but there was something about the pale young man's intense expression that forbade any such jovial remark. Instead he said, "Hardly surprising. New York in winter can be a damned chilly place."

"Indeed it can, Colonel," and Lord Rupert bowed as Gage climbed into the coach ahead of him.

A few minutes later it drew up before The Bunch of Grapes, and Colonel Gage and his companion made their way inside. Within, the air was heavy with smoke, and a whole assortment of smells greeted their nostrils, the pungent stink of unwashed humanity contrasting violently with the scents of those who affected to be beaux of fashion. Overriding all this, however, there was the smell of cooking: onions and pork and vegetables all melding together in one great and glorious stewpot.

Gage turned to his companion, who looked even frailer in such rough surroundings. "Not too much for you, is it?"

The minute the words were out of his mouth he regretted them. For Lord Rupert flushed angrily and said, "No, Sir. I've been in worse dens than this, I assure you."

Tom was about to ask of what sort, but he held the question back, simply saying, "Really?"

They found a seat at a dimly-lit table and ordered from a youthful potboy, who stared at Gage's uniform very pointedly — or so Tom thought.

"I believe we're not altogether popular," he murmured as the boy withdrew to see to the order.

"Who cares?" said Rupert, full of a sudden bravado. "We're the governors, after all."

"Yes," said Gage, then repeated, "yes," more softly. Then he steepled his fingers and put his chin on them reflectively, saying nothing.

Rupert stared at him, aware that he had said something out of turn but uncertain as to what it was. So they sat in silence until the potboy returned, surly as before, banging the pots of ale down in front of them. Gage looked up. "Thank you," he said.

The potboy grunted by way of reply and moved on to serve another table. Tom followed him with his eyes. "Fortunately, he is in the minority — at least for the moment."

"What do you mean, Sir?"

"Precisely what I say. The Colonies are ours by right. Yet there are those — and he is one of them — who despise us and would love to be independent."

"Surely not."

"Mark my words, my Lord."

Two high spots of colour appeared in Rupert Germain's normally pallid cheeks. "If you say so, Colonel, then I will believe it. But I would not credit such a thing from anyone else. The Colonies seem well contented to me."

Tom half emptied his tankard. "It could be that I am imagining things and that all will be well, of course. Anyway, enough of that. What of your future? Do you intend to stay in America?"

Rupert Germain took a sip from his alepot. "That depends, Sir."

"On what?"

"Rather on you."

"What do you mean?"

Rupert's colour increased a little. "Well, now that I've finished drawing up the plan for the chasseurs, I wondered if you had any further work for me."

Gage emptied his tankard. "Well, no, my Lord — not really."

To say that the young man was disappointed was only to describe half his reaction. His jaw lowered, his lips quivered, and he hid the expression in his eyes, covering his face with his alepot, drinking busily — and somewhat noisily.

The Colonel thought furiously. What could he offer a young civilian by way of work? The answer was absolutely nothing.

"I'm sorry," he said.

Rupert drained his tankard and placed it back on the table. Then he looked up, his features controlled once more. "It appears that it will have to be my second plan," he said brightly.

"And what might that be?"

"I thought of starting a newspaper, Sir."

"A newspaper?" Gage could hardly credit what he was hearing. "But have you any experience? I mean, surely one should have some knowledge of such an enterprise."

Lord Rupert Germain's colour deepened so that he now looked unhealthily flushed. "Well, actually, I thought of employing staff to manage that side of affairs. Fact is, I've lately received some money. A rich

childless aunt has died and left funds to her nieces and nephews. I've inherited enough to start such a thing. The only question remains as to where."

The Colonel was speechless. True to his word, he had paid Germain for the time and effort he had used in planning the new regiment. And all the while the young devil had been in possession of a handsome bequest. Extremely handsome if his plans were anything to go by.

He stared, bereft of words, then eventually burst out laughing. "And to think I believed you penniless. But then I should have guessed. The Germains are not generally short of money by all accounts."

Rupert looked terribly earnest, adopting an expression that was vaguely amusing. "Oh, but I was devoid of cash when I arrived, Colonel Gage. It is only the legacy that has set me up beyond my expectations. But if you so wish I can refund the money you have paid me. To be honest, I no longer have need of it."

Tom smiled at him, laughter only an inch away. "Lord Rupert . . ."

"Rupert, please. We are friends, are we not?"

"Rupert then. You did a great service when you drew up those plans for me. I have been far too preoccupied fighting the French and the Indians to concentrate on them. You earned that money and I would be deeply insulted if you returned it to me."

"Then in that case . . ."

"Look, why don't you buy me a drink to celebrate your inheritance? How about a bottle of claret, if they have such a thing in this extraordinary place."

Full of enthusiasm, Rupert rose to his feet. "You shall have the best in the house, Colonel."

"I wonder what that will be," said Tom Gage, and laughed.

Two days later, Colonel Thomas Gage set out for Brunswick, accompanied by several others, one of whom was his old companion-in-arms, Major Henry Gladwin. They rode horseback, making a fine sight as they clattered down Broad Way and out of New York City, red uniforms standing out in the pallid winter sun.

Tom could not recall a time when he had been in such a state of anticipatory pleasure, his mind full of memories of Margaret. Had it really been a whole year since they had met? He could hardly believe it. Then he started to wonder what had happened in that year. Had she fallen in love with anyone else? Her letters had been so full of gossip and names of people she had been to see, met at social events, out riding and enjoying herself. Had one name been more important than the others? Thomas Gage made an irritable noise and spurred his horse onwards, anxious to get there, anxious to learn what fate held in store for him.

He had ridden the length of Broad Way, going south, and now the fort and the Governor's House, together with the bowling green, lay before him. He recalled his arrival, almost a year ago to the day, and the great pleasure he had felt when introduced to Margaret. The memory of it stirred him slightly even while he rode

60

along and despite the freezing weather conditions, he felt himself grow warm.

"The ferry's due in at any moment," said Major Gladwin.

"Good. I'm longing to be away."

"That's obvious." The Major added "Sir" as Gage shot him a sideways glance.

"Why? Why is it obvious?" asked Thomas, decidedly prickly because of his high emotions.

Major Gladwin looked at him, wondering whether to tell the truth, which was that the Colonel had been twitching with impatience ever since they had met that morning. He thought better of it.

"Nothing, Sir. Just an idea I had. Probably wrong."

Thomas sighed heavily. "No, truth to tell, you're right. Fact is, Henry, there's a woman involved."

"Really?" lied Gladwin, who had been wondering if the Colonel would confide in him.

"Yes, I met her a year ago, and she has been corresponding with me ever since — off and on. She seems like a social gadfly, but that wasn't how she struck me at the time."

"Go on, Sir."

Thomas sighed again. "There's not much more to tell except that I was instantly attracted to her and, I think, she to me. But a year's a long time, Henry, and now I'm not sure what I feel. Whether it was just infatuation or something deeper, I'm not certain."

"Well, Sir, it's as well that you find out. And find out you will by the end of Christmas."

Colonel Gage looked at his comrade. "Yes indeed, and do you know the thought makes me slightly nervous."

"Why, Sir?"

"Because for some reason I want it to work. I don't want to arrive there and find that she has feet of clay and is not the woman I thought her. I'm thirty-eight years old, Henry. It's high time I settled down."

"Plenty of days for that, Sir," said Henry Gladwin gallantly, but secretly he believed that Gage, if he wanted a family life, should think seriously about his future, and now was as good a moment as any.

They arrived at the ferry just as it was docking, disgorging the many passengers travelling to New York for the festive season. Bright-eyed youngsters rubbed shoulders with merchants, satisfied with themselves and the lives they had created in the Colonies. The Colonel, watching the stream of people set foot in the city, thought back to the surly potboy and wondered if, perhaps, he had been wrong, if the Colonies would continue for ever, pleased with the way George II and his parliament were running things. Yet the attitude of that boy, particularly to the red coat Gage had worn, had both surprised and shocked him. But then, Tom thought, the potboy was just one amongst hundreds, a small and inconsequential minority.

As the last of the passengers got off, Gage and his party dismounted and led their horses aboard. The ferry plied between Brooklyn and New York Island, constantly crossing to and fro, and the plan was to ride down beyond Yellow Hook and to take the Narrows

Ferry to New Jersey, then make the final push on horseback, arriving, hopefully, by nightfall.

Gage turned to Henry Gladwin as, with much creaking of chains, they set off once more.

"Where are you spending Christmas, Henry?"

"With some friends, not far from Brunswick."

"Well, enjoy yourself. You know we assemble for recruiting duty immediately after the festivities?"

"Yes, Sir. I'll be there."

"I couldn't manage without you," and the Colonel gave Major Gladwin a friendly pat on the shoulder.

They reached their destination at sundown, and Gage, having repaired to a hostelry to remove the stains of the journey and have a drink to give him courage, set forth once more on his weary horse. As he turned up the drive he wondered, yet again, just what his reaction to Margaret would be. Yet, as the front door opened, the girl who had been uppermost in his mind for some days was standing just behind the Negro servant. The Colonel took one look and was immediately entranced. As for Margaret, she gave him the most delightful smile imaginable and dropped a curtsey, quite deep. Thomas, on foot now, having taken his mount to the stables first of all, bowed formally.

"Miss Kemble," he said, making his way into the hall.

"Colonel Gage," she answered, then took him by the hand. "Welcome to our home, Sir. Did you get my letters?"

"Every one, Madam."

"And do you know them all by heart?"

Her smile was beguiling, and Tom felt the year that had passed slip away even as he looked at her.

"Again, Madam. Every one."

"Then that's as well," she answered, and, turning, led him into the house.

CHAPTER
FOUR

Christmas, 1757

It had started to snow during the night of his arrival and continued throughout the next day. But the day after that, namely Christmas Eve, it stopped, leaving a cold, clear morning to look out on as Tom Gage got from his bed and threw open the window. As far as the eye could see there stretched flawless white, the trees laden with glittering diamonds, the fields an uninterrupted view of total purity. But despite the early hour, there were those who had risen before him. For from quite close to the house came the sound of voices, laughing and frolicking, and Tom could swear that Margaret's was one of them. He was just about to turn away and dress hurriedly when a snowball, pitched with unerring aim, hit him clean in the face. As he wiped it off with the sleeve of his nightgown, he leant out further to see who was responsible, and there, hurrying round the side of the house, was the young lady in question.

"I'll get you for that," Tom yelled in his barrack square voice, and hurrying into his uniform, the jacket of which he left unbuttoned, he descended the staircase at double speed. Two black faces regarded him, both thoroughly startled, but the Colonel merely gave them

a friendly nod as he wrenched open the front door and went, helter-skelter, in hot pursuit of his assailant.

She was nowhere to be seen but the snow, of course, held its own clues. Two sets of footprints led from the front door and round to the back, where Tom slept, his room giving him an unsurpassed view to where, in the far distance, the River Delaware curled snakily through the landscape. Several outbuildings, including the stables, the coach house, and a hay store, lay ahead of him. But here the footsteps parted company, one lot doubling back into the house, the other crossing and crisscrossing in an attempt to hide where their owner was lurking. Thanking God that he had picked up quite a lot of tracking skills from Calico Joel, Tom set about stalking his quarry, suspecting that it was Margaret and hoping profoundly that it was.

The footprints leading to the coach house seemed to him to have been made most recently and, throwing open the great door, Tom stepped inside. That the Kembles were a prosperous family he already knew, but that they ran two coaches, to say nothing of a one-horse chaise, surprised him. But he did little more than give them a cursory glance for from within the shadowy space ahead of him came a muffled laugh. It was Margaret all right, he felt certain of it.

"I know you're there," he called, "and I'm coming to get you."

He pulled his hands into his chest and growled fiercely, then was struck by the thought that it might be Judith, Margaret's younger sister.

"Oh well, too late," he muttered to himself and started the search.

She was nowhere to be seen, but Tom took a shrewd guess that one of the conveyances would provide an excellent hiding place and set about searching them. The first coach revealed nothing, as did the second, so it was to the chaise that he tiptoed carefully, determined to give her a fright. The cover of the chaise was drawn up, as if for bad weather. With a wild cry, Tom suddenly pulled it back, only to reveal an empty space.

"Goddammit, woman," he exclaimed. "Where have you hidden yourself?"

"Look up," said a voice over his head.

The Colonel did so and burst out laughing. For there she was, sitting on the cross-beam, swinging her legs, eating an apple and generally having a good time. With an athletic leap that startled even him, Tom ascended to the coachman's box and from there clambered on to the beam to sit beside her.

"Have you just done that?" he asked.

"Yes, does it surprise you?"

"Greatly. What did you do with all your skirts?"

"I picked them up and climbed with them round my ears."

"Oh dear, not very ladylike."

"No, perhaps it wasn't." She smiled broadly. "You'd better leave before I descend."

"I most certainly will. I don't need two shocks in one day. And talking of that, was it you who threw that snowball?"

She looked mischievous. "It could have been."

"Or it could have been Stephen. Listen, I'll have you know that he is a member of my regiment and showing disrespect for a senior officer is a court martial offence. Now what do you have to say?"

"That your jacket is undone and you might get cold."

"I dressed in a hurry. I'm sorry."

"There's no need to be. It shows that you're human."

"And my human behind is beginning to ache. Do you mind if I get down?"

"Not in the least. If I jump, will you catch me?"

"I'll try, Miss Kemble."

"Thank you, Colonel," she answered solemnly.

Tom lowered himself onto the coachman's box and put his arms up for her, and a minute later she was in them, all the warmth and beauty of her closer than she had ever been before. Unfortunately, he wasn't standing completely true and toppled backwards as she landed so that they both ended up on the box, she virtually on top of him.

"Well," said the Colonel, "it's a good thing your father can't see us."

"Why?"

"He might get the wrong impression."

"Yes, I suppose he might," she answered, but made no effort to move herself.

"If you stay like that I will probably kiss you," he went on.

"Will you?" she answered provocatively and closed her eyes.

Just for a second, Tom studied her face, noticing the curve of her lashes, the way her nose was just a fraction too short for classical beauty, the sculpted look of her cheeks, then he kissed her on the mouth, revelling in the sweetness of her.

Very gently she moved away from him, so that she sat beside him. They stared at one another for a minute, neither speaking. Then eventually he said, "Did that upset you?"

She shook her head, saying nothing.

"Then why are you so silent?"

"Because it was wonderful, that's why."

"Really?"

"Yes."

Tom said nothing, realising in that moment that since the death of his fragile beloved his first kiss had been given to Margaret, exactly a year previously, and there had been no encounters with women since. Suddenly he felt drained of confidence and decidedly middle-aged.

"I'm too old for you," was out of his mouth before he had had time to think of the full import of the words.

Margaret Kemble sat up straight. "Are you now? And how old might that be, Colonel?"

"I've just celebrated my thirty-eighth birthday."

"Oh, when was it?"

"December the fifteenth. How old are you?"

"Bluff soldier indeed! That is a question you should not enquire of a lady. But as it's you I'll answer. I shall

be twenty-five in August. And before you ask the date, it's the fifteenth."

He smiled. "An odd coincidence."

"Very. Worth celebrating, don't you think?"

She moved closer to him, and Gage felt himself respond despite his sudden lack of self-esteem. "How would you suggest?" he asked.

"By kissing me again, just for good luck of course."

She was an inch away from him and he could see her amber eyes and the mocking expression in them.

"Oh, to hell with age," he said suddenly, and embraced her once more.

The intensity of her response surprised him, unprepared for it as he was. It told him many things about her. Firstly, that she had been kissed on many occasions before. But, more importantly, that she genuinely liked the way he kissed her and was happy for him to continue. Tom Gage opened his mouth and let his tongue explore her lips which, after a moment or two, parted. Thus, they were kissing deeply when a voice from outside called, "Margaret? Where are you?"

They drew apart reluctantly, both of them rather flushed.

"It's my mother," she whispered in his ear.

"Then you'd better go."

"Yes. Follow in about five minutes. I don't want anyone to know I've been in here with you."

"Very well. But Margaret . . ."

"What?"

"I'm not too old, am I?"

"In my opinion, Colonel, you're as young as you feel."

And with that, and a swift peck on the cheek, she swung athletically down the side of the coach and reached the floor beneath, turning to give him a smile before she left the building.

Fond though he was of Stephen Kemble, a young ensign in his own regiment, Tom Gage was hardly in the mood for him. Yet it was almost as if Margaret had mentioned something to him, for he hardly left the Colonel's side from that moment on.

Gage had waited the necessary five minutes then, having taken the precaution of buttoning his jacket and trying desperately to look presentable, he had sauntered back to the house in time for breakfast, at which he had been joined by Stephen, brimming with enthusiasm and obviously delighted that his commander should be a house guest for the festive season. Much to his annoyance, Tom had been forced to make polite conversation when all he had wanted to do was be alone to marshall his thoughts. For this was the first time since the death of his mistress that he had felt a stirring of the blood. And how deeply it had stirred when Margaret kissed him.

". . . marvellous news about your new regiment, Sir."

With a mighty effort, the Colonel wrenched his thoughts away from Stephen's sister to the conversation in hand.

"Yes. It is indeed," he said, over-heartily. "We're to set up recruiting headquarters as soon as Christmas is over."

"And where will they be, Sir?"

"I thought here in Brunswick to be as good a place as any," Tom answered in the same hearty tone.

The young man looked astonished. "Oh. Oh, I see."

Oh no you don't, Tom said mentally, though aloud he said nothing.

"Yes, a dashed good spot, Brunswick," poor Stephen blundered on. "I expect you'll be inundated with volunteers."

Tom permitted himself the luxury of a laugh. "Hardly rushed off our feet, I would have thought."

Stephen seemed lost for words but eventually said, "Why did you pick Brunswick, then?"

"Perhaps because of the proximity of your good selves," Gage answered truthfully.

The ensign took this as a compliment to himself and glowed a smile. "Well, thank you, Sir."

Gage made a suitable face and at that moment Margaret walked into the breakfast room, changed and ready to go out.

"Where are you off to?" Stephen asked.

"Mama, Judith and I are going to visit the poorer people and take them some gifts," she announced. "And what will you and Colonel Gage be doing in the meanwhile?"

"I expect we'll go for a ride. What do you say, Sir?"

"A good plan," Tom answered. But already his thoughts were elsewhere, back in the coach house, with her in his arms and the sweet surprise of her response.

"I'll see you tonight, then," he said.

"Yes, tonight," she answered and turning on her heel, went out.

It got dark early, but in the gloaming the men of the household went out to fetch the Yule Log, which had been specially chosen on Candlemas Day and stored to dry out during the summer months. This was lit, with much ceremony, with the unburnt parts of last year's log which had been saved especially for that purpose. The females, meanwhile, brought holly into the house and wove it round decoratively, and when they were finished hot glasses of Yuletide punch were served. Then everyone went to change because the Schuylers, yet more cousins, were coming to dine.

Alone in his room, Tom sat on the edge of his bed and remembered for the hundredth time the feel of Margaret Kemble in his arms, lived again the moment when his mouth and hers had met. He was certain now that he was falling in love with her, and he wondered dismally where the future lay. He was thirteen, nearly fourteen, years older than she was, and no doubt she was only playing with him, leading him on for her own amusement. But, dammit, he could not treat her as he would a camp follower and take her to bed. The very rules of hospitality decreed that he must tow the line and behave like a gentleman. But it wasn't easy when she was giving him all kinds of signals which indicated otherwise.

"Damn the woman," he said aloud, and reluctantly shrugged his shoulders into his dress uniform.

Downstairs everyone was at fever pitch with excitement, and Tom felt his spirits rise. At the very least he could have a good Christmas and a pleasant flirtation — and leave it at that. But even as the thought came into his mind, he knew that he stood on the brink of something far more serious. That Margaret Kemble had that indefinable something that could quite easily lead him into deep water.

She was late, the last to arrive, and when she did it was with such style and splendour that Tom caught himself staring and blushing. She chose the moment to descend the stairs when he was attending to the Yule Log, so that his back was averted. But when he turned and saw her, dressed in dark green and red as if to echo the colours of the holly that decorated the place, his mouth fell open like a schoolboy's.

Her gaze swept everyone and finally alighted on him. Pulling himself together, Tom gave a small, ceremonial bow to which she replied with a deep curtsey, smiling at him in her beguiling way as she straightened again. It was going to be difficult to resist her, the Colonel thought. He deliberately turned to her younger sister, Judith, to make conversation.

The room was full of people, all related one to the other. Mrs. Kemble, a woman of skinny frame and delicate health, had borne seven children, five boys and two girls. The two eldest, Samuel and Richard, had recently married but had arrived to spend Christmas with their parents. The rest of the brood, Peter, Stephen and William and their sisters, were single, though Peter was courting seriously. Tom, who

had only one brother, thought of the advantages of plenty of children and felt slightly envious and out of place in the midst of such a happy family gathering.

Then, quite literally, the worst happened, and he found himself smiling wryly and taking himself to task for being a besotted fool. With a peal of the front doorbell the man he had envisaged for Margaret — only this one was no New Jersey farmer but a buck of the very first order — came into the room and looked about him.

He was stunningly handsome, his black hair tied back with a bow, his dark eyes lustrous, his tall figure superb. Further, he was dressed by a London tailor, while his white shirt must have been new on that evening. Tom Gage found himself violently disliking him for no obvious reason. But, deep down, he knew that he was jealous of so much youth and beauty, and was aware that in a straight choice between him and the newcomer, he, Tom, must bow out of the picture.

Peter Kemble Senior was making the introductions. "Thomas, I would like you to meet Philip Schuyler Junior. Philip, this is Colonel the Honourable Thomas Gage."

Tom bowed to the limit of formality and said, "A pleasure to meet you, Sir."

Philip gave a studied bow and answered, "How dee do, Sir. What a fine English accent. I was at Oxford until I came down two years ago."

"Really?" said Tom, affecting an interest which he did not feel. "Which college?"

"Magdalen, Sir."

Philip waited expectantly for the Colonel to tell him whereabouts he had attended, but instead Tom said, "I did not go to university. I went straight into the army."

Schuyler made the very slightest of faces. "How commendable."

"I don't know about that. All I can say is that I became an ensign at seventeen and have been in military service ever since."

"Very interesting I'm sure," said Philip. His eyes wandered round the room and alighted on Margaret. "Excuse me, Colonel, if you would. I see my cousin Margaret and must go and pay my respects to her." He gave another small, elegant bow and left Tom standing alone.

So that was it, thought the Colonel. The minx had led him on, probably for something to do, but now her real lover was here. He decided to get very slightly drunk and took his glass back to the punch bowl where a Negro slave, dressed in livery, was silently serving.

It would have been socially incorrect to have conversed with the man, but nonetheless Tom studied him idly. He was a match for Philip Schuyler in every way except for the colour of his skin. Tall, supple, with an even better physique than the white man's, the slave was handsome by anybody's standards. The white wig which he wore set off his features, while his dark eyes — which met Tom's for a second before looking away — were superb. The Colonel reckoned him to be about twenty years old and as full of vigour as any of the Kemble brothers whom it was his lot to serve. Then, quite suddenly, Judith, all eighteen years of her,

approached the punch bowl and murmured something in an undertone. The Negro filled her glass and murmured something back. Their eyes met for the briefest of seconds, but the look told Tom Gage all he needed to know. They were not lovers yet but by God they were going to be. Clearing his throat, the Colonel turned away.

The call came to go in to dine and Tom found himself seated with Mrs. Kemble's unmarried sister, Agnes, on his right and Margaret on his left. Next to her was the ubiquitous Philip, dripping charm, a diamond cravat pin sparkling in the candlelight as he turned between the ladies who flanked him. The Colonel, watching him covertly, found nothing to like about the fellow at all. Margaret, however, was very charming and seemed to find time for her companions on both sides, sharing herself equally between the two. Tom, not to be outdone, concentrated hard on Miss Agnes and managed to elicit a few whispered sentences from her. Eventually, though, it was time for the ladies to withdraw, and he was left alone with the assembled masculine company. Despite earnest conversation with the various brothers Kemble, it was Philip Schuyler who leant across and spoke to him.

"Are you enjoying yourself, Colonel Gage?"

"Yes, very much."

"However, it must be difficult being away from your family at this time of year. Surely you would give anything to be back home."

Tom gave a short laugh. "My dear Sir, I have been here two years and am perfectly used to it."

"Still, it must be hard for you."

The Colonel fought back a rising irritation. "No, believe me, I am content."

"And Mrs. Gage?"

"There is no Mrs. Gage."

"I see," said Schuyler, and his look said it all.

Tom turned away angrily, the inference that he was a bung-boy unspoken but made abundantly clear. He drained his port and refilled his glass, wondering whether to take Philip to task, then deciding that the laws of hospitality forbade him from doing any such thing. And he was still sitting thus, quietly fuming, when the ladies came back in.

Margaret ran her eyes over the assembled company, then, for reasons best known to herself, came straight up to Tom.

"Well, Colonel, we have some Christmas games ready, and I am relying on you to give me a helping hand."

He had already risen to his feet, but now he took her fingers and raised them to his lips, watching her all the time as he did so. She looked at him, and he saw that she knew that something was wrong and was sympathetic.

"It will be my pleasure, Miss Kemble."

"I hope you will be amused by our diversions, Colonel Gage."

"I can think of nothing more delightful than being diverted by yourself," he said, and kissed her hand again.

She removed herself from his grasp but not before he had seen an unreadable look cross her face. "Then please follow me," was all she said.

The Kemble family had laid on a splendid entertainment which included games and carol singing. Tom, his spirits restoring fast, joined in with enthusiasm. And when, finally, Miss Agnes sat down and played music for dancing, he approached Margaret confidently. His hopes, however, were dashed as she announced, "I always have the first dance with Philip, I'm afraid. It's a family tradition."

Tom bowed and turned away, but immediately found himself cornered by Mrs. Schuyler. She was one of those women whose every wish must be pandered to, and so he made a set with various young Kembles, all of whom threw themselves into the dancing with gusto. Fortunately Philip's mother ran out of breath and was escorted back to her seat with much use of her fan. Thus Tom found an excuse to step outside and get some air.

It was a bitter night lit by a huge silver moon, the trees, still snow covered, etched blackly against the indigo sky. Tom, having taken several good deep breaths, a therapy in which he had a great belief, was just about to go back inside when he realised that he was not alone. Two dark figures stood beneath a tree, talking. Without meaning to, he drew back into the shadows and listened.

". . . let's announce it tonight, sweetheart. It will make their Christmas if we do."

It was the dreaded Philip who had just spoken and Thomas realised that he was stuck where he was. If he went back inside now, they would know that he had been there eavesdropping.

"Philip, no." It was Margaret's voice. "Let's not do anything in a hurry."

"But why not? I've been asking you since the summer."

"That's not the point."

"But it is. I want to tell them of our engagement when everybody is together, enjoying themselves. Of course, the public announcement will have to follow later, but why not now as far as our families are concerned?"

"Because I'm not ready."

"What do you mean exactly?"

"Just what I say, Philip. I'm not ready. I've got to do some serious thinking."

"Why?"

"Because I have. Because I'm not sure what I want."

Gage heard Philip make a noise of exasperation and could picture him clearly, dark eyes narrowing in the moonshine, the elegant lips going into a hard line.

"And what is that supposed to mean?"

"Oh." Now she was getting annoyed, but Tom steered his mind away from how she would look, finding it too painful to fill his thoughts with her.

"Well?" Philip continued.

"I'm just not sure about anything any more."

"Not sure you want to marry me?"

"As you mention it, no. I really don't know,"

"It's nothing to do with that Gage fellow, is it?" Philip's tone was sharp with suspicion and, despite himself, Tom craned his ears. "You're on a loser if it is," Philip continued nastily. "He's not interested in your type, my dear."

"Meaning?"

"Something I can't explain to a lady. Just take it from me that he's not interested in women."

"Oh really? I hadn't thought that at all."

"Why? Don't tell me he's made overtures to you. I find that hard to credit."

"Stop it, Philip. Your hideous innuendos are completely without foundation. He's as good a lover — better — than most men of his age."

"And how do you know that, my dear?"

"I know it because I do. How dare you? You are to consider any understanding we might have had as over."

Philip lost control. "You arrogant girl. I'm not only your cousin but heir to the Schuyler fortune, I'd remind you."

"I don't care if you're the richest man in the Colonies, Philip. Our understanding is over."

And with a tremendous rustling of her skirts, Margaret Kemble swept from the balcony and back into the house.

Gage stood motionless, terrified lest Schuyler should discover his presence. But after a few moments, during which Philip cursed wildly under his breath, he, too, returned to the house.

So that was that. She had been engaged to her cousin, at least unofficially, but had ended it this very night. With something like hope in his heart, Colonel Gage went back into the mansion.

He woke suddenly and quite automatically reached for his pistol, which he always kept beneath his pillow. It wasn't there, and after a few seconds he remembered where he was and that his gun had been stowed away safely for the duration of the Christmas festivites. It also occurred to him that it was Christmas Day, and the sound he had heard could well be someone creeping along with presents. He lay utterly still and listened for the noise again, and sure enough, heard it once more. Somebody was scratching faintly at his door.

Swinging his legs out of bed, Tom, very aware of the fact that he was naked except for his nightshirt, crossed to the door and opened it a crack. It was pushed, quite hard, so that momentarily he lost his footing and staggered backwards. The person outside took advantage of this and came in, closing the door behind them silently. The Colonel stared at Margaret Kemble, wearing nothing but a nightgown and rail.

"Miss Kemble!" he exclaimed. "What are you doing?"

"I have broken my engagement to Philip Schuyler," she said and promptly burst into tears.

He did the only thing he could to comfort her, taking her into his arms, realising that without heels the top of her head only reached to his shoulder, all the while

82

making soothing noises, much as one would do to a child.

Eventually the weeping abated, and she looked at him from eyes awash with tears. "Oh, Tom, have I done the silliest thing?"

"Probably," he answered, sighing despite himself.

"Why do you say that?"

"Because Philip Schuyler is rich and going to get richer. He is what is known as a good catch, Margaret."

"But I don't want to catch him," she answered and started to weep once more.

"Listen, be quiet," he said comfortingly. "If you don't love him, there's your answer."

"I used to love him, at least I thought I did. But now . . ."

"Yes?"

"But now I know I don't."

Gage felt his heartbeat start to speed up. "And why is that?"

She looked at him, eyes glistening. "Haven't you guessed?"

His heart was now so loud that surely she must be able to hear it. "No, I haven't," he answered huskily.

"Because, Colonel Thomas Gage, you came into my life, didn't you?"

And with that she fled from his arms and out of the room, leaving Tom to stare after her, feeling the first thrill of pure joy as he gazed at the place where, but a moment before, she had been standing.

CHAPTER
FIVE

January, 1758

"Did you have a good Christmas, Sir?" asked Major Henry Gladwin, somewhat amused by the faraway expression on his Colonel's face.

"Um?" said Thomas.

"I said, did you have a good Christmas?"

Tom Gage returned to reality, though not without a certain struggle. "The best of my life," he answered expansively and then grinned broadly.

He was sitting in the living room of a private house in Brunswick, commandeered by the army as a recruiting headquarters, the freshly hand-painted sign outside the front door, complete with arrow to indicate exactly where the applicants should go. So far that morning they had received one person who was already drunk despite the earliness of the hour. Nevertheless, the man had looked fit and had been young, the two main criteria, and they had signed him up on the spot. The fact that the fellow couldn't write but had signed with an X had also been disregarded.

As for Gage himself, he still hadn't returned to reality following the festivities. He was by now deeply in love with Margaret and had high hopes that she had the same feelings for him. On every possible occasion they had slipped away from the others to be alone together.

And then the ardour that they aroused in one another had been almost uncontainable. Yet, by sheer will power, Tom had controlled himself, knowing that this girl was special, that she could not be treated like one of the hordes of women who followed the army wherever it went. In other words, he was behaving like an officer and a gentleman — and hating every second.

He sighed aloud, knowing that the gap in age between him and Margaret was his main cause for concern, and Henry Gladwin looked up from the bundle of papers he was reading.

"Anything wrong, Sir?"

Gage smiled a little sadly, taking himself to task for being a besotted old fool. "Only myself, Henry."

"How do you mean, Sir?"

Gage teetered on the brink, wondering whether to confide or not, then, because he longed to talk to someone else about his problem, blurted everything out in a rush.

"It's Margaret Kemble. The trouble is I'm falling in love with her. But she's considerably younger than I am; fourteen years to be precise."

"So?"

"So it fills me with doubt. I can't decide whether she really cares or whether she is playing some intricate game."

"Why don't you ask her. Straight out. Tell her you're unsure of the situation and would like it clarified."

Tom pulled a face. "The trouble is I don't want to end it."

"But why should it end? She is probably waiting for you to say something."

"Like what?"

"Oh, for heavens sake, Sir. Ask her to marry you if that is what you want."

Gage grew quiet, thinking about spending the rest of his life with such a delightful girl as Margaret and wondering if he was man enough. Something of what he was considering must have shown on his face, because Gladwin said "You do want that, don't you, Sir?"

Tom hesitated, beset by doubts about himself, then answered, "I would love it, if I thought I could make her happy."

"Give her plenty of children, Sir. That's the way to keep her occupied," Major Gladwin answered, then, realising how bold he was being with his commanding officer, blushed. But Tom, suddenly happy at the thought that other people did not frown on the age gap, laughed uproariously.

"I've a mind to do as you say, Henry. I think I'll propose."

"It will bring things to a conclusion, one way or the other, Sir."

"It certainly will."

There was a noise in the doorway as a man appeared, looking hopeful. "Are you the recruiting sergeant?" he asked Tom, his accent clearly of the Colonies.

"I suppose you could call me that," Gage answered, and with a smile motioned the young fellow to take a seat.

★ ★ ★

Despite his show of bravado, Tom found it almost impossible to bring himself to the point of proposing. During the next few days, he called at Margaret Kemble's house with as much frequency as possible and finally managed to slip out with her into the gardens, cold though the weather was. Walking beside her, he took her small, gloved hand in his own, but said nothing, instead walking onwards, his eyes firmly to the front. Eventually, though, she stopped and turned to face him.

"What have I done to upset you?"

"Nothing. Why?" he asked, surprised.

"You've been so edgy the last few times we have met."

"I'm sorry. I didn't realise." He put his hands on her shoulders. "Can we continue this coversation in the summerhouse? It's damnable cold out here."

"It will be damnable cold in there as well."

"At least we'll be out of the wind."

"There isn't any wind."

"Margaret," said Tom, and this time his voice did have an edge to it, "do as I want for once, will you."

She gave him a deep look from those incredible eyes of hers but, without further argument, strode before him to the summerhouse, locked up and desolate at this time of year. However, there was an old and somewhat well-used key in the lock, which she turned. Inside it was dim, full of metal garden furniture, stacked carefully in a perilous pile, but pushing this slightly to one side she made room for herself and Gage to sit on the wooden seat.

"Now then," she said.

The Colonel was completely nonplussed, not having an idea what he should say. Eventually, though, he managed to blurt out, "You know that I hold you in the highest regard."

She muttered something which sounded like, "A bit too damned high."

"I beg your pardon?"

"I said, 'A bit too damned high'. "

"And what is that supposed to mean."

The wondrous eyes turned on him again. "I know that you hold back sometimes."

Gage gave a bitter laugh. "Well, what else can I do? You are the daughter of my host; you come from a good family. I can hardly treat you as if you were a camp follower."

"Did you not tell me that some of them are ladies of rank and fortune?"

"Possibly."

"Well, then."

Half angry with her, Gage, turning, took her in his arms. "Margaret, I'm serious. I can't take you to bed, much as I want to."

She gave him a look that melted his soul. "Why not?"

"Because I can't," he answered crossly, aware that even while she was speaking to him he was becoming aroused.

"But I want you to."

"Is that what you said to Philip Schuyler?"

She drew away from him. "That never happened with him. Oh, you foolish man. It's you who awaken these thoughts in me, don't you understand? For some

reason, God alone knows what, you have made me wish that I was one of those women."

"What do you mean?"

"A camp follower. I want to be your mistress, Tom. I want you to make love to me."

In distress he answered, "I mustn't, Margaret. Don't you understand? I would dishonour your father's hospitality if I did."

She wept, genuinely upset. "Then what am I to do?"

"Marry me," he said, and the words came out of his mouth so easily he wondered that he had been afraid to say them.

She took his face in her hands, holding it tightly so that he could not look away. "Repeat that slowly."

He laughed, suddenly knowing what the answer was going to be, suddenly sure that she wanted him as much as he wanted her. "I said, marry me."

She kissed him, very gently, first on the nose and then on the lips. "I thought you weren't going to ask me," she said and looked as vulnerable as a child, her old laughing, teasing self completely vanished.

"Do you love me?" Tom said seriously.

"Oh yes. I think I loved you right from the start, when I heard your funny English accent on the stairs."

"Going to meet Mrs. Van Cortlandt?"

"Yes, then. You looked so dashing in your uniform, I found it impossible to resist you."

"Is that why you wrote to me?"

"Yes, you know it is. But what about me? When did you fall in love with me?" Her face changed. "You do love me, don't you."

"You know damned well I do. Anyway, you haven't given me an answer yet."

"What answer? Oh, neither have I. Well, I'll have to think about it."

"For how long?"

She was her old tantalising self again, shooting him brilliant looks. "I don't know. Five minutes."

"Then let me ask you again — properly." With certain difficulties, given the very cramped space they were in, Tom Gage went down on one knee, disturbing a large spider as he did so. "Miss Kemble, will you do me the honour of giving me your hand in marriage?"

She smiled naughtily. "I daresay." Then seeing his downcast expression, Margaret relented and threw her arms round his neck. "Yes, my darling, yes, yes, yes. Now please get up. That poor spider longs to return to its web."

He stood up, pulling her to her feet with him, and they indulged in a long, deep kiss; a kiss during which he allowed his hand to caress her breasts, actually slipping one inside her bodice and bending his lips to kiss the small, round bosom thus exposed. She stood silently, eyes closed, enjoying this new sensation.

"You've never done that before," she said eventually.

"We have not been betrothed before."

"Does that mean . . . ?"

"No," said Tom firmly, removing his lips and tucking her back inside. "Now, let us go indoors. Your parents will think us lost."

She loitered for one minute more. "A final kiss before we tell the world."

"I must go to New York and get you a ring." He paused, then said, "Margaret, you are quite sure you want to proceed with this? I am fourteen years older than you are, remember."

She smiled her delightful smile. "My darling, that is the least of my considerations. The point at issue is that I truly care for you, and I want to be your wife. Is that good enough?"

He looked at her seriously, then grinned. "It's quite good enough for me, my dear."

The Kembles, mother and father, bore such knowing expressions that Tom immediately guessed that they had been expecting something like this for days. None the less, Colonel Gage asked if he might make an appointment to see Mr. Kemble privately, expecting to be told to come back in a day or two. But yet again he was to be surprised by the fresh outlook of the colonists.

"Well, Colonel, if you have the time, I most certainly have. How about now?"

Tom bowed and clicked his heels, suddenly nervous. "Certainly, Sir. It is very kind of you," and he followed Peter Kemble down the corridor, wondering what he would do if Margaret's father were to say no, citing the age gap as his reason.

The house, which had been built some thirty years earlier, was square and tall, rising three storeys in height, with servants' quarters on the top floor under the roof. Coming to the foot of the elegant staircase, Kemble motioned Gage upwards, passing many fine

rooms as they made their ascent. The Colonel had seen the interiors of many of them but was still astonished at just how good a life the rich could have in the Colonies. Yet, by contrast, other, poorer people lived very plainly and worked very hard. But then, he supposed, it was ever thus, and all he was seeing was a mirror of England, though with a certain restless energy that the old country lacked.

They reached Peter Kemble's study, a room Tom had not seen before, lined with bookcases and with extremely good Dutch paintings on the walls. A fire had been lit before which were two large and comfortable chairs. Tempted though he was to accept Margaret's father's offer of a seat, the Colonel felt it better if he remained standing. Kemble, meanwhile, settled himself and looked at Gage with an enigmatic smile.

"Well, Colonel Gage?"

"Sir, I have something important to ask you."

"And what might that be, pray?"

"The fact is, Sir, that I . . ."

"Yes?"

"That I wish to pay my addresses to your daughter."

"I have two, Sir. Which one did you mean?"

"Margaret, of course," Tom said rapidly.

"Ah," said Peter Kemble, and steepled his long fingers, resting his chin on them.

"Would that be in order, Sir?" Gage asked, feeling decidedly tense.

Kemble chuckled, a reassuring sound. "I take it you have mentioned this to her."

"Yes, Sir, as a matter of fact, I have."

92

"And her answer?"

"Was yes. So now it is up to you, Mr. Kemble."

Kemble laughed once more. "I had hoped for someone with better prospects than an English army colonel for my daughter."

Philip Schuyler came into Gage's mind, but he stood silently, mouth firmly closed.

"But," said Kemble, with a definite twinkle in his eye, "no doubt you have hopes of rising high."

"Yes, indeed I do, Sir," Tom answered stiffly.

"In that case, what can I say?"

"I hope, Sir, that you will give me your blessing. That you will give us your blessing."

Kemble stood up and shook Tom's hand firmly. "My boy, forgive me for teasing you a little. My wife and I have watched your growing attachment for Margaret with interest, wondering when you were going to say something. Naturally we are delighted that she will become part of such a well-established English family."

Tom smiled at last. "I shall write to my brother forthwith. Though I must admit that I have mentioned my feelings for Margaret already in a letter."

"Will the Viscount be pleased with the outcome?"

"He will be delighted."

"And so am I. Pray have a drink in celebration, Colonel."

"Tom, please, Sir. And, yes, I would love one."

Outside night drew in over the New Jersey countryside, still mainly snow covered though men had dug paths and tracks for easy access for themselves and their carts. But inside the Kemble household that night

fires crackled and people celebrated. Toasts were proposed and healths were drunk, and in the midst of the circle of happy faces stood Tom and Margaret, blissfully bright, very much in love, and totally unaware of the future that fate had lying in wait for them.

CHAPTER
SIX

July, 1758

The snows had long since gone, making way for another hot, unrelenting summer. And in the heat sweated fifteen thousand soldiers, half of them Regulars, trudging through the ruins of what had once been Fort William Henry towards Ticonderoga. Gage, in the uniform of full colonel, could feel the sweat running down inside his shirt and was more than aware of the fact that he stank, washing facilities being of the poorest, even for the officers, when the army was on the move. He was unaware, however, of the fact that he was a good-looking man, with his long, aristocratic nose, his firm chin and full, rather sensual lips. Nor did he understand the power of his eyes, which were an unusual shade of blue, quite light, the colour of a spring sky. Yet he did know that his looks had made him popular with members of the opposite sex all his adult life, although he had never considered the reasons why. And now he was betrothed to that captivating beauty Margaret Kemble, she of the dark hair and amber eyes, and planned to marry her before Christmas. That is, if he survived the present campaign.

At the moment, the army was making its way northwards, up the shores of Lake George, its aim to conquer Canada and drive out the French, still in an

unholy alliance with the Indian nation. And, for once, they were full of hope as, from England, the dominating Prime Minister Pitt infused new life into the troops. In fact, spirits were high and Gage, in command of his own regiment, the 80th Foot or Gage's Light Armed Infantry, part of the advance guard, found himself whistling as he rode along at the head of his men.

"Happy, Sir?"

It was Major Gladwin who had spoken, riding rapidly to join Gage in the forefront.

Gage smiled. "Yes, I suppose I am. As happy as one can be in this sort of situation."

"Why do you say that? We haven't come across any French so far."

"My dear Henry, they could be watching us at this very moment. As a matter of fact, I don't like all this quiet. I don't trust it."

"I know what you mean," Gladwin answered, glancing round him.

Tom Gage laughed. "But that's just my superstition. There's probably not a Frenchman for miles."

"If there is we should have glimpsed them by now."

"Yes, we should. I've sent Calico Joel on to have a look."

Gladwin appeared relieved. "Well, if anyone can find them, it will be him. He's invaluable. Can't say that I like him any better though."

"He's an odd cuss," Gage agreed, nodding. "He's so damnably taciturn, that's the trouble."

"That's his Indian blood. What happened to his French mother, by the way?"

"She wouldn't go back to her own people. They returned her to civilisation but she ran away, back to her Cherokee. I believe she died some years later."

"And the father?"

"God knows; maybe he's still alive. Who can tell?"

"Calico Joel presumably."

"Presumably," answered Tom, and they both laughed.

As soon as the light began to fade, Colonel Gage, still at the head of the column, called a halt for the day, and the men began to light fires and put up the small tents which they carried in their backpacks. As he had originally intended, the men travelled light and fast, carrying no more than somewhere to sleep and a tin mug and plate. Their guns and ammunition they wore, quite literally, about their person. Yet the Colonel had insisted that they should get a decent night's rest. For himself, he had a full-sized tent, carried by a packhorse, which was in process of being erected when Calico Joel appeared silently by his side.

"I wish you wouldn't do that," said Tom, jumping, his mind at that moment firmly on Margaret, whose latest letter he had received just before he left civilisation.

"It is the Indian way."

"To creep up soundlessly?"

"To move without making any noise, yes. *Mon Colonel*, I have much to impart."

"Tell me."

"The enemy is just ahead of you. You are walking into a trap."

Gage drew in a breath. "I knew they wouldn't be far away. Where are they exactly?"

"At Ticonderoga, five miles ahead. The Marquis de Montcalm is fortifying the fort there with much haste. He knows you are coming."

"I see."

Glancing over, Tom saw that his tent was ready for him and motioning the scout to join him, he went within. Once inside, he poured two glasses of spirit into tin mugs and sat down on a folding camp chair, indicating the other to Calico Joel.

"Tell me from the beginning. What did you see?"

"I saw a breastwork of logs and a rampart of sharpened stakes hastily being put together."

Gage stroked his chin. "Um. We must get word to General Abercromby. And fast at that."

Calico Joel drained his mug and held it out for a refill, saying nothing. Tom automatically filled it, together with his own.

"I will go an hour before first light, *mon Colonel.*"

"He'll be moving his troops then, as will I."

"What better time to catch him?" the scout replied simply.

"What do you mean?"

"He will be fresh from a night's sleep. His decision will be clearer than one grasped at this hour."

It was said as a statement, quite finally, and the Colonel was left with no choice but to accept the man's word.

"Where will you sleep?" he asked.

"On the ground, close by."

"Is there anything you require for the night?" asked Gage.

"Nothing, *mon Colonel*."

"Calico Joel, tell me something."

"What?"

"Is your father still alive?"

"Yes. He is a chief of the Cherokees. He is not on the warpath."

"Why do you scout for us; surely your allegiance should lie with the other side?"

"You treated me well, *mon Colonel*. When we first met. Remember?"

And Tom Gage did. It had been in the woods east of Fort Duquesne. Gage had been newly arrived in America, and he had, quite literally, stumbled over a wounded Indian lying on the ground, preparing to die. He had done what any man would and carried the fellow, thin to the point of starvation, back to camp and put him in the hands of the army surgeon. And there Calico Joel had made a miraculous recovery and instead of leaving when he was better, had gone to see the Colonel — then of lesser rank — and offered himself as a scout. The fact that he spoke English and French had been amazing enough, but his abilities as a scout had been overpowering. He had joined Gage forthwith and from that day forward had been his bond man. Yet an extremely strange one.

Now he simply said, "Goodnight, *mon Colonel*," and moved out of sight, leaving Tom alone to finish his drink.

Colonel Gage unbuttoned his uniform and stared up at the sky. The moon was new, a mere crescent, but the stars shone in their thousands, as they had done since time began. So a trap lay in wait for them, he thought, and a cruel trap if Calico Joel's word was to be trusted. And tomorrow, General Abercromby would be informed and make a decision, no doubt, to take evasive action.

Tom sighed, finished his drink and pulled the flaps of his tent together. Then, pouring some water recently drawn from a nearby river into a basin, he washed away as best he could the stinks of the day. Then, last thing, before he blew out his candle, he put his head outside again. There was no movement anywhere, the men all asleep.

"Oh God," he found himself praying, "Let me stay alive. Let me survive whatever happens. Let me know the happiness of being married to Margaret, even if it is only for a few months."

Thus saying, he closed the flaps once more and fell asleep on his hard camp bed.

"What do you mean he said we're to march ahead?" Tom said incredulously.

"That was his answer, *mon Colonel*."

"I can scarcely credit it."

It was dawn, and the entire camp was up and preparing to move. Breakfast, what there had been of it, had been eaten as the sun first came over the horizon. And now the men, dressed and ready in their brown coats with black buttons, awaited their orders for the

day. However the Colonel, closeted still in his tent with the chief Indian scout, had so far not emerged to give them any. So they rested as best they could until their instructions were issued, wondering what they were going to be called upon to do.

"I can't believe it," Gage continued, his expression askance.

Calico Joel's face remained as impassive as ever. "I told General Abercromby what I had seen, but he said there was to be no change in orders."

Tom shook his head slowly. "Is the man stupid or what?" was out of his mouth before he could control the words.

The Indian shrugged. "I repeat what he said only, *mon Colonel*."

"Yes, and don't repeat my reaction or my arse will be well and truly kicked."

A momentary grin crossed the Indian's features before it vanished as quickly as it had come. "I'll keep quiet," he said, short as ever.

Gage stood up from his camping chair. "I'd best say nothing to the men," he remarked grimly.

"No, best not."

"So we'll go forward — straight into the trap."

"Yes," said Calico Joel simply. "Straight into the trap."

They marched for two hours, during which time the Colonel kept away from General Abercromby and his men, moving more slowly with their heavy baggage. So it was that he and his troop were first on the scene, gazing with horror at the abatis of fallen timber that

had been prepared for them. Calling his men to halt, he awaited the General's arrival. And eventually, after an hour's delay, the heavily laden force caught up with them.

"Well, Sir," said Abercromby, squinting at Fort Ticonderoga with its gruelling defences, "what do you think?"

"I think we would have been better to have gone further west and avoided trouble, General."

"Hm." Abercromby, a short, somewhat bad-tempered man, studied the fort through his telescope. "We can take the place, easy. We'll charge 'em and be damned."

"We'll be damned all right," Gage said under his breath. Aloud, he turned to Major Henry Gladwin. "Are the men ready, Major?"

"Ready as they'll ever be, Sir."

"Then order them to charge."

"But . . ."

"I said charge, Major Gladwin. The General has ordered a headlong frontal assault."

"Yes, Sir, but . . ."

"You can tell them I'll be at the fore."

"Right, Sir."

So began yet another brave but hopeless challenge to the might of the French. Again and again, Gage's Light Armed Infantry charged with incredible courage into an impenetrable abatis. Meanwhile, Abercromby's men, gallant to the last, ran alongside them. But as they approached the fort the most deadly crossfire opened up. The Marquis de Montcalm had positioned his men

brilliantly, on either side of the oncoming British forces. The oncomers were indeed caught in the most terrible snare they had ever encountered.

Colonel Gage was beyond worrying about his personal safety and charged recklessly towards the defences, throwing caution to the winds. On either side of him his regiment, formed with so much love and care, dropped in their tracks, or, worse, became entangled in the dead branches, suspended in grotesque positions, brown coats alongside red.

"Bastards," shrieked the Colonel, wildly firing at the unseen enemy. "Bastards. How dare you bring my boys down."

All around him his men were struggling with ferocious courage to get through the trap and dying for their pains. Bullets were flying everywhere, singing in his ears, so that when one hit him in the arm it hardly came as a surprise. None the less, it halted him, and he clutched at the wound with his hand. But he would have gone on running forward if Calico Joel had not appeared from nowhere and put himself directly in the way.

"Leave the field, Colonel," was all he said.

Tom stared at him. "I can't do that."

"You're wounded. Let the surgeons dig the bullet out or Miss Kemble will have a dead man for a bridegroom."

It was the mention of her name that brought him back to reality, that and the tight grip on his good arm that he simply couldn't shake off. With a crab-like persistence, Calico Joel would not release his hold until

the Colonel, reluctantly, allowed himself to be led to the medical tent, where he waited his turn amongst the dead and the dying.

"You were lucky," said the doctor, as he extracted the bullet. "That bullet probably saved your life."

"How do you mean?"

"If you'd stayed out there you would have been killed for sure."

"How many are fallen? Do you know?"

"Over a thousand," said the surgeon, and started to stitch the wound

"A thousand!" repeated Gage, and turned away to hide the tears in his eyes.

In fact it was more than one thousand and six hundred men who fell that day. Eventually, Abercromby admitted defeat and ordered what was left of the regiments to withdraw. So, that night, Thomas Gage sat in his tent and reflected on the horrible losses of the encounter and wept, privately, once more, that his own regiment should have been so decimated.

After midnight, with his single candle still burning, Calico Joel slipped silently through the flaps of the tent and stood before him.

"You called for me, *mon Colonel?*"

Tom, drunk and depressed, his arm aching wildly, looked at him. "No, I didn't call."

"Then your soul must have done. Here, let me rub some of this on your wound."

"What is it?"

"An Indian balm, it is made from cornflowers. Here."

And before Tom could object, the scout had removed the bandage and begun to gently rub in his ointment. It was very soothing, the Colonel had to admit it, and so he fell asleep, sitting in his chair, the Indian massaging his arm and singing, very quietly, a Cherokee prayer for a safe recovery.

When he awoke in the cold grey dawn it was to find that the pain in his arm had reduced to a dull ache, and he knew then that it would only be a flesh wound and would heal completely. Of Calico Joel there was no sign; indeed, there was little sign of anyone as Gage stepped out of his tent and gazed on the remnants of his regiment, lying on the ground, too tired to put up their shelters. Turning away, Thomas Gage walked into the darkness of the quiet forest to contemplate the horror and futility of war.

CHAPTER
SEVEN

December 8th, 1758

He stood in the small white church, happier than he had ever been in his life before, yet decidedly nervous for all that. For this was the moment he had been awaiting for most of his adult life, the moment when, after many amorous adventures, he finally settled down and took a bride. He was just days away from his thirty-ninth birthday, his future wife was twenty-five and beautiful into the bargain. Thomas Gage, the fighting done for the year, had every right to be well pleased with himself.

Yet the happiness he felt was tinged with sadness. It was doubtful whether the 80th Foot, otherwise known as Gage's chasseurs, would be kept on after the close of hostilites. Still, they had given him a consolation prize by raising him to the rank of brigadier, which couldn't be overlooked. But for all that, his regiment, swelling in numbers again after the massacre at Fort Ticonderoga, was dear to his heart, and he would be sad indeed to see it disbanded.

The church overflowed with people, some of the congregation being forced to stand at the back. Gage, surrounded by his fellow officers — who had nicknamed Margaret 'the Duchess' — were as nothing compared with the gathering of the Kemble clan

including, of course, the usual smattering of De Lanceys, Van Cortlandts and Schuylers. Philip was present, dressed to cause a stir, a beautiful young woman accompanying him, tightly clinging to his arm and gazing winsomely at everyone who looked at her. Tom wondered whether this might be a new love or simply an adornment, brought along to show the world how little he cared about Margaret.

There was an organ in the church, having been bought and donated by Peter Kemble himself, and this had been rumbling away with pieces by Bach and Haydn from the moment the first guests set their foot across the threshold. But now it piped a fanfare, and there was a rustle in the congregation. With his dress uniform of brigadier chafing his neck, Tom allowed himself a peep round and saw that there was movement in the porch. He swiftly turned his head and stared frontwards, aware that the bridegroom's witness — who else but his old comrade-in-arms, the Duke of Devonshire's protégé, Henry Gladwin — was having a good look at the bride's arrival.

"Here comes the Duchess," Henry muttered, and at that moment, Tom felt so many conflicting emotions that tears stung his eyes but fortunately did not fall.

She was making a slow progress up the aisle, leaning on the arm of her father, no doubt smiling at all who caught her eye. Meanwhile, the organist, a middle-aged man with a flowing wig and a pair of folding spectacles on his nose, leaned closer to the organ as he applied pedals and pulled out stops in order to give as grand an

accompaniment to the bridal entry as possible. Then, in a rustle of skirts, she was beside him.

Tom turned to look at Margaret and could not help but stare at her in admiration. She could have worn white or tawny, but had chosen the lighter colour. Her fantastically embroidered petticoat was of a slightly bluish shade, above which her rounded neckline, cut dramatically low, fell away in an open robe of white tafetta. On her head she wore a headdress of ribbons and flowers matching those she wore at her neck.

"You look beautiful," he whispered.

"Beautiful for you," she murmured back.

The service began, conducted by an Anglican clergyman, a tall colonial, well pleased with his flock, as they were with him. Eventually though there came a pause in his long-winded oration and Tom, realising that he was being regarded by a pair of commanding steel-grey eyes, knew it was the time to exchange vows. Taking Margaret's hands in his, he spoke the words, "I, Thomas . . ."

But though he continued to speak and pledge himself to her, his mind roamed far away, back to the expanse of the family estates at Firle and Highmeadow and the loveliness of them both. He wondered, briefly, if he would ever be able to take his bride back to England, let her see for herself the exquisite glory of the church of Staunton rising above thousands of acres of woodland, the swelling majesty of the distant hills.

He came back to reality as he put the ring upon Margaret Kemble's finger. She was his, for better or for worse. Then the most curious thing happened. Just for

108

a moment it seemed as if time had hurried forward, as if he and she stood in a corner of it as yet to be experienced. He heard a voice say, "I have been betrayed," and recognised it as his own. He saw her eyes, her gorgeous dark eyes, slide away from his, unable to meet them. But when he forced her head round so that she had to look at him, he saw that they had become hard and cruel, glittering like a snake's.

". . . those whom God hath joined together . . ." the clergyman was saying, and with an enormous effort of will Thomas Gage came back to reality. He looked at his wife and saw that she was smiling at him, her eyes as soft and teasing as ever. He bent his head and kissed her and with an effort put his terrible premonition behind him.

The wedding breakfast was held at the Kemble mansion and was as luxurious and resplendent as only one of the leading colonial clans could make it. Dozens of little tables had been set up, round which gathered the guests; the officers splendid in their uniforms, the ladies dressed in the very latest fashions from London and Paris, for they had had a whole year to prepare for the great event and were now vying with one another. At the head table sat Tom and Margaret, surrounded by the best flowers that the gardens could provide for the time of year.

He was madly in love with her, realising how lucky he was that the beautiful young daughter of one of the governing families should have given him her hand in marriage. But still the odd occurrence in church, that

moment when time had frozen and he had seen into the future, haunted him.

"Tom, what's the matter?" Margaret said in her forthright way.

"Nothing, my darling. Why do you ask?"

"You looked at me so oddly in church. Just as if you didn't know me. I didn't care for it at all."

Tom hesitated, wondering whether to confide something of what he had felt. Then, realising how completely crazy he would sound, decided against. His marriage was tremendously important to him, the last thing he wanted was to frighten Margaret off.

"I must have been concentrating hard," he lied. "I do it at really important events. That's all it was."

Even as he spoke the words, he knew they sounded absolutely feeble, that he was making matters worse.

"Listen," he murmured urgently, "I love you, and that's what matters. I can say, with my hand on my heart, that I have never met anyone like you in my entire life. Today, in church, I promised myself to you. And that's a promise I intend to keep."

Her face softened. "You're sure?"

"As God is my judge," Tom answered solemnly.

And why then, at that moment of saying sincerely what he was feeling, should a frisson of fear possess him again? With a visible shrug of his shoulders, Brigadier Gage thrust the sensation away and turned to pick up his glass.

"Let me drink to you, my darling."

"And I to you."

They clicked glasses and gazed, smiling, into each other's eyes, his a vivid blue, hers the colour of good cognac. "To the future," they chorused and drank deeply.

Later, when all had had their fill, there was dancing in the great hall — or what passed for it in this massive colonial dwelling. Tom and Margaret, by this time both tired and longing to be alone, led the first set, then as soon as it was polite to do so announced their intention of withdrawing. This gave rise to much hilarity amongst Tom's fellow officers, somewhat inebriated to a man. It ended with them carrying him upstairs, shoulder high, then stripping him off and making lewd remarks about his private parts, before dressing him in a new nightgown made especially for the occasion. They had all forgotten his recent elevation in rank and this night acted as boys together, with much laughing and rudery.

However, there was a respectful silence when they finally led him down the corridor to the room in which Margaret awaited him, sitting up in bed. Dressed in white, a lace nightcap on her head, she looked so young and vulnerable that Tom fell even more in love with her, thinking of how well he was going to look after her; that she was, quite literally, a child bride compared with a man of his experience. He climbed into bed and sat solemnly beside her. Then Major Gladwin, with a great deal of winking, drew the curtains round them and there was a lot of noise as the merrymakers left the room.

Not certain that they were entirely alone, Tom put his finger to his lips, crawled down the length of the bed and cautiously looked out. Everyone had gone. He turned back to his bride and saw that she had removed her nightcap, letting her luxuriant hair spread over the pillow. Then, before he could say a word, she had slipped her nightgown off and lay there naked. It was the first time Tom had seen a woman nude since the death of his frail mistress, and the effect on him was profound. In one move he removed his nightshirt and knelt up so that she could see his toned and muscular body. Then he lowered himself slowly onto her.

But first they kissed and caressed. Gage, with infinite love, kissed every part of her, including her feet, which made her plead with him to enter her. Finally he did, trying to be gentle, knowing this was her first time, yet in the end carried away by his own feelings, so that he pushed hard and exploded inside her with a great shout. But afterwards, knowing well what women liked, he fondled her, using his hands, until she, too, let out a great cry, then died a little in his arms.

A long time afterwards he said, "Did you enjoy that?"

"Enjoy isn't the right word. I flew to heaven."

"So did I," he whispered close to her ear.

She turned to look at him, propping herself up on her elbow. "Do I please you, Thomas Gage?"

"Enormously."

"More than any other woman you have known?"

"Far more."

"Do you like being married to me?"

"I love it," said Thomas, closing his eyes.

"And will you always?"

"Of course I will." He was dropping off to sleep.

Margaret snuggled down beside him. "Think of years and years like this. With things between us just getting better."

Tom opened one eye. "Do you mean what I think you mean when you say things between us?"

She giggled. "Yes, I do."

He stretched out his arm and pulled her head into the crook. "Will you always love me the way you love me tonight?"

"Yes, I swear it."

A smile played round his mouth. "No, don't do that. You might go off me, and then where would you be."

"I could never go off you," she answered and yawned.

"Tired?" he asked, waking up again.

"No."

"Are you sure?"

"Yes, I'm sure."

"Then kiss me and show me how sure you are."

She moved her head so that her mouth was opposite his and then, quite slowly and deliberately, she put out her tongue and slid it between his lips.

PART TWO — SARA

CHAPTER
EIGHT

May 17th, 1774

It was a wet morning, the rain lashing across his face as he came up from his cabin below and stepped onto the deck of the *Lively*. Before him, amazingly long and decidedly intricate, stretched Boston harbour, a myriad of wharves and jetties, filled with great ships, and, more ominously, further out to sea but very much present, British warships. General Gage, commander-in-chief of the British forces in the American colonies and newly appointed royal governor of Massachusetts, returning from a pleasant sojourn in England, was about to take his first step into the city over which he had recently been given total authority.

The rain was coming down in torrents, forcing him to take a handkerchief from his pocket and wipe his eyes so that he could see the crowd awaiting him on the wharf. The town, heaving with revolutionaries he knew for a fact, certainly seemed docile enough. In fact, with the bosun's pipes whistling a greeting and the drums on board rolling, to say nothing of the bells of Boston cheerily ringing a bright carillon, Tom felt a lump in his throat, a moment of emotion which hit him unexpectedly.

He eyed the crowd once more as the ship slowly slid into its mooring. Standing stiffly to attention was the

Independent Corps of Cadets, his personal guard of honour. Gage stared at them, all buttons and finery, well aware that they had been responsible for taking possession of the tea ships during the infamous Boston Tea Party, when tea had been dumped in Boston Harbour by locals disguised as Indians. It had been an ignominious affair, and the British government had duly responded. Gage had been chosen to take the severest measures and close the port of Boston. He had been told to rule with an iron fist.

The gangplank was being moved into position and secured and in a few moments it would be up to him to descend and be greeted by the town officials. Tom composed his features, aware that he looked fine in his uniform — red, heavily embroidered with gold. He would cut a dash, he thought, more than conscious that literally dozens of pairs of eyes were upon him.

Time had been kind to him in the fifteen years since he had married Margaret. Unstooped, he still presented a tall figure, and his waistline had stayed slim, as had his wife's despite the fact that she had presented him with several children, all of whom were being educated in England. Indeed his latest child — a girl called Charlotte — had been born there. Yet despite his pleading that that is where they should remain, Margaret, in company with the baby and her brother Stephen, had set sail for New York on May 9th.

"We belong together," she had said when he had told her that America was no longer safe. "Anyway I am American. Nothing will happen to me."

And because, deep down, he needed her company and was warning her out of a sense of duty, he had given in and agreed that she should join him after visiting friends and relations in New York.

The gangplank had been finally secured to satisfaction, and Gage, drawing himself up to his full height, put his foot upon the top plank. At that moment the crowd burst into loud huzzahs, the guns from the moored men-of-war suddenly let fire in salute, and so with the sound of cheering and churchbells ringing in his ears, the General descended into the city of Boston.

An official stepped forward. "Welcome to Boston, Governor. On behalf of the citizens, I greet you."

Tom's light blue eyes, which had hardly aged, crinkled at the corners. "Thank you, Sir. I am looking forward to living amongst you."

With that he waved to the crowd, who were yelling lustily, and climbed into the carriage which awaited to take him to the Court House, where he would be sworn in. It was only a stone's throw away, at the top of King Street, where Queen Street intercepted, but the coach proceeded slowly, passing through lines of cheering people. Tom thought, as he bowed and waved his gloved hand on either side, that he would have presumed the population of Boston to be the most loyal supporters of the Crown, had recent events not proved otherwise. Still, he acknowledged their greeting with dignity, keeping his face composed for the duration of the short journey into the heart of town.

Outside the Court House there were even more people, and Tom noticed a group of blacks, standing

together, clearly slaves, shouting their greeting, though in somewhat more subdued tones. And then, quite suddenly, one face leapt out at him, one pair of eyes caught his. Just for a moment he forgot everything else and simply stared.

It was beautiful, its skin like polished amber, its hair long, dark and straight. But the eyes of the girl were totally arresting. Slanting and lovely, they were the colour of jet, shining and deep in her contrastingly light skin. That she had European blood was crystal clear, yet she stood with the slaves, quite unassuming. For a moment his light eyes and hers, dark as night, met and held and then, shyly, she dropped her gaze to the cobbles and would not lift them again. Curious as to who she was, Tom Gage swept into the Court House.

Once inside, all was formality. The General, playing his part, went up the stairs, climbing to the second floor, to where the Council and its President awaited him. With a bow, he presented his commission, after which he was sworn in by the President. This done, to the roar of cannons, he stepped onto the balcony and again acknowledged the cheers of the packed crowd. Looking down into their midst, he saw that the slaves, all of them, had gone.

"Well, Sir," said Andrew Oliver, the Lieutenant-Governor, "may I tempt you to a glass of champagne?"

"Indeed you may, Sir," Gage answered heartily, taking a glass and downing a good mouthful.

"I would like to propose a toast," Oliver added in a slight undertone. "To a successful outcome to all your endeavours."

Gage pulled a face. "There's trouble brewing; I feel it in my bones."

Andrew Oliver gave a hollow laugh. "Trouble — I'll say there is. There are so many of them, all members of the Committee of Correspondence. But the chief incendiary is a rag-and-snatcher man called Samuel Adams."

Gage looked genuinely surprised. "What do you mean? A rag-and-snatcher?"

Oliver lowered his voice even more. "Not literally. But he's a filthy bastard. His clothing is stained and rumpled; he forgets to wash. His one aim is to return Massachusetts to a Puritan community, black hats and all."

"Sounds a bit like Oliver Cromwell."

"There are similarities indeed. But beware of him, Governor. He can organise a riot in a minute — and does. He's the most dangerous man in the Colonies, and that's saying something."

Tom let out an involuntary sigh. "My God, I've got my hands full."

"Yes, Sir, you have."

"Well on the first of June, I close the port of Boston. Let's see how they like that."

"They're going to hate it."

"Still, those are my orders, and I am here to carry them out, hate or no hate."

It was Oliver's turn to sigh. "I don't envy you your task, Sir. Truly I don't."

Gage squared his shoulders. "It has to be done, and that's all there is to it."

Andrew Oliver looked him straight in the eye. "We will await developments," he said.

The next stop, with the formalities in the Court House done and the crowd dispersing, was the carrying of his goods to Province House, the mansion owned by the state in which the Governor and his family were to dwell. With the crates of personal possessions coming directly from the *Lively*, General Gage made his way by coach wondering what sort of building it was to be his fate to live in. He was pleasantly surprised.

For a start, it was large and imposing, standing back from the street in its own grounds, with stabling and a coach house behind. The house was railed off, with a porter's lodge on either corner, between which marched sentries. But it was to the roof above that Gage's eyes were drawn. For at the very top, above the cupola and dormers, stood a weather vane in the form of an Indian, with bow and arrow aiming at the spire of the Old South Church, executed in copper and gilt, with one glass eye looking down at the world below. Even seeing such a whimsy made a grin creep over the Governor's features, and he stretched in the coach, putting his arms above his head and breathing out.

The house was reached by passing through an imposing gateway and climbing a broad flight of stone steps to the grand pillared entrance. Very impressed, Tom Gage duly made his way up and found himself in a large hall, in which was standing a group of people.

The steward, a black slave, stepped forward. "Governor, so glad you arrived safely, Sir. My name is

Robin. Now, if you would like to meet your other servants."

Gage inclined his head graciously. "Of course."

"This, Sir, is Beulah . . ."

Automatically Tom smiled but his eyes had already been drawn to the back row. For there, amidst the slaves, was the girl he had noticed earlier, this time firmly looking downwards, very mindful of her lowly station in life.

With a conscious effort, Tom dragged his eyes away and concentrated on the others. "Which is the coachman?" he asked.

A grinning jackanapes, his face almost split in half he was smiling so broadly, broke the line and bowed so low that his tight curly hair touched the ground.

"Hello Governor," he said. "Welcome to Province House. The last coachman, he died recent. But I look good in livery. I can drive your coach for you."

"And your name is?"

"I am Andrew, Sir."

"And these, Governor, are Isaac, Mildred and Sara."

Sara, so that was her name. As Robin mentioned each one, the servant concerned stepped forward and bowed or bobbed, and she came at the end. Again, there was tremendous decorum, keeping her glance to the floor, not meeting the Governor's gaze.

He repeated her name, "Sara", and fleetingly she looked up. Just for a second she stared at him, her glorious dark eyes devoid of any expression except one of fear. Then again, she dropped them to the ground.

"And now, Governor, if you would like to inspect the house," said Robin, and led the way.

It was indeed a magnificent building. A huge staircase rose up through the centre, grandly designed and carved. On each floor it terminated in a square landing, from which the ascent continued towards the cupola. Tom climbed to the very top and stood there, looking out through the windows. A magnificient view was waiting to be seen from every angle; the harbour, the gardens, Boston Neck, that thin promontory of land which joined the mainland by means of a causeway. Turning once more, the Governor studied the port.

Soon, he knew, it would become deserted when his order to close was carried out. But now it was alive with ships of all kinds, though, he noticed, some were already sailing away, knowing that the future of Boston was numbered in days. His eyes swept the deeper blue of the millpond, the rolling of the great ocean, taking in the mass of piers and shipyards, warehouses and wharves, great platforms for drying fish. And there, out at sea, loomed the British men-of-war, ready to see off anyone entering the port once his order became law.

Gage turned to look in the other direction, remarking the thinness of the Neck. When storms blew or there was a particularly high tide, waves would rush over the mudflats, and then Boston would become an island. An island over which he would have total control. Shuddering suddenly, the Governor turned away.

He was just about to begin the descent when he recognised a figure in the grounds far below. Sara, the

slave, had gone to peg out washing. What kept him standing there he never afterwards knew. But the fact remained that he stayed motionless, simply staring at her, wondering about her mixed ancestry and who her parents might have been.

A cough brought the Governor back to reality, and he climbed down the narrow staircase and found himself facing Robin.

"These are the servants' quarters, Sir. The women sleep in those rooms, the men in the others. We thought we would place your valet in the small guest room on the floor below."

"That will be fine," said Tom.

"It is so arranged at the moment that the receiving rooms are on the ground floor, the bedrooms above. The master bedroom opens onto the balcony, which is very pleasant. But should Mrs. Gage be desirous . . ." His voice trailed away.

Tom turned to look at him, a smile crinkling his eyes. "Mrs. Gage will be arriving when she has visited her friends in New York."

"And approximately when will that be, Governor?"

"About September I would imagine."

"Very good, Sir."

The tour continued, terminating in the master bedroom, where a large four-poster awaited.

"I'll rest for a while, Robin. Can you make sure that I'm called at six."

"I'll send your valet as the hour strikes, Sir."

Robin bowed his way out, and Tom, removing his shoes, his formal jacket and his hose, lay down on the

bed and closed his eyes. The noises of the house grew distant even while he listened to them. A few minutes later he was fast asleep.

He woke to the sound of voices. A girl was saying, "Take your hands off me, Isaac. I told you I ain't interested. Leave me alone."

A man's voice, clearly Negro, replied, "Just one little kiss, Sara. I sure as hell think you ain't going to miss that."

"I said no, and I meant no. Now go 'bout your business."

"You're my business, Sara."

There was the sound of somebody catching someone, followed by a muffled scream. In one move, Tom was off the bed and padding silently and bare footed to the door, which he threw open, taking the couple by surprise.

Sara was in the arms of one of the black slaves, struggling violently, turning her head this way and that to avoid his kisses. They both whirled as they heard the door open, and the male slave let go of her so violently that she rocked on her feet as he made off at speed down the corridor.

Tom raised his eyebrows. "Well, well."

The violence of her reaction startled even him. Flinging herself at his feet, she burst into sudden tears.

"Oh Masser Governor, don't dismiss me. I have nowhere to go. Don't put me on the street, I beg you."

Bending over her, Gage pulled her to her feet, then fetched a handkerchief from his pocket and wiped her

eyes. "Sara, don't cry like that. I'm not going to put you out. I just want to know what happened."

She looked at him, her face awash with tears. "It's Isaac, Sir. He wants me bad. But I don't want him and I wish he would leave me alone."

Despite her tragic look, the Governor could not help but grin at her strange accent, half of it Negro, the other half with the flat Boston sound. Seeing him smile, Sara yet again dropped her gaze, suddenly aware that she had said something amusing.

It was he, the Governor, who suddenly felt awkward, not quite certain what to do next, "Run along now, there's a good girl," he said lamely.

"Yes, Sir," she answered and scuttled away, not looking behind her.

Tom went back into his bedroom, conscious of the fact that he had probably made matters worse for her. Crossing to the window, he stepped out on to the balcony, still in his bare feet, the feel of the cool slabs beneath his toes giving him a sense of freedom Then he heard six o'clock chime and a simultaneous respectful knock on his door.

"Come in," he called.

The door opened, and his personal valet stood there. "Good evening, Sir. I have come to help you get ready for dinner. I've pressed your dress clothes."

Glad to have one familiar face on his staff, Gage answered cheerfully, "Good evening, Perkins. Are you settling in all right?"

"Yes, Sir. Very comfortable I'm sure. Would you like a bath, Sir?"

"Do you know," Tom answered, "I would like that very much."

So it started. The tin bath was carried into his dressing room, and the slaves began to labour in and out with pails of boiling water. Meanwhile, Tom stood in his shirt and breeches, still barefoot, supposedly looking through papers but in fact watching the black people, feeling that he was learning about their characters from the very way they carried the buckets. First came Andrew, grinning as broadly as ever, obviously wanting to make an impression and, in fact, succeeding. He would make a fine-looking coachman, Tom thought. He visualised the black man in livery and had to smile at the mental picture.

Isaac appeared terrified and would not meet the Governor's eye. In fact on the one occasion he did glance up, Tom was looking at him with a stern reproving gaze that would have frightened anyone who caught it. I doubt he'll give Sara any further trouble, Gage thought, and wondered why he felt pleased by this.

Robin and Beulah were married to one another and were older than the other slaves. They had been together so long that they had started to look alike, both having gentle, kindly expressions and greying hair. It appeared that Mildred, the youngest of the slaves at fifteen, was their daughter, and they also had a son, Peter, who was twelve and worked at fetching wood for the great fireplaces. This, of course, left Sara.

Yet again, Tom tried to decide her ancestry. She was a half-caste, he could have sworn it, and whichever

parent had been white had given her her long straight hair, her amber skin and the setting of her eyes and nose. She was totally beautiful to look at and, so the Governor thought, as yet unaware of it. He wondered about her age and came up with seventeen or eighteen, thinking to himself that whatever slave married her would be very lucky indeed. In fact she was almost too good for that, Tom thought, then remembered her accent and smiled rather sadly.

The pail procession was almost done, the honour of the last being Andrew's. With his empty bucket in his hand, the slave bowed low, his jackanapes grin wide and happy.

"Don't forget Masser, I can drive horses real good."

Tom, who was undoing his shirt, looked up. "What happened to the last coachman? Did you say he died?"

"He did, Sir, and there ain't been nobody to replace him. We all take it in turns."

"Tell you what, Andrew. You can drive me tonight to Fanueil Hall. Be ready, clean and dressed in one hour."

The grin spread even wider. "I'll be ready, Sir. You can rely on Andrew."

He bowed briefly and was gone, leaving Tom Gage in peace to soak in a hot bath, to shave himself and then to prepare for the banquet being given in his honour.

He thought afterwards that it had been a great success. The townspeople had toasted him liberally, there had been expressions of goodwill and loyalty to the English Crown, indeed the whole atmosphere had been one of conviviality and good humoured ease. The only sour

note had been when Tom had risen and proposed a toast to the retiring governor, Thomas Hutchinson, and had been greeted with hisses. However, he had overcome the embarrassment, and one or two people had risen to drink with him. In fact one of the figures had looked vaguely familiar and after the banquet, when people were mingling, Tom had approached him. The man had turned at the sound of footsteps, and Governor Gage had found himself looking straight into the face of Lord Rupert Germain.

"Rupert, my dear chap, what on earth are you doing in Boston? Last I heard of you you were in New York running a newspaper. What a wonderful surprise."

The other man, slightly older, slightly greyer, but slim as ever and still with that tendency to flush, went very red. "Governor," he said, "I had hoped to be able to speak to you."

Gage clapped him on the shoulder. "Speak to me! Dammit, man, there would have been trouble if you hadn't."

Rupert's colour faded, but only slightly. "Truth to tell, Governor, I've a great deal to say to you, what with one thing and another. Quite a lot has happened in the — how many years is it since we met?"

"It has to be twelve."

"Has it really?"

It was out of Tom's mouth before he could control the words. "Are you married by any chance?"

The flush again. "No."

"Ah, well." Tom did not add, I thought not. Instead he said, "Look, Rupert, can you join me for a drink

after the banquet? My carriage is outside, and I'd appreciate a chat. But this is hardly the place."

The younger man looked immensely pleased. "I'd be delighted, Governor. Actually I have a coach here so I'll meet you at Province House at half past ten. Would that suit?"

"It would suit very well indeed. Thank you."

"I'll see you there, Governor."

Gage was being called away to meet official dignitaries, struck by the thought that he would rather they paid loyal service to the Crown than hung flatteringly to his coat-tails. For tonight, as with earlier in the day, it would have been almost impossible to guess that this town, Boston, was the seat of insurrection, the boiling point of the whole damnable rebellion. A rebellion that it was his avowed intent to avoid, come what may.

An hour later and it was all done. The Governor descended the staircase in Fanueil Hall and swept out to his carriage, where Andrew, in full livery, a fanciful hat with a low brim on his head, awaited him. Pulled up close to the Governor's coach was another, very finely appointed. Tom was amazed to see Lord Rupert Germain swing into its dark interior as he got aboard his.

"Andrew, hurry," he called up to the Negro, still grinning cheerfully at this hour of the night. "That's my guest in there."

The slave rolled his dark eyes. "Why, Governor, that be Mister Germain who is one of the richest folks around. Do you know him?"

"I certainly do."

"Well, bless me," said Andrew, and applied the whip.

In the event they arrived at Province House about a minute or so before Rupert Germain. The gates had been opened, and it was the Governor himself who informed the guards that he was expecting a visitor. Thus the two men ascended the steps side by side and made their way into the room that Tom, on his first inspection of the house, had noted as the withdrawing room.

It was large and spacious, thick curtains drawn over the windows, a harpsichord imported from France against one wall, several large chairs and a chaise placed discreetly. A fire had been lit which was flickering rather feebly as they entered. Tom, ringing the bell, placed the dried wood on it himself and watched the flames catch almost straight away. There was a pause as Robin came in with the tray and poured the brandy, then Tom turned to his guest.

"My dear man, tell me everything."

"You were right about where we last met. It was in New York, but it was ten years ago, not twelve."

Tom laughed and sipped his brandy. "Time rushes by; I wouldn't have known."

"You do recall that I was going back to England and came to say goodbye?"

"Yes, of course. That's why it was such a surprise to see you tonight. I rather thought you had stayed."

The flush crept up Rupert's neck again. "Fact of the matter was that I went back to see my mother who was

far from well. Then she died, quite suddenly, while I was there." Tom made sympathetic noises. "Anyway, to cut a long story short I stayed a year, didn't like it as much as I thought, so I returned."

"So your future lies in this country, does it?"

"Yes, I think so. I sold my interest in a New York newspaper before I departed. Now I own the *Boston Mirror*."

Tom gaped. "Do you? Good gracious. And to think I knew you when you were struggling along. Why, Rupert, you have come a long way."

Rupert permitted himself a slightly satisfied smile. "Yes, I have. But I mustn't overlook my competitor, the *Boston Gazette*, otherwise known as the Dung Barge."

"I'm sorry. I haven't come across that yet."

"Oh you will, Governor. It slants stories, fabricates events, distorts and suppresses the truth. In other words, it is an inflammatory rag, a revolutionaries' handbook, and it is my avowed intent to bring it down."

He emptied his glass rapidly, and Tom refilled it.

"What you say interests me enormously. I must get hold of a copy." Then, realising that this sounded tactless added, "But, of course, I shall makes yours my regular read."

Rupert nodded, "It would certainly be wise to keep an eye on the enemy. It is only a weekly but is packed with sedition."

"And you? How often do you publish?"

"Three times a week. Our next edition will be full of a tribute to yourself, Governor."

"How very kind. But please call me Tom. My close friends do."

Rupert finished another brandy, and again Gage refilled his glass, wondering as he did so whether Germain had developed a liking for alcohol over the years.

Rupert sipped, then said, "And Mrs. Gage? Will she be joining you?"

There was a certain edge to his voice which Tom ignored. "Margaret presented me with a daughter, Charlotte, last August and, quite frankly, I wanted them to stay in England. For their own safety. But she set sail in May, three weeks after I did. A nursemaid accompanied them, and they are headed for New York where they will remain for a while. I'm expecting her in September."

"I see."

"You'll like her, Rupert." Tom realised that a cajoling note had crept into his voice and tried desperately to erase it. "When you called on me in New York she was in Brunswick, visiting her parents. But I really want you to meet her. She's truly delightful."

"I'm sure she is," answered the other man, still with that same tone. "Anyway, I must be off, my dear fellow. I have quite a way to travel."

"Oh, where do you live?"

"In Milton, near old Governor Hutchinson's place. It's very beautiful there. You must come and visit."

"I should like that. Thank you."

Lord Rupert stood up. In all the years since Tom had last seen him, he had not gained an ounce of weight.

His hair, still long, now had some fine grey strands, but other than for that, there was little change.

"Allow me to escort you to the front door."

"Gladly."

The house was quiet, other than for Robin snoozing in a chair in the hall. He sprang to his feet as he heard the two men approach, hurrying to get Rupert's cloak. Having seen Tom Gage's guest safely into his coach, the slave bowed.

"Will that be all, Governor?"

"Yes, Robin. You can lock up and go to bed. Goodnight."

Suddenly exhausted, Tom walked slowly up the great stairs, unbuttoning his formal red coat as he went. He hadn't felt so tired in an age, yet it was the tiredness of contentment. For today, at least, had been good. When he closed the port on June 1st no doubt the situation would change, but tonight he was happy.

He walked into his room whistling to himself, taking his coat off and throwing it over his arm as he went. Then he stopped short. Somebody was there ahead of him, standing in the shadows cast by the four-poster.

"Who's there?" he called.

Sara emerged from the gloom, her eyes as usual cast downwards, the warming pan in her hands.

"Oh, it's you," Tom said abruptly.

"Yes, Governor. I'm sorry to disturb you, Sir. I was just warming the bed."

Just for a moment, Tom was a young soldier again, stationed in Dublin, and was opening his mouth to say

something mildly rude when the full import of who he was came flooding back.

"I see. Well, goodnight."

"Goodnight, Governor."

She raised her eyes, and Tom stared straight into them, drawn in spite of everything. Then, again, he recalled his position and turned away.

"Goodnight, Sara."

"Goodnight, Sir."

And she was gone, leaving nothing but the shadows behind her.

CHAPTER
NINE

July, 1774

It was a thrilling sight. With a great roll of drums and tramp of booted feet, the King's Own and the 43rd regiments landed in Boston the day after Governor Gage closed the port on the first of June. The inhabitants, strangely silent, sullen indeed, stood to one side and watched them pass. Nobody cheered or shouted as the soldiers, scarlet-coated, upright, looking neither to right nor left, marched through the streets of Boston, standards fluttering in the breeze, bands playing, towards the Common where the men were to camp.

And down on the waterfront, other than for the transports which had brought the regiments in, the wharves were also strangely silent. There in the bay rode the warships, the transports lying to close by, but there was not a topsail vessel to be seen. General Gage had come to close the port — and close it he had. But the British had misjudged the situation. Salem and Marblehead had offered the use of their jetties to the Boston merchants rather than make a profit at the expense of the town. In other words, there were signs that the colonists were starting to hang together.

A fortnight after the grand military display, two more regiments came into port, the 5th and 38th. Leading

the 5th, to Tom Gage's great relief, was one of the most able young men in the British Army, Hugh, Earl Percy, son of the powerful Duke of Northumberland, to act as second-in-command, only superceded by the Governor himself.

Gage, in full uniform, was at the port to meet him and had never been so grateful as when Hugh stepped onto the gangplank. With an ill-disguised grin, the young Earl hurried downwards and arrived at the bottom where he gave an impeccable salute.

"A good journey, Brigadier?" asked Tom, his eyes twinkling.

"Very good, Sir. Thank you."

"Your men all ready?"

"Ready for inspection in forty minutes, Sir."

"Right. Order disembarkation, my Lord."

Hugh turned to shout to his second-in-command, and shortly afterwards there came the tramping of feet as the men left the ship and lined up on the quay. Gage and Percy drew to one side.

"My dear boy," said Tom quietly, "it's so good to have you here."

"Has it been difficult, Sir?"

"Not really, not yet. But it's shaping up. Adams and Hancock are blowing hot. But we'll see what difference the troops make. I'll wager that people will be glad to see them and might now be able to act and speak freely. Without fear of retribution from the Faction."

Hugh Percy looked thoughtful. "Perhaps. We can only wait and see." He deliberately changed the subject. "What news of Mrs. Gage, Sir?"

138

"She's landed safely in New York. She'll be joining me in September."

"It will be good to have her here," Hugh Percy said with enthusiasm.

Gage looked thoughtful. "I tried to persuade her to remain in England, you know."

"Why, Sir?"

"I thought she — and Charlotte — might be safer."

"But surely with the army . . ."

Gage shrugged his shoulders. "Who knows? Anyway she insisted on coming so that's an end to it. Now, time I inspected your men."

The two regiments were lined up on the quay, and Gage began his slow progress amongst them, pausing to chat with as many troops as he could. Also present on the dock, standing at a respectful distance and making little noise, were the soldiers' women. These were the wives and camp followers who accompanied the army wherever it went. They were under the absolute control of the commander-in-chief who, eventually, turned to them.

"There will be no plundering on this expedition, absolutely none. Is that understood?" he said.

"Yes, Sir," answered an older and more senior woman, speaking for the rest.

"I want no offence caused to the local population," Tom continued. "Most of them are loyal and deserve to be treated with courtesy. Do I make myself clear?"

The women bobbed their understanding, though Gage trusted them about as far as he trusted the men, namely hardly at all. To him the soldiers were low-grade

individuals, who operated best in packs, which was the way they had been trained, unlike the men of his own regiment, sadly long ago disbanded, who had been hand-picked and individually trained.

He turned to Percy. "Very good, Brigadier. Take them away."

"Yes, Sir."

"And you are to call this evening at Province House. We need to talk privately."

"Very good, Governor."

The Earl saluted, nodded to the bandmaster, and to the tune of "The British Grenadiers" mounted the white horse that had been brought specially to the quayside for him. Then he was off at the head of his regiment, making as brave a showing as any as he made his way through the silently staring people of Boston towards the Common.

He had walked through the streets and, on a whim, decided to call in at the Blue Bell and Indian Queen before returning home. Having ordered a cognac, Tom settled himself in a corner and drew a copy of the *Boston Mirror* from his pocket. Just getting into it, he was disturbed a few minutes later by a small and very nervous cough. Glancing up, he found himself looking into the spectacular eyes of Sara.

Since his first day in Province House, he had seen little of her and what glimpses he had had been of her back view, disappearing rapidly down a corridor. So now it was something of a shock to find himself face to face with her in the unlikely surroundings of a tavern.

As he looked up she gave a small bob and said, "I am sorry to disturb you, Governor, but you have a visitor waiting in the house."

"Who?" he asked shortly.

"Mister Germain, Sir. He said you arranged to meet him."

"Goddammit," Gage said, swallowing his drink in one. "I'd forgotten all about it." He folded his paper, then said, "How did you know I was here?"

The exquisite face coloured. "I saw you come in, Sir."

"Saw me?" Tom said, puzzled.

"Yassir."

And that was all she would say, though the Governor had a shrewd suspicion he knew the answer. She had been down on the docks watching the soldiers arrive and had probably taken the same route home and seen him go into the tavern.

The girl turned to go, but Gage, for no logical reason, leaned forward and caught her wrist. "Wait a second. You can walk with me."

The poor thing did not know where to put herself. "No, Sir. I couldn't do that, Sir. It would be unfitting, Sir."

He couldn't help but laugh at her, yet part of him wanted to comfort her, as if she were a sad child.

"Why would it be unfitting?" he said, smiling.

"Because it would, Sir, and you know why. The Governor walking with one of his slaves. Why, Robin would put me clean out the house."

"Damn Robin," Tom remarked, feeling the cognac hit his stomach. "But I take your point. It wouldn't be right."

She gave him a look which, despite everything, he felt himself responding to. "Goodbye, Excellency," she said, and she gently removed her wrist which he still grasped.

"Goodbye."

He felt outwitted, yet why Tom could not explain. But he was so overcome by the encounter that he ordered another cognac which he downed in haste before heading back to Province House. There, he found Rupert Germain, looking slightly tense.

"Ah, Tom, you're here. I must speak to you urgently."

"My dear friend, what is it?"

"It's this wretched business of Sam Adams and the locked door."

For a minute Tom couldn't think what he was talking about, then he remembered. Wrenching his thoughts away from Sara, he listened while Rupert repeated the story of Samuel Adams, the unwashed revolutionary, calling an Assembly then, when Gage had sent his secretary to dissolve it, locking the door to prevent him entering.

"I shall present it as a shameful gesture to you," Rupert announced.

Tom looked thoughtful. "Why mention it?"

"Why? Because it is a disgusting and flagrant insult, that's why."

"Then refer to it on your inside page, and give it nothing but small attention. I declare that Sam Adams

142

wants publicity, indeed he craves it. So why satisfy him?"

Rupert rose to his feet and paced round the study. "You're right, of course. Yet on the other hand it is my duty to keep the public informed."

Tom Gage, who was extremely on edge himself, though he couldn't have explained why, rose from his chair and poured two cognacs, passing Rupert one.

"The public will believe what it wants to believe, and there is nothing you can do about it. The Dung Barge will present the incident as a great victory for Adams and say that this town is now under military rule. You will tell the truth as you see it."

"Yes, I must."

"Oh Rupert, Rupert," said Gage wearily. "I know you do your best — and thank God for the *Mirror* — but it will all be the same in a hundred years' time."

He sank down in his chair again, suddenly tired beyond belief.

His friend looked at him. "You could do with a day off. Come out to my place on Saturday. There you can get away from everything for a few hours."

Tom smiled at him, a certain fatigue in the smile. "I most certainly will if I can."

Rupert stood up. "I'll expect you for dinner, but come well before. Come in the morning, and then you can see the house and grounds at their best."

"I will make a point of trying. Thank you."

After he had gone, Tom toyed with the idea of having another cognac but decided against. Drinking in the daytime was the last thing he needed in these difficult

and dangerous times. Still, he had an hour to kill before Hugh Percy's arrival and nothing in particular to do. He turned to his desk to attack some paperwork but at the last minute decided to put it off until the morning. Yawning slightly, he climbed the staircase. However, when he reached the floor on which his bedroom was situated, he continued to ascend until he came to the narrow set of stairs that led into the cupola. He had only taken two steps when he realised that somebody was there ahead of him. Without even seeing who it was, he knew it was Sara. Smiling wryly to himself, the Governor continued to clamber upwards.

There was a small wooden bench fixed to the wall, running round the entire structure. The slave was sitting there, staring out at the harbour but turned with a start at the sound of his footsteps. She gazed horrified for a moment, then jumped to her feet.

"Oh, Excellency, I didn't think it was you. I didn't know you came up here."

"Sara, sit down, there's a good girl. I do come here occasionally when I want to get away from everything. Why do you?"

She stood looking at him, wondering whether to fly down the stairs and out of his way, or whether perhaps to remain. For the second time that day, he caught her wrist.

"Look, I'm not going to hurt you. And if it will make you any happier, I won't tell anyone that we've spoken. But you interest me — as do all my servants," he added hastily as he saw a sudden wary look in her eye. "Tell me about yourself, please."

144

Slowly she sat down again, opposite him. "There's not much to tell, Masser."

"Everyone has a story. Tell me yours. Who was your mother?"

"I never done meet her."

"But what of her? Where did she come from?"

"From England," Sara answered surprisingly.

"Really? So she was white?"

"As white as you, Governor. But she didn't have such a good start."

He smiled at her encouragingly. "Go on."

Sara smiled as well, and her face transformed. It was as much as Tom could do not to draw breath audibly at her beauty.

"She was born in prison, Sir. In Bridewell. Her mother was a young prostitute, put away for her crimes. I don't know any more about her, but I guess it was prostitution or starve."

Tom was silent, thinking about the Bridewell prisons, one near Fleet Street, the other off Tothill Fields, where it was considered sport to go and watch the women whipped for their crimes. However, the men who hired the poor wretches suffered no such fate. But Sara was continuing.

"Anyway, as soon as my mother, Lucy, was eight she was taken from the poor house and sent off to work in the plantations. That was the way of it with all the Bridewell kids, provided they was healthy and strong."

Again, Tom said nothing, his mind full of his own children and their golden days. He pictured them as he had seen them, smiling at him so recently on his eagerly

145

awaited visit to England. For all of them, girls too, were sent home to his brother for an English education. He loved every one of them, though he had to admit that William had a most endearing way with him and was possibly his favourite. But the thought of any of them being put to work at the age of eight filled him with horror.

He realised that Sara had stopped speaking and was studying him.

"What was you thinking, Sir?"

"I was thinking about my children."

"Are they back in England?"

"All but Charlotte. She's in New York with her mother. She'll be coming here in September."

Sara's face lit once more. "It'll be good to have a baby in Province House, Sir."

"Yes, I suppose it will. Anyway, continue with your story."

"You really want to hear it?"

"Yes, yes I do."

"Well, my mother was shipped out to Virginia, and there she worked until, at the age of fifteen, she had a baby too."

Tom looked at her. "There has to be more to it than that. Who was your father? Do you know?"

She gave him a cynical smile, her face looking momentarily hard. "Oh yes, I know all right. He was another slave, a black slave, name of Jordan. He loved Lucy, but she died giving birth to me. My black grandmother brought me up, and I lived. Eventually I was sold off at the age of ten. I was taken to the slave

market in New York and bought by a dealer, who got a better price for me here in Boston. So that's how I come to be in your house, Governor."

Tom shook his head slowly. "What a sad tale."

She looked annoyed, the first sign of spirit he had seen in her. "No, Sir, it ain't sad. It's a true story of working folk and how they survive. I'm proud of my Mammy. Yes, and I'm even proud of my Grandmammy too. I reckon she sold her body in order to keep it going."

The Governor burst out laughing, delighted by her strange phraseology. Then stopped as he saw her mortified expression.

"Sara, Sara, don't look like that. I'm just amused by the way you say things. You're so direct, so straightforward. Please don't be annoyed."

She got to her feet. "Forgive me, Excellency. I said too much."

Tom looked at her and stated honestly, "If you go now our friendship will never continue, you know that."

She stared at him, straight in the eyes. "How can it continue anyway? The Governor and a black slave? I don't believe so."

He, too, stood up, taller by far than she was. "The fact is that I like to have my mind diverted from the difficulties of reality. I enjoy talking to you." An inspiration came to him. "Tell me, can you read?"

She shook her head mutely, lowering her eyes. "No, Sir."

"Well then, let me teach you." He gave her a very straight look. "And that is what I mean, Sara. There'll be no question of payment of any kind whatsoever."

He gave particular emphasis to the last few words he had spoken and waited for her to respond. Eventually she did. After gazing at the floor for a while, she looked up. Then she gave a slow, stunning smile.

"Thank you, Governor. I would like that. When shall I come?"

He found himself speaking rapidly, anxious to get the words out and go before she changed her mind.

"Perhaps tonight. After I've finished work. I've Lord Percy coming to see me. After he has gone. Now, if you will excuse me." And he had turned and was going down the narrow staircase before she could say a word.

That night Tom Gage dined in solitary splendour, sitting at one end of the huge dining table, missing Margaret and wishing she would conclude her business in New York and join him. He drank rather more wine than he should and felt distinctly mellow by the time the meal was ended and he was at liberty to leave the room and take a pipe into the garden. It was five o'clock, still light, and he sat beneath an apple tree and thought of the situation in Boston. It seemed to him that the only way forward was to fight fire with fire, to be as tough and as hard as the British required. To keep the port closed until such time as the colonists paid for the tea they had thrown so carelessly into Boston harbour. Yet, in his opinion, there were only a handful of rabble-rousers leading the gullible with them. He felt certain — well, almost — that the Bostonians would come to their senses with the arrival of the army.

He closed his eyes and must have dozed off, for the next thing he remembered was the face of old Robin saying, "Masser Governor, Lord Percy is here."

"Gracious me," said Tom, shaking himself. "Have I been asleep?"

"Just for half an hour, Sir. You looked so peaceful that I didn't like to disturb you."

"Well, thank you for letting me rest. Where is Lord Percy?"

"In the withdrawing room, Sir."

Just for a moment Gage stood in the shadow of the doorway and let his eyes take in the face of the Duke of Northumberland's son, thinking to himself what a fine figure the young man presented. Yet, as far as looks were concerned, he had few. It was his general manner, the way he had with him, that was so attractive.

He was thirty-two years old but already suffering from hereditary gout, though this he stoutly refused to accept, marching miles with his men, declining to go on horseback when the soldiers were on foot. He was thin, almost to the point of being bony, and had a large nose and receding forehead. But his eyes, wide and with an endearing ability to give sidelong glances, caused by the fact that he was short-sighted, were extraordinarily arresting. And now they lit up as he caught sight of the Governor, standing in the doorway, watching him from the shadows.

"Well, Sir. How are you this evening?"

"More to the point, my boy, how are you?"

They sat down and waited until Robin had served cognac and withdrawn.

"I'm as well as can be expected, Sir. Under canvas for a few days until I find somewhere to rent. Then I'll be well away."

Gage smiled. "It takes a bit of getting used to, I warn you."

Percy gave a confident grin. "The locals seem very pleasant to me. I've already been chatting to several of them."

"And who might they be?"

"Mostly residents of the houses in Beacon Street, come out to watch the men setting up camp. One of them was a *femme formidable* named Lydia Hancock. Quite frankly, Sir, she's huge. But she's invited me in for meals until I find somewhere of my own."

The Governor raised a cynical brow. "Mrs. Hancock, eh? You know who she is, don't you?"

"No."

"She's the aunt of John Hancock, the other part of Sam Adams. And who is Adams, I hear you ask. He is the most dangerous and deadly of all the rabble-rousers. He is obsessed with returning the Colonies to Puritanism, black hats, Bibles and all. But to achieve this end, he uses methods that others of his belief would shun. He causes riots, stirring the waterfront mob into a frenzy; he tars and feathers his critics; his propaganda is inflammatory and untrue. In other words, he is the most ruthless individual it has ever been my misfortune to encounter."

"And Hancock? Where does he fit in to this?"

"He is Adams' other half, a necessary evil. He is as fine a buck as Adams is a rumpled ascetic. Hancock

150

dresses within an inch of his life, has a gilt carriage, custom-made in England, liveried servants, caparisoned outriders; his nickname is the 'King'. He is proud and handsome, tall and slender. Adams on the other hand is short and portly, crumpled, with shaking hands and head. Yet one needs the other."

"I don't understand, Sir."

"It's very simple really. Sam Adams wants power; the other is after glory. Thus, they complement one another."

"And where did Hancock get all his money?"

"Inherited the lot. From the late Thomas, husband of Mrs. Lydia. No doubt they will cultivate you because of your position in society, but be on your guard with John, my friend."

Earl Percy was quiet for a moment, then said, "I think perhaps I can learn more by becoming their associate rather than their enemy."

"If you think that is the best way forward, then so be it. But remember that everything you say will probably be repeated back to Adams, and he is implacable in his hatred for all things British."

"I shall say only what I want them to hear, Governor."

"Then I wish you luck."

There was rather an awkward silence during which Gage became aware of other sounds. People were conversing quietly in the hall, a clock was ticking nearby, somewhere outside a dog was barking frantically. He looked at the young nobleman with a brotherly affection, thinking how little he knew and

how much he had to learn. But he had given his warning, the rest was up to Percy himself.

The Earl finished his cognac and stood up, his thin frame almost melting into the shadows.

"Well, Sir, if you'll forgive me I really could do with some sleep. It's been a long and difficult day."

Gage also rose. "Of course, it was good of you to come. Anway, as I told you this morning, I'm glad you're here. I'm sure your presence will make a lot of difference."

Percy saluted. "Thank you, Sir. I'll do my best. And I'll heed your warning, never you fear."

"Hancock himself is a fool. It is the power behind him that concerns me."

"I understand, and I will observe," was Percy's parting promise.

Gage escorted him to the front door, where Robin sent Andrew on the double to fetch round the nobleman's mount. Then he was gone into the moonlight, leaving the Governor alone in his mansion.

Wearily, Tom made his way back to the withdrawing room and settled in his chair by the fire. He closed his eyes and almost immediately fell asleep, so deeply that he did not hear the gentle knocking on the door, nor did he see it open and Sara come in.

The slave stood for a moment, looking down on the sleeping Governor, thinking how young and vulnerable he looked, how innocent somehow. Then, having gazed on him for several minutes, the girl smiled to herself and left the room as quietly as she had entered it.

CHAPTER
TEN

August, 1774

"V, W, X," said Thomas Gage patiently.

"V, W, X," repeated his pupil, laboriously putting them into her copy book. "X — why that's how I used to sign my name."

"Well, in future you must put S, A, R, A. Can you write that?"

"I can try, Governor."

She bent her head over her book, her tongue sticking out of the corner of her mouth, and slowly wrote the letters, each one individually, not joined up at all. Tom, meanwhile, watched her, an extraordinary expression on his face. For mixed in with his kindness to Sara was something else, an intangible element of which he was not consciously aware and would have denied vehemently if anyone had challenged him with it.

He had been teaching her for four weeks now and was pleased with the progress the girl was making. She could already write all but the last two letters of the alphabet and was longing to read, though he had explained that this skill would be more slow in coming. However, he had managed to secure a child's primer from a local bookshop and together, phonetically, they were going through it.

Every day, at about ten o'clock in the evening, she would come to his study, and there they would spend an hour working before they both went their separate ways to bed. To Tom it was like a light relief from all his troubles — which grew daily. To Sara it was the opening of a whole new world, a world in which educated people held sway and to which she, through the goodness of one man, was at last getting a glimpse.

Of course, the other servants had found out. After the first rumours that the Governor was seeing Sara, that he was sweet on her, Tom had sent for Robin.

"I think you should know, Robin, that I am giving Sara reading and writing lessons. And you can take that look off your face. There is nothing of that nature involved, and I would be grateful if you could tell the other servants as much."

"Yes, Sir."

Tom had got up and paced from his desk to the window which looked out over the beautiful gardens of Province House.

"Why is it," he had said, half to himself, "that people always jump to the wrong conclusions in life?"

"Who knows, Governor," Robin answered. "I guess it be just the nature of folks."

Tom had turned round to look at him. "Well, I won't have any of that amongst my staff. Kindly put a stop to it at once."

But he had been hoping for too much. The rumours, though dying down now, continued to be whispered about the place.

Now he watched her as she wrote 'Sara' again and again.

"That's very good," he said. "Very good indeed. Tell me, do you have another name?"

"No, Governor. Some slaves only have one name. Didn't you know that?"

"I don't believe I'd consciously thought about it."

"Well, it's true. Though I guess in England things might be different."

"Probably. I can think of one chap, Jack Beef, who was servant to John Baker, a magistrate acquaintance of mine. He was considered very highly; in fact, Baker said he couldn't have run his household without him."

Sara stood up. "Well, I think he was lucky. Anyway, Governor, it's eleven o'clock, and I got to go."

"Stay another few minutes. I'm going to have a nightcap, but can I offer you some tea?"

The slave shook her head. "No, Sir, it wouldn't be fitting."

"Oh, for God's sake," Tom answered irritably, "stop thinking about what is fitting and what is not. I am inviting you to have a cup of tea. Now, would you like one or wouldn't you?"

Sara looked at him, then smiled. "Best not to cross you in this mood, Sir. Yes, I would like tea."

"Then go to the kitchen and make it. But bring it back here, mind. No slipping up to bed."

"I'll do as you say, Governor."

Something about the way she made that remark stung Tom, and he sat at his desk after she had gone and wondered whether he was turning into a bully. It

was probably the atmosphere of Boston, he said to himself. For a more contrary bunch of people he had yet to meet.

He was doing everything possible to bring them to order; had closed the port and sent to London for permission to enact other important regulations regarding the government of the province. But still the Bostonians resisted. He knew well that the Faction had secret meetings, knew who the ringleaders were. Yet he didn't want to be seen openly taking measures against them. If only I could win their confidence, he thought. Yet even as he had the idea, he knew it would never come to fruition. He was being forced into the role of a dictator, and he detested every second of it. But duty came above everything, and he had given his word to both King and country that he would make Massachusetts — and Boston in particular — come into line.

The door opened, and Sara stood there with a tray. Instinctively the Governor rose to his feet and went to help her carry it through, setting it down on a side table. Then, while she poured he gave himself a large brandy, then settled down in a chair on one side of the fire. Sara, however, went to sit in a back seat, not the one opposite.

He glanced over. "Sara, come and sit with me, please. And before you say it's not fitting, I am inviting you, and it would be rude to refuse."

She moved into the other chair with a certain reluctance and sat quietly, sipping her tea. And then, as if something in him gave way, he suddenly satisfied

his desperate need to talk, to lay bare everything he was thinking. Tom Gage found himself telling Sara how much he wanted to succeed and how the odds were stacked against him, so that the only choice open was to fight fire with fire, to be as hard as the rebels themselves. In fact he was telling her things that he would normally only have discussed with Margaret, who continued to absent herself in New York, much to his chagrin.

He must have gone on for about half an hour, but when he finally fell silent, Sara looked at him and smiled. "It must be terribly difficult for you, Master Governor."

Tom smiled back. "Yes, I'm sorry to bore you with all that, Sara. Accept my apologies. It was just that I needed to tell someone other than my fellow officers."

"I understand, Governor. There is no need for an apology. It is very interesting."

"You think so? So what would you do in my position?"

"Sir, how can I answer that? You must remember that, even though my mother was English, I was born here. I am an American. And now, Sir, if you will excuse me. I have to get up early."

He got to his feet. "Of course. Goodnight, Sara. You have worked hard tonight."

She lingered a moment in the door, her beautiful face earnest beneath its white cap. "Goodnight — and thank you, Sir."

Overcoming a sudden, quite mad desire to kiss her, Thomas turned away to the fire and stared into the dying flames.

★ ★ ★

In the darkness of Boston that same night, a meeting was being held in the long room above the printing office of Benjamin Edes and John Gill, publishers of the *Boston Gazette*, nicknamed the Dung Barge and the most influential competitor to Rupert Germain's *Boston Mirror*. The print shop lay behind the Court House in Dassett Alley, a narrow, noisome bit of a street, to which several men had gone once darkness had fallen. Now they sat, wreathed in blue pipe smoke, drinking rum and listening to Samuel Adams holding forth.

John Hancock, handsome and fine, a dandy, a buck — 'a milchcow to the Faction but whether public spirit or vanity has been his governing spirit is uncertain', as a contemporary said of him — was leaning back in his chair, one thin white hand holding a glass, his eyelids lowered as he gazed at the floor. Next to him sat Paul Revere, a complete contrast. Dark, stocky, short, very French looking, he had dark brows and eyes, a strong nose and a full, passionate mouth. He was already onto his second wife and his second family, his first wife having given him eight children and having died of her labours.

Sitting across the way from them was thirty-three-year-old Joseph Warren, a medical graduate from Harvard. Already a widower, he was as fair as Revere was dark, with light, bright blue eyes and mobile features. He looked amazingly alive and alert, and was currently balanced precariously on his chair as he leaned forward, taking in every word Adams had to say.

158

It was sad about his wife, was the consensus, but he really should remarry. In fact many of the more practical couldn't think what he was playing at, still mourning the frail creature who had died two years ago. But Warren was a doctor and entitled to do as he wished. Nowadays he lived with a housekeeper and three young children, Elizabeth, Joseph Junior and Mary, in a handsome house near Fanueil Hall. There was absolutely no woman in his life.

There were others sitting amongst the pipe smoke, most of them Harvard graduates. Josiah Quincy, with a beautiful voice and a wall eye; the Reverend Samuel Cooper, pastor of the Brattle Street Church, handsome and intelligent; his brother William, who had been town clerk for many years; Thomas Melville, young and vigorous, with a roman nose and cheeks like a rose in snow. There was also another doctor, Benjamin Church, always short of funds, highly-strung, bombastic and keeping a mistress. These men, all so different, were united by a common bond. They were all members of that most secret society, the Long Room Club.

In the darkness below, silent for the moment, was their servant the printing press, ready to do their bidding and publish articles by their members, all under the cover of pseudonyms. Above, however, Sam Adams stopped talking, more to draw breath than anything else, and there was an inadvertent sigh of relief.

"Well, gentlemen," said Dr. Church, rising to his feet, his face reflecting a kind of roguish charm which

was instantly attractive. "I'm afraid I must away. I have an early appointment."

Dr. Warren also stood up. "I too. My first patient is due at seven-thirty."

Sam Adams, having had a few minutes in which to breathe, returned to the attack. "Must you go?" he said in his shaky voice, affected occasionally by palsy.

"I must for sure," Warren answered.

"But there is much left to discuss," Adams insisted.

"Then you will have to discuss it without me," the doctor replied, reaching for his hat.

Church took his lead. "I must away, my dear fellow. Honestly."

Adams gave in with a bad grace. "Oh, very well. I shall leave our further plans till the next meeting."

"Yes, do so, old boy. When will that be?"

"In a week's time. You will be there?"

"Assuredly," said Church, and putting his hat on his head, bowed his way out.

Revere winked an eye as the older man puffed down the stairs. "He's off to see his mistress," he whispered.

Warren, more serious, pulled a bit of a face. "He's a funny one all right."

"I think he's rather sensible." Revere's unsaid thoughts hung in the air.

Warren gave him a look which forbade any further intimacy. "We are all entitled to our opinions."

Revere grinned. "Come on, my friend, I meant no harm. I'll walk back with you."

The two men went silently down the staircase and through the darkened print shop, passing the silent

press which lay like a sleeping dog awaiting instructions from its master. Quietly stepping out into the little alley, they slipped like shadows past the unlighted Court House. Then they turned left, making their way up Corn Hill and into the darkness of Dock Square. Here they shook hands and parted company, Warren making his way to the houses close to Fanueil Hall, whereas Revere went over the drawbridge and out of Boston proper into the North End.

Inserting his key in the lock, Joseph Warren stepped inside the hall, taking off his hat and cloak and dropping his stick onto a settle. Then he went through into his study, his private place, leading from the room where he dealt with patients, empty now but for the examination couch. Shutting the door between the rooms, Joseph poured himself a small cognac, then took a book from the shelves and settled down to read. But the words floated before his eyes, and he found it almost impossible to concentrate. Eventually he put the book down and stared into the dying flames of the fire, wondering what tremendous things the future held.

It was essential that he and his fellow revolutionaries should resist every attempt by the British to get them to cooperate. However hard they were ground down, however hard Gage intended to be with them, they must fight back. Yet Joseph abhorred the methods used by Sam Adams; the mob violence, the tarring and feathering, the unbridled disrespect for other people's property. Yet, despite this, he was a member of the Sons of Liberty, a trained gang who had established a rule in Boston stronger than that of any law court.

161

With a sigh, Warren put down the book and closed his eyes briefly. Minutes later he was fast asleep in his chair, dreaming of a woman, a woman he could not see but who he knew he adored. This woman meant more to him than his fragile wife ever had, more than any woman before or since. Slipping into a deeper level of unconsciousness, Warren gave himself up entirely to the dream.

He must have dropped off before the fire because he knew he was dreaming. In the dream, the door of the study opened, and Sara stood there, totally naked. Gage simply sat, gazing wide-eyed at her incredible body, at the rise and fall of her breasts, at the suppleness of her waist, the narrowness of her hips, the spread of dark hair between her thighs. He did not speak and neither did she, but slowly, slowly she turned so that he might admire her from every angle. Which he did, silently worshipping her loveliness. Then she closed the door again and left as quietly as she had come.

Tom moved into another phase of sleep, but when he woke and looked at his watch he saw that only a quarter of an hour had elapsed since he had last consulted it. The fire was on its last gasp, and he raked it out, then made his way sleepily up to his bedroom. There was nobody about, and the very quietness of the house struck him to the heart. Then he was seized by the notion to go on to his balcony. In his shirtsleeves and breeches he made his way outwards and looked across at the Old South Church.

162

In front of Province House the night sentries were patrolling up and down, and Tom could hear their muttered conversation as they passed one another. Other than for them, Boston seemed deceptively quiet, the good citizens all abed. For no reason at all Calico Joel came into Tom's head, and he wondered where the scout had gone and what he was doing. Then his thoughts turned to Margaret, and he wished with fervour that she would leave New York and come to him.

And then an idea stopped him in his tracks. Would she approve of Sara, he wondered, and, even more, would Margaret let him continue to teach the slave girl? Somehow he knew the answer even before the event and Tom sighed deeply, then turned back to his bedroom where, having stripped, he flung himself into bed and immediately went to sleep.

It certainly was a beautiful view. To the west, the Governor could see fifty miles to where rose the blue mass of Mount Wachusett; to the east, the fields stretched and rolled, taking their leisure as they descended to the Neponset River, which meandered lazily into Boston Harbour. Behind the house stood gardens, very fine and formal, and then by contrast behind them, in turn, a wild orchard. Apple trees hung low with crops; plums and pears were ripe; and birds of every description flew down to attack the provender. Tom let his eyes feast on bluebird and blue jays, on the common brown thrashers who also came to eat the

fruit. It truly was an earthly paradise, and Tom turned to its owner with enthusiasm.

"Well, Rupert, you have a fine place here. Tell me, from whom did you buy it?"

They both looked at the stately house, the shutters back to greet the day, a wisteria clambering over its front door up to the windows.

"From Augustus Hamilton. He had raised a family here, but after they had all left home and his wife died, he sold the estate to me and went to New York."

"Do you ever get lonely here on your own?" Tom said thoughtlessly.

"Never," Rupert Germain answered immediately. "I like my own company. I'm used to it. I could never live with anyone else. Too dog selfish."

Tom smiled lazily, feeling more relaxed than he had for weeks, basking in the August sunshine, enjoying himself.

He had at last kept his promise to visit Rupert at home. And how glad he had been to leave Province House, get into his coach with merry black Andrew — who had got his wish and now was permanent coachman — seated above. He had watched with interest and a certain kind of childish delight as they had passed through the heavily guarded Boston Neck and then turned south, heading past Dorchester to the attractively situated Milton.

He wondered now, sitting on the terrace in the sunshine, why Rupert Germain should chose to be so reclusive, why he had elected to live out of Boston and come in on a daily basis. Yet what was there to stop

him? A man could live where he liked when he had no responsibilities, no family to consider.

These thoughts brought Tom back, yet again, to Margaret. She had had more than enough time in New York now and was daily due to join him. Yet, for some strange reason, he hadn't written to ask her to come back, knowing that his moments of escape with Sara would be doomed to end. For he could not see a woman of Margaret's temperament allowing him to teach a slave the basic elements of reading and writing. Nor, indeed, the pleasant interludes that followed the lessons when he and Sara often sat in a comfortable silence, he drinking a nightcap or two, she content to drink tea, quiet and still, almost like a lady.

"What were you thinking?" said Rupert.

Tom laughed a little. "About my wife, Margaret," he said.

He saw Rupert stiffen. "Oh yes?"

"Wondering when she was going to leave New York and join me. She landed there in early July, you know, and her brother, Stephen, has already reported for duty. Anyway, it's her decision. She'll come when she's ready."

"Assuredly," said Rupert, and put his fingertips together.

Tom Gage smiled somewhat cynically. Despite the fact that he had been married nearly sixteen years, he knew full well that Rupert still disliked the thought of her.

"I'm sure you will take to her," Gage said for the twentieth time. "You don't recall her from that party we were all at?"

"My dear fellow, no. There were so many people there. Anyway, I shall meet Mrs. Gage in due course I expect. Now, would you like some more punch?"

"Thank you." Tom held out his glass, closing his eyes against the sun. Rupert got up from his chair in order to pour, standing closer to the Governor than was utterly necessary. As he leant forward his cheek brushed that of Gage and held for a second before it was withdrawn. Tom opened his eyes, realised what had happened but decided to say nothing. Yet it was of interest that in seventeen years Rupert's feelings had not diminished.

A beautiful black slave, male, came out of the house. "Dinner is served, Sir."

Rupert looked up. "Thank you, Jamie."

Tom, watching, thought he knew how Rupert whiled away the hours of solitary existence. And what could a slave do but agree? His mind, for no reason, flew to Sara and his erotic dream of her. Angrily he pushed the vision away and stood up, preparing to go in to dine.

"It is truly a pleasure to have you here, Tom," Rupert said suddenly.

"It is truly a pleasure to have been invited," Tom replied and followed his host into the house.

CHAPTER
ELEVEN

September, 1774

"And that, Sir," said Hugh Percy with a grin, "should show 'em whose in charge."

Gage lifted a glass of claret. "I'll drink to that."

They were seated opposite one another at the dining table, the room lit by candles, the servants dismissed.

"If this little venture comes off," the Governor continued, "it will give those damned rebels something to think about."

"There's no reason why it shouldn't," the Earl answered. "Dammit, we've planned it hard enough."

And he was right. The secret manoeuvre of September 1st, 1774, had been discussed down to the finest detail; now all that awaited was the execution.

It had been a grim summer. Gage's retreat from Salem back to Boston had been undignified to say the least. He had gone there to swear in the newly appointed royal councillors, only for the radicals to challenge the regime, preventing several members from attending by threat of physical violence. Others they had forced to resign, others still to flee to Boston for their own safety. In this last number, Tom himself had been included. He had left in a hurry at the end of August and was now safely back in Province House.

Yet was safely the right word? He had returned to Boston to find the place had deteriorated further. For now it was filling with people who sought royal protection. People who looked to the presence of armed troops for asylum. The Governor had seethed with anger, and out of this feeling a plan had been born, a plan which this very night was going into action.

"Do you mind, Sir?" Percy was asking, producing a pipe.

"Not if it helps you to concentrate. Tonight is going to be a long one."

"Indeed it is."

So saying, the Governor stood up and led the way to his study, the Earl following closely behind. There, he unrolled a map which showed in detail Boston Harbour, the Mystic River, and the surrounding countryside. Both men pored over it, Lord Percy taking a pair of spectacles from a pocket and putting them on. Tom gave him a sideways glance and thanked God that his sight still held out.

There was a knock at the door which opened to reveal Robin, looking slightly puzzled. "Colonel Maddison to see you, Sir," he said.

"Very good. Show him in."

The clock in the hall was just chiming midnight as the Colonel came into the room. Gage straightened up from the map, while Percy shot one of his brilliant looks in the direction of the door, partly because he was unable to see who had arrived until he grew closer.

"My dear George," said the Governor enthusiastically, and shook the new arrival warmly by the hand.

168

The Colonel saluted then bowed. "I await your final orders, Sir."

"Only one. That the men wear sacking over their boots. I want this done entirely in secret. If there is any noise and somebody wakes, then we may as well forget the whole thing."

George Maddison smiled. "It's already taken care of, Sir. Every man, all two hundred and sixty, has been issued with hemp."

"Good. You leave at four-thirty?"

"On the stroke, Sir. As you ordered."

"Then there's nothing left but to wish you success."

The Earl spoke, removing his glasses and giving them a quick polish with a handkerchief before thrusting both into his pocket.

"I've ordered the longboats to await the men, Colonel."

"Very good, my Lord."

"So *bon chance*."

Colonel Maddison saluted and bowed once more. "Goodbye, gentlemen, and thank you."

Percy turned to the Governor as the door closed behind him. "A very able man that. You chose well, Sir."

Tom looked grim. "Don't speak too soon, my friend. Anyway, I suggest we get a few hours' sleep before the event. You're welcome to stay here."

"I will, Governor, thanks. What time are you getting up?"

"At four-thirty when it begins."

"So shall I," said Hugh Percy, and bowing to Tom, took a candle and made his way upstairs.

On the stroke of the half hour, while the town of Boston lay asleep, Maddison and his men crept out from their various quarters and marched silently to the Long Wharf. Here, longboats from the King's navy, thirteen in all, bobbed on the morning tide. The men climbed aboard and when the entire company was seated, the coxswains pushed off, their mission to row across Boston Harbour to the Mystic River. Once the hand-picked battalion had arrived its orders were to march inland to the Powder House on Quarry Hill and there to seize the remaining gunpowder and bring it back to Boston, placing it under British control.

As soon as he had been forced out of Salem, it had come to Tom's attention that the powder was disappearing into the surrounding countryside. Angry with the way he had recently been treated, the Governor was determined to put a stop to such activities. Hence the surprise raid under cover of darkness.

Having crossed the straits, the soldiers came ashore at Temple's Farm and marched, in silence, to Quarry Hill, about a mile away. Here they waited in the dim light until morning, then they went into the Powder House — opened for them by the sheriff of Middlesex County, Colonel David Phips — and retrieved two hundred and fifty half barrels, which they carried back to the boats. Then they were rowed back to Castle Island, leaving behind a small detachment who marched

on to Cambridge and removed two brass field pieces that belonged to the Province. By noon it was all over, the munitions safely stored in Castle William, the men back in their barracks and snoring.

At Province House there was indeed cause for celebration. Earl Percy sent his coachman to his home to bring extra champagne and he, Tom and Colonel Maddison proceeded to get slightly drunk. The largest store of gunpowder in Massachusetts had been seized without a shot being fired. It was a triumphant exercise, brilliantly carried out.

"Well, Sir, here's your health," said Percy, shooting Gage one of his spectacular glances.

"Here's to all of us," said Tom, lifting his glass to the half dozen people who had crowded into his study.

"Hear, hear," came a general chorus, and there was a clinking of glasses.

Into the silence after they had swallowed, Lord Percy said, "This will give the Faction food for thought."

Gage refilled Hugh's glass. "Yes. I wonder what their reaction will be."

"Who knows?" came the reply. "Let them get on with it whatever it is."

In the event it was more, far more, than anyone could have imagined. While the officers were busy getting merry in Province House, the first rumours had started to fly. It was growing in the telling, of course, like a whispering campaign: war had broken out, the King's ships were bombarding Boston, the Regulars were marching. Bells began to toll in all the towns as the

men of Massachusetts responded to the gossip, none of which was true but which they implicitly believed.

As dusk fell fire beacons were lit, beacons that had been erected to warn against war with the French. The whole countryside began to arm itself and to march in the direction of Boston. By the morning of September 2nd, armed men in their thousands were heading for the town on both foot and horseback. Everywhere the leaders of the revolution found themselves trying to stop the people from perpetrating acts of violence and failing despite their best effort.

The mob turned ugly in Cambridge and marched on the local supporters of King George, forcing them to flee for their lives. One house had its windows smashed by boys and servants. Yet another unfortunate, Customs Commissioner Benjamin Hallowell, was riding in his chaise, complete with an accompanying servant. Suddenly surrounded by a violent mob he took his servant's horse and galloped for Boston full pelt. The mob, at least a hundred and fifty strong, came howling in hot pursuit. Behind, thundering along to no avail, were three of the rebel leaders vainly trying to stop them.

As Hallowell approached the safety of Boston Neck, the horse collapsed beneath him. Nothing daunted, the loyalist Tory had taken to his heels and sprinted through to the sanctuary of British lines, where he remained, telling his tale to anyone who would listen.

In Province House the Governor was astounded by the turn of events. That the people would have been mildly irritated by the seizing of their powder, he had

172

reckoned on. That the whole countryside should have risen against him, in force, frankly astonished him. Sitting quietly, he considered what was best to be done.

He was still alone, inasmuch as his wife was yet to join him. But now he no longer missed her so much, indeed had had hardly a moment recently to concentrate on his married life, or anything else for that matter. She had written that she would be arriving in early September but it was already the evening of the second and there was no sign of her. Gage sighed. When Margaret joined him, it would be the end of teaching Sara, he felt certain of that. Though even those enjoyable interludes had been shelved since the affair of the gunpowder raid.

Seized by a sudden restlessness, the Governor got to his feet and paced the room. A feeling of impending disaster gripped him and with it the conviction that he must defend Boston to the hilt. Sitting at his desk and starting to write urgent orders, he rang a bell, not looking up as it was answered almost immediately.

"Yes, Sir?" said Sara's voice.

Gazing in surprise, Tom allowed himself the brief respite of studying her. She had grown even more beautiful, if anything, since he had started to teach her. For now the girl had a poise, an air of calmness about her, which had been missing before. Despite himself, despite everything, Gage found himself smiling at her in pleasure.

"Sara. Where have you been hiding? I haven't seen you around for days."

She smiled back at him and instantly the atmosphere in the room lightened. "I've been here, Master Governor, but I think you've been rather preoccupied."

He gestured to the seat on the other side of the desk. "Come and sit down. I'm sorry about your lessons. But you're right. I've had a lot on my plate. You know about it, I take it."

"Yes, Sir. I know about it."

"And what do you think?"

"I think it's mighty difficult for you, Sir."

Gage gave a humourless laugh. "Yes, you could say that."

"So what are you going to do?"

It was the first direct question she had ever asked him, except for queries about their lessons together. And it was also the first time that she had not addressed him by a title of some sort. Gage stared at her for a moment, then laughed, pretending for a second that she was an old and intimate friend and rather enjoying the feeling.

"I'm going to close Boston, that's what."

"But how, Sir?"

"I am writing orders right now for the Neck to be defended by heavy cannon, put them on Roxbury Neck too. Then I'm going to call in all the weapons in the town and compulsorily buy any existing stocks of gunpowder."

"In case you're attacked from within?"

"Precisely." Gage put down his pen, thinking how bright the girl was and wondering, yet again, about the poor drab who had been her grandmother. Had she

perhaps been the daughter of some aristocratic house, run away to marry, only for her lover to let her down. But the girl was speaking again.

"Won't it annoy the Faction, though, Sir?"

Tom sighed again. "It's too late for that. The uprising of today was too big to take any further risks. Boston must be fortified."

The slave nodded and wisely changed the subject. "I can write all my alphabet, Sir. From memory."

"Good girl. Well done." His voice changed. "Sara, I can't teach you tonight. I have too much to do. But stay and have a cup of tea with me please."

She stood up, her plain dress making no sound as she did so. For an instant, Tom had a vision of her dressed in dark green silk, cut to enhance her beautiful body. Then he remembered his dream and felt guilty.

Sara noticed nothing though, merely nodding and saying, "I'll fetch the tray, Sir."

He worked on, writing orders, checking lists, aware that she was in the room — a comforting, soothing presence — but paying her no attention at all. Until, at one o'clock in the morning, he looked up, wiping his eyes, from which he could no longer see straight.

Sara slept in a high-backed chair, deeply unconscious, uncomfortable but tranquil. Gage laid down his pen and stretched, stiff with sitting. Then he got up and began to douse the candles. Finally he approached her and shook her gently by the shoulder.

"Sara, wake up. It's time to go to bed."

She opened her eyes, but he could tell by the expression in them that she was still asleep. "Yes, Governor."

"Come on, there's a good girl."

For answer she stood but collapsed against him, flinging her arms around his neck. The temptation to kiss her overwhelmed him to the point where, through tiredness and worry and general despair, he actually did so. Holding her close like that, he bent his head and engaged in a long, deep embrace. Then he felt guilty again and, candle tree in one hand, he escorted the sleeping girl up the stairs, opened the door to her tiny room, and put her inside. Then he hurried down a flight, flung off his clothes and finally fell into an exhausted sleep.

In Warren House in Hanover Street, Dr. Joseph Warren, similarly tired, was still sitting in his study wondering about the future. He had been one of the few Whigs, as the revolutionaries liked to call themselves, who had known the truth about the seizing of gunpowder during the small hours of September 1st. But communication being what it was it had been difficult to notify the country folk that war had not broken out, and they had marched on Boston regardless. Eventually, of course, the news had got through that this was not a state of high alarm, and they had withdrawn again. Yet there had been satisfaction in seeing that vast number rise as to a man. When the time came, thought the young doctor to himself.

He rose from his chair and poured himself a small cognac. But three sips were enough, and he dropped off to sleep with the glass still upright in his hand. Almost at once the dream which had been recurring recently

came to him. The woman who haunted him stood before him, her eyes dancing and laughing, holding out her hand. He took it and they entered a dark dwelling together, a dwelling he could not identify except that there was the smell of straw and animals in the air.

"Tell me your secret," he whispered.

She laughed at him. "Why should I?"

"Because I need to know it. It is vital that I do."

She drew close to him, and her eyes, the colour of topaz, gazed into his. "What will you give me in return?"

"My love," he said, "for ever and ever."

She laughed once more and Joseph Warren woke up, sweating.

It was cold in the house. The fire had gone out and the candles burned low in their sticks. Yet for all the loss of temperature he was hot, pouring sweat.

Joseph stood up, putting his glass down onto a tray. He had been at a meeting in The Green Dragon Tavern, a meeting of the Faction called in haste as a result of the gunpowder seizure. At this gathering they had sworn never to be taken by surprise again. A committee had been formed whose intended purpose was to watch the movement of British soldiers and gain every intelligence of the Tories, as the rebels thought of Gage and his crew. That had been all very fair, but it had gone on late, until after midnight, and Warren could not help but wonder if it was his tremendous mental excitement that brought about the recurring dream.

Yet the woman was so clear to him, as clear as if he knew her, though he realised that he had never met her, nor anyone resembling her. For with her dark hair and gorgeous eyes she was in a class on her own. Warren gave a bitter little laugh and started to ascend the staircase to his lonely bedchamber, thinking that he would mix himself a sleeping draught. For he was over-fatigued; he knew it. Yet how could it be otherwise in view of recent events.

He undressed and put on his nightshirt, then went to a cupboard and mixed himself a dose containing laudanum. After that he fell into bed and almost immediately slept, this time to dream of Paul Revere and, strangely enough, of Dr. Benjamin Church, whose roguishly charming face seemed changed and somehow sinister.

CHAPTER
TWELVE

September, 1774

He had been waiting impatiently all day, despite the fact that she had written to say that it would probably be the afternoon before she arrived. But now, at last, shortly after four o'clock, there was the sound of carriage wheels outside, which drew to a halt at the entrance to Province House. Tom, seated at his desk, dealing with mass upon mass of official papers, leapt to his feet, calling to Robin to gather the servants into the hall. Then he threw open the front door.

Margaret was in the street, supervising the handing out of her daughter to a capable girl, extremely tall and decidedly English-looking. Just for a moment, Tom stood watching her, thinking she was thinner than when he had last seen her. Then, because it was so long since he had had her company, just for a second he regarded her as if she were a stranger.

She was still beautiful, there could be no denying that, though now her beauty had an indefinable edge to it. The lines of her jaw were more clearly defined, the lips tended to close more firmly, while the look in her lustrous eyes was deep and knowledgeable, aware of things that she had not understood as a girl.

Feeling someone looking at her, Margaret turned, then gave a cry. "Tom."

Years ago she would have flown into his arms, thrown her own around his neck, and kissed him. Now, murmuring some instructions to the nursemaid, she walked briskly up the path, and stood before him. "How is it with you, my dear? Are you well?"

He gave a wry smile. "I will be better now you have arrived." And, giving her a swift kiss on the cheek, Tom Gage escorted his wife within doors.

Robin had hustled as many of the servants as he could find into a small welcoming group, and now they stood stiffly, awaiting inspection. Tom went along the line introducing each one. Isaac he had turned out some while ago, not replacing him, saying that the others could easily perform his duties. Andrew, on the other hand, had not only risen to the post of full coachman, but was helping Robin, taking on most of what Isaac had done and more. A jackanapes he truly was, but he was so cheerful and so bright that Tom begrudged him nothing. Now he gave a magnificent bow and said, "It will be an honour to serve you, Mam."

Margaret smiled at him, it was difficult not to. "I look forward to it."

"And this," said Tom, passing to the next slave, "is Sara."

The girl was shaking, very slightly but still obviously. Margaret ran her eyes over her and for no reason Tom, suddenly remembering the kiss he had given her, went red. Turning to look at him, Margaret noticed his change in colour but said nothing, merely raising her brows slightly.

180

The introductions done, Tom turned to his wife. "Let me show you our room. I am sure you will love it as much as I do."

She smiled. "Let me reintroduce you to Charlotte first. I think you'll find her much grown."

For the second time in as many minutes, Tom felt guilty again. He had actually forgotten the arrival of his daughter. It had been five months since they had last met, and he simply wasn't used to having a baby round the house. He over-compensated by saying, "May I hold her?"

"Certainly you may," answered his wife, and gave a nod to the nursemaid who had been silently standing in the background, holding the child, who had slept, angelically, throughout the proceedings.

As soon as he touched her, she woke and started to scream, yelling for all she was worth. Much abashed, Tom, unused to fatherhood as he was, attempted to placate her. But Charlotte merely grew redder and redder, while her crying grew louder and more forceful.

"I'm afraid she doesn't recognise you," said Margaret with a slight smile on her face.

"No," said Tom, and handed his weeping daughter back to the maid.

"If you could show me the nursery suite," Margaret went on, "we'll settle her down for a nap. She's all out of routine with this travelling."

"Yes, of course," the Governor replied and led the way up the staircase, turning left at the top.

Two rooms, one for the nursemaid and one for the child, had been aired and prepared, and though

Margaret queried that there was no day room for them, she decided that that could be organised later. She turned to her husband. "I'll leave her for the present. If you could show me our establishment."

"Certainly, my sweetheart. This way."

He led her along the corridor and threw open the door of their room, then proceeded to lead her onto the balcony. Margaret stepped out and breathed deeply. Then she stopped.

"There's a strange smell. What is it?"

"Too many people," he answered baldly.

"What do you mean?"

"Hundreds have poured into the town, seeking refuge from the rough handling they are experiencing outside."

Margaret looked thoroughly shocked. "What sort of people?"

Tom sat down on the bed, his expression grim. "Doctors, lawyers, merchants, landowners; in short anyone loyal to the King. They've decided to come to Boston for their own protection. The result is horrible — overcrowding and high feelings. The revolutionaries truly believe that all supporters of the King are enemies of and traitors to their own country."

Margaret sat down beside him, her expression grim. "As I passed through Boston Neck, I saw that it had been heavily fortified. Why is that?"

"Because I ordered that a powder store be raided and the powder seized. The whole country rose against me. Twenty thousand men were on the move. They truly believed that war had broken out. They disbanded

182

eventually, but I decided there and then that Boston must be protected at all costs."

"Against such a thing happening again?"

"Precisely."

She looked at him earnestly. "And will it? Will they repeat a rise like that?"

"Not if I have anything to do with it," he answered and sighed.

Margaret put an arm round his shoulders. "Have you missed me?"

Tom automatically answered, "Of course I have," but, in truth, he hadn't greatly, particularly of late, too preoccupied with the situation and — he had to admit it — watching Sara blossom as she learned.

She pulled his face round to look at her, a questioning expression on her own. Thinking quickly, Tom said, "Have you missed me? Or was the social scene too bright in New York?"

"I was visiting friends and family," she answered firmly.

He smiled and patted her knee. "You won't find it so jolly here, though Lord Percy attempts to burnish the place."

"How does he manage that?"

"He has become friendly with the Hancock family, particularly Miss Dolly if one is to believe the rumours."

"And who might she be?"

"The youngest daughter of an old Boston family, the Quincys. She lives with the Hancocks for his aunt,

Lydia, is determined to marry her to John, damn his eyes."

"Why?"

"Because the beastly buck is a revolutionary through and through, despite his posturing and airs and graces. Anyway, Hugh Percy takes meals with them, much to Dolly's delight and joy."

Margaret laughed, and it was wonderful suddenly to hear the sound. "And what other gossip is there?"

"Plenty. Mostly about the Earl. He lives in a grand house in Tremont Street, formerly the home of Governor Bernard. There he entertains lavishly and has made many friends in the town and garrison."

She laughed again. "Are you jealous?"

"No, strangely I'm not."

"Why, strangely?"

"Because I have you," the Governor answered, but even as he kissed her, an image of Sara came into his mind and the fact that she had trembled when she had been presented to Margaret.

That evening they were to dine alone, the two of them together again. But before that Tom had an irksome duty. He was to receive Dr. Joseph Warren and the unlovely Samuel Adams, petitioning him about something or other. Warren he quite liked, though he hated his politics, but for all that there was something wholesome about the man, and his reputation as an excellent doctor preceded him. Adams on the other hand was revolting; palsied and pale, unscrupulous in his methods, always in rumpled, soiled clothing. If Tom

had had his way, he would have pitched the fellow into Boston harbour with stones in his pockets. And good riddance. Now, however, he must do his official duty and receive them.

It was Margaret who suggested that they should be greeted in the withdrawing room and not in his study.

"Offer them a drink, my dear. Be kind."

"Kind!" snorted Tom, shrugging into his formal uniform coat. "The rats could do with stringing up. Well, no, that's not quite true. Warren's a decent enough chap but as to that other fellow. Dear God, you ought to see him."

"I'd like to," she answered, turning from her dressing table and looking at him.

At that moment, dressed in dark green, emerald earrings in her ears, she looked truly lovely. Tom, staring at her, was totally enraptured.

"Would you?" he said.

"Very much indeed. Could I not be introduced to them and then leave you when you have personal matters to discuss?"

"Why not?" he said. "It can't do any harm and may perhaps do good. I'll give word to Robin that when they arrive they are to be shown into the withdrawing room."

She stood up, coming close to him. "I'd like to help you, Tom. I thought how careworn you looked when I arrived."

He pulled a face. "Anyone would be given the amount of effort I have to put in."

"Well, I'm here now, sweetheart."

She snuggled close, and he took her in his arms, then bent his head and kissed her. After a few moment she drew away, laughing.

"What about your visitors?"

"I'd say damn them but I can't. Duty calls. But when they're gone . . ."

"Yes?"

"You know perfectly well," he answered and gave her a playful smack on the bottom.

Downstairs, all was harmonious. The candles lit in the withdrawing room, the curtains drawn against the autumn evening. Margaret, her dress swishing as she walked, settled herself in a chair by the fire and accepted a glass of sherry from Robin. Tom, uneasy at the thought of entertaining revolutionaries, stood before the fire, one arm behind him, the other holding his sherry glass. Punctually at six o'clock, the front doorbell was pulled and echoed in the hall.

Robin's head appeared. "Should I really show them in here, Governor?"

Tom gave a slightly rueful smile. "Yes, Robin. Mrs. Gage has a mind to meet them."

Robin's eyes rolled slightly, but he braced himself. "Yes, Masser. Whatever the lady wants."

As he vanished, Margaret caught Tom's eye. "Oh dear, am I really acting so extraordinarily?"

But there was no time to reply. Robin appeared once more, solemnly intoning, "Mr. Adams and Dr. Warren, Governor." And the two men, looking decidedly

186

surprised, were ushered into the room, where they stood fidgeting and turning their hats in their hands.

Margaret stood up. "Gentlemen, how do you do? I am Margaret Gage, the Governor's wife. Won't you sit down and have a sherry?"

"I do not drink, Madam," replied Adams at the same moment that Dr. Warren said, "Thank you, Ma'am. How kind of you."

On hearing this Samuel Adams lowered himself onto the very edge of a chair, while the doctor, staring at Margaret as if she were a visitation, accepted a glass from Robin, who was busy at the sideboard.

There was a silence broken by Dr. Warren saying, "It is a pleasure to meet you at last, Ma'am." And he gave Margaret a look of obvious admiration.

She smiled. "How nice of you to say so. My husband was telling me earlier about you — and about Mr. Adams — and I asked him if it might be possible for me to meet you both."

Adams, who was maintaining a pointed silence, cleared his throat noisily. Tom raised a brow but said nothing while Margaret gave Adams her sweetest smile, a smile which he completely ignored.

Dr. Warren said rapidly, "I take it from your accent, Ma'am, that you and I are fellow countrymen."

"Yes, indeed, Sir. I am extremely proud of being a member of the Kemble clan from New Jersey."

"I had no idea," answered the doctor. He swallowed his sherry rather rapidly, and Margaret indicated to Robin to refill the glass. She turned to Adams.

"Would you like some water, Sir?"

"No, thank you," he replied gruffly and shifted his body from one side to the other, his head shaking of its own accord as he did so.

Margaret turned her attention back to Warren. "Are you married, Sir?"

"I was. My wife died two years ago. I'm afraid that she was not strong."

"Oh dear. I'm so sorry. You must miss her."

"Truth to tell, I do. It's not easy bringing up three children on your own."

"It must be a great struggle." She turned to Tom, who had remained standing, listening to the doctor and ignoring Adams. "Our youngest child is here in Province House. I felt she was too small to leave behind in England. That is where our other children are being educated, you know."

Samuel Adams growled, "American schools not good enough, eh?"

Margaret gave him a glowing smile. "No, they're not really, are they."

"You're entitled to your opinion."

Warren drank his sherry rapidly, then said, "Thank you for inviting us to join you, Mrs. Gage. Now if we could speak with the Governor privately."

Tom gave an audible sigh which he attempted to disguise as a cough.

"Of course, gentlemen. If you would like to follow me."

Adams gave the briefest of bows and left the room, but Dr. Warren lingered, raising Margaret's hand to his

188

lips. "It has been a great pleasure to meet you, Ma'am. I hope I will have the opportunity to do so again."

"No doubt you will," she answered. "I believe that Boston is a very small community."

"It is indeed," he replied, and, giving an elaborate bow, left the room.

"If you will excuse me, my dear," said Tom.

"Of course."

After they had gone, she helped herself to a second glass of sherry and sat staring into the flames. In company with her husband she had not taken to Adams at all, considering him a slovenly rag-bag of a creature. But the doctor was entirely different, fresh-faced and fine-featured, his blue eyes blazing beneath his own powdered hair. She wasn't sure whether she liked him, but she certainly found him arresting, attractive even. With a laugh, Margaret settled down to read until the time came to go in to dinner.

The meeting over, the usual plea not to fortify Boston being listened to politely, gravely, then ignored, the two men made their way out from Province House. Feeling enormously like being on his own, Dr. Warren, making an excuse about seeing a patient, bade a scowling Sam Adams goodnight and disappeared in the direction of his own house. But he did not go home, instead he made his way to the harbour, deserted and empty since the closure, and into The Sun Tavern, close to the waterfront, where he sat in a corner and ordered a rum.

It was extraordinary, probably coming from not sleeping well, but Margaret Gage's apparent resemblance

to the woman who haunted his dreams was uncanny. The topaz eyes, the black hair, everything about her. Joseph sat like a schoolboy thinking about her, planning how he could meet her again, how he could get hold of a sketch of her, realising that, for once, she was occupying his thoughts even more than those of the troubles of Massachusetts. As he ordered more rum he felt a stiffening in his breeches, a sensation he had not experienced for a while.

"My God," he said to himself, "what has she done to me?"

Wild thoughts went through his head. He pictured the Governor dead as pork, out of the picture. He envisaged the battle for independence won, America belonging to the Americans, the British chucked out for good and all. Then he briefly allowed his mind to wander over a picture which became more and more appealing. The widow Gage throwing in her lot with him, becoming a mother to his children, them starting out as a family in a brand new country full of golden opportunity.

Acting completely atypically, Dr. Warren ordered another rum and remained silently sitting in the corner, dreaming his dreams.

At Province House, dinner eaten early according to British custom, Margaret and Tom retired to the withdrawing room where they both sat reading. He, official documents, as usual, she, a novel by Henry Fielding, *The History of Tom Jones*. Where Tom grunted and sighed, Margaret laughed and chuckled, a

welcome sound which, even though he was not joining in, Tom enjoyed. Eventually, though, she put down the book and yawned.

"My dearest, I am so tired. The journey to Boston has really drained me of energy. So, if you will forgive me, I shall make my way to bed."

Tom put down the report he was reading and took off his glasses. "Of course. I shall be up in half an hour. It's just that I've got to get through these wretched things tonight. Forgive me."

She crossed over to where he sat and leaned over the back of the chair. "Of course I do. But don't stay up late. You'll exhaust yourself and then where will everyone be?"

"Bloody glad, I should imagine."

"How can you say that? Hundreds of people are relying on you."

"And unfortunately for everyone of those there are thousands who wish me out of the way."

Margaret kissed him lightly on the cheek. "Now stop it. Such gloomy talk does not become you."

He leant up and returned the kiss. "You're right. I must be optimistic. Anyway, I won't be long, I promise."

She went from the room, and Tom heard Robin leave his post in the hall and escort her up the stairs. He half-listened to their progress, scanning the report at the same time, and was slightly startled when there was a gentle knock on the door.

"Come in," he called. Then again, "Come in."

191

The entrance opened a fraction, and Sara stood there, her face anxious, her children's primer in her hand.

"Is it all right, Master Governor?"

"Sara. Come in and sit down."

She obeyed him quietly, taking the chair vacated by Margaret. Tom, who had put his spectacles back on, looked at her over the top of them. Yet again, the girl's singular beauty made his throat constrict slightly as he did so.

She said nothing, regarding him silently, so that he was finally forced to say, "How can I help you?"

She spoke. "I realise this must be the last lesson, Sir, 'cos of the arrival of the lady. But I wondered if I might read my primer to you. I been practising."

He put down his papers. "Go on then. It will be a relief after this lot."

She opened the book and started to read, slowly but clearly. Gage got up from his place and poured himself a cognac, then returned to his chair. His eyes closed and for a while he listened, as intently as he could at this hour, then sleep finally overcame him.

He was awoken by silence and by the fact that Sara was shaking him gently. It was a complete reversal from the last time they had been alone together.

She smiled at him. "Come on, Governor. Your wife will be waiting."

He opened his eyes. "Sara, I'm so sorry. But I heard most of what you read. It was excellent. You've really worked hard."

Her face clouded. "Thank you for everything, Sir. But I still couldn't read an adult's book."

"Why don't you try?"

"'Cos I ain't got any," she answered simply. She moved away from him. "Goodnight, Sir, and thank you again."

"Think nothing of it. Goodnight, Sara."

She went out, still moving silently, and Tom, left alone to look at the dying embers, thought to himself how different it could have been for the girl if she had been the illegitimate child of another father, a sea captain perhaps. Or even someone like himself. He smiled briefly, got up, raked out the fire and went upstairs.

Entering his room quietly, carrying a candle tree, he heard regular breathing coming from the bed. Holding it high he saw that Margaret was fast asleep. Silently he undressed, put on his nightshirt — something he hadn't done in a while — and climbed in beside her. In a few minutes he was deeply asleep as well.

CHAPTER
THIRTEEN

October, 1774

The situation remained stable that autumn. Stable, that is, as far as one could tell. Three thousand more soldiers arrived during this time, together with the promise of four hundred Royal Marines to be there before the end of the year, to join the forces already camping in Boston. Yet against the twenty thousand men of Massachusetts who had been summoned within a day to march against the town, it was a pitifully small number. Meanwhile, the Governor wrote home begging for further reinforcements. To Viscount Barrington he implored, 'If you think ten thousand men sufficient, send twenty; if one million is thought enough, give two; you save both blood and treasure in the end.' But the answer had come, 'such a force cannot be collected without augmenting our army to a war establishment'. The British powers had promised him four hundred Marines and told him to get on and do the job.

During this time the rebel leaders of New England were gathering strength. At a convention held on September 27th, 1774, they urged that special bands of minutemen — men who could literally be ready to fight in one minute — be formed, so that one third of them would constantly be on hand to march. It also recommended that a means of communication, of

alarms and express riders to give notice of what was happening, be set up throughout the whole of Massachusetts.

In Boston clandestine meetings continued at The Green Dragon Tavern, attended by Paul Revere, Samuel Adams, John Hancock, and the two doctors, Warren and Church. But though Joseph appeared to concentrate, to give his all to the cause, he had a secret, a secret which he kept entirely to himself. A secret which had sent him in his own private world into a kind of frenzy of excitement.

After the night when he had met Margaret, a night which had culminated in him drunk and unsteady, returning home late, he had gone to bed in an agony of deadly fascination. But in the morning, sick and sorry, he had resolved to put her out of his head forthwith — but with scant effect. The only moment when she departed from him was when he was dealing with patients. Thus he had decided that if you can't kill the feeling then let it all emerge, and had taken to hanging round Province House whenever he had a spare moment. Eventually, after two weeks, he had been rewarded. Mrs. Gage herself, pushing the bassinet, emerged, with no sign of the nursemaid. He had stepped forward, sweeping his hat from his powdered hair.

"Mrs. Gage, what a delightful surprise."

She had flashed her great eyes in his direction. "Why Dr. Warren, what brings you this way?"

"I was just walking past, Ma'am. May I accompany you?"

They fell into step beside one another. "How are you liking Boston?" he asked.

"Tolerably well. Though the town seems to be getting more and more full."

"Full of my fellow countrymen who would prefer to be British," was out of his mouth before he had had time to think that he was addressing the Governor's lady.

"Are they not forced to come here?"

"Indeed they are. Because of the behaviour of yet other of my countrymen who are giving them a difficult time in their own surroundings. So they hurry to Boston for protection."

Margaret turned to look at him, closely scanning his face. "And what of you, Dr. Warren? Would you pester loyal subjects so that they are obliged to leave their homes?"

Aware that he was being tested in some way, Warren weighed his words carefully. "Yes, I probably would, Ma'am. You see, to me the bigger picture is all."

"And what bigger picture would that be, pray?"

"Madam, listen to me." Joseph had stopped walking in his anxiety to get through to her. "I truly believe — indeed would die for — my conviction that America is for the Americans, that British rule here is oppressive and, dare I say, tired. Surely you as an American, a Yankee, must see that."

"I certainly don't. America is a British colony and as such should remain loyal to the King."

"The American people have rights too," said Dr. Warren, then realised how he must be sounding to her,

a mad doctor spouting forth political doctrine, a provincial besotted with the idea of freedom.

"I'm sorry," he continued hurriedly. "Those are my beliefs, but I should have kept them to myself, particularly in view of who you are."

"No, you have a right to express them to whom you choose, Doctor."

"But not to you," he said lamely. He gathered himself together. "Good day to you, Madam."

They had reached the junction of Winter Street and Marlborough Street, and she was apparently going to make her way towards the Common because she was already starting to turn up the narrow thoroughfare.

"I'll be on my way. Goodbye," the doctor added for good measure.

She smiled at him. "Despite our differing views, I have enjoyed speaking with you, Dr. Warren. Perhaps we can do it again another time."

His heart soared in his chest, and he snatched his hat from his head and gazed at her, his blue eyes blazing sincerity.

"You've enjoyed it? Truly? Oh, my dear Madam."

Her smile deepened. "Until next time then."

"Next time it is." He swept her gloved hand to his lips. "Shall I wait here at this hour tomorrow?"

"No, Sir. In three days from now. I shall take Charlotte to the Common to see the soldiers drilling. She enoys that."

"I will be here unless I have a visitor. Good day, Mrs. Gage."

"Good day, Dr. Warren."

And with another smile, she rounded the corner and headed away. Joseph stood watching her until she was out of sight then quite literally took to his heels and ran all the way back to his house, close to the Fanueil Hall, terrified he was going to be late for his next patient.

In Province House, Governor Gage was attempting to decipher a letter which he had received that morning. For a start the writing was crabbed and difficult to read, for a second it was written in appallingly bad French. Indeed it was not until he got to the end and saw the signature 'Joel' that he realised who it was from. With a suppressed whoop of joy, he carried the letter to the window, the better to read it.

"Your Excellency," it began, "I find myself able to put my hand and heart at your disposal. I shall report for duty shortly. Please be so good as to give me a safe conduct through Boston Neck and its environs. I will come soon."

He was still reading it, delighted by its contents, when Robin knocked and put his head round the door.

"Lord Percy to see you, Governor."

"Show him in, would you?"

"Yassir."

Hugh came through the door, and Tom was struck again by the man's apparent fragility. Today he moved as if he were in pain and even saluting seemed to hurt him.

"Sit down, man. You don't look well."

Hugh gave him one of his sidelong glances. "I've been better, Sir. It's this damnable gout. I've got a bad

198

attack today. It's hereditary, don't you know. My poor father is riddled with it."

"Damn shame, unfortunate fellow. Well, my friend, on another topic, how goes it with the men?"

"Reasonably well. They are clothed against the winter and relatively fit."

"Thanks to yourself I believe."

And it was true. Lord Percy, ever watchful of his troops, had provided their winter uniform personally. Now the younger man looked at the Governor.

"I was wondering, Sir, if you and Mrs. Gage might be free to dine with me tonight."

"Yes, I'm sure we are. She is out at the moment, taking the child to the Common to see the soldiers. But I will ask as soon as she returns."

The Earl hobbled to his feet. "Will you send word?"

"Of course. Now, did you come by carriage?"

"I did today. The pain is considerable."

"Are you sure you want guests tonight? Would you not be better resting?"

"No, quite honestly having company seems to help. That and the alcohol."

"What time would you like us to arrive?"

"I thought perhaps six o'clock. After all, we're not in England now."

"No," echoed the Governor, "we're not in England are we."

It had been the merriest of parties at which Margaret had been the belle. Admittedly she had every opportunity to shine for the only other woman present

had been the wife of the Lieutenant-Governor. Unfortunately Abigail Oliver had several chins, all of which bounced as she spoke, together with a long pointed nose. She had also grown plump with the passing of the years. In short, it was no contest, and Margaret, in a dark red gown with black petticoat, effortlessly rose to the occasion.

Sitting down at the table, for once relaxed and enjoying himself, Tom let his eyes linger on his wife of sixteen years. He felt immeasureably proud of her, for she had kept her figure despite having the children, and her dark hair and amber eyes had picked her out as a beauty many years ago. These had not changed; indeed, although he stared at his wife's hair quite closely for signs of grey he could see none. Percy, meanwhile, was looking at her with his ravishing glances which meant he could scarcely see her. But she, unaware of this, flirted and laughed with him and generally acted as hostess. Eventually, though, Margaret and Mrs. Oliver retired and left the men to their port and pipes.

At this, several gentlemen called for the chamber pot and relieved themselves at table. Gage, however, preferred to step outside, even though it was somewhat cold. He had just finished his affairs when a voice spoke suddenly out of the darkness.

"Greetings, *mon Gouverneur*."

His hand flew to his pistol; he couldn't help it. "Who are you?" he hissed.

There was a soft chuckle, and the speaker stepped into the light of the porch. "Do you not know me, *mon ami?*"

It was Calico Joel.

Tonight he was dressed in buckskin trousers, with a strange jacket which appeared to be made of patches atop. His long black hair was tied back in a ponytail, his dark eyes gleamed with thoughts. He had abandoned the cocked hat — which had probably died of sheer wear, Gage considered — and now had a broad-brimmed chapeau, with the scarlet feather, presumably a new one, stuck into the headband.

"My friend," said Gage delightedly, "I only got your letter this morning."

"Letters take their time, I travel swiftly."

"I contacted the troops guarding the Neck as soon as I received it."

"They were suspicious but eventually they let me through."

"How was it in Canada?"

"Everyone wants to be French," said Joel, and laughed shortly.

Gage looked at him. "Have you been to Province House yet?"

"I saw the outside. Very important-looking place. I did not try to gain entry because I feared being turned away."

"Then how did you know . . . ?"

Calico Joel allowed a flicker of a smile to cross his taciturn features. "Shall we say I followed your trail, *mon Gouverneur.*"

"Where are you going to sleep tonight?"

"I have no plans, Excellency."

"Then you must stay with me. Indeed, you must remain with us until you find alternative accommodation."

"Very well, but I shall sleep in the garden."

"But, my friend, it is getting cold."

"I shall not be cold, *mon Gouverneur*. I have my things with me." And the scout indicated a large rucksack which was lying on the ground.

"If you insist. But now I must get back within. What about you?"

"I shall go to a tavern. I will return in three-quarters of an hour."

"As shall I." The Governor looked at him. "I can honestly say that I have never been happier to see anyone." He added as an afterthought, "Mrs. Gage will be delighted too."

The scout nodded but made no comment, and then, quite literally, he was gone, disappearing into the night from which he had suddenly sprung. Tom, smiling to himself, went inside.

Whether he had had too much brandy, whether it was the strange turn of events with the sudden arrival of Calico Joel, or whether it was worry about the state of affairs generally, but the Governor found it impossible to sleep. Beside him in the great bed, Margaret slumbered deeply but Tom lay awake, staring through the curtains to where the balcony lay bathed in moonshine. His thoughts ran wildly, wondering if he would ever bring the Colonies to heel, wishing he were

out of the whole damn business and back in England again.

After an hour enduring this, during which his mind went over the same problem again and again, he decided to get up. Moving very quietly so as not to disturb his wife, he got out of bed and put on his slippers and a night rail, then, almost acting on impulse, he climbed the stairs up to the floor where the servants slept. Then up the narrow flight to the cupola.

Here, standing up, he could see the darkness of Boston, one or two lights here and there, spread out before him. Gazing down into the garden, he could vaguely make out a small tent and knew that this must be where Calico Joel had bedded down for the night. Then he froze, went utterly rigid, as for the second time that evening, something moved in the darkness. The Governor whirled round.

"Who's there?" he whispered.

"It's Sara," said a muffled voice.

"What are you doing here? You should be in bed asleep." His fear had made him sound harsh, abrupt almost.

For several minutes there was no reply, then she whispered, "I'm going now. Good night, Sir."

"Wait." His hand shot out and grabbed her arm, and he pulled her close to him. He could see in the moonlight that she had been weeping, for her eyes were red and puffy, even her face was swollen with tears.

"Sara, what is it?" he asked, his voice completely different.

"Nothing, Governor."

"Don't be ridiculous, girl. Nobody gets into a state like yours over nothing. Tell me what is wrong."

He sat down on the wooden seat, pulling her to sit beside him. She folded her hands in her lap and gazed at the floor.

"I couldn't sleep," she said eventually.

"But why should that make you cry?"

"I don't know, Sir."

"Sara, pay me the respect of treating me like an adult. Tell me why you're crying."

"Because . . ."

"Yes?"

"Because I miss my lessons, Sir."

"Oh, is that all," said the Governor, and instantly regretted it, for the slave wept again, profusely.

"Sara, come on. I didn't mean any harm. Come here."

He put out his arm and placed it round her shoulders. Reluctantly, she drew a little closer.

"Come along, my dear. There's no need to upset yourself. We'll think of something," he said, as if he were placating a child.

From where he was sitting, his nostrils were full of her essence. Clad in her nightclothes, away from the kitchen smells, she was extraordinarily fresh and clean, an overriding scent of some exotic flower, something unidentifiable, emanating from her.

"If the lessons mean that much to you, we must continue them," he said, wondering where he was going to find the time in his busy life.

She put a small hand out and touched his arm, the one that lay resting on his lap.

"Just occasionally, Master. I know how committed you are."

"I tell you what," he said, looking down at her, "if I get you an adult book to read, will you read it to me when next we meet?"

"Oh, yes, Governor."

"And what would you like?"

"Nothing too difficult, Sir."

Her voice was slowing, as if sleep were coming.

"I'll see what the bookseller has to offer."

There was no answer and looking at her again he saw that she had indeed fallen asleep, sitting up and leaning against him. In repose he studied her perfect face, admired its angles and contours, the sweep of the dark lashes on the damask skin. The he, too, closed his eyes and felt the pressures of the day drain away from him as he fell asleep at last.

He awoke in the steel grey light of dawn, rigid and uncomfortable. Sara still slept deeply, her head in his lap. Gently but firmly, the Governor shook her till her eyes opened and looked into his.

"Sir, what are you doing here?"

"I came into the cupola late last night and found you here. As seems customary with us, we both fell asleep whilst talking about books."

She was on her feet in a matter of seconds. "Oh my, I'll be put in the street for lateness. The other slaves will be round the house by now. Forgive me, Sir, but I've got to fly."

And she was down the ladder and out of his sight on the instant. Aching in every limb, Tom stood up and looked out of the window of the cupola. Far below in the streets of Boston, two figures were walking along, patrolling. He smiled grimly. It was the rebels, watching the soldiers, who, in turn, watched them from behind the window panes of their lodgings, leaning towards the fire, sipping their mugs of mulled wine and laughing their heads off.

"And so, you see, Ma'am, why I am a devoted member of the Faction."

Joseph Warren, sitting beside her on a rug on the Common, paying no attention to the marching soldiers whatsoever, leaned slightly away, having made his point.

Margaret played with the baby, who sat utterly still, watching the military men with fascination.

"I must say, Dr. Warren, that when you explain certain things they most certainly give me cause to think. But what say you to the mob violence? To the tarring and feathering? How can you justify them, pray?"

The young physician sighed and, forgetting himself, removed his hat and ran his fingers through his hair. Specks of powder fell onto his coat which he brushed at with a truly beautiful hand.

The hand of a doctor, Margaret thought, watching the gesture.

"It's mainly the work of Sam Adams," he said apologetically. "He can start a riot on the instant if so

required. He has the ear of the common man." He paused then said, "And that last remark makes me sound like a diabolical snob. For what are we, after all, but common men? I went to Harvard so I have a good education. But stripped naked I am the same as all the rest."

Margaret sat silently, watching him, thinking that he was a true patriot, a truly decent man, whatever the differences between them might be. But were they so different? They had both been born in this enormous country, this country that even now was going through birth pangs trying to free itself of British tyranny. Shocked with herself for that last thought, she bent over Charlotte.

"Come along, my sweetheart. It is time we were getting back."

Joseph was immediately all contrition. "Was it something I said?"

"No, of course not. It is just that the baby needs to go home now."

He scrambled to his feet. "Of course. Let me help you pack up."

He bent over the rug, folding it carefully, corner to corner, and for the first time it occurred to Margaret that he might be falling a little in love with her. She had thought to begin with that he was meeting her merely to talk about the Colony's future. But now she wasn't quite so certain. After all, he was a widower in his thirties, she just forty-one. She gave him a brilliant smile.

"Well, Doctor, are you going to walk back with me?"

"It will be my pleasure, Ma'am."

"Do you then enjoy my company?" she asked, testing the water.

"I love it," he answered frankly, and Margaret's suspicions deepened.

"It will be too cold soon to sit and watch the soldiers," she answered as they started to saunter back.

"Then perhaps I might be permitted to take you to a coffee house."

"I don't know if it would do for the Governor's wife to be seen in company with a well-known rebel."

He sighed. "No, I don't suppose it would. However, there is a small place little used by other people."

She laughed at his depressed expression, certain now that he was more than interested. "Well, I'll think about it."

"Would you," Joseph said.

"Of course I will."

They had reached the street corner that indicated the parting point.

"Till next time then," said Dr. Warren, and raised his hat.

"Till next time," answered Margaret, and gave him a small bobbing curtsey.

Then she turned the corner and made her way to Province House, nursing a small secret which, if truth be told, brought a smile to her lips and a sudden lift to her heart.

CHAPTER
FOURTEEN

November, 1774

The winter of 1774 was one of the most severe the country had known. Snow fell early, and the seas were rough and icy. For the warship sailing from Britain to America, carrying the long-awaited troop of British Marines, it was a journey of pure hell. Gales battered the rigging, the ship plunged crazily through foaming green waters, the hands had to beat the ropes with sticks to remove the ice. But as well as the four hundred men promised to Governor Gage on board, there were personal letters for him, one of which bore terrible and tragic personal news.

The ship finally managed to stagger into Boston harbour in mid-December. Lord Percy was there to oversee the landing of the men and personally took possession of the letters intended for his superior officer. These he stored in a bag and later that day, when the Marines were safely ashore, he called at Province House to deliver them.

He found the Governor in his study, his usual retreat, and handed him the letters which Gage sifted through, glancing casually at the various writings on the outside.

"Ah, here's one from my brother," he remarked, breaking the seal and opening it.

"How is he?" asked the Earl.

There was no reply and, looking at him, Lord Percy saw that the Governor's face had turned the colour of ash, and his shoulders were hunched, as if he had some great burden on them. A great rush of concern filled Hugh Percy, and he put his glasses on to make sure he had not misinterpreted the events. But Tom was reading the letter again, his face drawn and haggard.

"Bad news, Sir?" the Earl ventured quietly.

At length the Governor glanced up, and Hugh could see that the man had tears in his eyes, tears only barely held in check.

"It's my son," he said softly. "It's William. He died on October 30th."

"Oh my God," exclaimed Percy. "What a tragedy. Oh, my dear Sir."

And it was at that moment that Margaret, giving the lightest of knocks but not waiting for an answer, swept into the room. She stopped short as her eyes took in the scene before her.

"What's the matter?" she said. "What's happened?"

Tom rose from his seat behind the desk and crossed to her, putting his arms round her. The Earl immediately felt *de trop* and started to make his way out. But the Governor stopped him.

"No, Hugh. Don't go. Not now anyway."

"Then I'll wait in the other room, Excellency. You two should be alone." And with that Lord Percy made his way into the hall.

Robin was there, hovering as usual, waiting for his master to ring for him. Hugh hesitated, not certain

what to do for the best. Eventually he said, "Robin, your master has received some very bad news today. I would advise that you and the other servants treat him with the greatest care."

Before the slave could answer, the two men heard a cry from inside the study. "Oh no! Oh no!" said Margaret's voice. "I can't bear it. Not my darling William."

This was followed by the sound of her starting to weep. Gage could be heard murmuring to her, gently and comfortingly.

"I think," the Earl said to Robin, "that this might be the moment when I take in brandy."

"Not me, Sir?"

"No, not you. Not at present."

"Very good, your Lordship."

The two men, Percy still wearing his spectacles — a fact that he loathed but thought necessary on this occasion — went into the withdrawing room and assembled a tray. And then, as in the way of high drama, the front door chimed, and Robin, smart in blue livery, went to answer it. Rupert Germain stood there, his smile fading as he saw the Negro's grim expression.

"Is anything wrong?" he asked.

Lord Percy stepped forward, rapidly whipping off his glasses. He gave a very small bow. "Lord Rupert, how nice to see you," he said.

The newspaper proprietor made his way into the hall. "Is everything well here?" he asked.

The Earl lowered his voice. "Your friend the Governor has received some very distressing news. His young son, William, has died in England. He and Mrs. Gage are currently in the study together."

Rupert looked stricken. "What a terrible thing to happen. Do we know what killed the little fellow?"

Hugh shook his head. "There may be details contained in the letter. But I have no idea. You'll have to ask the Governor."

"I will, obviously, but not now. I'll go again. Goodbye . . ."

But he got no further. The study door flew open, and Margaret stood framed in the entrance, her face crumpled up like that of a small girl. She stared at the two men blankly, then ran into Percy's arms.

"Oh Hugh, Hugh," she said between her tears. "That he should have died without me being there. That my little boy should have died by himself."

"He was not alone, I feel positive," Percy said softly. "The Viscount would have been with him, I'm sure of it."

"But he needed me, and I wasn't there."

"Madam, your place is here with the Governor. Your son must have known that."

"I have left my children by themselves for too long."

"But Mrs. Gage," ventured Rupert, "could you have saved him if you had been there?"

She shot him a look of pure anguish, disentangled herself from Hugh Percy's grasp and fled, sobbing, up the stairs.

"Oh dear," said the young man.

The Governor appeared in the study doorway. "Let her go. She's mortally upset. As for you two, come and have a drink with me for God's sake. I feel so low."

Putting on his spectacles briefly, Percy shot a look at Tom Gage's face. He was holding back his tears, just, but his face was still ashen white.

Rupert hesitated. "Tom, I feel I should go."

"You'll go to hell if you leave now. If you care for me, you'll spend half an hour with me."

"Very well."

The Governor called out quietly. "Robin, no more visitors today. Tell them I am indisposed."

"Yassir. I'm sorry, Sir."

"You're a good man," Tom said by way of reply, then, ushering in his two guests, he closed the study door.

He got amazingly drunk. So drunk, indeed, that he fell asleep at his desk. A gentle tap at his door, a tap which grew progressively louder, woke him again, and he stared round angrily, then realised where he was. This was followed almost at once by an awareness of what had made him get drunk in the first place. Sighing deeply, Tom straightened his uniform as best he could.

"Come in," he called.

Sara entered silently and stood regarding him from the other side of the room.

"What do you want, my girl?" he asked, irritable even with her.

"Just to say I'm sorry about your little boy, Sir."

"Oh, oh. Thank you."

"Is there anything I can do to help, Master?"

He regarded her bleakly. "Just tell me where he is now. Where his small soul has journeyed to."

"Don't you believe in Heaven, Sir?"

"No, not really." Tom let out a sigh in which the weariness of years was voiced. "I've seen too much of death and dying. Seen soldiers fall all around me. Seen . . ." But his voice choked and was silent as again, unbidden, the memory of Culloden field came back.

He stared at Sara silently and then, at last, the tears came and the Governor wept bitterly. She said nothing but came to stand behind him, her fingers seeking out the nape of his neck where all the tension and pain were centred. Thus they stayed in silence, he sobbing without restraint, she quietly massaging his neck and shoulders. Eventually she spoke.

"Go to Mrs. Gage now, Governor. She needs you."

"Yes," he said, wiping his eyes and blowing his nose. "She must be so distressed."

"She's asleep, Sir. But she'll want you beside her when she wakes. And I also have an answer to your question."

"About William?"

"Yes. He's in Heaven, for certain. Whether you believe it or not makes no difference. He's gone there."

"Gone to Jesus, eh?"

"I don't know about that, Master, but he's sure as Hell gone to God."

Her choice of words made the Governor give a short laugh. "Thank you, Sara. You're a good girl."

Just for a second her hands lingered on his shoulders, then she collected herself and giving him a

214

little curtsey, left the room. He stood staring at the space where she had been then, moving like a man suddenly grown old, he went out and made his way upstairs.

There was to be no peace for him. Paul Revere, hearing a rumour that the storm-embattled ship, HMS *Somerset*, was heading for Portsmouth, Massachusetts, to seize gunpowder and armaments, rode off to warn the people. Heading through the frozen slush, he arrived in Portsmouth on December 13th. There he made himself busy rousing the town folk. But if he thought his ride had been in secret, he had another think coming. On the very day of his arrival in Massachusetts, the Governor had a visitor.

"Well?" he said, as Calico Joel made his way silently into the study.

"Revere's gone," said the scout briefly. Then, thinking that maybe that explanation was too brief, he continued, "He thinks we're after the powder in Fort William and Mary. He's rousing the people to fight."

"God damn the bastard," shouted Tom, throwing his arms aloft. "The miserable little prick. He must have had word of the *Somerset* battling its way up the coast and thought it was after the powder."

"But you are going after the powder, Excellency."

"Yes, but not yet. I was waiting for the weather to improve. Now I've got to send out a ship to protect the fort. In these conditions. Merciful heaven, is there to be no end?"

Calico Joel looked at him wryly. "Not till we beat them or get out."

"Get out? Yes, I sometimes think that will be the answer." Gage looked at the scout very directly. "Joel, have you heard the bad news?"

"Yes, Sir," the scout answered quietly.

"It's been a terrible blow to me and Mrs. Gage."

The Indian nodded silently. "When did you hear?"

"When the *Somerset* docked, two days ago."

"I see. You must not cry for him, my Governor. He is everywhere now."

"What do you mean?"

"The Navajo people have a prayer. It goes, 'Do not stand at my grave and weep; I am not there. I do not sleep. I am a thousand winds that blow. I am the diamond glints on snow. I am the sunlight on ripened grain. I am the gentle autumn rain. When you awaken in the morning's hush, I am the swift uplifting rush of quiet birds in circled flight. I am the soft stars that shine at night. Do not stand at my grave and cry; I am not there. I did not die."

It was said very simply, with no pretence, and Tom sat silently, staring at the scout. Eventually he said, "Could you write that down. I would like my wife to read it."

Calico Joel gave a rare grin. "No, *mon Gouverneur*, I could not do that. I only write French."

"Then you will have to say it slowly while I do so. Now, start again."

Calico Joel waited until the Governor had a sheet of paper and a pen, then he said the prayer once more, this time with many pauses. The Governor scratched away until the Indian fell silent. Then he looked up.

"Thank you, Joel. I am deeply touched."

The Indian remained impassive. Then he said, "Do you want me to ride to Portsmouth and find out what Revere is up to?"

"How long will it take you to get there?"

Calico Joel shrugged. "A day. But if I set off now and go through the night I can be there tomorrow morning."

"Very well. Go like hell but take care."

The scout shrugged, turned and was gone, as silent and impassive as ever.

Gage sat for a moment, looking at the prayer, then, taking it, he left the study and went to the first floor bedroom. Entering quietly, he saw that Margaret was lying on the bed, staring at the ceiling and that she had put on deepest black. She did not turn her head as he came in.

"My darling, how are you?" he said tentatively.

"I am distraught," she answered him.

"Why?"

"I cannot get over the fact that our son died without seeing me again. That I deserted him."

"Margaret, how could you know what was going to happen? You came to Massachusetts and brought our youngest child with you. You did what you thought was best."

"If I had had an inkling."

"Don't reproach yourself, sweetheart. You are but human."

"I wish I were dead," she said bitterly.

Instead of arguing with her, Tom said, "Yes, I sometimes wish that too."

She looked at him, not expecting that response. "Why?" she asked.

He sat down on the bed and started to remove his boots. "Because I get heartily sick of the whole bloody business here. Whatever I do seems to no avail. Yet somehow I must contrive to convince these rebels that British rule is best. That is often what makes me think to end it all would be preferable."

"How can you say such a thing?" Margaret asked, sitting up.

"Because that is how I genuinely feel."

"Oh Tom," she said and subsided back on the bed, weeping once more.

He lay down beside her and took her in his arms. Then they wept together until every tear had run dry. Finally out of their despair there arose a need for each other. Fully dressed as they both were, Tom first kissed her, then, raising her skirts, lifted her on top of him, meanwhile undoing the flap of his breeches. She slid down on him and then rose and fell in a rhythm that drove them into a frenzy, forgetting William, forgetting everything except their desire for one another. Tom controlling himself as best he could, eventually could hold back no longer and coursed into her just as she, too, cried out in ecstasy. Then, lowering herself down beside him, the two of them fell asleep, arms around each other, until they were woken by the gong which announced dinner.

Tom got to his feet. "Do you want something on a tray, my dear?"

She smiled at him. "If you can delay proceedings by half an hour, I'll join you. Are we alone tonight?"

"Yes, we are."

"Good. I won't be long." She rose from the bed and rang for her maid, looking at him over her shoulder. "Tom . . ."

"Yes?"

"Do you still love me?"

"You know I do," he answered.

And he did love her for all the years she had been his wife and for all the things they had shared together. Yet the love had changed from that first spellbinding delight which had held him in its grip. Now his love had almost become a habit, even though he was ashamed to admit it. Unbidden, the memory of that stolen kiss with Sara came back to haunt him, and he mentally upbraided himself for being an old lecher.

With an effort, Tom straightened his uniform and slowly went down the stairs.

What became known as the Portsmouth Alarm was a heavy defeat for Governor Gage. Even though Admiral Graves, a rough sea dog with an uncontrollable temper, ordered the sloop HMS *Canceaux*, with a company of Marines on board, to sail to Portsmouth, the ship could not leave until December 17th. Meanwhile, Paul Revere had done his work and four hundred New Hampshire men had gathered and attacked the Fort, paddling eerily down the Piscataqua River through the

gentle white snowflakes that were falling. Others marched overland to the Fort.

They had no opposition to speak of. Six men, all invalids, guarded the place. The New Hampshire men swarmed over the ramparts, took everything they needed and ran down the British flag. When the Captain of the Fort tried to resist and drew his sword, he was wounded. Another British soldier going to his aid had a pistol snapped in his face and was knocked senseless by the butt of it.

By the time the *Scarborough* sailed from Boston, backing up the *Canceaux*, it was all far too late. The commander of the expedition landed to find the Royal Governor furious, a looted garrison and the news that a thousand men had marched on Portsmouth but had now gone home again. Admiral Graves, hearing the turn of events, almost had a seizure. Governor Gage, despairing of ever succeeding in his quest to tame the colonists, felt resigned to his fate.

Yet, interestingly, he made no move to arrest Paul Revere, believing strictly in the rule of law. Even Percy, who supported his superior through thick and thin, wrote home, 'The general's great lenity and moderation serve only to make them more daring and insolent.' He, who had arrived so open-minded and almost pro the colonists, was learning to hate them.

So, with passions running high and feelings never more acute, the town of Boston began to prepare for Christmas.

CHAPTER
FIFTEEN

Christmas, 1774

They met in the small, secluded coffee house he had mentioned on a previous occasion. He, as usual, fresh-faced and eager, his own hair powdered; Margaret, desperately trying to conceal who she was, even down to wearing a veiled hat on her dark head. It was the day before Christmas Eve, and Joseph Warren was bearing a small gift for her, even though he realised his behaviour in giving it might be considered excessive.

News of the loss of William had reached his ears, and his heart had bled for her. He had three children — Elizabeth, Joseph and Mary — bringing them up by himself, and he had imagined how he would have felt if one of them had died. Devastated was the only word that seemed to sum up his emotion. Now, he felt her sadness as if it were tangible, and leaning forward across the table, he put his hand over hers.

"I'm sorry about your son. It must have been a grievous blow for you."

"It was for both of us," she answered quietly.

"Yes, yes, I'm sure it was." He kept his hand where it was. "Is there anything I can do to help?"

"Just tell me why he died. You're a medical man; surely you must know."

"Did the Viscount not say?"

"He just said he got a fever and never recovered."

Dr. Warren shook his head slowly. "The description is so vague. It could have been anything. Several of my friend Paul Revere's children have died, to say nothing of his wife."

Margaret withdrew her hands from beneath his. "Don't mention that man. Why my husband hasn't clapped him in gaol long ago I truly can't imagine."

"You refer to his part in the Portsmouth Alarm?" asked Joseph gently.

"I most certainly do. He seems to me to be a rabble-rouser."

"As am I," Joseph answered with a slight touch of humour.

"I never think of you as that."

"But, Mrs. Gage, that is exactly what I am. I rouse the people of this country to exert their rights. Because I truly believe they have such rights. I cannot think how you, an American born and bred, could hold opposing views."

Margaret sighed deeply. "Because I am married to who I am. But, deep down, though you should be the last person to admit this to, I do have a feeling that you could be right."

Because he loved her so much and because he was an emotional creature, Warren's eyes filled with sudden tears.

"God bless you," he choked out.

Margaret extended her hand and took one of his, beautiful and clever, in her own.

"Not totally right," she hastened to add, "but I admit you do have a point."

The doctor, producing a sensible workaday handkerchief from his pocket, wiped his eyes.

"Forgive me. An excess of emotion."

Margaret laughed softly. "I never realised you felt so deeply."

The brilliant blue eyes sought hers and held them. "I feel deeply about many things, Madam."

She knew at once what his hidden message was, and a wave of fear tinged with excitement coursed through her. That she still loved her husband was beyond dispute but here was this man, younger than she, clearly telling her that he, too, cared. Margaret deliberately placed her hands over his.

"Do you, Doctor?" she said quietly.

"Yes, I do."

"Such as?"

"Well, I love my country above all things — well, almost all things. I love my children more, of course. And . . ."

He paused and his cheeks flushed brightly.

"Yes?"

He dropped his voice to a murmur. "And I love you."

It was a fraught moment, and Margaret was at a loss for words. To gain time, she repeated what he had just said.

"You love me?"

"Yes. I have right from the time I first saw you. It was just one of those amazing things. I fell in love at first

sight. I'm sorry if this has upset you, but the fact remains."

She remained poised and calm, though her heart was thudding wildly. "Dr. Warren, I don't know how to answer you."

"Are you furious?"

"Furious? No, of course I'm not. I am amazingly flattered."

"And will you continue to see me?"

"You know I will."

His grip on her hands tightened. "Mrs. Gage, might I be allowed to call you by your Christian name?"

She laughed. "Yes, certainly you may. May I call you by yours?"

"I would be honoured."

"Then, my dear Joseph, why don't you buy me another coffee."

He laughed and wept again, relieved that she had not been angry, relieved that she had not resorted to feigned dignity and silly phrases.

"Of course. At once."

He signalled to the waiter and as he turned away Margaret studied him. He was fine-looking, there could be no doubt of that. Indeed, had he not been so serious and intense, he could have been one of the most handsome men in town. But his expression was set and earnest, giving his features a sullen look in repose. Yet when he turned back to her, he transformed, and she decided that it was all to do with the expression in his eyes.

"Margaret," he said, his voice low, "I have a Christmas present for you."

"How very kind."

"Please accept it, and think of me when you open it."

She looked down. "I have nothing to give in return I'm afraid."

"I expected nothing. Nothing that is except your friendship."

"You have that always."

And she really meant it. The revolutionary doctor was proving to be a considerable influence in her life, an influence that in some mysterious way was starting, very subtly, to make her think like an American.

On Christmas Day, the Governor called the entire staff into the withdrawing room for them to have a glass of hot punch with him and his wife. This they did, toasting his health and that of Mrs. Gage, and admiring little Charlotte, who was in her best clothes and behaving angelically. In fact all would have been serene had it not been for an odd underlying current of sadness.

Tom and Margaret had decided that they must now put the death of William behind them and concentrate on the future. Yet, secretly, they still grieved, despite the show they were putting on for the benefit of the servants and each other. The Governor was, to add to his problems, growing increasingly worried about the situation in Massachusetts. Further, a report had come to him only yesterday, Christmas Eve. It had been Calico Joel, his most trusted man, who had brought it to him.

"Greetings, Excellency," he had said as he had walked into the study.

Tom had looked up from his usual mound of documents. "Greetings, Joel. Compliments of the season to you."

"Thank you. I come to report something."

"Oh yes?"

"It is about Dr. Warren, the rebel medicine man."

"What about him?"

"He is meeting someone."

"So?" said Tom, losing interest and starting to study his papers once more.

Calico Joel had stood silently, observing the man to whom he had sworn allegiance, knowing perfectly well who the mysterious woman was but not daring, not even he, to tell the Governor her true identity.

"That is all, *mon Gouverneur*. He meets a woman. You must be careful."

Tom had looked up. "Why? Why should I be careful?"

Everything hung in the balance, but the Indian chose the path of discretion and said nothing.

Tom had persisted. "Why? Is this woman important? Tell me."

"I believe her husband is close to the British high command."

"An officer's wife?"

"Possibly, yes."

Tom had stared at him, then had finally shrugged and returned to his papers. "Keep an eye on the situation in your usual way." He had looked up again. "What are you doing for Christmas, my friend?"

"I shall be around, *mon Gouverneur*."

"Then come and have a drink with us tomorrow at noon. You will be most welcome."

And now the scout had entered the room, dressed as extraordinarily as ever but bearing himself well. He removed his hat on entering, and his black hair, which had been tucked up inside, cascaded to his waist as he did so. He bowed solemnly to Mrs. Gage, then he turned to the Governor.

"Excellency," he said and put his hand to his heart.

One glance at Margaret had been enough to confirm that she was the woman secretly meeting Dr. Warren. But this was a matter on which he must keep his own counsel. Bowing again, he accepted a drink. And then he saw Sara. He had never observed anyone as beautiful before. Today the girl seemed burnished, a glow about her skin and hair that came from within. Standing very still, Calico Joel noticed the way she looked at the Governor and knew at once that she was in love with him. Then he saw the little glance that Tom gave her and realised that they shared a secret of some kind. He also knew, instinctively but certainly, that they had never been to bed together.

Mrs. Gage was speaking. "Charlotte, you are to behave yourself."

But the child was reaching for Calico Joel's hair, wanting to stroke it and play with it. Instantly he sat cross-legged on the floor and picked the girl up in his arms. He heard Margaret's slight intake of breath but ignored it. Then he and Charlotte stared at one another, he most directly, she too at first, before she

227

grew shy. Finally she put out a hand and touched his hair and then, laughing, seized great handfuls of it and ran them through her fingers. Sara, who had been watching, gave a laugh of pleasure and, squatting down, joined in.

Margaret gave a sound of annoyance and bent to put an end to the child's game. Joel caught her eye as it grew level with his and said, "It is Christmas, Madame. She enjoys herself."

"Yes, of course. I just did not want her to annoy you, that is all." She straightened up as did Sara, who blushed and looked away. Margaret gave the girl a very odd glance then turned her attention back to the rest of the room.

Calico Joel, imperturbable as ever, remained on the floor with the little girl and played quietly, speaking to her in bad French, telling her Indian stories of which she did not understand a word but listened enraptured to the sound of his voice.

Tom bent forward. "She's not pestering you, is she?"

"No, Excellency. I am content."

"That's all right then."

But Calico Joel, playing with the child, was also observing and thinking, wondering where it was all going to end, not only the political situation but also the other, more personal, drama that was destined to unfold within the walls of Province House.

She had been delighted with her gift which she had unwrapped secretly. It had been made of silver, a little mirror, and she suspected that Joseph had ordered it

from his friend Paul Revere, whose trade it was to fashion that particular metal. Yet she felt guilty about using it, knowing it came from revolutionary hands. But as she sat on the bed in the silence of her room, Margaret fell to thinking about everything that Dr. Warren had said to her since her arrival in Boston.

His declaration of love, of course, had both thrilled and excited her. Indeed, though her first loyalty lay with her husband, and always would, she loved him in a fashion. The fashion of infatuation, which, together with the delicacy of secrecy, was almost overwhelming. Yet it was the broader message that he was telling her that she was presently considering, the message that America had outgrown the yoke of British rule and was ready to govern itself. So much he said made perfect sense to her, American-born herself, that it was hard to know these days who was right and who was wrong.

Peering at herself in the little mirror, Margaret saw that she was frowning and immediately changed her expression to a smile. Did she look forty? she wondered. She traced the lines at her mouth and eyes with an extended finger, pulling the corners upward. Next she examined her chin, raising it high and staring fixedly at the consequent sharpness of her jawline. Finally she stood up and turned to right and left before the big cheval mirror in the room. Her figure was still fine, that was certain, but her face did look a little older, there could be no denying it.

Suddenly she burst out laughing and twirled round. However she looked, Dr. Warren had fallen in love with her, and it was the greatest secret of all time. She was

giggling away to herself when there came a sudden knock at the door and without waiting for a response, one of the slaves entered.

"Governor . . ." the girl was saying.

Angry because she must have been seen acting stupidly, Margaret looked at the slave closely and saw that it was Sara, and felt a totally unjustified dislike of the young woman rise within her.

"The Governor is not here," she said, her voice like ice.

"Sorry, Mam. I thought . . ."

"You thought what?"

"That he might be around."

"He is still downstairs entertaining our guests."

"No, Mam. The party broke up a quarter of an hour ago, and he ain't there."

"Has the Indian man gone?"

"He's in the kitchen, Mam. He is going to have dinner with us servants."

What came over Margaret she couldn't possibly tell, but she acted totally uncharacteristically. "The only fit place for him in my view," she said.

She saw the colour rise in Sara's cheeks, but the girl made no reply, merely looking at the floor.

"Which is where you can go as well," Margaret added, compounding the felony. "If the Governor should require you he will no doubt send for you. And I would advise you in future, my girl, if you value your position in this house, not to treat him in such a familiar manner. Is that understood?"

"Yes, Mam."

"Now go. And you may send my maid to me."

"Yes, Mam."

The girl bobbed a curtsey and left the room, and Margaret flung herself down on her dressing table stool, staring at herself in the mirror. How could she have been so horrible to the child? And yet there had been something terribly free about the way Sara had called out to Tom as she came in. A seed of suspicion was sewn in the mind of the Governor's wife which resolutely refused to go away.

On Boxing Day, Lord Rupert Germain threw a magnificent party for the British high command at his great estate at Milton. Everyone was there, from the Governor down to the lieutenants. And, for once, everyone put the thought of the trouble brewing out of their minds and concentrated on having a splendid time.

Margaret, beautiful in a gown of ice blue with silver trimming, wafted amongst the guests, being charming to one and all. Yet inwardly she was in turmoil, wondering what Joseph Warren would have made of such a gathering of the intelligentsia of the British rulers. Her husband, for once, seemed devoid of tension, laughing and at ease with everyone except Admiral Graves, to whom he was cordial but that was all.

Eventually, she wandered outside, onto the beautiful terrace that overlooked such incredible views. To her left, she could see the purple height of Mount Wachusett, a good fifty miles away by her reckoning. To

the east, the fields dropped away, gradually descending to the Neponset River, where it meandered into Boston Harbour. Very faintly, she could hear the distant tolling of church bells coming from Boston. It was a scene of immense calm, peaceful almost. Margaret found herself wishing that everything was different, that she was in her mother country in a time of settled behaviour, that the trouble brewing between the British and the colonists was over and done, one way or the other.

She turned as she heard someone step from the house behind her and saw that it was Lord Rupert Germain himself, to whom she had finally been introduced two months earlier. She gave a slight curtsey.

"Admiring the view?" he asked.

"Yes. It's beautiful. So peaceful."

"If only it really were," he said, echoing her thoughts.

"Yes, if only."

They looked at one another, and Margaret saw, quite distinctly, the fact that he did not really like her. That deep down he resented her, the reason why she could not even guess. She decided to be utterly charming and make him squirm.

"So how is the newspaper business, Lord Rupert? I hear you are one of the richest men in Boston now."

"Am I? Yes, perhaps I must be."

She slipped a hand through his arm. "Oh come now, you can't deceive me."

"I wouldn't wish to, Madam. The truth is that circulation is falling because I am loyal to the British.

No one wants to read what I write any more. They want the hysterical stuff put out by the revolutionaries."

"So what do you intend to do?"

"If things get any more difficult, I plan to sell up and go back to England."

"Surely not."

"Indeed yes, Madam. I do not jest about so serious a matter."

She let go of his arm and stood looking at him in the bright light of that clear fine day. He was painfully thin, his long greying hair unpowdered, his slight frame hardly befitting a man approaching forty.

"Lord Rupert, do you think war is going to break out?"

He paused, considering his answer, and finally said, "I am surprised that it hasn't done so already."

"Are you positive?"

"Utterly."

"Then who will win?"

"The Americans," said Lord Rupert Germain simply. "We just don't have the manpower to defeat them."

"My God!" answered Margaret, with much feeling. "I wonder if my poor husband is aware of how you feel."

"In his heart, he knows," Rupert answered her. "He knows that it is only a matter of time."

CHAPTER
SIXTEEN

December, 1774

They came home in the coach, Andrew on the box, smart as paint and cracking his whip. Tom, who had, quite frankly, got drunk during the course of the day, dropped off to sleep almost as soon as they started to move. Margaret, staring out of the window, seeing nothing because of the early darkness, felt a restlessness that prevented her from relaxing, a restlessness brought about by the wildness of her thoughts.

If Rupert Germain were right and the Americans were going to win the war which seemed to be inevitable, where did this leave her husband? Blamed, no doubt, for losing the Colonies and being generally incompotent. She looked at the slumbering form beside her, head sunk on chest, gentle snores emerging, and felt a great warmth for him, putting out her hand, taking his and squeezing it. He did not respond, being deeply unconscious, but his snores became slightly more subdued. Margaret turned to the window again and then, unbidden, a picture of the slave Sara came into her mind. What was it about the girl that she didn't altogether trust? And why had she come into the bedroom, almost as if she'd forgotten that Margaret was there, calling out to him in that familiar manner?

Did they share something, something that had happened before Margaret arrived in Boston?

Suddenly she froze in horror as a terrible thought occurred. Five months had passed between his sailing for America from England and her joining him. Supposing, just supposing, that he had warmed the space in his bed with the half-caste. Knowing him as she did, knowing his needs and desires, he would have been quite capable of it. Yet surely he wouldn't have betrayed her, her whom he professed to love.

Then she thought of herself and how attracted she was to Dr. Warren, with his bright blue eyes and innocent expression. How easy it would be to forget her committments and comfort him for the death of his wife with the oldest magic in the world. Suddenly, Margaret found a tear running down beside her nose and falling onto her chest. She felt deeply depressed and nothing could lift her spirits as they hurried through the darkness towards Province House.

Once within, she abandoned her husband, weaving slightly, and made her way up the stairs, calling for her maid. The girl came rushing from the servants' quarters, apologising, and started the business of undressing her mistress. First the elegant headdress was removed and set on a wooden stand, then the jewellery, the open robe, the ornamented petticoat beneath, came off. Finally Margaret stood naked except for her stays, hoops and, quite daring, hip pads. Eventually, though, these encumbrances having been taken away and stored

in a clothes press, she slipped into her chemise and permitted the maid to brush her long dark hair.

"Where is Andrew?" she asked casually, as the girl set to with the brush.

"In the kitchen, Mam. He thought you wouldn't be needing him again tonight."

"And Robin? Where is he?"

"He is in the hall, Mam. Can he get you anything?"

"A cup of hot chocolate perhaps."

"I'll tell him directly."

"Good." Margaret's voice became almost over-casual. "And where is Sara?"

"I don't know, Mam. I ain't seen her around. But she won't have gone to bed just yet."

The Governor's wife smiled and nodded but said nothing.

Eventually, when the girl had brushed her hair sufficently, Margaret turned towards the great bed. "I think I won't have the chocolate after all. I'm so tired. I'll just say goodnight, Lucy."

"Goodnight, Mam. Do you want me to help you to bed?"

"No, I can manage. Goodnight."

But she remained where she was, sitting at her dressing table, until the sound of the girl's footsteps had died away. Then, taking a candle and slipping a night-rail over her chemise, she crept across the bedroom floor, through the door and down the stairs.

It was dim in the hallway below, full of shadows and dark spaces, her solitary candle doing little to lighten the gloom. Margaret stood silently, listening. There was

no sound except for a distant solitary voice, a female voice, holding forth in what appeared to be a soliloquy. There was also a light coming from beneath Tom's study door. Noiselessly, Margaret advanced, and stood on the far side, all attention.

She could hear Sara, apparently reading aloud, though with immense difficulty and a certain amount of pausing. Margaret waited a fraction longer, her hand on the door knob, then she slowly and silently opened it and stood in the entrance.

Tom sat in the chair behind his desk, sound asleep. Sitting on the other side was Sara, reading from a book that she held open on her lap. Just for a moment the girl did not hear her, and Margaret was able to stand and take in the scene. Even though her husband slept there was something intimate about the two of them, as if they were old friends. Sara continued to read for a few more seconds, hesitating over the longer words which she pronounced phonetically. Then, even though Margaret had made no move, she became aware of her presence and suddenly looked up.

Panic filled the girl's eyes, and her face equalled their expression. She leapt to her feet, clutching the book, and started to back away. Margaret said nothing, merely fixing Sara with a glance guaranteed to frighten her out of her wits. Then with a loud bang she slammed the door closed and ran up the stairs once more. Finally she crashed into her bedroom and turned the key in the lock before she flung herself onto the bed.

She should have wept, she knew that, but for some reason she lay dry-eyed, staring round the dim confines

of the bedroom. After about ten minutes, she heard Tom come upstairs and try to open the door. He called her name softly, but she did not respond. Eventually she heard him go down again. After that there was silence.

She was behaving appallingly, and she knew it. Yet she was furiously jealous and hurt. Sara had better watch her step in future, Margaret thought. It was clear that before she had arrived in Boston the girl had done her best to seduce Tom and had probably succeeded. Well now the day of reckoning was at hand. No more secret meetings at which the girl read aloud. She would put the black bitch out on the street tomorrow. With this triumphant thought, the Governor's wife finally went to sleep.

He had asked at breakfast next morning why she had locked the bedroom door. Margaret had gazed at him, large-eyed.

"Did I? Oh, Tom, I'm so sorry. What could I have been thinking of?"

He had fixed his eyes on her firmly, and she had been forced to stare directly into them, noticing as she did so how tired he looked, weary indeed. She regretted locking the door now, imagining him tossing and turning on the chaise in the drawing room. But had he? Perhaps he had spent the night in the cell-like room that the slave girl occupied, held tightly in a pair of dark arms.

She must have made some noise of disgust for Tom said, "What's the matter? Have I done something to

238

offend you? I can only think I must have behaved badly at Rupert's yesterday."

She paused, weighing up what to say next, then eventually asked, "About that slave, Sara . . . ?"

"What about her?"

"I came downstairs late last night and found you together with her in your study. You were asleep; she was reading aloud."

Tom laid down his knife and fork, and there was an edge in his voice. "As a matter of fact, I've been teaching the girl to read. It seemed a harmless enough occupation. I told her that when you joined me from New York the lessons would have to stop. This upset her, so, since then, she has been struggling her way through adult books borrowed from my library. That is the beginning and the end of it, and is all I have to say on the matter."

Margaret stared at him, and Tom suddenly remembered his premonition that one day she would somehow betray him.

"Why?" she asked.

"Why what?"

"Why is it all you have to say."

"Because there the story begins and ends," he answered loudly, snatching his napkin from beneath his chin, his chair scraping as he suddenly stood up.

Margaret rose also. "Is that the truth?" she hissed.

"Of course it's the bloody truth. What else did you expect? That I rogered the wretched girl? Good day to you, Madam. Perhaps you will join me when you can keep a civil tongue in your mouth."

And he marched out of the dining room and into his study, where he closed the door, very firmly.

They had been alone for those few moments while Robin fetched more toast from the kitchen, but now his head appeared, rather too promptly for Margaret's liking. In fact the minute he approached her, the toast rack on a tray, she could tell by the roundness of his eyes that he had heard every word of the argument and was bursting with it. She decided to be direct.

"Robin, his Excellency and I have had a slight disagreement. I would appreciate it if you didn't mention it to the other servants."

"No, Mam." But she knew from his expression that he hadn't been the only one to overhear.

"And you may repeat my instructions to anyone else who was in earshot."

"Yes, Mam."

"You may clear away now. I have had enough to eat, thank you."

"Why, Mam, you've hardly had a thing."

"I've eaten enough," she snapped and left the table, her clothing rustling as she walked.

Upstairs, she turned left towards the nursery, hoping to catch her daughter being bathed in the tin bath before the fire. Thrusting open the door, she greeted the nursemaid who was busy warming the clothes on a clothes-horse.

"Where is Charlotte?" she asked, pleasantly enough, though she was aware that there was an edge to her voice.

240

"In the other room, Madam. One of the slave girls is playing with her while I get the bath ready."

She knew who it was even while she had her hand on the door handle. But even she was shocked by the sight she saw. With so much love on her face, Sara was throwing Charlotte in the air and catching her again in outstretched arms. The baby was laughing in delight, relishing every second. Margaret caught herself thinking that Sara was possibly the most beautiful girl she had ever seen — and at that moment she knew pure hatred.

"Put that child down," she ordered from the doorway. "How dare you play with her in that free manner?"

Sara deposited Charlotte beside her, and the child, seeing the look on her mother's face, cowered into the slave's skirts and started to cry.

The black girl tried nobly to defend herself. "I was only helping out Nanny, Mam. She asked me to mind the baby while she got the water warm. I thought I was doing good."

"You have no right to even be in these rooms. This is the nursery suite. It is not the duty of slaves to enter it. But then you make yourself pretty familiar with most of the rooms in this house, don't you, my girl?"

Sara grew pale. "What do you mean, Mam?"

"You know perfectly well what I mean, you scheming little minx. Sidling around the Governor while I wasn't here."

"Mam, I never . . ."

"I've seen it with my own eyes, and last night was the final straw. You are dismissed from service, Sara. You are to leave the house immediately. Go to your room and pack your things, then out with you. And no going to the Governor with your tales of woe. Your days of manipulating him are over."

Sara's head was held high as she extricated Charlotte from the depths of her dress, then left the room, passing right beside Margaret, who held the door, as she did so. The nursemaid, scarlet-cheeked, stood opening and closing her mouth, but any thoughts she might have had of speaking in the girl's defence were quashed by the expression on the face of her employer.

"Good riddance," said Margaret loudly from the nursery door. She turned to Nanny. "I've decided not to see Charlotte bathed this morning. I am going out. I shall come and play with her this afternoon. Good morning."

"Good morning, Madam," answered the girl, too stupefied to make any remonstrance whatsoever.

Once again, she wore the hat with the heavy veiling, leaving the house by the garden entrance and making her way past the coach house and stables. She found herself in the narrow confines of Governor's Alley, which ran directly behind the buildings in which Margaret dwelt. It was narrow but soon led out to School Street, from where Margaret made her way into Cornhill.

There seemed to be soldiers everywhere, out in their twos and threes, presumably off-duty, idling around.

But they were disciplined. Despite the insults mouthed at them, some said aloud, they did not respond but kept their eyes to the front and continued to talk one to the other.

Margaret hurried on till she drew level with the Long Wharf and automatically looked right. Once when the great harbour had been in its heyday it would have been bustling, alive with every kind of vessel, for the wharf stretched out to sea for half a mile so that even the largest ship could come in at low tide. Now, other than for the British men-of-war, it lay deserted. Yet nothing could take away the raw, edgy excitement of Boston. There was still the cry of fishermen selling their wares, the shout of little black sweeps, the sound of horses' hooves on cobbles and the rattle of carts.

But dominating all was the joyful sound of bells. From Christ's came a royal peal, from King's Chapel a sonorous, sad sound. Every church could be identified by its individual tone. Markets were opened and closed to their peal; on the Sabbath they called in the faithful to pray. And underneath their huge cacophony came the sound of smaller bells. The local hostelries had hand bells to indicate that they were about to serve dinner. Shops rang bells to muster trade, doorbells rang, schoolmasters called in their pupils by their use. And above all came the wild sound of the sea, forever pounding onto the headland, and the high uninhibited shriek of the gulls.

Margaret turned left into Queen Street and from there made her way to Hanover Street where, opposite the entrance to Elm Street, stood the house in which

Joseph Warren was bringing up his family with the aid of a housekeeper. Looking to right and left, hoping and praying that no one would recognise her, Margaret rang the bell.

It must have been the housekeeper who answered the door because a tall, spare woman whom Margaret did not know, stood there.

"Yes?"

"Is Dr. Warren in, please?"

"Are you a patient?"

"Yes," Margaret lied wildly. "Yes, I have a very sore throat."

"Well come in and sit down, Ma'am. He has somebody with him at present, and there's one person ahead of you."

"Very well. I'll wait."

She was ushered into a small waiting room in which sat a respectable looking woman, conservatively dressed, with a pained expression on her face.

Margaret sat down opposite her, hoping that she would not be identified. But there was scant chance of that, for the woman was emitting a series of small groans and moans, closing her eyes in apparent agony, then shivering. Eventually she spoke.

"Forgive me, please. I feel so ill. I keep coming over faint."

"I'm sorry," ventured Margaret, terrified of being given a list of the woman's ailments. But there was to be no avoiding that. Fixing her with an eye that defied resistance, the other launched forth.

"It all started with the death of my husband, you know. Poor soul, I nursed him till he passed over, then I was left, alone to face the world. No sooner had he gone than I felt this searing pain in my knee. Of course I immediately bound it tightly but it swelled up and grew worse. I had to tear the bandage off, layer upon layer of unendurable agony. Then I got these acute pains in my stomach. To be honest with you, I thought my end had come. No sooner had that cleared up than I got the sniffles. A permanent cold, if you understand me — I've had it for nigh on two years now. Then I started sweating in the night, and that, together with my lack of sleep, has fairly finished me. I have taken now to settling down on the day bed whenever I feel the need. Of course I have the most beautiful hand-crocheted coverlet which . . ."

It was at this moment that, mercifully, she was cut short by the patient before her leaving and the housekeeper calling out, "Mrs. Paine, you are next if you please."

The woman, who had become quite animated during her monologue, now assumed an expression of acute suffering and made her way into the doctor's consulting room. Margaret, wondering what she was doing there and beginning to regret that she had come, shrank into her chair and meekly awaited her turn.

It came half an hour later; a half hour during which she had twice risen to go, then thought better of it. For she really needed someone to talk to, someone to whom she could communicate her feelings, or rather her version of them. Finally, though, there had been the

245

sound of heavy footsteps approaching the surgery door which had opened to reveal Mrs. Paine — could any name have been more suitable? — leaning heavily on Dr. Warren as he escorted her.

"Mrs. Bradlee," he was calling, "could you go to The Orange Tree Tavern and bring back a hackney for Mrs. Paine? She is feeling unwell and needs to lie down at once." There was some muttering, but the housekeeper, pulling a shawl round her shoulders, hurried out. "Next patient," said Dr. Warren, without looking up.

He led the way to his consulting room, courteously standing to one side to let his visitor pass. As she drew level with him he recognised her, despite the thick veiling, and she heard him draw in his breath in astonishment.

"Margaret," he said, as soon as the door was closed. "What are you doing here?"

Sitting down opposite his desk, Margaret drew back her veils. "I'm sorry; I felt I had to see you. I have so much to tell you."

He sat down opposite, his fair skin flushing with the pleasure of her company. Then he put his hands over the desk and took hers. "Tell me," he said.

Strangely, when it came to it, Margaret told him the whole truth, even down to details of her own hypocrisy. How, despite her cooling feelings for the Governor, she had still been wildly angry with Sara.

"Yet I was condemning him for something I'm not sure of."

Joseph Warren sat silently, considering.

246

"Are you certain there was anything untoward in the Governor's relationship with the slave? Surely it was as the girl said. He taught her to read, that is all."

"Yes, but . . ."

"I have always considered the Governor an honourable man. I totally disagree with everything he says, but that does not take away from the fact that he is a man of integrity."

"So you don't believe he and Sara shared a bed?"

Joseph looked at her, realising that he had a golden opportunity, an opportunity to win her affection quite solidly. But he, too, was a man of integrity. "No, I don't."

Yet Margaret left out the final detail, that she was jealous of Sara's youth and beauty.

"Then I'm content," she said, making to get up.

He came round the desk and put his hands on her shoulders. "Stay a while and have coffee with me."

"Yes," she said, raising her hands to touch his. "I would like that. Thank you for listening to me, Dr. Warren."

"It is my job to do so," he answered and wondered why his heart had started to speed up.

CHAPTER
SEVENTEEN

December, 1774

The Governor worked hard all the morning, trying to lose himself in writing reports and reading others. He had taken the minimum time off for Christmas, three days in fact, and was now busy catching up with what scant information had come in in that time. There had been one or two cases of drunkenness amongst the soldiers, three had deserted, and another deserter had been captured and shot at the foot of the Common. In short, it had been a quiet time.

Shortly after ten o'clock, the Governor had heard a quickly-hushed commotion in the hall but had not bothered to investigate its source. Therefore, when, at eleven, he rang the bell on his desk, he had not been surprised when Robin had answered punctually, though with a long face.

"What's the matter?" he had asked, giving the servant a quick glance.

"Nothin', Governor."

"Um. So what was that racket I heard in the hall about an hour ago?"

"That was Beulah, Sir. She let out a little scream."

"Why?"

"'Cos she was upset, Sir."

Tom put down his papers and said rather irritably, "That much is obvious. Why was she upset?"

"Because of Sara, Governor."

"Oh for Heaven's sake, man. Don't go on beating about the bush. What has happened?"

"The Lady sacked her, Sir. Told her to get her things and get out of the house. Beulah was in the hall to see her go. They both cried."

Tom sat staring at him. "Sara has gone?" he said. "Yassir."

"But why? What did she do wrong?"

"I don't know, Governor. Apparently she was playing with little Charlotte, and the Lady took against her. Anyway, she's gone."

"But where? Has the girl any relatives in Boston?"

"No, she ain't, Sir. She's on the streets, and that's all there is to it."

Tom sat motionless, trying to take in what he had just been told. The more he thought about it, the more he felt he must take action. For how could he let Sara spend even one night sleeping rough? He must find the girl and get her into lodgings. That was the least he could do.

He stood up. "Send Andrew to me, would you?"

"Yes, Masser Governor. At once, Sir."

When the coachman arrived, Tom, who had crossed to the window and stood looking over the garden, turned and said, "Andrew, I've got to go out, but I don't want to take the coach. Prepare the chaise as swiftly as possible. I'll join you in five minutes and get

inside in the coach house. The less attention we draw to ourselves the better."

As soon as the slave had gone he ran upstairs, straight to his room. He half expected to find Margaret there, angrily lying in wait for him, but the place was deserted. Quickly he stripped off his uniform jacket and put on plain black, then he covered everything with a dark cloak and a plain tricorne hat.

Andrew was still saddling up the small grey horse that drew the chaise when he got to the coach house. But five minutes later all was done, and the Governor swept out of the side entrance leading from the stabling block.

"Andrew, we've got to find Sara and put her into lodgings," he called.

"Where is she, Governor?"

"That is what I don't know. It is up to us to locate her."

Yet where in those crowded streets was the girl?

They decided to sweep the town, going backwards and forwards. First Andrew took the chaise to Boston Neck where enquiries revealed that no one answering Sara's description had passed through to the countryside beyond. Then they careered up Orange Street, to Newbury Street and Marlborough, looking in all the little alleyways and wharves that led off the main thoroughfares. There was no sign of her.

Andrew was sent into the many inns and coffee houses — The Blue Anchor, The Indian Queen, The Bull's Head, The Sun, The Blue Ball, The Orange Tree — all to no avail. Thomas, fearing recognition on so

delicate a mission, went into the churches. But it was in The Feather Store, which was in fact the apothecary's shop, that the Governor got his first clue.

"Good morning, Excellency," said John Stanbury, son of the man who had built the shop. "What may I do for you this morning?"

"One of my slaves has run away," lied Tom, gallantly covering up. "A girl, name of Sara, rather beautiful. Have you seen her by any chance?"

"Yes, Sir. I have."

The Governor stood staring, having expected yet another negative reply. "You have? Where?"

"As a matter of fact she came in about half an hour ago. Came to remind me to send up some stomach medicine for Beulah. Brought me the money for it. Not really the action of a runaway, eh Governor."

"Very odd behaviour," Tom answered, but his heart had quickened its pace. Half an hour meant that Sara must still be in the vicinity. "Anyway, thank you Mr. Stanbury. Good day."

"Good day, Governor. Call again."

Outside stood the chaise, but there was no sign of Andrew. Tom waited for a moment then obeying some strange instinct cut down Crooked Lane into King Street. Then he set off to walk the length of the Long Wharf, filled with the feeling that this was the way she had gone. He was halfway along when he spotted her in the distance, a desolate little figure staring out to sea. It was all he could do not to break into a run, but he quickened his pace and walked firmly towards her.

She heard his booted feet approach and turned to see who it was, her face undergoing a rapid change of expression, from fear to a kind of joy, rapidly hidden by the lowering of her head. She bobbed a curtsey as he drew nearer.

"Sara," he said.

"I'm sorry, Excellency," she replied. "I was only playing with Charlotte. Mrs. Gage entirely misunderstood."

"You don't have to explain," he answered. "Naturally I can't go against my wife's decision, but I don't condone it."

She looked up at him, her dark eyes holding back tears. "I'm sorry, Sir," she said again.

He took her by the shoulders. "There's no need to apologise. I accept that there was a misunderstanding. However, to go back is impossible. I know my wife, and she won't hear of it. So, let's to business. Do you have anyone to go to?"

"No, Sir. You know I don't."

"In that case you must find lodgings. I shall help you. Then, once you're settled, we can make plans for you to get employment."

The tears descended, and Sara wept silently. Tom, looking at her, felt himself torn with anguish. He tightened his grip on her. "Come now, my girl, everything will turn out for the best. Just you wait and see."

She fell against his chest, her hair clean and sweet-smelling, crying with relief. Tom remained holding her, standing like that for several minutes until she regained her composure and drew away from him.

Determined to be kind but stern, he said, "Come along, Sara. The chaise is waiting. Let's try and find you somewhere to live."

"I'm coming, Governor." She stooped and picked up her little bundle of possessions, then walked obediently back beside him, looking straight ahead of her.

Proceeding like this, he became aware of several things. Firstly, how much taller he was than she; secondly, how much he longed to offer her his arm to support her; thirdly, how much he cared for the child. For that was their relationship to be sure, father and daughter. And he was acting like a father in his attempt to see her safely settled.

In Dock Square, they caught up with Andrew, whose great grin almost split his face at the sight of Sara.

"You found her, Excellency."

"Yes, Andrew. Here she is, safe and sound."

"Now we get her some lodging. I think there's a woman in Salem Street that lets out rooms."

"Then let's go there."

Tom handed the girl into the chaise and squeezed in beside her. It was originally built for one and he was pressed tightly against her. So tightly, indeed, that his arm could feel the curve of her breast. Fiercely putting down such alarming thoughts, he stared solemnly ahead of him, refusing even to glance at her.

Andrew, with much whip-cracking and cries of "Get on, boy" to the horse, negotiated the narrow confines of Wings Lane and turned left into Hanover Street. Next they crossed over the Mill Creek to Middle Street, then turned into Princes Street, off which Salem Street lay.

The house Andrew headed for was at the end, the door being opened by a middle-aged woman with a suspicious face.

"Yes?" she said.

"I've come about lodgings, and I ain't from the army," Andrew stated.

The woman stared at the chaise, trying to see who was sitting inside. Much against his better judgement, Tom got out, determined that Sara would be found somewhere to stay, and quickly.

He bowed. "Madam, I have with me a young female of exemplary character. She is seeking lodgings, and I believe you have a room to spare."

She curtsied. "Sir, all my spare rooms have been commandeered for the officers. I have nowhere extra."

Tom, delighted that he hadn't been recognised, reverted to the oldest tactics in the world and produced cash from inside his jacket.

"I will pay you well."

The woman's expression altered, indeed became quite pleasant. "Well, I suppose my sons could share. As long as it wasn't for ever, of course."

"Should I bring the young lady to meet you?"

"Yes, if you would, Sir."

"I warn you that she is black. You have no objection?"

Yet again those most mobile of features transformed, then the woman clearly thought of the money being offered. The Governor was subjected to a long scrutiny from a pair of extremely shrewd brown eyes, then she

said, with a strange, secretive smile, "No. Not at all. Bring her in, Sir."

Wondering what she was thinking, Tom helped Sara from the chaise and took her up the front steps.

Yet again those brown eyes flew up and down, taking in every inch of the girl's general bearing. Then she said, "I am Mrs. Wells. I'll show you the room. It is presently occupied by my son Benjamin, but he can move out in half an hour." She turned to the Governor. "May we discuss rent, Sir?"

"When Sara has seen the room, yes."

"Of course. Come this way — Sara."

The room was small but it was comfortable and clean. The Governor left the black girl starting to pack up Benjamin's things and went with Mrs. Wells into the parlour. Here that most canny widow drove a hard bargain which he accepted. Reluctantly Tom agreed to pay twice what the room was worth and gave her bills to the value of a month's rent in advance. He went upstairs again and found Sara sitting on the window seat, staring out. She turned as he came in.

"Master Governor, how can I ever thank you? You have done a very kind thing this day."

"Think nothing of it. I'll come and see you soon, Sara. Take care of yourself and continue with your reading."

"Very good, Sir." She hesitated, then added, "Will you return tomorrow?"

It was on the tip of his tongue to refuse but then he saw her pleading expression, and his resolve melted.

"Yes, I'll be here tomorrow."

"Thank you, Sir. Thank you."

He turned and went downstairs, bade farewell to the landlady, then left the house, climbing into the chaise which was waiting outside. Looking up he saw that Sara was waving and gave a salute in return.

"Home, Andrew. And as quickly as possible," he said.

"Yassir."

He could not know that as soon as he was out of sight, Mrs. Wells hurried out and round the corner to see her neighbour.

"Well, my dear," she began before the other woman had had a chance to speak, "you'll never guess what."

"What?"

"The Governor himself, dressed incognito, has been to my house and taken a room for his mistress."

"Never!"

"Yes, and to crown it all, she's a black slave."

"Well I'll be blowed, so I will. For now I've heard it all."

CHAPTER
EIGHTEEN

New Year's Eve, 1774

It was New Year's Eve, the end of the year 1774, and a more solemn occasion Tom could not recall. He had invited Lord Percy and one or two other officers to dine, but despite his best effort, despite the attempts of everyone present to put some enthusiasm into the party, conversation had been sporadic, laughter at a premium. Even Mrs. Gage, who had earned something of a reputation amongst the British high command as a belle of fashion, had dressed sombrely, as if echoing the general atmosphere.

Hugh Percy, surreptitiously putting on his dreaded spectacles for a few minutes and studying his host and hostess, found them changed. Yet it was an indefinable difference, something he could not have described even to himself, but for all that they had altered in some way. Yet the circumstances in which they were presently living were enough to transform anyone, he thought. And that statement applied to all those present. All faced with the fact that war was almost inevitable. The only question was when and how it would break out. He removed his glasses again as the Governor started to speak.

"Gentlemen, I can tell you frankly that I am extremely perturbed."

Instead of asking why, there were murmurs of assent from those present; Stephen Kemble, Margaret's brother, nodding his head wisely.

"It is the business of the Government at home to make the decisions," Tom continued. "It is my job to execute measures, not to choose what they are."

"I think," said Lord Percy, selecting his words carefully, "that they are going to procrastinate."

"Deliberately?"

"Yes, I believe so. I think they are rather hoping the situation will resolve itself."

Gage let out a deep sigh. "In my opinion the Yankees are spoiling for a fight. It's just a matter of time."

Margaret spoke. "But you must admit the colonists have a point."

There was an akward silence, broken by the General himself. "Which is?" he asked.

To give her her due his wife looked uncomfortable but still said, "There are thousands of people, many of whom were born here. Surely they have a right to feel they could govern themselves."

"Just as you have a right to your opinion," Tom replied calmly. He turned back to his fellow officers. "Gentlemen, let me give you a toast. To 1775, whatever it might hold."

They stood up, raising their glasses, and there was a chorus of, "To 1775."

Margaret got to her feet a second or two later and drank with them. Then she said, "If you would excuse me, gentlemen. I am sure there is a great deal you want to discuss privately. Goodnight to you."

And she left the room, her skirts stiff and crackling. There was another silence broken by Lord Percy saying, "Mrs. Gage has an outlook, Sir. After all, she is American born."

Tom muttered something almost inaudible which sounded suspiciously like, "I am more than aware of it," but Hugh let it pass. He turned to the Governor. "Well, Sir, do you wish to discuss plans?"

"No, not tonight." He turned to the assembled company. "Is it your wish that we have one evening free of this worsening situation? That we forget it and enjoy ourselves?"

"Yes, indeed," answered several heartfelt voices drowned out by Major Pitcairn, a tough Scotsman who swore great oaths yet had a gentle exterior and soft, large eyes. "By God, it will do us good, Sir."

"In that case let me ring for the port," Tom answered, and pealed the handbell loudly to attract Robin's attention.

Upstairs, lying fully dressed on the bed, Margaret heard the sound and thought that the evening might well end in cards and dice. For she had guessed that there would be no serious talk this night. She felt ashamed now of her outburst, felt she had said too much. Not that she didn't believe in the cause but to speak so in front of her husband and his officers had been going too far. Suddenly full of nervous energy she rose and opening the doors, walked out onto the balcony.

Below her she could see the gardens and beyond the two sentry boxes with the sentries marching between

them. Then suddenly her heartbeat quickened and she hastened to the balcony's edge to get a better look. A man stood in the shadows, a man whom she recognised instantly. She could dimly make out his dark cloak and the white blur of his upturned face. He was holding something, perhaps a book purchased from young Henry Knox, a big fat boy who had a shop close to Province House. But he had been unable to resist lingering a moment in the hope of seeing her. Quickly, almost surreptitiously, she briefly raised her arm to wave, and was rewarded with a similar gesture from Dr. Joseph Warren. Then she stood silently, watching him walk away, seeing him turn his head once more for a final brief glance.

Going back into the room, Margaret thought of Joseph's blazing sincerity, of his passionate belief in the cause of freedom, of his willingness to lay down his life for it. Lying on the bed once more, she saw herself as a woman torn between two opposing factions. Out of her loyalty to her husband she must support the Tory cause, yet when Joseph spoke to her of the Whigs, of his belief in the future of the country of which she herself was a native, then she knew that was where her beliefs lay.

Downstairs the party continued, the port being passed, the men swapping stories, Lord Percy giving brilliant glances from his short-sighted eyes. But eventually there seemed a silent consent and several of the officers stood up to take their leave. The Governor, who was exceptionally weary himself, bade them

farewell, ill concealing a fit of yawning, until eventually all had gone with the exception of Hugh Percy.

"Half an hour to the new year, Sir."

"Yes," said Tom, and gave a small, bitter laugh.

"Do you dread it as much as I do?"

"Every bit, I imagine."

"War is inevitable, isn't it?"

"Indeed it is, my dear Hugh, indeed it is."

After the Earl had left, Tom poured himself another brandy and sat alone, dousing the candles and pulling back the curtains to allow the moonlight to shine through. He found his thoughts turning to Sara, wondering whether she was up to see the new year in or had gone to bed, tired as he was.

She had settled in comfortably enough with Mrs. Wells, and the Governor had booked further reading lessons for her with a certain Francis Borland who lived in Milk Street. Because Tom regarded her as a kind of daughter — that is what he told himself, anyway — he called on her once a week, desperately clawing the time out of his busy days.

With no work other than helping Mrs. Wells to keep the house clean, Sara had devoted herself to her studies and was now reading well, frequently aloud to the Governor, who sat in the chair while she perched on the end of the bed. He had said to her once, "Sara, do you never go out with people your own age?"

She had smiled at him just a trifle wistfully. "Sir, where could I go? I think you sometimes think you are back in England and that I am a young woman of position. As it is I run errands during the day for Mrs.

Wells. I visit the shops and go to church on Sundays. But as for meeting people like myself, no I don't."

Terrible feelings of guilt had suffused him. "But, my dear . . ."

"Don't worry about it please, Master Governor. I have visits from you. They are quite enough."

Time went on a loop, and he said to his wife, "But I'm years older than you are," then had wondered why Sara's cheeks had suddenly flamed and realised he had spoken aloud.

Now, sitting alone in the moonlight, he thought of that remark and cursed himself for making it. Sara could have been forgiven for imagining he was meaning something entirely different. Yet, he had said the words, had thought momentarily that he was speaking to Margaret, then realised that it was Sara, so young and innocent, who sat there.

The Governor rose and paced the room, hoping that his former slave was happy yet having the sneaking suspicion that his visits alone kept her going. He wondered how much longer he could continue making them in view of the worsening situation. Not only that, the journeys to the other side of town were shrouded in secrecy, yet Andrew was aware, driving the coach through the winter nights as he did. At least, Tom thought to himself, his disguise had not been penetrated. Nobody was aware of who he actually was, of that much he was certain.

He jumped as the door behind him opened slowly. Turning, he saw that Margaret stood there, clad in her nightclothes. She smiled at him.

"I've come to see the new year in."

He was filled with relief, half imagining that she had found out where he went occasionally, that his excuse of overseeing the troops had been penetrated.

"My dear," he said.

She came to stand close to him, her familiar perfume pervading the atmosphere.

"Shall we drink to it?"

"For better or worse, yes," he answered, and going to the bottle stand drew out a bottle of champagne. "This is probably the last we'll have for a while."

"What do you mean?"

"That supplies are beginning to run short."

"Don't let's discuss it, Tom. Lets pretend that we've rolled the years back."

It was his turn to ask her what she meant.

"Can't we just be us for half an hour? As carefree as we were when we started out on our life together?"

"I don't see why not." He poured two glasses and, as he did so, the longcase clock that he had bought in England and shipped out with him struck midnight.

"Happy New Year, darling," she said and snuggled close to him.

"Happy New Year," he answered and wished with all his heart that it would be for both of them.

CHAPTER
NINETEEN

February, 1775

The spies had been called for duty to the office of
Major Stephen Kemble, who had been put in charge of
intelligence. And nobody, thought Margaret's brother,
who had grown older and wiser and no longer affected
an English accent, could have wished to see a more
contrasting bunch of men. First there was Captain John
Brown, an eager young sprite, willing to do anything
and go anywhere. Then there was his companion,
Lieutenant John De Berniere, also young but a veteran
of Gage's old regiment, the 44th. Seated at the back of
the room was Major Thomas Pitcairn, he of the terrible
oaths and soft, gentle eyes. While standing was the
oddity, Calico Joel, clearly sizing up the other men in
the room and not being particularly impressed by what
he saw.

There was one spy missing, of course — Dr.
Benjamin Church, on the surface an avowed patriot,
but secretly, silently on Governor Gage's payroll. His
mistress was a woman of expensive tastes, and he had
been forced to sell out to the other side in order to
satisfy her whims — or so he told himself. In fact he
was a greedy man and liked the power and pleasure of
extra money. Simply enjoyed feeling it and having it

around him. He was also, strangely for a medical man, totally devoid of conscience.

Everyone looked in Stephen Kemble's direction as he started to speak.

"Good afternoon, gentlemen. I am sure you all know why you're here. It is the Governor's intention to learn as much as possible about the nature of the country round Boston so that the troops, should they receive the order to march, can do so with maximum efficiency. And that is where you will come in. I would like each and every one of you to scout out certain places and report back directly to me. In this way I can make a plan of the area with particular notes as to manpower, arms and so on. This will be invaluable."

Kemble turned his attention to individuals.

"Major Pitcairn, you are to scout round the area looking for possible ambush sites. Captain Brown and Lieutenant De Berniere, you are to venture towards Concord and beyond, absorbing anything of interest. As with Howe, sketch maps will be invaluable to us." Major Kemble cleared his throat. "Any questions?"

"We won't wear uniform, surely to God." This from Major Pitcairn.

"No, you will dress as countrymen. Even you, Sir."

"Me?" Calico Joel spoke for the first time.

"You. I want you to take up residence in Concord and report back every move the people make. I also want you to seek out information regarding military equipment and stores gathered by the Whigs and give me the dates, names, places. Is that clear?"

"Perfectly," the Indian answered succinctly. "But I would prefer to dress as I do normally."

"Then please be as inconspicuous as possible," Kemble answered and grinned broadly. "Perhaps you should start by cutting your hair."

Calico Joel looked at him very straightly. "I would not do that, not even on the Governor's command. But then he is too great a man to ask it of me. Don't worry, Monsieur, you will have your information whatever my attire. Now, may I go?"

The request came as such a surprise that the Major answered "Yes," and even before the word was out of his mouth Calico Joel had saluted and left the room. There was a moment's silence after his exit, then Lieutenant De Berniere said, "Queer sort of a cove, ain't he."

"He certainly is. But say nothing against him before the Governor. He can see no wrong in the fellow at all."

"If this was any other time, I'd be tempted to take him down a peg or two, damnable half-breed."

"Well it isn't so you can get that thought right out of your head."

Major Pitcairn let out a crack of laughter. "You're all jealous of the man's reputation, I'd swear it. The chap's an excellent scout, and there's an end to it. I warrant he'll do the best of any of us."

"That, my dear Sir," Lieutenant De Berniere replied with dignity, "remains to be seen."

It was so easy to change into ordinary clothes and slip round to the stables to take out the chaise, or so the Governor thought as he hurriedly took off his uniform

and put on plain dark breeches and coat. Yet tonight it seemed as though fate were conspiring against him because as he descended the stairs, Margaret, who was frequently out herself at this time, came from the living room and stood regarding him.

"Going to inspect the troops?" she asked him pleasantly.

Some instinct made him say, "No, not tonight."

"I thought not."

"Why?"

"Because tonight you are dressed as a civilian. Tell me, my dear, what is it you do when you are garbed thus?"

"I drive round Boston in the chaise. Anonymously."

"With what purpose?"

"To see how the people are faring," he answered smoothly.

"But surely that is something you already know."

"I like to keep my finger on the pulse."

Margaret pulled a face. "What a nasty thought. Do you go to the taverns and mix with the lower orders?"

"Sometimes."

She gave a humourless laugh. "You sound as if you are a Whig."

Thomas made a great effort to be agreeable. "My darling, I have been doing this for some time now. I may have sent my spies out of Boston, but I think it is imperative that somebody knows how the people within are reacting."

"People or person?"

"What do you mean?"

"I sometimes think that you are going to meet a woman."

He hated lying to her, had always prided himself on his truthfulness, but the consequences of her knowing that he went to see Sara were too terrible even to contemplate.

"I resent that remark," he defended himself. "How would I have had time to meet anyone, let alone see her on a regular basis?" Margaret suddenly looked unbelievably weary, and Thomas's heart bled for her. "Darling, don't be suspicious. Let me assure you that I have always been utterly faithful to you."

She leant her head against his chest. "I know, I know. It's just this beastly place and the situation which gets worse daily. Go on, mix with the populace if that's what makes you happy."

"Strangely enough, it does."

"Then go on. I won't wait up for you. Go and enjoy yourself."

Such a sudden capitulation brought out the reverse in Thomas Gage. "My darling, I won't go tonight," he said. "Let us sit together in the candlelight and talk of England and how one day we will return there."

In the way of all human beings, having won her victory, Margaret promptly answered, "No, Tom. I insist that you go. It is clearly essential that you keep your eye on the citizens. Now, run along do."

"No, darling, I've decided to stay."

"No, I insist that you go."

In the end, the Governor was practically pushed through the front door, where, having returned the

salute of the two guards on duty, he went round to the stables and persuaded the small grey horse into the traces of the chaise. Normally this would have been Andrew's job, but when he went to visit Sara, Governor Gage considered it more private if he did the whole business himself. He was blissfully unaware, of course, that the entire staff of Province House knew exactly when he called on the girl and made lewd jokes about it. A fact that would have infuriated him had he been aware of it. But now, having got the horse in position, he climbed aboard the chaise and set off through the darkening streets of Boston.

He could see the light in her room as he turned the corner into the crowded alley, huddling beneath the shadow of Christ's Church. In Christ's, Gage had a boxed pew with his name on it which he dutifully attended every Sunday. On those days, accompanied by Margaret and driven by Andrew, he could not even look at the place where Sara lodged, indeed averted his eyes. Yet he often wondered if she attended divine service, sitting somewhere at the back, leaving hastily before he had time to catch a glimpse of her.

Tonight, though, she must have been watching from the window because she was standing on the stairs as Mrs. Wells opened the front door and curtsied.

"Good evening, Sir."

"Good evening, Madam. Is Sara within?"

"Oh yes, Sir." Mrs. Wells looked upwards. "There she is; waiting for you. And what a sweet smile she's giving," she added archly.

The Governor merely nodded and went up the stairs with measured tread, giving the slave girl a small bow as he passed her and went into her room. Once inside he turned and looked at Sara, removing his hat as he did so.

"Oh, Governor, it's so good to see you."

He put his finger to his lips. "Shush. She might overhear you. Nobody must know who I am."

"Oh, Sir, she don't know nothing. She just thinks you're some gentleman who takes an interest in me."

"I'll bet she does," Tom answered with a grin and sat down on the one and only chair.

He studied the girl as she busied herself fetching glasses and a bottle of wine.

"Sara, where did that come from? You mustn't spend your money on me. Really, that's naughty of you."

She turned on him a brilliant face. "It's all right, Governor, truly. I've got more work. Money ain't a problem."

"What is this work, child?" asked Tom, a horrid suspicion clutching his heart.

"I'm cleaning people's houses, Sir. Mr. Borland suggested a lady who is too frail to do her own. And she suggested another. What with that and my lessons, I'm pretty busy."

"Thank God," breathed the Governor.

"Talking of God," Sara said cheerfully, "I saw you in church last Sunday."

"So you *were* there. I wondered if you might be."

"I comes at the last minute, and I leaves early."

"It's 'came' and 'left'," said Tom, accepting the glass she held out to him.

"Sorry, Master Governor. Anyway, I saw you in the front, singing away."

"Yes, I enjoy the hymns. Do you, Sara?"

"Oh yes. I enjoys them fine. Mrs. Gage looked well," the girl added in an undertone.

"Yes, she keeps her spirits up," Tom answered, thinking, even as he spoke, that it had been some weeks since he had actually asked Margaret how she was. Momentarily his mind wandered, wishing that their relationship had retained the fervour of their early years together, then conceding that marriage and children and the hardships of everyday life made that hope impossible.

Having poured herself a glass of wine, Sara sat on the floor, looking the governor straight in the eye.

"Tell me, Master, how is this situation going to end?"

"Your guess is as good as mine, my dear. I have no idea. In armed conflict I dare swear."

"But what will happen in the end?"

"The government in Britain will force the Whigs to back down I imagine."

"Oh."

"Why do you say it like that? What do you mean?"

"I ain't sure, Governor. But I guess I admire them just for standing up for themselves."

Tom stared at her. "How can you say such a thing? What are you thinking of?"

"You forget, Master, that I was born here. I am a Yankee."

"But your mother was English, your father African. Surely that is your primary alliance."

The look of anguish on Sara's face was indescribable. Springing to her feet she said, "Oh Sir, please don't speak like that. I spoke out of turn, I know it. I should never have said what I did."

It rapidly went through the Governor's mind that this was not destined to be his night as far as relationships with members of the opposite sex were concerned.

"No, no," he answered, "you have a right to express an opinion."

She gave him an agonised glance, her lovely face a study of misery. "Please don't go, Sir." Then she flung herself into his arms, more affectionately than Margaret had done an hour previously.

Tom stood there, more than aware of her closeness, of the exotic smell of her. His mind was racing, remembering the time he had kissed her, of his dream of seeing her naked. In an agony he said aloud, "You must regard her as a daughter."

Sara looked at him, startled. "Why do you say that?"

He looked down at her, snug in his arms. "Because I must," he answered, though the words did not come out as firmly as he would have wished.

"But, Sir, I am not your daughter, nor could I ever be so."

"Oh Sara, don't say that. Have I not treated you with respect?"

"Oh, indeed you have, Master Governor."

They stood staring at one another, looking deeply into each other's eyes, till eventually Sara whispered, "Don't you want me at all?"

Tormented, Tom could only murmur back, "You'll never know how much."

A smile crossed her face and standing on tiptoe she brushed his cheek with her lips. It was more than human flesh and blood could endure, and the Governor bent his head and gave her a kiss, a kiss in which all his longing for her was mixed with the months of hardship he had been enduring.

"Shall we go to bed?" Sara asked, almost innocently.

Tom shook his head. "No, let's just continue like this. If I slept with you, I would never forgive myself."

Sara smiled, an ancient smile that spoke of centuries of old, old wisdom. "Very well, Master. We shall do as you say."

It must have been midnight before he left, walking out into the cold air with his heart on fire and his body freezing. He had kissed her and embraced her and loved her but had held himself back from seducing her. For that, he told himself now, was something he must never do. But even as he thought it, even as he climbed into the chaise and set the little grey horse into a brisk trot, he knew how close he had been to doing just that.

"She's dangerous for me," he said aloud.

And he felt certain that the only way to stop himself was to stop seeing her for a while. Stop until he had got over this mad and passionate infatuation. For surely that was what this feeling was. Yet the thought of it

made him cringe, indeed brought tears stinging behind his eyes.

Quietly he turned into the stables from the back of the building and settled the horse for the night. Then glancing at his pocket watch and seeing that it was approaching one in the morning, he finally rounded the corner and made for the front door.

"Who goes there?" cried one of the sentries.

"The Governor," came the reply.

"Pass, Sir, all's well."

But is it, thought Tom as he made his way quietly upstairs. Is it really?

CHAPTER
TWENTY

March 6th, 1775

The spies had been moderately successful, thought Gage with a slight air of cynicism. Major John Pitcairn returned with some crudely drawn maps. Lieutenant De Berniere and Captain Brown, however, did not fare so well. Taking with them their batman, who they referred to as 'our man John', they banished him to a separate table when they stopped for something to eat at a Whig tavern in Watertown. This immediately aroused the suspicions of the black girl who served them. Warning them — none too pleasantly — not to go further inland, the pair hurried away. Menaced by horsemen who rode up to them, glared, then galloped off, the two soldiers, having got as far as Worcester and drawn some maps of the hills and roads, plodded back to Boston through heavy snow. Most of the time they had been fearful for their lives.

But as Major Pitcairn had predicted, it was Calico Joel who triumphed. Getting a job as a hired hand on a widow's farm, he studied the people of Concord and noted their military equipment and stores. Then in the evenings, by candlelight, he wrote memoranda to his beloved General in amazingly bad French, detailing exactly what the Governor wanted to hear. He was

precise and to the point. In other words the Indian was providing just what was needed.

With Joel's latest missive in his hand, the Governor leaned back in his chair and sighed. It would be obvious to anyone that the revolutionaries were building up their military reserves in preparation for combat. Yet how could he, without specific instructions from London, order his men to go on the move? As it was he had started regular marches of troops into the countryside, had written to everyone in command to be on full alert. Personally he believed that decisive action against the insurgents now would cure the problem once and for all. But would it really end it? As long as there were people like Sara around, people who had been born in this vast and frightening country and believed themselves to be part of it, how could there ever be peace?

Tom leaned back further and let his mind wander over the last evening he had spent with the black girl, remembering with pleasure the kisses he had given her and her eager response to them. Unconsciously his hand went to his collar and loosened the top button, the very memory making him grow hot. He had deliberately kept away from Sara since, throwing himself into his work, plagued by pangs of conscience regarding his wife. But Margaret, almost as if she knew, had been strangely distant, as though her thoughts were occupied elsewhere. In normal circumstances Tom might have been worried by this aloofness, but in the present tense atmosphere he put it down to concern for the future.

276

There was a knock on his study door, and in response to his call, Major Pitcairn put his head round.

"The meeting is due to begin, Sir. I'm making my way there. Any instructions?"

Tom stared blankly, his thoughts a million miles away. "What meeting?"

"The anniversary of the Boston Massacre . . ."

"In which five people died." Tom snorted.

"Some massacre. However, the meeting's due to begin in half an hour. Dr. Warren is to be the speaker."

"A good man other than for his political views."

"I'd give him good man straight up his arse," Major Pitcairn exploded.

"Well not this afternoon you won't. Let him speak in peace."

"The trouble with you, Governor," the Major said daringly, "is that you're so bloody fair."

Gage did not respond, merely staring at his nails.

"Oh well, I'll be off, Sir."

"Goodbye." The Governor looked up. "Pitcairn, you're to make sure there's no unruly behaviour. And that's an order."

The Major saluted. "Very good, Sir. I'll see to it." The door closed behind him.

With the flash of a hatpin, Margaret secured her second best hat to her head and stood up, smoothing out the folds of her pink silk open robe before a full length mirror, turning to see herself from every angle. Then, on an impulse, she crossed her bedroom and went out onto the balcony, looking across Marlborough Street to

where the people of Boston were already beginning to make their way into Old South Church — or Meeting House, as it was known. For today the man she had come to hold in high regard, the young revolutionary doctor, Joseph Warren himself, was about to make the oration celebrating what was known as the Boston Massacre. Margaret leaned forward, her hands on the stone balustrade, wishing that Boston didn't smell quite so rank. But the fact was that people from the country, people loyal to King George and therefore open to all manner of insults against both their property and their persons, had come flooding into the town for their own protection. Overcrowding had meant shortage of both food and water, and it had also meant that the stink got worse. With a look of resignation, Margaret left the balcony and slowly started to descend the stairs.

Despite the fact of his ever-increasing activities, she had seen quite a good deal of the physician recently. It had been relatively simple to organise. She had taken to walking daily, sometimes with Charlotte, sometimes on her own, but always telling him the general route she was taking. Sure as fate, somewhere along the way Joseph Warren would hurry up to her, begging her pardon for being late. On occasions, too, she had visited his house for an hour or so, in between his seeing patients, of course. They had talked about the revolution that was coming, for by now she was firmly convinced that it would. He had even extracted a promise from her that she would help him if necessary and had worked out a simple code for him to warn her that he needed her. There had never been any

wrongdoing, other than for him sitting closer to her than was strictly necessary, putting his hands over hers occasionally, turning his blazing blue eyes on her. Yet Margaret knew as well as if he had told her that he loved and wanted her and all she would have to do was encourage him minutely. Yet how could she betray the husband who had been through so much with her all these years? Stangely, though, when she spent time with Joseph Warren she forgot all about that and merely lived for the present.

Making her way down the stairs, Margaret saw Major John Pitcairn leave her husband's study and go out of the front door. She knew instinctively that he had the same purpose as herself, that he was going to hear Joseph's oration. She hesitated, wondering whether to say farewell to Thomas, then deciding that he was too busy to be bothered. Cautiously, she went quietly out of the front door.

Crossing Marlborough Street, she entered the Old South Church to find the place packed. Every head turned as she entered and Margaret saw that — much as she had expected — a goodly number of British officers were there ahead of her. One nudged another, they all stared, then politely rose to their feet in a body. There was little option but to proceed forward to the front pew, aware that there was a whisper of, "The Governor's wife has arrived. Fancy that!" buzzing all round her. Raising her head, glad that she was wearing a becoming hat, Margaret sailed along the aisle.

As luck would have it, Major Pitcairn bowed her into her place.

"A pleasure to see you, Ma'am."

"I thought I should attend."

"Yes, yes indeed," he answered over-enthusiastically.

Margaret looked round and saw that Lord Rupert Germain was also present, a notebook and pencil surreptitiously balanced on his knee. She gave him a brief nod of her head, and he stood up and bowed.

By now the church was full to overflowing, British officers sitting on the steps of the pulpit completely blocking the way in. Wondering how on earth Joseph was going to manage, Margaret could not help but think that so many British present indicated a plot to seize Samuel Adams and John Hancock, who sat behind the pulpit in the deacons' seats, together with Dr. Benjamin Church and Paul Revere. Praying that Dr. Warren was going to escape such treatment before a vast and partly hostile crowd, Margaret waited.

When he did come, she let out a gasp of surprise. Not sure how he was going to get into the pulpit, she was amazed to see a head appear at a window behind it and Joseph himself climb into the church. Making his way through his few allies, he clambered into the pulpit from the back and stood silently surveying his enemies, who sat like a murder of red-coated crows waiting for him to make the slightest slip.

This day, the doctor was garbed in breeches and a Ciceronian toga which, though dramatic, did not altogether become him. However, despite his odd costume, he looked amazingly attractive with his spectacular eyes lit with their own inner fire. He caught

Margaret's gaze and hastily looked away again. Then he cleared his throat and began.

"My ever honoured fellow citizens, it is not without the most humiliating conviction of my want of ability that I now appear before you . . ."

His voice, by nature soft and gentle, had developed a harsh edge to it which rang round the church to the accompaniment of hisses and catcalls from the British officers. Despite these, Joseph continued to speak, ignoring the interruptions and even dropping his handkerchief over a handful of bullets, which a Captain Chapman, sitting on the pulpit steps, handed up to him. Margaret was lost in admiration, thinking how remarkable it was that a physician should be able to speak at length about something which he held so dear. Occasionally, he looked straight at her, and she could tell by his glance that he couldn't actually see her, that he was lost entirely in his oration. Eventually though, he drew to a close.

". . . and take your seats with kindred spirits in your native skies."

He left the pulpit amidst thunderous applause and a slow handclap from the British. Margaret sat in silence, thinking that though the speech had been too flowery for her taste, it made one thing obvious. Joseph Warren believed so passionately in his cause that he was prepared to die for it.

When the uproar had calmed down, Samuel Adams, scruffy as ever, got to his feet.

"The thanks of the town should be presented to Dr. Warren for his elegant and spirited oration." More

thunderous applause. Adams held up a large hand. "And now let us make plans for next year's celebration of the bloody massacre . . ."

But he got no further. Only five people had died during what had come to be known as the massacre, and this was pushing the red-coat officers too far. There was a storm of hissing and several cries of "Oh fie! Oh fie!" Margaret stood up to go but was pushed to one side by a crowd of citizens heading rapidly for the doors. The people of Boston, not used to such elegant turns of phrase, had mistaken the word for 'Fire' and were leaving in a panic. Others, meanwhile, seeing the doors were jammed tightly with fleeing folk, hurled themselves bodily out of the windows. Margaret stood, being shoved and knocked on all fronts, staring in horror as the scene of panic unfolded.

"Mrs. Gage, come with me," said an English voice, and she turned to see Lord Rupert Germain holding out his hand to her.

She had never really liked the man, but now she took his hand willingly enough as he led her towards the back of the church. They passed right by Joseph Warren, who was sitting, exhausted and unmoving, in a deacon's chair. He looked up as they passed, and his eyes widened, but he said nothing, merely getting to his feet in order to follow them. Ignoring him, Lord Rupert headed straight for the window which the doctor had used to come in, and checking that the ladder was still in place, climbed out.

"Mrs. Gage, you are to follow me," he said. "If you fall I will be there to catch you."

So saying he started to climb down and after a moment's hesitation Margaret raised her skirts and followed him, Dr. Warren forming the third part of this extraordinary triangle. They reached the ground safely, all three, only to discover another diversion. Marching past the Old South, drums and fifes going for all they were worth, was the 43rd Regiment, blasting out military music with gusto. The townsfolk of Boston, now on edge, hearing the noise thought they were under attack, and started screaming again.

"Oh for God's sake," said Rupert irritably.

Margaret turned to Joseph. "Dr. Warren, can't you do something to calm them? Many of the men are armed. Any violence now will be a signal for battle."

The doctor showed his steel. Stepping into the midst of the yelling crowd, he shouted, "Good people, be easy. They're not going to hurt us. It's merely a military band."

But nobody listened, and several people were shaping up for a fight. Lord Rupert turned to him.

"Warren, are you armed?"

"I carry a pistol, yes."

"Then fire it into the air, man. For heaven's sake get them to pay heed to you."

Reluctantly the doctor fished beneath his toga and drew out a gun which he proceeded to fire, pointing skywards. Several women screamed but the crowd grew quiet.

"Good citizens, be calm. There is no danger. I beg you to disperse and go to your homes in peace," he yelled.

At this point there was a huge drumroll followed by a fanfare of fifes.

"I said it was a military band," the doctor added wearily. "Please go away."

Reluctantly they started to drift off. Dr. Warren gave a bow and began to follow the crowd but not before he had given Margaret a deep look. Her colour came up; she couldn't help herself. Nothing could have been more obvious, and he had done it in public too.

"Mrs. Gage, I insist on seeing you home," said Lord Rupert.

"No, truly, I shall be quite all right."

"Nonsense," he answered briskly. "You have had a nasty shock. Allow me." And he offered her his arm and bowed to the doctor, dismissing him.

"Good day, Warren."

"Good day Mrs. Gage, Lord Rupert."

And with another bow they parted company.

Rupert crossed the street with some care, waiting for the regiment to march out of sight, and entered Province House, which was strangely quiet after the noise they had just been subjected to.

"Tom," called Margaret, "you have a visitor."

And she flung open the study door only to discover the Governor and Lord Percy bent over what looked like a somewhat crude map. Much to her astonishment they folded it away immediately.

"Oh, I'm sorry," she said. "I didn't realise Hugh was here."

The second-in-command gave her a glance from eyes from which spectacles had been rapidly removed.

"Mrs. Gage, how nice to see you."

Margaret smiled. "Lord Rupert Germain is here."

"Excellent. Take him into the withdrawing room. I shall be out in ten minutes."

"Very well."

Somewhat surprised, Margaret turned to her visitor. "If you would like to come with me, Lord Rupert."

"Gladly, Ma'am." He followed her into the salon and sat down in a chair opposite hers. "What did you think of Warren's oration?" he continued.

"Politically biased but relatively good. What did you make of it?"

"I thought it was inciting the mob to violence."

"Oh, surely not."

"Oh, surely yes. I tell you, Madam, Warren is a very dangerous young man."

And Lord Rupert shot her a look which made her go suddenly quiet.

CHAPTER
TWENTY-ONE

April 14th, 1775

It had come. The letter from London authorising Gage to start hostilities. It was dated January 27th, 1775, and arrived on April 14th of that year. It was carried by a cousin of Margaret's named Oliver De Lancey. This red-faced, stout young man was a Yankee by birth but had been educated at Eton and had got himself a commission in the British army. Disembarking at Boston from HMS *Nautilus*, he had hurried to Province House bearing the sealed documents marked 'Secret'. Puffing and even redder in the cheeks than usual, he had swept through the front door and demanded of Robin that he must see the Governor.

"I'll find out if he can be disturbed, Sir."

"Nonsense, man. It is imperative that I see him immediately."

"Yassir."

Tom, hearing a noise in the hall, had sent Earl Percy out to discover what was going on. Clapping his eyes on the second-in-command, Captain De Lancey came to a smart salute.

"Sir."

"At ease. I don't think I know your face." Gingerly, Hugh placed a pair of spectacles on his nose. "No, I don't. Who are you?"

"Captain Oliver De Lancey, Sir. Just disembarked from the Nautilus with secret instructions for the Governor."

The Earl's face transformed. "So they've come — at last. Come in, my dear Captain, come in." And Hugh Percy waved him into the study and closed the door behind them. "Captain De Lancey from London," he announced briefly.

Tom looked up, taking in the fact that De Lancey was a member of a British regiment, the 17th Light Dragoons and was looking exceptionally business-like in his crested cavalry helmet, with the distinctive badge of a grinning death's head rising over crossbones adorning it.

"My dear Captain, when did you arrive?"

"About an hour ago, Sir."

"I see. Well, you must stay and take refreshment. But first of all let me see the documents."

The Captain reached into his leather belt, undid a pocket and drew out sealed papers. These he handed to Thomas, giving a little bow.

The Governor paused, feeling the weight of destiny on his shoulders, putting off the moment when he would finally know the wish of the British government. The other two men were silent as if they sensed something of what he was feeling. Then Lord Percy said, "Best open them, Sir."

Gage nodded and broke the seal, briefly scanning the contents. Then he picked up a pair of spectacles that were lying on the desk and read the papers through thoroughly.

287

"It's war, gentlemen," he said without looking up.

Captain De Lancey squared his shoulders and said, "Good." But Hugh Percy turned away and wiped his glasses with his handkerchief, silently.

Gage continued to read, then finally, sighing, he put the letter down. "It's from the Earl of Dartmouth," he said.

"Saying?" prompted Hugh.

"That the rebels of Massachusetts are . . ." Gage picked the letter up and read, ". . . a rude rabble without plan, without concert, and without conduct."

"How easy," said the Earl, "for men over three thousand miles away to make pronouncements."

"Easy indeed," the Governor answered and sighed once more. "None the less, they make themselves abundantly clear. In the name of the King, we are required to arrest the leaders of the rebellion, disarm their followers, and impose order on the Province of Massachusetts by martial law if necessary."

"I see," said Hugh, and put his spectacles back on.

Captain De Lancey, meanwhile, had been standing rigid, waiting to see how his superiors were going to take the news. Now he moulded his rubicund features into an expression vaguely resembling sympathy.

"Not quite what you wanted to hear, Sir?" he ventured.

"Not quite," Gage answered without cynicism. He turned to the young man, "Why don't you go and seek your cousin? I believe she's in. You must be so tired from travelling." He could simply have said "Dismissed"

288

and had done with it but politeness, as was customary with him, ruled.

Captain De Lancey came smartly to the salute, "Thank you, Sir," and turning on his heel, he marched from the room.

Gage shook his head. "Strange how the bearer of ill tidings comes in many guises."

"Yes indeed. We have no option but to obey, I suppose?"

"Oh yes, we have the final choice. Listen to this." He read from the letter once more. "It must be understood, however, after all I have said, that this is a matter for discretion."

"How sickening," exclaimed Hugh. "In other words, whatever happens, they can lay the blame on us."

"On me, you mean," Tom replied drily.

"Yes, probably."

There was silence for a few moments, then the Earl said briskly, "So what's your plan, Sir?"

"How many of the revolutionaries are still in town?"

"Dr. Warren's, here but he's sent his children and housekeeper away, and Paul Revere is around. Samuel Adams and John Hancock have left."

"I see." Tom paused, then said, "I suppose that it was inevitable that we march on them. They've been behaving insufferably."

Percy nodded. "Indeed they have."

"But . . ." said Tom, and the word was weighted, ". . . they may have an argument."

"Argument or not, we have our orders, and now it is up to us to carry them out."

"Indeed, indeed," said the Governor, and for the third time during that meeting, sighed.

Margaret had been on the point of going out for her walk when Robin came to her and breathlessly announced that Captain De Lancey awaited her pleasure in the withdrawing room. Surprised and pleased, she hurried in, arms outstretched.

"Cousin Oliver, how good to see you."

"Margaret, my dear. You look radiant."

And she did, lit by some inner fire, her luminous eyes alive with a secret she did not intend to share with anybody.

Oliver stood a moment, thinking that of all his cousins Margaret Gage was truly the most spectacular, still dressed to the inch despite all the shortages in Boston, more beautiful than ever now that she had become a mother several times. At that moment he fell a little in love with her and accordingly embraced her with enthusiasm.

"Tell me, how is England?" she asked, drawing him to sit beside her on the sofa.

"Tolerably fine, Madam. I called to see your children before I set sail, by the way."

"Did you?" she asked breathlessly. "Oh, tell me how they are?"

"Fit as little fleas." His face changed. "I was sorry to hear about young William though."

Margaret's entire demeanour suddenly changed. "The Governor . . ." She used the phrase quite unconsciously. ". . . wrote to England, and both my

290

brother and sister-in-law were with him when he died. There is some comfort in that."

"Indeed there is. Now . . ." Oliver altered his voice to sound cheerful once more. "I come with many reinforcements for General Gage."

"Really?"

"Yes, seven hundred marines, three regiments of foot and De Lancey's dragoons — a company belonging to my father of course."

"Those last have a fearsome reputation."

"They certainly do, Ma'am. They are particularly effective in the suppression of civil disturbances."

Margaret gave a small shudder. "I suppose that is what you would call this situation — a civil disturbance."

"Yes, Ma'am, it certainly is."

The door opened, and Thomas stood there, looking partly excited and partly very weary. He crossed to the wine cooler.

"Would you like a drink, Captain De Lancey?"

"Yes please, Sir."

"The only thing that is plentiful is rum — that's because the Yankees drink it."

"That would be fine, Your Excellency."

Thomas nodded silently and poured Margaret's cousin a neat shot and a brandy for himself.

"To success," he said, raising his glass.

"To success," echoed Oliver De Lancey.

As she left the house, accepted the salute of the guards and turned left down Marlborough Street, Margaret

thought about that toast and wondered what its actual meaning might be. One reason suggested itself but was too horrible to contemplate.

Today the town was very crowded but she scarcely noticed the other pedestrians as she made her way along, heading for no particular reason towards the harbour, where, it seemed, there was great activity. The *Nautilus*, the ship which had brought her cousin into port, was moored up, and troops were still disembarking. Knowing nothing of the secret documents or their great importance in determining the future of the Colonies, Margaret slowed her pace and stared.

At the back of her mind, as it always was when she went out alone, was the thought that she might meet Dr. Warren, accidentally of course. Today she would have something to tell him, that more troops had arrived to protect the colony. Sheltering in the doorway of the Fanueil Hall, staring down the length of the Long Wharf, Margaret felt herself grow cold with anticipation. And then there was an unexpected but so welcome touch on her elbow, and she turned to see Joseph, removing his hat and giving a small bow before her.

"Madam," he said, and the smile that lit his face told her everything.

"Oh, Joseph," she said, inexplicably glad to see him, and she gave him a hasty kiss on the cheek.

He was embarrassed, that was certain, but also pleased. For he put his hand up, pulling off his glove and touched the place where her lips had rested momentarily.

292

"How are you faring, my dear?" she asked.

"The better now that I have seen you, Madam." And he offered her his arm that they might walk together.

"You know that more troops have arrived?"

"Oh yes. I've been watching them most of the morning."

"Oliver De Lancey is here with his father's dragoons."

Dr. Warren nodded and smiled but said nothing, then suddenly turned away and fiddled with something in his mouth. Margaret stared.

"What's the matter?"

Joseph grinned carefully. "Truth to tell, Paul Revere has made me a couple of false teeth, carved them from ivory and fitted them on a silver wire."

"Gracious. Why?"

Joseph smiled ruefully. "Vanity I guess."

Margaret knew, as clearly as if he had told her, that she was the reason why Joseph had decided to have them.

"Let me see," she said now.

"There." Joseph pointed to an eye tooth and the one beside it.

"How very clever. I wouldn't have been able to tell." She leaned closer, peering into Joseph's mouth in a very intimate way. And it was at that moment that her eye was drawn to a figure standing quite close behind him and staring at her, wide-eyed.

"Damn that girl," she muttered.

"What is it?" asked Joseph, and turned round.

Sara stood there, dropping her eyes as soon as she realised she had been observed. Margaret was just able to note that she wore a simple but good muslin gown, before Sara turned on her heel and started to walk away.

"Who was that?" Joseph said.

"A slave who once used to work in Province House."

Joseph nodded. "I see." He tucked her arm through his once more and started to walk towards the Long Wharf. "Listen, I can't stay long. I have a patient to attend to. But, Mrs. Gage, I feel a sense of impending danger. I think the British are going to make a move against us."

Margaret grew pale. "Oh don't say those dread words. I simply could not bear it if my husband became the instrument of shedding Yankee blood."

Joseph looked grim. "Do you mean that?"

"You know I do."

"Then you haven't forgotten your promise to help me should I ever need it?"

"Your signal will be a letter apparently written by Quincy the glovemaker. If when it arrives I am to expect you after dark. We will meet in the stables of Province House."

"If I am not there by midnight, then you are to retire to bed. You know I won't be comng."

Margaret turned to him. "Joseph, won't it be a terrible betrayal of my husband if I do this thing?"

"Madam," he answered her seriously, "it will be a choice between him and the country into which you were born. Certain matters transcend family loyalty."

"Do you believe that?"

"Sincerely," he said and put his hand on his heart.

Looking back, Margaret could see that Sara had vanished, and she breathed a little more freely. None the less she had the feeling that this day she and the physician were being watched.

"I think I'd better go," she said. "It seems there's too much activity today."

Dr. Warren reached beneath his greatcoat to look at his pocket watch, and Margaret saw the gleam of pistol butts in his pocket.

"You're armed," she said.

"I have to be," he answered unsmilingly. "I'm known as a dangerous man."

"Joseph, be careful. Don't let anything happen to you."

"Why? Would it bother you?"

"You know it would."

They had reached the beginning of the Long Wharf, and the numbers of people out and about had started to lessen. Joseph leaned forward and did something he had never done before. He kissed her swiftly, full on the lips. Just for a second his mouth lingered on hers and then he withdrew it as quickly, bowed, and turning on his heel hurried off in the direction of the town. Margaret, staring as his figure grew distant, raised her hand to her mouth — just as he had done earlier to his cheek — then thoughtfully made her way home again.

"Christ Almighty!" exclaimed the Governor in a fury, "the bastards know what we're up to."

A letter had arrived that very afternoon, brought by a special mounted messenger, and yet again it was from Calico Joel so its authenticity could not be doubted. It said very simply, ". . . last Saturday the 7th of April P — R — toward evening arrived at Concord, carrying a letter that was said to be from Mr. W — n."

"Telling him, no doubt, that we are going on stand-by."

"But we weren't then."

"You must admit, Sir, that that was the day when Admiral Graves ordered every ship in the harbour to lower their longboats and have them at the ready."

The Governor quite literally ground his teeth. "That idiot. I order him to do something, but can he be subtle? No. Blatant as you please he just does it, in full view of the passing populace. Small wonder they warned Concord where they've got so much stuff hidden."

"Quite right," said Hugh Percy sympathetically.

"There's one item of good news. Joel has offered to act as scout and guide the regiments wherever they want to go."

"And will you take him up on it?"

"I can't think of a better man. I shall send a letter by this very same messenger recalling him to Boston."

He looked up as Robin's face appeared in the doorway. "Sir, Lord Rupert Germain has called."

"Oh God, not now."

"I think it might be wise to see him," said the Earl. "After all, his paper is still read by some people. Surely he could put something in to calm the situation.

296

Remember, no one as yet knows about your secret orders."

"You're right as usual, Hugh. But how much do we tell him?"

"Very little. Next to nothing, in fact. Only what you want him to put in his paper."

But it seemed that Rupert had other things on his mind. Coming in, he sat down on the edge of the seat on the far side of the desk and fiddled somewhat nervously with the buttons at his sleeve.

"Ah, Rupert," said the Governor, putting on a jolly manner he was far from feeling, "I haven't seen you in quite some while. How goes it with you?"

"As well as anyone else in these difficult times." He looked up. "Sir, I must ask you. Do you intend to arrest Dr. Warren?"

Startled, Tom answered, "No, not particularly. Why do you ask?"

"Because the man's a menace. His Boston Massacre oration was highly inflammatory and designed to work on the susceptibilities of those who listened to it."

"But only his followers did that."

"Plus your officers."

"Well, of course. They went deliberately to provoke him."

"And Mrs. Gage?" Rupert said quietly.

There was a profound silence, eventually broken by the Governor saying, "What do you mean?"

"Mrs. Gage was at the meeting also."

"Yes, of course she was," said Hugh Percy. "She told me of it. Said it was very amusing."

"Hardly the word I would have used," Rupert responded drily.

The two men stared at each other, and it was the Governor who broke the slightly hostile silence by saying, "Well, Rupert, what did you come to see me about?"

"Have you any particular news for me? Something I can put in my paper?"

"Reinforcements have arrived, of course."

"But surely the Yankees will imagine that to be some kind of challenge."

"Possibly." The Governor spread his hands. "Then I don't know. What can one say at a time like this?"

Rupert looked at him very straightly. "I'll think of something." He stood up. "Well, goodbye Sir."

"Goodbye, Rupert. Always a pleasure to see you." The Governor looked down at his desk. "If you'll excuse me, I've a mountain of paperwork. Percy will see you out."

"Of course."

Once in the hallway, Rupert Germain gave Hugh Percy a searching look. "Get him to arrest Dr. Warren if you can," he murmured.

"Why, for God's sake?"

"Because he's dangerous, more dangerous than you imagine. And the trouble is that he has friends in high places."

"What do you mean by that, my Lord?"

"I'm not quite sure — yet."

And so saying, Rupert Germain walked from the house, leaving his lordship with many things to think about.

CHAPTER
TWENTY-TWO

April 18th, 1775

Thomas Gage, Governor of Massachusetts and commander-in-chief of the British forces stationed there, appointed as such by His Majesty King George III, rose at daybreak on the morning of Tuesday, April 18th, 1775, leaving his wife still sleeping. Creeping into the dressing room that led off the bedroom, he shaved and washed himself in the hot water brought by his valet, then he dressed and hurried downstairs to snatch breakfast before the seven o'clock conference of officers.

Robin, looking somewhat bleary-eyed, was up, while Beulah was lighting the fires. They both looked round, somewhat surprised, to see the Governor had risen so early.

"A quick breakfast, please," he said, and even to his own ears his voice sounded harsh. So saying, he went into the study, and started to study maps of the local countryside.

Half an hour later, he was joined by the cream of his men, alert and glad that the order had come at last and that they were destined to see some action.

"Good morning, gentlemen," he said, looking round the room. "First of all I must warn you that Revere and

his cronies are completely au fait with everything that is going on," Tom advised the general company.

"How so, Sir?" somebody asked.

"I had a letter from a British officer saying . . ." He picked it up. ". . . 'that the inhabitants of the villages local to Boston conjectured that some secret expedition was afoot and that they are on the look-out.' This follows a visit by Revere. Further, Calico Joel wrote this morning from Concord that most of the military stores had been removed, but that stocks of provisions are still there, along with several large cannon and powder. You may draw your own conclusions."

Lord Percy spoke up. "If I may suggest, Sir, I think we should send out a mounted patrol to intercept any American messengers and stop them from giving the alarm. Because, mark my words, if one of them gets through and gives the danger signal, there's going to be trouble."

"Good plan," the Governor answered. "I'll write to Colonel Smith immediately."

He sat down at his desk and wrote a sentence. 'A small party on horseback is ordered out to stop all advice of your march getting to Concord.' Tom then handed it to a messenger who had been standing silently, close to the door.

"Take this to Colonel Smith and ask him to act on it immediately."

"At once, Sir."

The young man saluted and left the room. Gage addressed his fellows once more.

"Right. Let's hear how the rest of the plans are going."

"Following your orders, Sir, the elite corps of grenadiers and light infantry have been put on stand-by. The story given out is that they are to learn new evolutions."

The Governor twitched his shoulders. "Will it be believed?"

Hugh Percy gave a sideways grin. "Who knows? The citizens of Boston are a canny lot."

"Indeed they are. What else?"

"We move tonight at about ten under conditions of the strictest secrecy. The men will leave the barracks by the back way and move silently through the streets. They will then make their way to an empty beach on the edge of Back Bay, near the new Powder House. After that they will embark in longboats."

"And their destination, Sir?"

"At the moment I intend to keep that confidential."

The officers exchanged a glance but said nothing.

"What do we tell the men?" asked Major Pitcairn.

"Tell them to prepare and that is all. They will be given further details when they are actually on the move."

"Very good, General."

"Well, gentlemen, I think that will be all for the present. And, by the way, I believe we'll have a relatively easy time of it. I do not think those damned rebels will take up arms against His Majesty's troops."

"Let us pray that you are right, Sir," said Lord Percy as he left the room.

★ ★ ★

Joseph Warren sat in his office, staring into space. He had risen at dawn in his empty house — his children and housekeeper had been sent away long since — and had breakfasted sparsely. Then he had dressed himself in sensible clothes and gone to the room in which he saw patients. Today he had cancelled all appointments, preferring to be free to receive callers anxious to discuss the present situation.

There had been plenty of them, all bearing much the same message. It was obvious that the Governor was preparing to make a major move — something long expected — but the salient point was where and with what purpose. As the afternoon had worn on, the tension in the air became almost tangible. So much so that Joseph felt unable to sit still any longer. Putting on his hat, he went down to the harbour and there stood, watching the British activity.

The longboats had been lowered days ago but at the moment there seemed a lot of bustle round them. Over the air came the thin high pipe of boatswains', whistles together with the groaning screech of heavy tackle. Further, sailors were coming ashore on errands. In short, it was a scene of high activity, and it was clear to all who observed it that some important manoeuvre had been planned.

Thoughtfully, Joseph made his way back to his house in Hanover Street, calling in at The Orange Tree Tavern for a cognac before he went further. As he sipped, his mind filled with visions of Margaret; her midnight hair, her ravishing eyes, the smell of fine scent that wafted up

from her clothes. He was as passionately in love with her as only a widower could have been. For, for three long years now, he had been utterly devoid of connubial pleasures, had spent restless nights in his lonely bed. Sometimes, poor female patients had offered themselves to him but he always refused, though secretly he was often terribly tempted to say yes. But he had acted as a man of honour would. Not accepting a fee but not accepting a favour either.

Now, though, he was growing more and more certain that he must contact Margaret as once, not so very long ago, they had agreed he would, the day they had walked on the Long Wharf and he had kissed her for the first time.

Joseph thought, ordering another cognac, he had little choice now but to call the favour in. He had no real alternative. For it was imperative that he knew exactly what the British were up to if the country folk were to be warned to stand their ground and defend themselves. Yet she would risk all in telling him, he was very aware of that.

Margaret had slept late that day, in fact the sound of the officers leaving had been what actually woke her. Ringing a bell for her maid, she had been dressed and had her hair arranged, then she had gone to see Charlotte in the nursery. By the time she had played with her daughter — a child of some twenty months now — it was almost too late to take breakfast and Margaret had wandered downstairs to find her husband.

She thought, as she knocked on his study door, and on his invitation entered, that she had never seen him look worse. Beautifully dressed as always, his face was a travesty of what it normally was. His eyes were sunken, with deep shadows beneath, and his skin was the colour and texture of parchment. His fine nose looked long and thin, and his lips were pressed into a tight line. He looked up as she entered.

"Good morning, my dear."

"Good morning, Tom."

"Did you sleep well?"

"Perfectly, though I was woken by the sound of men's voices. Did you have an early morning conference?"

"Yes."

"Why?"

Tom looked down at his hands, laying down a paper he had been reading. "I'm afraid I can't tell you that."

"What do you mean?"

"What I say, my darling. It was a private matter."

Margaret felt strangely thwarted, unused, despite her years as an army wife, to that kind of treatment. But she smiled at him playfully despite her seething emotions.

"I expect you're sending the troops out."

The Governor had smiled back at her, though his eyes remained strained and drawn. "Just as an exercise, my dear."

She felt like telling him not to insult her intelligence, that it was perfectly obvious that something enormous was afoot. But yet again she dissembled. Laughing

lightly she said, "Of course. I quite understand. Discretion is all." Then she blew him a kiss and left the room.

Once outside in the hall, however, she quietly struck a blow into her cupped hand. If Joseph Warren were to ask her for information, she would have none to give. Before Margaret had had time to think about what she was doing, she found herself making her way up the stairs to the cupola, from whence she would have a splendid view over the whole of the town.

Standing up, she stared in the direction of the harbour. Even at this distance she could see signs of activity aboard the longboats. Men, small and dark as insects, were scurrying about. Further, some of the boats were being rowed across to the *Boyne* and were being tied up beneath the mighty ship's salt-stained hull. Picking up a telescope that someone had abandoned on the seat, Margaret put it to her eye.

There could be no doubt about it. The sailors were heavily engaged in some business of their own. Tom had belittled her by refusing to discuss the matter of what was taking place. And then, quite suddenly, Margaret felt terribly sorry for him. Sorry for all the stresses and strains and worry he was having to endure; sorry for the anguish she had seen staring at her from her husband's eyes.

Sitting down, she stared blindly out at the scene of immense activity on the waterfront, thinking about the import of what was taking place. She could never betray Tom nor his trust in her. If Dr. Warren were to contact her, then she would not answer. But even as

these thoughts tumbled through her mind, she felt the great call for freedom that her beloved country was making and the part that she might be able to play in it. Unable to fend off tears, Margaret wept at the dilemma in which she found herself.

Joseph Warren had seen Paul Revere an hour earlier and both men had agreed that the state of affairs had reached a critical stage.

"They're obviously on the move," Joseph said. "But where? And how are they going? By land or sea?"

Paul Revere had given a shrug which had been passed down from his French father.

"We must find out," Joseph persisted. "Otherwise how can we warn the country people to defend themselves? That the Regulars are clearly going on the offensive?"

"Yes. But how, where, and what for?" Paul answered, repeating what Dr. Warren had just said a moment previously.

"God alone knows that," Joseph stated reflectively.

Revere had laughed shortly. "God and your highly placed informant, no doubt."

"Even they might not know," Joseph answered, more to himself than to the other man.

And now Revere had gone, and he was left to face his great dilemma on his own. Should he ask Margaret for help and thus involve her in true danger? Or should he just guess at where Gage's men were heading and how they were going to get there? Eventually, though, Joseph went upstairs to his bedroom, and there he changed his

suit and his shoes. He had made up his mind. He would send her the coded message. He was about to alter both their lives for ever.

Both the Gages, Thomas and Margaret, had spent the day in turmoil; he poring over maps and in conference with various officers who had called at Province House; she like a caged tigress, prowling round the place, eventually going for a walk to the harbour where she had seen for herself the extra activity and had known by the very look of the men that something extremely serious was afoot. She had walked purposefully back home, determined to get at the truth before the end of the day.

Knocking, then popping her head round the study door, she said, "Darling, you look weary. I think you should stop soon and have a rest."

Thomas looked up from a drawing that he was studying intently. "I'll have a break at dinner time. But thank you for your concern."

She forced a smile. "I look forward to that, then. What time would you like to eat?"

"At about five. I've got to see Hugh first."

Margaret laughed lightly. "I would have thought you'd seen enough of him today."

"One more visit," Tom had said and smiled at her.

She closed the door and leant on it hard, thinking that she still loved him and that she was about to betray him. That is if she could discover the information with which to do so. Yet discover it she must. Tom had always confided in her, throughout their marriage, and

there was no good reason why he should suddenly stop now. But a part of her shrank from being so disloyal when he was obviously so concerned. Yet the birth pangs of the nation into which she had been born lay heavy upon her. Margaret felt herself caught up in the great sweep of destiny.

She dressed very carefully for the occasion, wearing dark red velvet, a gown that she knew Thomas admired. Having had her hair taken down and brushed until it had a sheen upon it, she had it put up once more and wore a feather headdress which matched her clothes. Then she took extra care painting her face, adding a patch to her left cheekbone. In the soft candlelight she looked young again, ready to seduce a man and find out his most intimate secrets.

Swishing down the staircase, Margaret had another pang of bad conscience. The trouble was that though Tom had paid her scant attention recently, she still loved him. And she knew for certain that he loved her in return. Yet she was contemplating a bitter betrayal of that love.

"Oh God help me," she muttered under her breath.

Then she braced up. How could she betray her husband when she didn't even have the information and, indeed, may never have it. And secondly, no coded message from Joseph had yet arrived. She was working herself into a state of anxiety for nothing. Yet still the feeling of disloyalty dogged her as she went into the dining room.

Tom was not there and Margaret stood hesitating, wondering whether to take a seat, but at that moment

she heard him in the doorway and, looking up, saw that he had come into the room. To say that he looked bone-weary was understating the case. She had never seen anyone so drained of vitality, so totally grey. Instinctively she went towards him, arms outstretched.

"Oh my dear, you look so tired. Come and sit down."

He hadn't changed into dress uniform as was his custom, nor had he shaved. In fact from where she was, so close to him, Margaret could see a growth of stubble on his face.

He smiled apologetically. "I'm sorry not to have dressed. I've had rather a hectic day."

She smiled. "This must be a particularly big exercise you're contemplating."

"You could say that," he answered and let her lead him by the hand to his chair.

Margaret rang a bell, and Robin came into the room with Andrew and started to serve their first course while Andrew poured the wine. When they had finished the slaves went to stand silently by the sideboard but Thomas looked up at them and gave them a weary nod.

"Thank you. Now if you would leave us."

"But Governor . . ."

"I'll ring when we have finished," Tom answered firmly, so that the two slaves had no option but to leave the room.

"I just didn't feel like having them stand there," he said by way of explanation.

"I understand."

"Do you, Margaret?" He sipped his wine.

"Yes."

Tom laid down his fork and looked at her from exhausted eyes. "I doubt you do."

"Why do you say that?"

"Because it's the truth. I don't think anyone, with the exception possibly of Hugh, knows what an ordeal it's been recently."

Margaret drank deeply, then stared into her glass. "I wish you would be honest with me, Tom. What is it that's troubling you?"

He sighed deeply, then said, "I've been ordered to march against the Yankees."

"What?"

Something of the horror in her tone must have communicated itself to him because he looked at her sharply.

"I see that I've upset you."

"I was born here," she answered wretchedly. "How do you expect me to react?"

"As my wife, dammit," he said irritably.

"I can't help feeling something for my native land."

"Then we cannot discuss the matter further."

Margaret's heart sank as she realised that there would be no confidences from him tonight. And at that moment she glimpsed through the window a black slave who looked suspiciously like Dr. Warren's man come running up to the house and be halted by the sentries before making his way to the staff quarters.

"I'm sorry, Tom," Margaret said, and she really meant it. "Forgive me. My loyalty lies with you, and it always will." Now the words stuck in her mouth.

At that moment she felt utterly contrite and ashamed of herself. Tom stared at her morosely.

"I understand your dilemma, Margaret. This situation must be impossible for you."

"It is rather."

"Come here," he said. "Come and sit on my knee."

She got up from her place and went round the table, glad that he was holding out his arms to her. She snuggled into them.

"You're right," he said, kissing the top of her head. "This is more than an exercise. We're sending the troops to Lexington and Concord tonight."

"For what purpose?" she heard herself ask.

"To capture the cannon at Concord and to arrest Hancock and Adams."

So that was it. He had told her everything in this moment of confidence while she sat on his lap and received his caresses. Without thinking, Margaret put her arms round him and hugged him tightly.

"Thank you," she said.

He gave her a sharp look. "What for?"

"For trusting me."

She felt low and cheap, and then she thought of the young revolutionary doctor and how much this information would mean to him. She steeled herself to ask one more question.

"Are the men travelling via Boston Neck?"

"No, my dear, they will go in longboats by sea, very secretly, tonight when the town is asleep."

"I see."

She went back to her place. "How is Hugh?" she asked brightly.

"He is about his affairs. He will call in after we have dined." He gave her a look down the length of the table. "I can trust you to keep what I have told you entirely to yourself."

"Of course you can," she answered, and as she said the words she felt that by her act of betrayal she had broken a faith with Tom that nothing could ever repair.

CHAPTER
TWENTY-THREE

April 18th, 1775

Earl Percy called at Province House shortly after eight o'clock that evening. Ushered into the Governor's presence, he came to the salute. Then, because his eyes were tired, he put on his spectacles and waited expectantly. Tom Gage looked up, and Hugh saw that he, too, was wearing glasses.

"Hugh, my dear chap, take a seat. Would you like a little cognac? I think we deserve it."

Lord Percy shot him a brilliant glance. "Thank you, Sir. I will."

They were in the library, Gage going back to his study for a while after dinner but finally settling himself in the other, more comfortable, room. He was quite alone, his wife Margaret announcing that she was going to have an early night. She had kissed him and departed, her manner slightly on edge. But Tom had put this down to the shattering news she had received, that he was sending troops in against her fellow countrymen. Not that he expected trouble of any kind. The sight of all those marching men in uniform would be enough to quell any uprising.

Now he said as much to the Earl, who looked at him quizzically.

"Are you sure of this, Sir?"

"Pretty positive. Why? Aren't you?"

"No, to be honest with you, I'm not. They've been so arrogant recently, almost as if they were challenging us."

"But that's my very point. When the challenge is taken up and they are faced with a great horde of men, they will back down. Just you see."

"I hope you're right, Governor," said Hugh Percy, and stared short-sightedly into his glass.

Tom cleared his throat. "Hugh, there is something I have to tell you."

So this is it, thought the Earl. All day long men had been asking him where they were heading and what their purpose was to be, but he could do nothing but shrug his shoulders. At last he was going to be informed and not before time.

"Yes, Sir?" he said, leaning forward in his chair.

"You've probably been wondering our destination and purpose."

"I have indeed."

"What I am about to tell you must be held in the strictest confidence. The officers and men must know nothing until they are actually heading there."

"Of course, Sir."

"The purpose of the mission is twofold. First we march to Lexington to arrest Samuel Adams and John Hancock, then on to Concord to capture the cannon and destroy the stores. As you know, we are going by longboat."

"I see," said Hugh, thinking he had guessed as much during the day. He was silent for a moment, then said, "Have you told anyone else?"

"Only one other," the Governor answered, and looked away.

His wife, thought the Earl, but said nothing.

The Governor cleared his throat again. "The men are ready?"

"They've been ordered to have an early night. They will be woken later and marched to Back Bay. Then they will set off."

"Very good. And the troop of riders I ordered this morning?"

"Gone long since. Twenty of them, ten officers and ten sergeants. Their orders are to intercept any messengers and stop them from raising the alarm."

Gage nodded. "Excellent. Then all we have to do is wait."

Lord Percy stood up. "Then if you'll forgive me, Sir, I think I'll be off to my bed. I plan to oversee the early embarkation."

The Governor rose too. "Goodnight, Hugh. I'll have one more drink, and then I'll join Margaret. There is nothing further any of us can do tonight."

In that he was going to be proved terribly wrong.

Joseph Warren trembled violently as he left the stables of Province House. Not only was he in possession of the vital information but, even more importantly — or so it seemed to him at that delicious sensation-filled moment — he had kissed Margaret as he had been longing to do for weeks. He could still smell her perfume where it lingered on his clothes.

He knew that he must hurry home, that the Governor had ordered none of the citizens should leave Boston that night, but he lingered a moment longer, staring at the stables where he had received the worst news yet briefly known his greatest joy. Then, turning, he made his way through the darkness towards his house.

It was nearly nine o'clock, and Lord Percy, having called in briefly at a tavern for another cognac, was making his way to Boston Common where the vast majority of his men were camped. Soon, he knew, they would be woken and ordered to march, still in ignorance as to the purpose of their mission. He had a feeling that it was going to be much more difficult than the Governor imagined, but though he had expressed his views there was nothing further he could do about it. Head down, he walked on, his bad eyesight making him unaware of a group of Bostonians standing together, talking earnestly, almost directly in his path.

"Good evening, Brigadier," a man called out when he was almost upon them.

Hugh rapidly put on his spectacles. "Good evening."

"Fine night for a march," said another, his flat Boston accent grating on the Earl's ears.

Hugh peered at them, recognising a couple of the men as being friends of the mad doctor, Warren. "What's that you say?" he asked.

"I said your troops may march tonight, but they will miss their aim."

A thrill of sheer horror ran the length of Lord Percy's spine. Somehow the secret must be out. But how?

"Oh really." He spoke in a terribly English voice. "And what aim might that be?"

"You know as well as I do, my Lord. The cannon at Concord."

He gave them a furious glance and strode on but once out of their line of sight he doubled back and broke into a run as he headed once more for Province House.

At just before nine o'clock, Joseph Warren let himself into his house in Hanover Street, calling for his slave as soon as he had crossed the threshold.

"Jake, come here. I need you."

The slave had appeared from the kitchen. "Yassir?"

"I want you to take two messages for me. One to William Dawes, the other to Paul Revere. Say to both that they are to come at once. The matter is extremely urgent."

"Yassir."

"And Jake . . . "

"Yes?"

"Well done. The other message you took arrived safely."

"Thank you, master."

And with that Jacob was gone, loping from the room, already exhibiting the speed he would use through the brightly moonlit streets of Boston.

It took Earl Percy a few moments to collect himself after his run from the Common to Marlborough Street.

Cold though it was, the sweat was pouring off him, and the inside of his mouth had gone dry as a stone. He stood in the hallway, panting and gasping, wiping his face with a handkerchief, while Robin knocked tentatively on the door of the library.

"Yes?" he heard the Governor say.

"It's Earl Percy to see you, Sir. He says it's important."

"Very well. Show him in."

He was still sweating as he went through the door where he just stood, gazing speechlessly at the Governor, his mind racing down a track at the end of which lay a terrifying truth.

"What is it, Hugh? You look ghastly."

"Sir," Hugh said — then stopped, not sure how to proceed.

"Yes? Go on, man."

"Sir, the mission has been betrayed. The Bostonians know where we are going." And he repeated the conversation he had had on the Common.

Gage sat so still that for a moment he appeared to be in a trance. And during that moment, the colour drained completely from his face, which turned the colour of a sail.

"I see," he said.

"I'm afraid I don't understand, Sir."

"No, you might not, Hugh, but I do. Only too clearly. My confidence has been betrayed because, other than for yourself, I communicated my design to only one other person."

Lord Percy felt his legs go suddenly weak. "May I sit down, Sir?"

"Of course. Let me pour you a brandy."

Tom turned away to get the drink, and when he turned back again, Hugh saw that there were tears in his eyes. Lord Percy decided to ignore them and said, "Will you still proceed with the mission, Governor?"

"Oh, yes," Tom answered, his tone subdued, "I have no choice but to do so. We are in too deep to pull out now. Hugh, when you have finished do you mind if I ask you to leave? I find that I have to go out after all."

"Not at all, Sir." The Earl drained his glass. "I'll return to the Common. The men should be preparing to set off."

"If you would. Thank you, my friend."

"No need, Sir."

And Hugh saluted and left, thinking he had never seen a man so shaken as Tom Gage had been that night.

At a quarter-past nine, Paul Revere arrived at Joseph Warren's house and was shown immediately into his study. There he found his friend and co-revolutionary in a strange state of heightened awareness, presumably because he had seen his contact who, Revere had suspected long since, was a woman about whom the doctor nursed passionate feelings. But nothing of this came into the conversation.

"The Regulars are on the move as we suspected. They are going to Lexington to arrest Adams and

Hancock, then on to Concord to seize the cannon and burn the stores."

"Are they going by land or sea?"

"Sea."

"Then I must warn the people of Charlestown as arranged."

"I want you to do more than that. I want you to get across the Charles River yourself and warn the countryfolk that the British are on their way. Now, I've already sent out Billy Dawes to ride through Boston Neck and take the message to the people in the west."

"Will he get through? I thought all the exits from Boston are closed."

"He might just make it. He's mounted on a slow-jogging horse, with saddle bags behind him, and a large flapped hat upon his head. In other words he looks exactly like a countryman on a journey."

Revere gave a short laugh at the description. "Bless him. But I'll do my best to get across, you know that Joseph. Anyway, there's no time to lose. We must hang lanthorns in Christ Church steeple as arranged. So I'll be off."

"Good luck."

"I'm going to need it," said Revere over his departing shoulder.

As soon as Hugh Percy had gone, Tom Gage gave in to his anguish. He wept bitterly, blaming himself repeatedly for having passed the information on to Margaret, thinking that if the mission failed it would be all his fault. But very soon his distress gave way to

another emotion. He felt furiously angry; indeed he could have killed his wife for betraying what he had told her was a state secret. And then, unbidden, the thought of Sara came into his mind, and he knew that he wanted to see her and hold her in his arms again.

He had deliberately not called on her since that last visit three months ago but now, he thought, he no longer owed loyalty to his wife. The bitch had divulged his most private and secret plans to the enemy. She must take the consequences of her actions. Trembling, and very slightly inebriated, Gage rose to his feet, allowed Robin to help him into his cloak, and left Province House by a side door.

Revere left Dr. Warren's surgery and hurried straight to Salem Street where, on the corner with Sheafe Street, stood the Newman house. Hearing a great deal of noise from within, Paul peered cautiously through the windows and saw to his horror a party of British officers, boarding with the widowed Mrs. Newman, playing cards at the parlour table and making an enormous jovial uproar about it.

Earlier that day he had been to see her son, Robert, knowing that he supported the Whig cause and knowing too, and more importantly, that he was sexton of Christ Church, commonly referred to as the Old North. He had warned him that great things were probably afoot, and had also enlisted the help of John Pulling, a vestryman of Christ's, together with a third man, a friend and neighbour, Thomas Bernard. He had alerted all three to stand by that night.

Now, staring through the window at the Redcoats, he wondered how on earth they were going to manage. Somewhat daunted, Paul Revere went round to the back of the house and, moving quietly for such a stocky man, went through an iron gate into a garden of shadows. He was just staring round disconsolately when one of the shadows detached itself and plucked at his sleeve.

"I'm here, Mr. Revere."

"Thank God," Paul whispered. "Now, let's get out of here."

The four men passed silently through the iron gate and out to the street beyond, then all of them suddenly pulled back as a chaise, driven at speed, went roaring past.

"Gracious, that looked just like the Governor," John Pulling said.

Revere gave another short laugh. "You've got the wretch on the brain," he answered, and playfully cuffed John's ear.

CHAPTER
TWENTY-FOUR

April 18th, 1775

Tom drew the chaise up in the alley which huddled beneath Christ Church and, late though it was, knocked on the door of Mrs. Wells's house. There was no reply. Stepping back into the street he called out, "Sara. Are you there?" Then he threw a pebble against the girl's window.

I must be mad, he thought, behaving like a schoolboy in the middle of this terrible crisis. Yet the fact was that he felt like a child, longing to behave as if he were a young soldier again, escaping from the mass of responsibility that had been thrust upon his shoulders and was about to go horribly wrong if the betrayal by his wife was anything to go by. Above his head, a window opened and somebody thrust their head out.

"Who is it? Who do you want?"

Tom moved irritably and a flash of his red uniform must have shown from beneath his concealing black cloak.

"Oh, it's you, Sir," said a woman. "I'll send someone down to let you in."

The Governor could have died of embarrassment. He had always tried to act with tact and diplomacy as far as his dealings with Sara's lodging house went. But now neighbours were opening their windows and

staring out curiously. Wishing that the rising moon weren't so bright, Tom did his best to hide himself in the shade of the chaise.

There was the sound of bolts being drawn back and a key groaned in the lock before the door swung open. One of Mrs. Wells's sons stood there, glaring.

"Who is it?"

"I've come to see Sara," Tom answered, still hiding in the shadows.

"Best enter then."

The door was opened wider, and the Governor slunk past the fellow, holding his cloak tightly round him to hide the uniform beneath.

"You'll know your way, no doubt," the young man continued, with more than a note of sarcasm.

The Governor did not speak but walked stiffly up the stairs and knocked on the door of Sara's room, aware of a pair of eyes following his every move. There was no answer so he knocked again, this time more urgently. Once again there was no reply, but Tom could not bear the close scrutiny from below a second longer. Turning the handle, he went inside.

Sara was fast asleep, her face lit by the moonshine, which had turned it from ebony to silver. The Governor stood silently, regarding the darkened planes of her cheeks, the droop of her silvered eyelids, the exquisite nose and mouth etched against the argent rays. Her long hair was tumbled about her, spread over the pillowcase like lace, and one hand tossed carelessly back resembled a flower, the curling fingers dark stamens.

Every emotion he had welled inside him at the sight. Quietly, sitting in the only chair, the Governor put his head in his hands and cried out his grief.

He must have made a sound, for Sara woke and said, "Governor, are you ill?"

He looked up at her, smiling through the tears that were running down his cheeks. "No, my dear. I'm sorry I woke you. Go back to sleep."

She sat up in bed, and her hair cascaded round her shoulders. "No, Governor, I can't do that. You have come to see me. Let me give you some refreshment."

He shook his head. "Sara, I've had enough to eat and drink today. I don't want that."

She smiled at him. "Then what do you want, Sir?"

He looked at her and said very simply, "You."

If she was surprised she did not show it. Instead she pulled back the bedcovers and answered, "Then come in, Master Governor."

He stood up and removed the all-enveloping cloak, then his coat, then started on his waistcoat buttons. In a second Sara was out of bed and helping him. And suddenly it was fun to get undressed with a woman to assist. Thanking God that his years of service had kept him lean and muscular, Tom just stood there and, wiping the tears away, started to laugh as she took off his boots and finally his trousers, till eventually he stood before her as naked as Adam.

"You're finely made, Sir."

"Stop calling me Sir. If I am to be your lover you must call me Tom."

"I never could be that familiar, Governor. I must always address you by your title."

"Do whatever pleases you," he answered carelessly. "Just kiss me."

The girl needed no invitation, nestling in his arms as if she had always been there. She raised her head to his, and he caressed her lips with his own until they were kissing deeply and long. Then, feeling himself grow hard, he carried her to the bed, pulled off the long, white nightdress and mingled his flesh with hers with utter enjoyment. But it was not easy for him, and he realised that Sara had been a virgin until he had taken it away from her. Yet by now he was shuddering in the throes of ecstasy and, crying out, released into her with a great shout of triumph. Then slowly he relaxed, and turned to her.

"Did I hurt you, Sara?"

"Yes, Governor. It was painful."

"I'm sorry. I should have realised. It just never occurred to me that I would be the first."

"Didn't it?"

"No, not for a second. You're such a beautiful girl."

His hand was running over her as he spoke, caressing her breasts and lower. Then he began to fondle a certain spot, rubbing and kissing it until she too let out a cry of triumph.

"Oh, Governor, that was good," she gasped.

Tom smiled and kissed her, before he entered her again.

The three men crept across the street in total silence. Paul Revere, having whispered their instructions to

them, had vanished into the night about his own affairs. But by now they were anxious to carry out his wishes and so, looking round to see whether anyone was watching and finding the place deserted, Robert Newman inserted his sexton's key into the lock of Christ Church.

"Thomas, you stand guard," he whispered. "John and I will make the signal."

A quarter of an hour later it was done. The two men, the lanthorns hung around their necks, had climbed the creaking staircase then ascended a narrow ladder above and gone, rung after rung, past the sleeping bells, to the uppermost window in the steeple. Throwing open the sash, they hung two lights out into the night, clearly visible to the watching eyes across the water in Charlestown.

But their descent was somewhat more perilous. Having at last regained the safety of the church and hidden their lanthorns in a closet, they were just preparing to leave when they saw a detachment of soldiers in the street near the church door. Of Thomas Bernard there was no sign. He had presumably been sensible and made his way home at the first hint of danger. Running through the church, Newman indicated a window near the altar. Both uttering a silent prayer, the two men pulled a bench up to it and climbed safely through. Their mission had been accomplished.

Tom, though he was longing to fall into a deep sleep and spend the night with the wondrous girl who had

327

changed his life, reluctantly forced himself to get up and dressed, gazing out at the moon which was rising, almost full, behind Boston. He stood still for a moment, memorising the scene, thinking about the beauty of the sight and the beauty of Sara, who had given herself to him so totally and without inhibition.

"What are you looking at?" asked her voice from the bed.

"The moon rising. It looks wonderful. Come and see."

She got out and stood beside him, the silver light once again highlighting the beauty of her body.

"How glorious it seems."

"Glorious to light an ugly scene."

He felt her grow tense. "What do you mean, Governor?"

"I mean that before it rises again a lot of people will know fear."

"And death? Are men going to their death?"

"I shouldn't think so," he said glibly.

But he was worried. Worried by what Lord Percy had said, worried suddenly that his men were going to meet resistance from the colonists.

Sara reached up and turned his face to look at her. "I hope not," she said. "I do hope that people aren't going to lay down their lives."

"Nobody could wish it more fervently than I," he answered her. He turned away, picking up his cloak from where it lay on the floor. "Goodbye, my darling, and thank you."

"That sounds as if you are never going to see me again."

The Governor turned to the girl and looked at her most earnestly. "Sara, you will never know how much I needed you tonight. I felt as if the whole of my life — well, the last twenty years of it at least — had been for absolutely nothing. I was desperate to find some solace, and I found it with you."

"So you will come back?"

"Of course I will. Every night I can. But I think you should find somewhere more private to live. Will you look for such a place in the morning?"

"But Master Governor . . ."

"I will cover the expense, Sara. You needn't worry about that."

"And you, Sir? Are you going to be all right?"

"I'll get through this with your help, my girl, don't you worry."

And so saying, the Governor kissed her once more and took his leave.

Margaret lay in bed, wide-eyed, unable to sleep at all. She had crept back from the stables unseen and had cautiously gone upstairs to her bedroom. There, without calling her maid, she had undressed herself and got into bed, expecting Tom to come upstairs eventually. But despite the fact she had not heard him go out, though there had been the sound of somebody calling later than planned, he had not come and for some reason she had felt uneasy. And that unease had grown with every passing hour. Lighting a candle that

stood beside her bed, Margaret stared at the decorative clock that stood on the mantelpiece. It was two o'clock in the morning, and Thomas had still not come to bed.

Slipping a night-rail round her shoulders, Margaret took the candle and started to make her way along the corridor, then down the stairs that twisted round before they reached the bottom. The ground floor was shadowy and somehow sinister, full of pools of impenetrable darkness that seemed to reach out with long fingers to pluck her into their depths. Skirting round them, she made her way tremulously into the study and, lighting more candles, gazed round.

There was no sign of Tom and no indication whether he had left in a hurry. Trying to recollect whether he had gone into the library, Margaret made her way there. And here she found the clues she needed. There were two glasses that had once contained brandy, still standing where they had been put down, and a sheaf of papers had been left tossed carelessly on the floor. She stood stock still trying to work it out.

Then the thought came that he had gone to see the men embarking, had been called for by Lord Percy and had accompanied him to Back Bay to watch the men set forth. Without really knowing what she was doing, Margaret poured a drop of brandy into one of the two dirty glasses and sipped it. And then she heard the front door open.

She stood frozen to the spot, racked with guilt for betraying her husband's secret. Then the thought of Joseph's passionate kisses came to taunt her and make her feel even worse about the meeting in the stable.

Utterly still, Margaret waited and eventually saw the study door open and Tom stand in the entrance. He stared at her, dumbstruck.

"What are you doing here?" he asked in a hoarse voice.

A thousand thoughts ran through Margaret's brain, the most paramount of which was to bluff it out should he accuse her.

"I got up to look for you, Husband. You did not come to bed."

"I do not sleep with traitors," he answered flatly and turned away from her.

At that moment of death, the death of everything they had ever meant to one another, Margaret felt nothing at all, just a blankness that seemed to start inside her stomach and spread throughout her body.

"What do you mean?" she heard someone say, and realised that it was her own voice that had just spoken.

He turned back to her. "Don't try and deceive me, Margaret. I only told two people where we were heading, and the other one I would trust with my life. The fact that you betrayed me speaks loud and clear. As far as I am concerned, our marriage is at an end."

She stood, icy and frozen, looking at him, while he returned her glance calmly.

"I shall send you back to England on the first available ship," he said. "Now I bid you goodnight."

He had dismissed her, just as if she had been someone from lower ranks that he had become bored with.

"Let me speak . . ." she started.

"No," he said crisply, "we have nothing further to say to each other. Now, may I suggest that you retire upstairs. I shall sleep here tonight and will make other arrangements in the morning."

And with that, he blew out the candles, handing her one to light her way to bed.

Margaret went up the stairs with her thoughts in turmoil. It was obvious that she could not plead her cause now. Matters like that must wait until tomorrow. So thinking she got into bed and finally fell into a fitful sleep.

CHAPTER
TWENTY-FIVE

April 19th, 1775

While Margaret slept, the American War of Independence, also known as the Revolutionary War, began. Dawn was just breaking in the hamlet of Lexington when the weary troops — they had left Boston five hours earlier and still had not been told where they were going or why — came marching round a bend in the road. Before them lay Lexington's meeting house, the largest building in the place, standing just beyond a big oak tree. Beside it lay the wooden bell tower, still pealing the alarm that the Redcoats were on their way. Beyond that again lay the Buckman Tavern. And there, standing on the village green, silently awaiting their arrival, were the men of Lexington, armed and ready.

"Bugger 'em," said Major Pitcairn, seeing the sight. "They've had warning."

Paul Revere had indeed escaped from Boston that night, as had William Dawes, despite the order that no one was to leave the town after nine o'clock. Crossing the Charles River, rowed by two friends with muffled oars, Revere had reached Charlestown by the skin of his teeth, sailing right beneath the hulk of the great ship *Somerset*, yet remaining unseen.

He had been greeted by William Conant and various other revolutionaries from the village. They had seen

the signal in the church steeple and had prepared for his arrival. A good stout mount called Brown Beauty, one of the fastest creatures in the neighbourhood, had been lent to him, and stocky Revere, his dark French face burning with intensity, had set off for Lexington to warn Hancock and Adams to make haste and go.

He had arrived at Lexington's parsonage, having escaped from a British roadblock, where the two men were staying, guests of the clergyman Jonas Clarke. The house was in darkness, guarded by local militiamen. But on his shouted insistence that the Regulars were on their way, he had gained admittance and delivered the warning to Hancock and Adams. Half an hour later, William Dawes had arrived and the five men had gone to the tavern on the green to refresh themselves. Then, with Lexington's bell tolling a warning, Revere and Dawes had set off for Concord.

Now Major Pitcairn said, "Bugger 'em," once more.

He had ordered his men to load as soon as he heard the clarion, much to their surprise. They had not imagined that they would be attacked or even molested on the march. But things were turning out very differently. So it was with loaded guns that they rounded that fateful bend in the road and heard a military drum beating a call to arms.

Nobody was quite certain what to do next, though they could hear the orders being passed down the line of Lexington men. "Stand your ground. Don't fire unless fired upon. But if they want to have a war let it begin here."

Then a young Marine lieutenant, Jesse Adair, fighting on the British side, made a momentous decision. The main road divided by the meeting house, left going to Concord, right to the Buckman Tavern and other village houses. He led his column to the right, shouting,

"Damn them, we will have them."

Major Pitcairn galloped forward, leading his company to the left, then halted them, managing to stop three of Adair's companies from advancing. But two units, following behind the charging lieutenant, were going at full thrust. Pitcairn was powerless and could only look on in anguish as the men broke into a run and started to shout the British infantry's battlecry, "Huzza! Huzza! Huzza!" Seventy yards from the men of Lexington, they deployed into a line of battle. The men in the rear came hurtling forward, the sergeants and subalterns dropped back. Major Pitcairn galloped his horse forwards, shrieking, "Disperse, you bastards. I order you to disperse, blast you." Then turning to the Lexington men, he shouted, "Lay down your arms, you damned rebels!"

The Lexington force's commander turned to his men and ordered that they comply, and some began to scatter, moving backwards and to both sides, though some did not hear the order and stayed where they were. And then a shot rang out, a shot whose echo would be heard right round the world. Nobody knew who had fired it or from which side it came. But to the British infantry, worked to a frenzy by their charge and

repeated battlecry, it was a signal, and they started to fire in response. Thus began the Revolutionary War.

Margaret having left the room, Tom threw himself into a chair and closed his eyes. Without doubt, this had been the most terrible, yet the most exciting day of his entire life. Yet he could not push away the feeling of unease that lay upon him. Indeed before he had faced Margaret with the truth, before he had fled through the night to Sarah, he had written one last note to the brigade major of Hugh Percy's regiment, Captain Thomas Moncrieffe. In it he had asked that Lord Percy's crack troops be under arms at four o'clock the next morning, ready to march if needed. He had given this note to a messenger, and then Tom Gage had faced his own nadir.

Now, though, thoughts of the fate of the men whose embarkation he had gone briefly to watch, haunted him. He had visions of the Yankees fighting back, of gunfire and wounding and death. Getting up and pacing the room, Tom eventually flung himself on a chaise longue and fell into an uncomfortable sleep.

He was woken at five o'clock by Robin's hand shaking his shoulder. Instantly Tom was fully conscious. He sat up, alert.

"What is it, Robin?"

"A rider is here from Colonel Smith, Governor."

"Show him in at once."

A minute later a dust-streaked and exhausted young man entered and gave a tired salute. "Sorry to disturb you, Governor, but I come from Colonel Smith. Sir, the

336

country people have risen against us, and we are in urgent need of reinforcements."

Tom struggled into his coat. "So the worst has happened." It was not said as a question.

"Yes, Sir. It started in Lexington and continued in Concord. They're fighting well organised, Sir."

"I've ordered Lord Percy's 1st Brigade to go on stand-by in case this very thing should happen. I want you to ride and see that Captain Moncrieffe has them ready. I'll follow in about ten minutes."

"Very good, Sir."

"Then you can go and get some rest," Tom added. To Robin, who entered as soon as the galloper had gone, he said, "Robin, bring me some coffee if you would. I shall wash myself then go out immediately." To the slave's unspoken question, he answered, "I slept down here last night for fear of disturbing Mrs. Gage."

Making his way upstairs, Tom passed through his bedroom on the way to his dressing room. Margaret lay with eyes tightly shut, not moving. Her husband had the strongest impression that she was actually awake but feigning sleep because it was the easiest course. He felt a cold fury sweep him and walked swiftly past the bed which, up till the moment of her betrayal, he had happily shared with her. Ten minutes, later he had hastily shaved and washed in cold water. He was ready for another day.

As it transpired, Captain Thomas Moncrieffe had not received the Governor's instructions that night. The sealed letter had been left with one of the servants, who

put it on a table waiting his master's return. The Captain, coming back early that morning, had fallen into bed without knowing that the message had come.

On discovering this, General Gage went beserk and shouted at everyone until, at seven o'clock, the brigade was finally summoned into marching order. By half past the hour they were ready to go but were kept waiting while someone went to summon the Marines, who were mysteriously missing but meant to join them. Their orders had been sent to Major Thomas Pitcairn, who was already fighting at Lexington by this time, and were awaiting his return in his room. Gage's fury redoubled, and it was left to Hugh Percy to calm him down.

"Sir, it cannot be helped. How could anyone have known that those instructions to Pitcairn were from yourself? We must remain calm."

"Calm!" Gage thundered in full voice. "Was ever a mission more ill-fated than this? I tell you, Hugh, it has the kiss of death upon it."

Because somebody betrayed your secret, thought the Earl, and I don't have to look too far to know who it was.

"We'll be ready to march soon, Sir. Mark my words; we'll give 'em a pasting if we meet resistance."

"Which you will," the Governor replied heavily.

"Well, Sir, with your permission, I'll inspect the men."

"Oh, do so, do so," came the somewhat testy reply.

So the Earl mounted his splendid sorrel horse and passed along the ranks of his soldiers, a brilliant sight in

his uniform of gosling green and scarlet, trimmed with silver lace.

At eight-thirty they were finally ready to march, making a stirring sight as they left town with colours flying and the fifes and drums playing "Yankee Doodle Dandy" as a particular insult to the locals. At the rear of the brigade had gone a set of mounted scouts, one of whom had been the faithful Calico Joel. He had bowed from the saddle to Tom as he passed him by.

The Governor, watching them go, felt every kind of emotion that it was possible to feel: proud that he was the head of such a fine body of men; in despair that he had been betrayed by his wife of seventeen years; stirring to a second youthfulness by his passionate interlude with Sara. How can a man cope with so much? he thought. Then, bracing up, he rode through town to see her, his heart lifting at the very idea.

He went on horseback, his usual disguise of a plain cloak falling back as he rode so that all the world could see it was the Governor who set forth. Wherever he went he received salutes. Some from the soldiery not involved in the present conflict, others given impudently by people of the town. He returned them all and felt a certain pride in the fact that he was such a recognisable figure and that, for once, he was abroad, not stuck in Province House as was his custom.

He spotted Sara before she had even seen him, making her way down Salem Street, past Christ Church, heading for a house at the far end. Tom reined in his horse and sat watching her, feeling his heartbeat

speed up as if he were a youth again. The experience of the previous night had sealed his fate. He was in love with her as only an older man for a younger woman can be. Yet for all that he could not help but notice her ragged clothing and the fact she had no cloak or coat. He decided there and then to fit her out with a new wardrobe.

Then he took himself to task. How could his mind be on such frivolities when men were dying in Lexington and Concord? But he knew, deep down, that only Sara and the magic she worked on him would give him sufficient strength to get through the bitter times that lay ahead.

He called out to her and she turned, smiled, and hurried towards him, standing at the horse's head and looking up.

"Master Governor, I didn't expect to see you so soon."

He shrugged. "These are busy times. Where are you going?"

"To the house at the end of the street. It's standing empty and I wondered if I . . . we . . . might be able to rent it."

Tom dismounted. "I'll come with you."

"That would be a pleasure, Sir."

They walked along, Tom leading the horse by the reins. "Last night was wonderful," he said, almost under his breath.

"It was for me too, Sir."

"It will get better, I promise you." She shot him a look but said nothing, and Tom continued, "I swear

that I will make you one of the happiest women in Boston."

"I think, Sir," she said, dropping him a small curtsey, "that you will make me one of the happiest women in the world."

They had reached the house but repeated banging on the door produced no result. Then from a dwelling further down the street a young female emerged.

"Can I help you?" she asked, giving the Governor an inquisitive stare.

He pulled his cloak tightly round him. "This house. Would you know who lives here?"

"It's empty, Sir. The owners got out of town. They left us in charge. I'm Maria Stillman, the Reverend's daughter."

"I would like to rent it for my ward. Who should I see about that?"

"Why, my father or me. We've been put in charge."

Thirty minutes later it was done, except for the embarrassing fact that Tom had left the house in such a hurry that he had very little money on him.

"I'll send some over immediately. Now, do you have any objection if my ward moves in straight away?"

The girl looked suddenly sly. "When the money comes, Sir, then she can."

"Very well. Sara, go back and pack up. I will get Andrew to call and tell you when the debt is cleared."

"Yes, Sir." But once Miss Stillman had gone, she looked up at him shyly. "What is a ward, Governor?"

"Someone put into my custody. Someone over whom I would have control."

She gave a sudden grin. "Guess I'd rather be a mistress, Sir." And with that she had walked away, leaving him alone.

The gallant troops of Brigadier Lord Hugh Percy saved the British force from being completely routed that day. As they arrived at Lexington, they saw to their intense horror that Colonel Smith's men had been reduced to a running mob and were being hounded by Yankee fighters. Ordering his artillery to open fire with the field guns, Percy pounded the rebels from above, the response to which was to send them scurrying for their lives.

But the battle was far from over. Having sent Andrew off to see to Sara, Gage had felt certain that lack of ammunition was going to be Lord Percy's problem and ordered two ammunition wagons, escorted by one officer and thirteen men, to set out. But the whole thing was ambushed and never reached the Earl, adding to his problems. He and Colonel Smith met to discuss the situation.

"We've fifteen miles to go and only thirty-six rounds to cover us," Hugh said, sitting in the Munroe Tavern, which he had made his headquarters.

"I am more than aware of the problem," replied the Colonel gloomily.

He was the opposite of Percy, lacking his flair and style. He had gained promotion by doing everything neatly and in good order, and thus had been chosen to lead the expedition to Lexington and Concord. It was the Earl, however, who had been sent to bail him out.

"There's nothing for it," continued Hugh, taking a nip of brandy to brace himself up. "We shall have to send a rider back to Boston for reinforcements."

"But surely the Governor . . ."

"The Governor must face facts," Percy replied harshly. "Either he helps us or we all end up dead."

Colonel Smith also took a glass of strong liquor. "What is it about these countryfolk that they have become so invulnerable?"

"They've been preparing, that's what. They've been drilling and marching and handling guns for some time now."

"Do you mean to say that they've been getting ready for war?"

Lord Percy finished his glass and held it out for a refill. "Yes. That is precisely what they have been doing."

"My God, then we're going to lose the Colonies."

"I think, Colonel, that we probably are. Anyway, back to practicalities. Who shall we send?"

"Lieutenant Rooke," Smith answered without hesitation. "He's a fine rider and should make the town fairly swiftly."

"Right," said the Earl.

Five minutes later, the handsome young aide-de-camp was saluting smartly before him. "Yes, Brigadier?"

"Rooke, I want you to ride back to Boston without discovery. Once there, you are to go immediately to General Gage. Tell him that Colonel Smith's command has been rescued but that we are going to have to fight

every step of the way back. Tell him that further reinforcement is of great importance."

"Yes, Sir. Anything else?"

"No, just good luck to you."

"Thank you, Brigadier. I shall do my damnedest."

Once he had gone, a heavy silence settled itself over the room. "Well, let's to it," said Hugh Percy. "We can fight 'em off as best we can."

"Death or glory," answered Colonel Smith, but his words had a hollow ring to them.

CHAPTER
TWENTY-SIX

April 19th, 1775

It was a sad and sorry army that eventually completed the long march back to Boston with the fighting men of New England following closely at their heels. It was twilight when the first men entered Charlestown, and it was blackest night when the last exhausted British troops crossed over and took up a position on the high ground. Men dropped down onto the earth and slept, the wounded lay shivering on Charlestown's landing stages, waiting for the Royal Navy to place them in longboats and escort them home. It was a scene of disaster, thought Earl Percy, walking amongst his men and giving them a word of cheer. And he wondered what the reaction would be in Province House.

In the event, the called-for reinforcements had not arrived. General Gage had not been able to spare a man to go to Percy's aid. Half his force was already in the field, the other was needed to hold Boston in check. He ordered the troops to remain under arms in barracks, prepared for the population of the town to rise. Like everyone else, Tom could only wait with drawn breath the outcome of this terrible day.

As soon as he knew the army had reached Charlestown, he left Province House and rode to meet them, waiting up at the Boston side to see the wounded

be ferried across. Eventually, after what seemed hours, Hugh Percy himself crossed the Charles River and set foot once more in Boston.

"Sir," he said on seeing the General, and gave a tired salute.

Despite etiquette, despite discipline, Tom Gage hugged him, he simply could not help himself. And Hugh, looking somewhat surprised, returned the hug after a second or two.

"It was extremely rough, Sir."

Tom looked at him, noticing how the elegant uniform was dirty and streaked with smoke, how Hugh had a black mark on his cheek and another on his hand, how exhausted he seemed.

"Thank God you're back in one piece is all I can say."

"We can no longer underestimate them, Governor. They fought well and hard. You can take it from me that this is but the beginning."

"You mean that they are set for war?"

"Quite clearly. I must confess that I never thought they would attack the King's troops with so much dedication."

"Neither did I."

"The way they shot at us was indescribable. Quite frankly, they are a force to be reckoned with."

Gage shook his head. "I would never have believed that this would be the outcome."

"Nor I. Well, Sir, if you will excuse me I would like to go home to bed. I'll report to you first thing tomorrow morning."

"Very good. I'll expect you at nine.

The last sight that Tom had of a shattered Lord Percy was riding his sorrel horse through the streets of Boston, both man and beast looking fit to drop.

Tom stood hesitating, wondering whether to call on Sara but deciding against it in view of the situation. Instead, he turned his horse round and trotted back to Province House. Knowing that confrontation with Margaret was inevitable, he made up his mind that tonight would not be the night. As he entered the house he saw her, clad in the dark red ensemble that he liked so much, coming down the stairs. He merely said, "Good evening," waited for her to reach the bottom, then went up to his dressing room. When he finally descended again, she was waiting for him in the library.

"Tom," she said directly, "for God's sake stop treating me as if I were a leper. Speak to me."

"I have nothing to say," he answered.

"But you will have to talk to me at some time. For the sake of Charlotte we cannot ignore one another totally."

Tom looked at her and for the first time saw that she was getting older. "Listen," he said, "I meant what I said the other night. You have betrayed me, and I want you and the child to leave Boston on the first available ship. But I agree that until that time we must observe the cordialities. But know that you have killed my love by your actions and that it will never return."

She let out a muffled sob and turned her head away from him. "I'm sorry," she gasped. "I was so torn . . ."

347

"I don't want to hear any more," he cut across her. "From now on I shall sleep in one of the guest rooms. We shall dine together if that is what you wish. But other than for that you may as well consider that our social contact is at an end."

"But Tom . . ."

"Margaret, I am too tired to discuss it further. Please accept what I say. I have had a day that I would not wish upon an enemy. Can we leave it at that."

She opened her mouth to answer, but Tom was saved by the arrival of Robin and Andrew with the first course. He was disconcerted to see that the coachman gave him the very slightest wink as he passed Tom a bowl of soup. The Governor did not respond.

They dined in silence, the noise of eating seeming to be magnified in the intense quiet. Afterwards Tom made his way into his study and firmly closed the door. But he was not to be left in peace. A ring at the front heralded a visitor, and a few minutes later Lord Rupert Germain was shown into his presence.

Tom stood up. "My dear boy, how are you? I haven't seen you in a while."

Normally pale, tonight Rupert was almost white, utterly drained of colour as he sank into a chair without invitation.

"Sir, I've decided to close down the paper," he said without preamble.

"Why?"

"I thought that would have been obvious. There's going to be a war, and there's no room for a sheet like mine which openly supports your cause."

Tom stood up and crossed to the sideboard. "Would you like a cognac?"

"No thanks. I haven't eaten as yet. I think I might be sick if I drink anything."

The Governor gave a wry grin. "Best not then. I'd offer you supper but we have just dined."

"Could you spare me a little cheese?"

"Yes, of course." Tom rang a bell. "Will you not eat when you return home?"

Rupert looked grim. "Fact is I'm too frightened to go back. I'm not popular because of the kind of paper I produce and mob violence is rife. When the fighting broke out yesterday I can tell you I packed up my things and left for Boston."

The Governor felt infinitely depressed, the news from his old friend seeming like the last nail in his coffin.

He sighed deeply. "I am so sorry to hear this. Your lovely house. It must have been a great sacrifice to leave it."

Rupert smiled sadly. "It was a choice between that and my safety. I prefer to live over the printing presses in Boston than risk another night in the place."

"You must do what you think best, I suppose."

"There was no question about it. I shall go back to England eventually and start all over again. But meanwhile, Sir, consider me at your disposal."

At that moment Robin arrived and was duly despatched to get some cheese. When he had left the room, Tom sighed again.

"I'm afraid that I can offer you nothing on my staff, Rupert. Though I must do my best to secure peace, I am certain that war is a real possibility, so I have surrounded myself with military personnel."

Rupert gave a grin. "I didn't really expect to come and work for you, Governor. I meant that if you need a friend I shall be here. Indeed you might well require someone to talk to, someone outside your immediate circle."

Tom gave him a suspicious look, wondering if he had heard anything. But Rupert sat there eating his cheese and fruit, which had just arrived, smiling amiably.

"Kind of you, my friend," the Governor said eventually. "I shall probably take you up on your offer."

Rupert nodded, his mouth being too full of food to speak.

Much as Tom wanted to see Sara, he was too exhausted to set foot outside again. Instead he went to a guest room at the other end of the corridor from his bedroom and there undressed and flung himself into bed. But he could not sleep. Thoughts came of the wounded; of the shot, of the bayoneted, of the dead. Tom found his mind had flown to the room at the barracks set aside for a hospital. How crowded it must be, how full of the sounds of the dying. By the morning the death toll would have risen even higher. What a grim way to spend a life, he thought. As the commander-in-charge of so much destruction. Then a vision of Sara came, and he felt a sudden peace. Thinking about her and

concentrating totally, clearing his head of any other thoughts, he finally fell asleep.

He was woken in the grey light of early morning by the sound of his bedroom door quietly opening. Margaret stood in the entrance wearing a nightdress and shawl, her feet bare. Just for a minute he stared at her blankly, then memory returned. He sat upright.

"What is it?"

"Thomas, we must talk."

"I said all I had to say last night."

"Did you mean it? For one mistake you would cast aside your wife of seventeen years?"

"One mistake, you call it," Tom said bitterly. "That mistake cost a host of British lives — and Yankee too. But no doubt you were thinking only of your country — this nation full of immigrants, mostly from Britain. Well, Madam, you should have thought more of the consequences of your action. Thought too, perhaps, of your husband, the man who, for a number of years, has cared for you and protected you. The man who gave you his heart. But forget that; it all lies in the past."

Margaret turned a tear-streaked face towards him. "Tom, for God's sake . . ."

He got out of bed and stood before her in his nightshirt. "Margaret, for the love of Christ stop it. You have done the deed; it is in the past. As soon as a suitable ship comes into port I am sending you and Charlotte back to England. Until such time, we will remain outwardly cordial but that is all. Have I made myself clear?"

She turned on him a look of pure dislike. "I always thought that you had a hard streak, and now I know it is true. Very well, two can play your hand of cards. I shall be civil but leave it at that. Goodbye to you." And she swept from the bedroom, closing the door with a bang behind her.

Tom sat on the edge of the bed, suddenly devoid of feeling, realising that another terrible day stretched before him. And in that moment he knew that he was going to confide in Lord Rupert, tell him everything, so at least there would be a sympathetic ear to listen when Tom was desperately in need.

CHAPTER
TWENTY-SEVEN

May, 1775

It was, thought Margaret Gage, one of the most depressing sights she had ever seen. Out through Boston Neck, a straggling but steady line of people was making its way. All supporters of the rebels, they had bundles in one hand and a string of children in the other, wandering out of Boston, which was now preparing for a siege. Equally, British supporters were making their way into the town from the country, fearing for their lives if they stayed where they were.

The Governor had demanded that all weapons should be handed over before any refugee could leave. Anyone who wanted could then theoretically get a pass to go. But in fact these passes were difficult to obtain and bore with them certain restrictions. Neither food nor merchandise could go with the applicant. And those who left could never return as long as the British held the town. Yet, despite this, the stream of people leaving equalled the stream of those coming into Boston for their own protection. Rupert Germain had started a trend that was growing daily.

Joseph Warren had left on the day of the Battle of Lexington and Concord, fighting gallantly alongside the revolutionaries. After that, he had decided to leave Boston behind and was currently staying in Cambridge,

where he had been made chairman of the Committee of Safety. He had written to the Governor on the day after the fight. A letter which had begun, 'I have many things which I wish to say to your Excellency, and most sincerely wish I had broken through the formalities which I thought due to your rank, and freely have told you all I knew or thought of public affairs . . .' He had not mentioned anything personal but still had felt compelled to write.

Margaret sat in the chaise, looking at the two sets of people, one group leaving, the other coming in, and felt at her lowest ebb for years. That her marriage was over she was utterly convinced. It was how she felt about it that was the crux of the matter. In one way her preoccupation with Dr. Warren had led her to a feeling almost of indifference. On the other she had spent all her formative years in the company of Tom Gage and was so used to having him there, of receiving his love, support and protection, that the thought of being without it truly hurt her. Yet there was nothing she could do. She had betrayed him for the sake of her country and now she must take the consequences.

If only Joseph were still in town, she thought. I could have seen him, explained what had happened and sought his advice. But he had gone, and she had heard nothing as to whether he had survived the fighting or not. Staring disconsolately at the lines of people making their way to the countryside beyond, Margaret felt the strongest urge to join them. To walk with them, offer to take a child or two by the hand, and leave Boston and all its political intrigue behind for ever. To go and find

Joseph and throw in her lot with his. To go and live in a quiet village in New England and perhaps have another child.

But even as she watched the pouring out of refugee families she knew that she must return to Province House and Thomas's grim expression and icy silence. Perhaps in time his attitude would soften and he would forgive her. Yet she knew that dream was over before it had even begun. Tom could forgive many things but betrayal was not one of them. And she, his chosen consort, had told his secret to the other side. She was, to put it bluntly, a traitor in his eyes. Margaret shivered, wondering what the punishment would have been if she had been a member of his staff rather than his wife. Being shot or hanged, she imagined.

She leaned forward. "Home, Andrew, I've seen enough."

"It's a funny sight, ain't it, Mam? All them folks leavin' and all them other folks comin' in. Hope there's going to be enough for us all to eat."

"Oh, surely there will be."

"I ain't so certain, Mam. I think hard times is comin'."

In the eventuality, Andrew was proved right. From plentiful supplies, rations were suddenly cut to salt meat and fish. The Governor ordered that his defences should be strengthened at both Boston Neck and along the Charles River. The flow, both in and out, had trickled off by May, during which time Tom frantically attempted to restore peace, while feeling certain that

the outbreak of further hostilities was merely a matter of time. It was a period of enormous tension for people on both sides.

Most evenings, as soon as he had dined — often in frigid silence — Tom would take the chaise and leave the house. The only exception to this rule was when he had business to attend to or some high-ranking officer coming to see him. Other than for that, he went out without fail, returning at about midnight, sometimes later. At first Margaret had lain awake, alone in the big marital bed, awaiting his return, but nowadays she simply went to sleep and ignored the whole thing. If it had been anyone other than Tom, she would have thought he had another woman, but this did not fit in with his rigid discipline. Or did it? In the silence of her lonely room Margaret grew suspicious.

Yet what could she do about it? She had chosen her country rather than Tom because she had listened to Joseph Warren, a man of great strength of character, not to mention the fact that she had been very much attracted to him. So she was as much to blame as anyone. But despite the facts, Margaret resented the idea that her husband sought consolation in the arms of another.

But what consolation it was. Tom Gage was like a man reborn into the joys of sex with a girl as uninhibited as any he had ever come across. He would lie for hours in Sara's close embrace, often in total silence, sometimes telling her that he loved her, other times simply making love to the best of his ability. It was such a total contrast to the grimness of everyday

living that he found himself longing for those evenings he could spend in Sara's company. He even had daydreams of sending her back to England and setting her up as his mistress in London, where she would instantly become the toast of the town. But, as ever, thoughts of Margaret would surface at this stage of his reverie. For reply he would stretch out an arm to Sara, pull her gently beneath him and, relishing every sensation, slowly sink deep inside her. At which she would give a cry of pure pleasure and hold him tightly. At moments like these Tom thought himself in heaven and wanted such intense feelings to go on for ever. But nothing can, and soon it was time for him to get dressed and leave her, driving home alone through the dark, empty streets of a town under siege.

Meanwhile more reinforcements arrived in Boston, including three British Major-Generals to help Gage in his present predicament. This brought the total number of marines, dragoons, artillery men and infantry to six thousand, all crammed together in that small town, all needing to be fed and watered and housed. Margaret could barely bring herself to smile at the newcomers, but smile she did, entertaining them at dinner and pretending to be interested in their talk of England and London life. But secretly her thoughts lay with Joseph — who was not only alive but corresponding with her through his old consulting rooms. He would send the letters there, and she would go and collect them and answer via the same route.

He was living in Watertown, seven miles up the Charles River from Boston. In one of his letters — all kept under lock and key in a secret drawer — he had suggested meeting Margaret. But she felt like a caged bird and wrote back that it was impossible. That was until one day in early June.

She was returning home from her walk to the harbour and vaguely noticed a countryman coming towards her, carrying his great baskets full of wares, which he had come into Boston to sell. She could not help but give him a second glance for he looked such a fright; a great flapped hat on his head, filthy hose, a shirt patched and worn, shoes with holes. Yet there was something about the way he carried himself, something in his bearing, that made her look at him twice. Seeing her stare, he approached her.

"I've a few things left, Mam. Want to see?" And before she could give an answer he had moved the apples to one side to reveal a piece of paper.

Margaret stared at it. "What's that?"

"Bless my soul, Mam. It's a letter. Guess it's for you."

She looked at him closely, and a pair of light blue eyes regarded her equally shrewdly. Then one of them winked at her. Margaret drew in breath, but before she could speak there came an urgent whisper.

"Don't say my name aloud or I'm a dead man. I've risked all to come here today. If you want to, meet me at my old house in fifteen minutes. Meanwhile, buy something from me for the love of God."

"I'll have a few apples," she said loudly, but her heart was racing with pure delight. Joseph had risked his life to come to her.

"Thank you, Mam."

She paid him with some money from her reticule, then walked on a little, then went through the pantomime of suddenly remembering something and turned on her heel. With a racing heart she made her way to Hanover Street where he was waiting for her.

The front door stood open and closing it behind her, Margaret stepped cautiously inside.

"Hello," she called. "Where are you?"

He came bursting out of his office, his hat cast aside, and she saw the gleam of his fair hair without powder or wig.

"Margaret," he said. "How is it with you?"

But before she could answer he had swept her into his arms and kissed her, just as he had on the night they had met in the stables. Except that these kisses were even hungrier, were even more highly charged than the others had been.

"Oh Joseph," she said, struggling to get a little air.

"Margaret, I've missed you so much. You'll never know how greatly. Oh my darling, does all go well with you?"

For answer she shook her head. "No. Tom found out that I betrayed him. My marriage is over. He no longer speaks to me."

"Bastard."

"No, Joseph. After all, I did tell you his plans."

"But only to protect the country that you love. But darling don't let's talk about it. Let's not ruin the hour we have together."

"An hour? Is that all?"

"Perhaps two. I passed through Boston Neck with Billy Dawes. He comes here every week, selling things. I begged him to let me accompany him. He did so but only on the strict terms that I would be back out before sundown."

"Will you return to Boston?"

"I doubt it. Mine is such a well-known face. They would be onto me like a pack of wolves."

"Well I didn't recognise you."

"That's because you weren't looking."

All the time they had been speaking he had been leading her to the room in which he used to see patients, and now they had arrived. Joseph sat her on the couch and went to a cupboard.

"Ah, it's still here."

"What?"

"A little brandy I used to keep for medicinal purposes. Will you have a drop?"

"Only a very little."

Joseph poured out two small glasses and handed her one, finishing his own in a single swallow. Then he came and sat next to her. He said nothing but she caught his light blue glance and in it she read passion and longing.

"I want you," he muttered.

"I know you do."

"And how do you feel about that?"

"Oh, God, Joseph, I want you too."

It was enough. He was upon her, raising her skirts to where she was naked underneath and putting his hand on her most vulnerable spot.

"Are you sure?" she heard him ask.

"Positive."

He let out a great sigh, and the next thing she knew was the feel of him entering her.

"I'm not going to take long. It's been such an age."

"Just to have you close is wonderful."

And it was, like heaven on earth, but as he had predicted it was over in a few moments. But then, after resting for another ten, he was ready once more and this time he made proper love to her, caressing her breasts and her body as he slowly undressed her. For the first time, Margaret saw him naked and longed for him, lean and muscular as he was. And he, laughing a little at the look of desire on her face, leaned over her and kissed her and entered her again, until they achieved the heights together and shouted loudly in the empty house.

Afterwards they dressed again quickly.

"You leave first," he said, "and walk slowly back home. I want one or two medical supplies which I shall hide in the bottom of the basket. Then I'll go too."

Margaret turned in the doorway. "Will we meet again?"

"Oh yes," he said quietly. "It is our fate to do so."

She looked up at him. "You have never said you love me."

"Haven't I? It's probably because we've been so busy. But I do love you, Margaret, with all my heart. You are the woman I have always dreamed of marrying."

"Will we marry one day, when Tom has divorced me?"

"Oh yes. You'll come and live with me in a New England village, and we shall have a sturdy little boy of our own. Would you like that?"

"I should love it."

"Then fix on to that dream, my darling. Hold it with you through all the dark hours ahead."

"I will think of it every night."

"As will I."

"And in that way we will never be separated."

"Never." She turned back to the door, which he opened for her. "Goodbye, my darling. Until we meet again."

He raised her hand to his lips. "Until that moment remember that I shall always love you."

CHAPTER
TWENTY-EIGHT

June, 1775

On June 12th General Gage issued a proclamation placing Boston under martial law. He also on that date reached a decision with his fellow Major-Generals to move against the neighbouring village of Dorchester, followed by the Charlestown peninsula. This time he kept the secret close to his heart, but did not take into consideration General Burgoyne. A loud-mouthed fellow who had arrived from England at the same time as Hugh Percy, Burgoyne enjoyed his various liquors, and after having had a drop or two too many, discussed the plans in what appeared to be every tavern in town. He may as well have made a public proclamation. It seemed to be only thirty minutes before the Yankees had heard them — all of them — and were acting accordingly. Consequently it became common knowledge that the British were about to launch an offensive and where it was to be.

Across the Charles River lay Charlestown, the place in which Paul Revere had collected his mount on that fateful April night. Beyond the town were two hills, Bunker and Breed's, and on the night of the sixteenth British sentries in Boston heard noises indicating that the revolutionaries were busily fortifying the place. They had chosen to entrench Breed's Hill, little

realising that this was a mistake. Properly fortified, Bunker Hill would have been impregnable. Breed's Hill, on the other hand, was lower and therefore more open to direct attack. Furthermore, it could possibly be flanked by the British landing from the Mystic River.

As usual, the British took their time about preparing, and it was not until the afternoon of the seventeenth that they finally landed at the end of the Charlestown peninsula. Then, after being drafted into wings, they slowly began to advance on the fortified hill, in two steadily moving columns of red.

Hearing that there was to be fighting at Breed's Hill, sightseers began to fill up the high places in Boston so that they could look across the river and see the action. The church steeples and rooftops were occupied first, then the balconies and windows, while Sara climbed upstairs to the attic floor and there discovered that by opening the small window and sitting on the sill, legs dangling outside, she had a fine view over the water.

She was dressed simply but finely in a muslin open robe of dark green, the Governor having thrown away her other clothes and rigged her out — to use her own expression — in better quality garments. Her daily life was dull, shopping and reading her main activities, but at night it metamorphosed into splendour. For at dusk, her Governor, the man who was the centre of her universe, the person she adored above all others, would come to her. Often they would make love, but equally often they would talk about his problems, or she would read aloud to him, or they would play chess, which he

had painstakingly taught her. She was never allowed to cook for him because he had always dined with his traitorous wife before he came to her. But for those few hours Tom belonged to Sara, and Sara alone. Now, putting a cushion under her behind to make it more comfortable to sit, she prepared to watch a battle that she knew he desperately needed to win.

Joseph Warren had left the house in Hanover Street feeling more happy and fulfilled than he had for years. He had longed for Margaret as only a young widower could and now, at last, she had given herself to him, and the consummation had been as glorious as anything he could ever have imagined. Further, they had a dream. A dream in which they were married and had a son. He had told her to hold onto that dream — now it was up to him to do so as well.

He had departed from Boston in a ramshackle cart with Billy Dawes, hardly speaking, full to the brim with emotion. After that he had returned to Watertown and the Hunt household, where he was staying, continuing his work as a doctor, organising the revolutionaries to the best of his excellent ability. Then on June 14th, somewhat to his surprise, he had been appointed a Major-General. Yet he had no troops to command, nothing, indeed, but the title.

At night, when he lay in his narrow bed, he would long for Margaret, think of her, dream the dream. Often he would be awake as dawn came creeping across the sky, when he would finally sleep deeply before rising a few hours later. It was not much of a life, but he

filled it with hope that one day he and she would eventually be together.

News came of the entrenchment being built on Breed's Hill on the evening of the sixteenth. As soon as it arrived, Joseph announced his intention of joining the Yankees in the inevitable fight and asked the women of the household to prepare lint and linen bandages for the casualties. Then he sat down to dinner.

Betsey Palmer, whose father owned the house, sat next to him, thinking how handsome he looked this night, how tanned and fit. She couldn't help but meet his light blue eyes, but every time she did so she looked away shyly.

"Will you have a glass of wine with me, Betsey?" he asked.

"Oh, no, Sir. Really."

"Why not?"

"You know I don't drink very often."

"Oh, come on, my little girl, drink a glass of wine with me for the last time."

She looked at him in blank astonishment. "Why on earth do you say that, Dr. Warren?"

"Because I'm going on the hill tomorrow, and I might never come off."

"Oh, don't speak so, Sir, please don't. You frighten me with such talk. Of course you'll come off. I insist upon it."

He laughed then, but not loudly, more in a thoughtful sort of way. "I'll try," he said and drank his wine, several glasses of it.

★   ★   ★

Margaret drank more than usual that night, thinking that perhaps in alcohol lay her solution. She knew that Tom was staying in for there was important business afoot, though naturally he had not told her what it was. But after dinner she loitered in the library, asking Robin to bring her a glass of port. She picked up a book she had already read and stared at the page, but her mind had wandered off. She wondered desperately how and where Joseph was, and prayed with all her heart that it wouldn't be too long before they met again.

She looked up, startled, as the door suddenly opened. The Earl Percy stood there.

"Oh, beg pardon, Ma'am. I didn't realise you were in here."

Margaret was very slightly tipsy; that is what gave her the courage to say, "Come and talk to me for a moment, my Lord. To be honest with you I could do with the company."

"Certainly, Ma'am, though I daren't delay too much. There's a great deal to be done."

"I'm sure there is. Pray sit down."

Hugh did so, taking the chair opposite hers. "You'll take a glass of port?" said Margaret, and rang the bell before he could answer. Once she had given the order, she gave the Earl a smile.

"So you will fight tomorrow?"

"That is the plan, yes Madam."

"And where is this to take place?"

A strange look crossed Hugh's face. "Round and about," he answered.

It immediately occurred to Margaret that he knew of her betrayal, that he was privy to Tom's innermost secrets.

"Oh, it is of no consequence," she answered lightly.

There was a flash as Hugh Percy produced his spectacles from an inner pocket and put them on his nose.

"Sorry to be so uncommunicative, Ma'am, but orders are orders. I'm sure you'll understand."

"Of course. I am an army wife." She paused, then said, "What news of Rupert Germain?"

"I believe he has been talked into producing a newspaper of sorts by your husband."

"I can well imagine. What is it like? I haven't seen a copy."

"It is very much the same as it was. All pro British and anti the colonials."

"Nothing changes then."

"No nothing." Percy downed his port in a swallow and stood up. "And now if you will forgive me, Ma'am, I must return to the meeting."

"Of course," said Margaret. "Be sure not to miss anything."

Once alone again her thoughts turned inevitably to Joseph. Where was he? she wondered. And, more importantly, was he going to be involved in the fighting tomorrow. She could almost hear him telling her to hold onto the dream. So, closing her eyes, Margaret did so, though with a heavy heart.

No sooner had the revolutionary forces opened fire on the British troops than the order was given for the

British to burn Charlestown to the ground. Admiral Graves, a man whom Gage disliked intensely, nonetheless was given the order to let loose his cannons, and the ships moored in the Charles River began to pelt the wooden town with hot shot. Up went the buildings in a conflagration, with flames roaring in the air and clouds of smoke everywhere. A rider immediately left for Province House to inform the Governor that his instructions had been carried out.

Sara, sitting in her window most of the afternoon, had a magnificent view of the blaze but felt her heart saddened for the people whose precious homes they once had been. Looking down, she noticed that the fire had attracted more observers and that underneath her in the street, standing on boxes and ladders to get a better view, was a crowd of men and women, all shouting out in protest. And then it happened. A familiar figure, wrapped in a scarlet cloak and riding a black horse, came into view, accompanied by an officer. Reining in, they sat side-by-side observing the blazing inferno across the water. They stayed like that, their faces expressionless, watching the destruction of an entire village. Then, knowing perfectly well that he was close to Sara's house, Tom glanced up and for a second their eyes met. However, they gave no outward sign of recognition, both of them looking quickly away.

Then Sara sensed rather than saw a movement below her. One of the men, standing halfway up a ladder, reached in his pocket and produced a pistol. Clearly incensed by the destruction of Charlestown beneath a rain of blazing shot, he suddenly raised it and took aim

369

at the Governor's head. Sara did not hesitate. Pushing herself off the sill, she launched downwards and onto the would-be assassin. The shot was deflected as both Sara and the man crashed to the street beneath. Instead of entering Tom's body the bullet went into hers. She had saved the Governor's life and in so doing had ruined her own.

Joseph had lain awake all night, thinking of Margaret and the battle that lay ahead of him and wondering if they would ever have the dreamed-of future together. As soon as it was light, he got up and washed himself in cold water. Then he dressed carefully in a light-coloured coat with a sprig on the buttons, a tie wig and a white-fringed waistcoat. Leaving the house quietly, he got on his horse and rode to Cambridge to see his friend Elbridge Gerry. There, after having talked a good while and breakfasted a little, Dr. Warren begged that he might have a few hours' sleep before the fight and was shown to a hot upper chamber where he flung himself onto the bed and slept at last. Seeing him, Gerry decided to let fate be the arbiter and not to wake him but see if he woke naturally.

At noon, however, there were sounds of stirring from the room above, and Joseph came down the stairs, buttoning up his sprigged buttons and putting on his tie wig.

"You're going then?" asked Elbridge.

"Yes, I said I would, so now I must follow through."

"Look Joseph, you might well get killed. Why don't you stay here? We need you to organise us. What use will you be to the cause if you end up dead?"

"It's no good, Elbridge. I've been through it a dozen times. I've decided to go, so go I will."

"Is there nothing I can say that will persuade you to stay?"

"No, nothing."

So Gerry had reluctantly seen his friend ride off in the direction of Charlestown, filled with the dreadful premonition that he would never see him again.

The shot that misfired startled the horses of the General and the young officer accompanying him and they both looked round to see what had happened. The sight that met their eyes was almost unreal. Lying flat in the street, unconscious, was a black girl, the would-be assassin conscious but groaning, a few feet away from her. Already a woman had rushed to the man's side and was vainly attempting to help him stand.

Tom, throwing caution to the winds, was off his horse like lightning, running to Sara and cradling her in his arms.

"Oh, my darling," he whispered, "what happened?"

But it was obvious without an explanation. She had seen the man below her take aim and had jumped on him to save Tom's life.

"Little girl, don't die," Tom murmured. Then he got up, lifting the unconscious Sara in his arms and carrying her into the house, ignoring the curious stares of the crowd which had formed. The young officer, not

certain what to do, followed behind, leading the two horses.

But once away from prying eyes, the General acted with the desperate calmness of someone who is utterly panic-stricken. Applying damp towels to the girl's forehead, he sat massaging her hands until eventually she showed signs of recovering consciousness.

"Anything I can do, Sir?" asked the young lieutenant nervously.

"Yes, go and fetch a doctor. Any doctor. If there is one left in this God-forsaken town. Hurry, man."

"Yes, Sir." And the lieutenant made a rapid exit, extremely puzzled by the General's attitude to the girl which, if he hadn't known him better, he could easily have mistaken for love.

Joseph Warren left his friend's house just after noon and rode to Charlestown, getting there in time to see the British ships fire hot shot and torch the timber town. British troops had landed, and the battle between them and the revolutionary force had begun.

Leaving his horse at the bottom, Joseph climbed Breed's Hill on foot and reported for duty to Colonel Prescott, a countryman by nature.

"Dr. Warren, Sir. You're here. Would you like to take command, General?"

The doctor gave a fleeting smile. "No, I most certainly would not. I've come as a volunteer."

"So you intend to stay, Sir?"

"Indeed I do."

So on that hot, airless day the battle of Breed's Hill, which would become known as the battle of Bunker Hill, raged. Joseph, who had come armed with nothing more than a book of poetry in his pocket, got a musket and a cartouche box from a retreating soldier. Then he fought hard and to the best of his ability.

Meanwhile the precise lines of English soldiers, beautiful in their red uniforms, did their best to advance uphill in the face of deadly gunfire. It was a slaughterhouse as, one by one, they dropped, men from both sides, and died a few feet away from one another.

Major Pitcairn, who had survived the battles of Lexington and Concord, was swearing a mighty oath, "Come on you goddamned bastards," when suddenly he fell, shot in the chest. His son, fighting close by, rushed to his side and carried his dying father on his back to a place where the high salt grass grew and the noise of battle was quiet. There he laid him down, kissed him and hurried back to fight on. The Major lay silently in the hot sun and bled to death.

Joseph, firing shot after shot, heard his name called out by an advancing British officer and half turned, a smile of recognition on his face. And then the most curious thing happened. He heard a loud noise and felt a sharp pain, and suddenly the battlefield faded away and he was hurrying up a lane to a weatherboarded house. Even as he approached it the front door opened and there stood Margaret, dressed as a New England wife would dress, and immediately behind her came a

stocky little boy with her great dark eyes and Joseph's fair colouring.

"Papa," he called, and as Joseph ran to catch him in his arms, he felt more happy than he ever had in the whole of his short, eventful life.

CHAPTER
TWENTY-NINE

June, 1775

Sara was fully conscious by the time the lieutenant returned with Dr. Silvester Gardiner, who was somewhat flustered and had been fetched from watching the battle through a telescope. Tom had carried the girl onto a chaise on which she now lay. He had earlier brought her a chamberpot to use and assisted Sara, who seemed incapable of moving independently. Thinking that he had never done this for anyone in his life, Tom had thrown the contents away. Then he had made her tea and waited for the doctor to arrive.

The expression on the medical man's face when he saw it was the Governor himself who had called him out, was almost amusing.

"Oh, your Excellency, I had no idea that it was you who sent for me." He turned to look at Sara, and his eyebrows shot up. "My goodness, what do we have here?"

"This is Sara," said Tom, barely curbing his irritation. "She is a former slave of mine but now lives here. Earlier today somebody tried to shoot me, and Sara saved my life by jumping on him from a window. In so doing I think she has somehow damaged her back."

"I see." Dr. Gardiner turned to the girl. "Now, young woman, I shall have to examine you. Gentlemen, I would suggest you leave the room."

No sooner were they outside than Gage turned urgently to the young lieutenant. "Hawkshore, I'm in serious trouble. I should have returned to my desk an hour ago. For God's sake go to Province House and make sure that my secretary, Samuel Kemble, takes my place. Tell him I have been delayed on business but do not say what it is, I beg you."

Now all was clear, thought Lieutenant Hawkshore. The old man was sleeping with the black girl. Well, good luck to him. To hide the grin that was creeping over his features, he cleared his throat and coughed a little.

"Very good, Sir."

"Now go," said Gage, realising that his secret was out but almost ceasing to care.

How long he waited in the little parlour, he was never sure, but eventually the doctor came through, wearing a serious face.

"Well, I've had a good look at her, Excellency."

"Yes?"

"I'm afraid the prognosis is not good. I would like to consult with one of my colleagues, but as far as I can see the bullet has entered her back and damaged the spinal cord."

"Well can't you get it out, man?"

"It can be removed certainly, but if what I think is correct, the girl will never walk again."

"Oh, my God! Are you sure of this?"

"As I said, Excellency, I would like the opinion of Dr. Eustis — he was trained by Dr. Warren, you know, and is a first rate physician. But it is my opinion that . . . er . . . Sara will have to spend the rest of her days in a bath chair, which will make life difficult for her when the child comes of course."

Tom sat silently for a moment, wondering if he had heard correctly, then he said, "The child?"

"Yes, Excellency. The girl is in the early stages of pregnancy. Didn't you know?"

"No, no. I didn't."

Dr. Gardiner shot him a look that conveyed a multitude of thoughts, the principal of which was that he knew damn well who the father was and was dying to go outside and have a good laugh. Tom struggled to keep his dignity in what were proving to be impossible circumstances and in the end gave up.

"Well, well. I had no idea," he repeated.

"Indeed, Sir," the doctor answered and made a strange gesture with his arm, almost as if he were slapping Tom on the back.

The Governor collected himself. "I'll be grateful if you can keep what you have discovered today to yourself. It could be most embarrassing for me if word of this got out."

"I shall remain silent as the grave," Dr. Gardiner answered, but Tom could see from the twinkling in the man's eye that he was going to do no such thing.

"How much do I owe you?" Tom asked, reaching for his pocket book.

"I shall send my bill when I have consulted with Dr. Eustis. Meanwhile, Sir, I suggest the girl rests as much as possible prior to the operation. Good day to you."

"Yes, of course. Good day," Tom answered and felt faintly surprised when the doctor gave a short bow before departing.

Sara had apparently dropped off to sleep when he went back into the room, looking so perfect in repose that Tom could hardly believe that she might well be seriously injured. However, she opened her eyes and gazed at him.

"Hello, Master."

"Oh, Sara, don't call me that. I am Tom to you and always will be."

She looked at him, and he saw fear in her eyes. "What have I done to my back, Tom? The doctor wouldn't tell me. He said he wanted to call another man in."

"You've bruised your spine, darling. That is all."

He simply hadn't the heart to tell her what the real truth might be.

"Will I walk again?"

"Yes, I'm sure you will. Now listen. I'm going back to Province House, and I will send Mildred to you directly. She can nurse you until you feel better. It means that you will be alone for about an hour. Is there anything you need?"

Sara pulled a face. "Perhaps the pot."

"I'll bring it. And Sara . . ."

"Yes?"

"About the baby. Why didn't you tell me?"

Sara hung her head, and a pinkish hue crept into her cheeks. "Governor, I wasn't sure. I thought maybe it was something else. Oh Sir, please don't be angry with me."

"Angry?" Tom said. "Why, I'm delighted."

And he really meant it. He may have fathered a family by Margaret but the thought of him at his age — fifty-five — once again being responsible for a life coming into the world, thrilled him immeasurably. Particularly with a mother as beautiful and perfect as Sara. Then he thought of what the physician had just told him and inwardly groaned. Surely when Dr. Eustis examined her he would find another diagnosis. Once the bullet was removed she would walk again for certain.

Sara slipped her hand in his. "Tom, do you love me?"

"You know I do. And I shall love our child when it is born, I promise you. But now I must go. There is a battle raging over on Breed's Hill, and I should have been in Province House some time ago."

The girl sighed. "It seems as if we are always saying goodbye."

Tom tightened his grip. "One day, when all this fighting is finished, I'll take you back to England with me."

She regarded him thoughtfully. "And what about Mrs. Gage? What will happen to her?"

"She will have left me, I feel certain of it."

"Why do you say that?"

Suddenly, Tom felt irritable, not with Sara but the situation in general. "My darling, I can stay with you

379

not one second more. When I come again I will tell you exactly why the relationship between my wife and myself has broken down. And before you start blaming yourself for being the cause, the answer is that you weren't. It was something else entirely. Now, I must go."

And kissing her swiftly on the lips, Tom went out, mounted his horse, and rode rapidly back to headquarters.

That night, after the battle, there was almost total silence in Province House. The British had won the day, but it had been a dark and bitter victory. Of the soldiers who had gone to Breed's Hill, two hundred and twenty-six had been killed and eight hundred and twenty-eight wounded. And many of the wounded were going to die anyway. Gage's particular friends Colonel Abercromby and Major Pitcairn were amongst the dead. It had been a terrible and sobering affray and one that the Governor had no wish to see repeated.

He had arrived home to find his wife had left the house without speaking to a soul and refusing any form of transport. Apparently, according to Robin at least, she had been dressed very soberly. The Governor, feeling he had enough to think about, closeted as he was with Lord Percy, had merely nodded when he had heard that Margaret was out.

"Will Mrs. Gage be returning to dine, Sir?"

"How would I know? Possibly."

"Very good, Governor."

And Robin had shaken his mournful black head and left the room, the gloom of the situation reflected in the droop of his shoulders, the slowness of his walk.

Margaret had gone to watch the battle, standing amongst a group of women who had turned out to be army wives and camp followers. Dressed in a black skirt and shawl, she had stood a little apart from them and had seen Charlestown go up in flames, then heard the rattle of shot coming from the opposite shore. But though some of the women had drifted off, several had remained, anxiously scanning the casualties as they were rowed back, lying in the bottom of the longboats, too weak to stand.

As it grew darker, she still waited, though what for she was not certain. There would be no news of Joseph on this side of the water. But some vague hope kept her standing there in the gathering dusk, watching the scores of pitiful wounded, some of them bleeding to death, being ferried back in those hard, uncompromising boats to the stark realities of military hospital.

One soldier, unwounded and standing, was helping an injured colleague ashore and passed quite close to her. Over his arm he had a coat, and as he walked by she thought she recognised it.

"What's that?" she asked, her voice strangely high pitched.

He turned to look at her, a hard-faced individual with not a shred of pity in him.

"A coat, lady. Want to buy it?"

"Let me see it."

He passed it to her without comment and just for a moment the world spun. It was a light lavender in colour and it had a sprig on the buttons. Joseph had often worn it when he had met her in another life, another time, and watched the soldiers drilling.

"Where did you get this?"

The soldier stared at her curiously. "Ain't you the Governor's lady?"

"No, no, I'm not. Where did you get it?"

"Up on the hill. It was on a dead man. I nicked it off 'im along with his westkit. Well, he won't have no use for it now. So I brought it back to sell."

Margaret grabbed his arm. "Did you know this dead man? Who was he?"

"Dr. Warren, Mam. Now do you want the coat or don't you?"

But she did not answer, instead flying towards the harbour where the boats were coming in, packed with the groaning and the near-dead. There were several women there before her, telling the sailors that they needed to go across and help bury their men. Because they knew them, because they were wives, or good as, of the Regulars, the soldiers were letting them into the boat, to sit amongst the blood and urine. Margaret, pulling her shawl up over her head, just went with them as if she belonged, speaking to no one and keeping her face averted as she crossed the Charles River to the ruins of what had once been Charlestown.

On the opposite bank, the injured were gathered in sad groups, waiting their turn patiently to be taken back. Many men were stretched on the ground, and

Margaret found herself picking her way round them as she headed up the slopes of the now quiet hill. Behind Breed's Hill stood Bunker Hill, its top turning purple in the fast fading light. But it was to Breed's Hill, alive with British soldiers digging graves for the fallen, that Margaret's eyes were fatally drawn.

As she drew nearer the top she felt her calmness begin to crack. Hesitatingly, she leaned down and touched a body, rolling it over so that she could see the face. A pair of sightless eyes gazed into hers, and she felt like screaming out her distress. But if she had done so they would have known that she was no army wife, used to such things, and she would be turned off the hill and sent back to Boston, at least that is what her imagination told her. In fact, as is usual at the scene of a terrible battle, nobody was taking any notice of anybody else, every man getting on with his own particular job.

She climbed higher, turning bodies as she went, her shoes hurting her, sticking occasionally where a dying man had urinated before he died. But she felt that she no longer cared what happened, as long as she could hold Joseph close to her heart before he was committed to the earth. Up she went until at last she reached the top and stood by the redoubt made by the Yankees.

"Joseph," she called, very softly, in case there was a chance of him being alive.

Ever afterwards she could have sworn that a voice answered, "Here," though of course it was only the chill little breeze that had come up.

She turned her head, and then she saw him, naked except for a sad pair of linen drawers, lying face down, the blood on his hands dried long since. She ran to his side, kneeling beside him, turning him, lifting him, embracing his poor wounded face, half of which had been shot to shreds. Then she saw to her horror that he was covered in earth as if he had already been buried, then disinterred.

"Oh my darling," she said, rocking him as if he were a baby. "What have they done to you? What have they done?"

"Excuse me, Mam," said a voice, "are you a relative of the deceased?"

She looked up to see a soldier regarding her, leaning forward on his spade.

"Yes," she shrieked, "I am his wife. What have you done to him? He looks as if he has already been buried."

"Well, he has. But discovering that he was famous-like, we dug him up again. Just as well from your point of view, ain't it."

"Leave him alone, you animal," Margaret hissed at him. "Leave him in peace."

The soldier shrugged and moved away, continuing his macabre trade of burying the bodies, seemingly with no thought to the fact that they had once been people.

In the darkness, Margaret sat, holding Joseph's icy corpse close, aware that she herself was growing cold as the grave. The bullet had entered the left cheek, just below his eye, and consequently that side of his face had been badly damaged. But she sat pressing the right

384

side of him to her, feeling her heart grow heavy as the flesh which she held so tightly.

As dawn came up, she knew what she had to do. Scratching at the earth with her bare hands, she started to dig a grave for Joseph Warren. Another soldier, taking her for an army wife, helped her and soon they had a hole big enough to put him in. Looking into its depths Margaret saw that another body lay within, a country fellow wearing a farmer's frock.

"You're going to have company, my darling," she whispered as, without ceremony, the soldier tipped the poor, sad corpse, wearing nothing but his linen drawers, into the dark hole.

"Wait one second, please," she called out, and the soldier stopped his shovelling of earth and stood silently while she dropped a brooch, the only jewellery she was wearing, into the place where Joseph lay.

Then she watched as slowly he disappeared from view beneath the rich soil of New England, he and the farmer side by side, forever joined in the earth they had died to protect.

CHAPTER
THIRTY

August, 1775

A ship suitable to take Margaret to England arrived in Boston Harbour in July, a month after the battle of Bunker Hill. It was called *Charming Nancy* and was due to carry back widowed army wives and wounded men, together with the orphans of the soldiers who had died on active service. The Governor at once booked a place for his wife and daughter on board, then plunged himself into the usual workload in order to avoid Margaret as much as possible.

They had hardly spoken since the battle, she utterly silent and withdrawn, he so sickened by recent events that he could no longer make the effort to talk. For, to add to his wretchedness at the number of British casualties, the news about Sara was not good. The two doctors had examined her for an hour, removed the bullet, then had both come up with the same prognosis: the slave girl was destined to spend the rest of her life in a wheelchair. Meanwhile, her pregnancy bloomed, the coming child clearly not affected by its mother's condition.

Then one day when the Governor was feeling desperately low, Calico Joel walked back into his life. Or rather sauntered nonchalantly, finding Tom in his study.

"Where the devil have you been?" was all that Gage could say.

"Ah, *mon Gouverneur*, do you remember me telling you that I got a job in Concord working with a widow woman?"

"Yes."

"Well, I returned there after the battle to see if she needed help. She did, so I stayed."

Tom stared at him severely. "I suppose that it did not occur to you that I was desperately worried. I saw you ride off but never saw you return. I thought you had been killed."

"Then why worry about me?" Calico Joel asked simply. "I would merely have gone to join my ancestors. What is the harm in that?"

Tom stared at him, too tired to argue, and the Indian immediately sensed his mood. "You have problems, my Governor?"

"A million," came the reply.

"Tell me of them."

"Let me get myself a drink first. Would you like one?"

Calico Joel shook his head. "You save it for yourself. I hear that food and water are short in Boston."

"They are indeed. We'll all lose weight at this rate."

"Perhaps that will be a good thing for some. Now, tell me what ails you."

Suddenly it was refreshing to speak to this impartial man to whom Tom would trust his life. But even though he had decided to censor what he said, the Governor found himself pouring out the whole story,

from Margaret's betrayal just before Lexington and Concord, to his impregnating Sara and the ghastly fate that had befallen her subsequently.

Calico Joel sat silently for several minutes, during which time Tom finished his drink and poured himself another. Then he spoke.

"Do you not think, *mon Gouverneur*, that you and Margaret have betrayed each other? And might not these acts of betrayal cancel one another out?"

"What do you mean?"

"What I say. It seems to me that both of you are at fault so why not forgive and start again?"

The Governor sighed. "You forget, Joel, that I must take Sara and her child into consideration. She is totally my responsibility. Soon they both will be."

"And Mrs. Gage would not overlook this fall from grace?"

Tom gave a short bitter laugh. "What a hope. She hates me enough as it is. If she found out the truth she would leave me for good."

"But she is leaving you anyway."

"I'm sending her back to England to get away from the situation. Eventually I hope to join her."

Calico Joel said nothing, merely nodding his head.

"Joel, will you visit Sara? She needs all the friends she can get," the Governor asked suddenly.

"I shall call on her today."

"Thank you. Tell her that I am ordering a bath chair to be especially made and that it will add greatly to her comfort."

"Yes, *mon Gouverneur*. I shall tell her."

On his way out, Calico Joel met Margaret coming through the front door. She had lost some weight, he thought, and was terribly pale. Under his breath he uttered an Indian prayer for the happiness of her marriage. Visibly, he bowed his head.

She looked at him as though she did not know him, then recognition dawned in her eyes.

"Oh Joel, how are you?"

"I am in good health, Madame. Are you also fine?"

"I am going back to England with Charlotte soon."

"That is as well," he answered. Then he bowed again and left the house.

In August, fully loaded, *Charming Nancy* sailed out of Boston. Tom had gone to the harbour with several other officers to see Margaret off. He had also been joined by Lord Rupert Germain who stood pale and quite grey about the hair, defying fashion and not wearing a wig as he did.

Margaret was in black, as she had been quite frequently since Bunker Hill, Tom noticed, almost as if she had lost someone in the conflict.

Stooping he picked little Charlotte up in his arms, thinking what a delightful child his baby had grown into. Then realised with a jolt that she was not destined to be the last of his children. That Sara, entirely paralysed yet still, despite everything, possessing that strange haunting beauty, was due to give birth in January. Guiltily, he looked at her as Margaret spoke to him.

"Goodbye, Tom. I wish you well."

She could have been addressing a stranger he thought. He made one last ditch attempt to behave like a husband.

"Goodbye, Margaret. I shall return to England as soon as we've sorted out these rebellious colonists."

She gave a twisted smile. "Is that how you think of them? But then it was ever thus. You have taken on a formidable enemy, my dear, as one day you will come to realise."

"I do realise it," he answered angrily. "I shouldn't have used that phrase to you who, after all, believes in everything they do."

"Yes, I am an American," she said with dignity, "and of that I am proud. Come Charlotte." And taking the child from his arms, she set her on her feet, turned, and made her way onto the gangplank.

"Margaret," called Tom in a sudden panic, beginning to pursue her on board.

She turned and gave him a look that he would never forget, because he saw in it that he had lost her, that she no longer cared whether he lived or died. She stared at him for almost a minute without speaking, then turned on her heel and slowly continued on her way aboard ship, the child trotting along beside her. Tom also turned, and in that turn knew that the future no longer contained the woman he had once loved with so much warmth and passion.

It was Rupert Germain who sensed that something was wrong. Tom found himself thinking that it would be, that of all the people in the world that he would prefer

390

not to know, it was poor Rupert who won. Yet one couldn't help but pity him. He had lost his glorious home, and his newspaper business had collapsed round his ears. Indeed if it weren't for the fact that he was enormously wealthy, one could regard him as practically destitute.

"Well, she's gone," he said, as the ship slipped its moorings, the band played and those who were capable of standing waved from the rail.

Tom ran his eye over the vessel, seeing that his daughter and her nurse were waving enthusiastically but that Margaret had remained below. He raised his arm in response and waved to the child for a good while, Lord Percy and Rupert joining him. Then, when *Charming Nancy* was well out to sea, he turned, feeling suddenly hopeless.

"Would you gentlemen care to join me for dinner?" he asked. Somewhat to his chagrin, Hugh said, "I'm sorry, Sir, I have to get back," but Rupert answered, "That would be delightful. Thank you very much."

"Shall we say six o'clock? I have some work to do beforehand."

"Thank you. I'll bring a bottle of very good wine that I managed to rescue from my cellar before I left."

"That would be splendid. Thanks."

Despite the fact that they had fallen out most bitterly, despite the fact that he was sleeping with another woman, the audible silence that had descended over Province House was almost tangible. It hit the Governor as soon as he came through the front door and enveloped him as he walked up the stairs and

entered what had once been his bedroom. The essence of Margaret was everywhere, filling his senses with the strange, alluring perfume that she always wore.

He stopped dead in his tracks for a moment, wondering how he could have let things come to such a miserable condition. Stuck in a hell-hole of a town, with no option that he could see other than to engage in an all-out war with these wretched colonists. And to compound his felony, he had managed to impregnate one of his slaves, who had paralysed herself whilst saving his wretched and undeserving life.

"Oh, fuck everything!" said the Governor loudly, and took a swiping kick at a low stool which sent it flying.

He sat down heavily on the bed and hung his head, feeling the tears start behind his eyes. Then he told himself not to be such a fool, that no weeping or kicking would right the situation and that he must try to make the best of it. Every instinct he had to survive manifested itself and, getting up, he went to the spare room and started to move his personal belongings back into the main bedroom. At least he would be in a comfortable bed from now on. And this set his thought stream onto Sara, and he determined to go and see her this very night.

At six o'clock, shaved and washed and in dress uniform, he went downstairs to find that Lord Rupert had already arrived, and was sitting in the library sipping a sherry. Judging by the brightness of his cheeks in an otherwise pallid face, Tom took a guess that the young man had been at the bottle ever since he had last seen him a few hours ago.

"My dear Sir," he said, rising as the Governor entered the room. "What a pleasure. At least we can still snatch at some vestige of civilisation in the midst of all this turmoil."

"Yes, indeed," Tom answered, somewhat over-heartily, thinking to himself that he ought to try and not drink a lot.

"A sherry, Sir?" asked Rupert brightly, as if he were the host.

"Thank you." And the Governor sat down.

Rupert took a chair opposite his, drawing it fractionally closer. "Well, it's farewell to Mrs. Gage," he said. Then without waiting for a reply continued, "Tell me your emotions as you saw the ship set sail."

"I was sorry to see my wife and daughter leave," Tom said carefully, "but it was better for them that they did."

"Quite so. And now you're going to be alone in Province House."

"Hardly that. There are the slaves in residence for a start. And to add to that this is also military headquarters."

"Indeed, yes," said Rupert, downing his drink and pouring himself another one without first obtaining permission. "But it occurs to me that you might be lonely. That you might crave some company occasionally."

Tom had a sudden dread feeling that he knew where this conversation was heading. Rupert was going to offer himself as a lodger. A terrible thought. Fond of the man as he was, he had no wish to have him under his roof.

"I have enough companionship, Rupert, truly. Quite honestly, when they are all gone, I am perfectly content with my own company."

"But how do you know that? You haven't been on your own so far."

"Margaret and I lived reasonably separate lives. A situation forced on us by circumstance. I know that we appeared as a couple before the world. But, believe me, we saw little of each other."

At that moment, Robin appeared. "Dinner is served, Excellency."

"Very good," Tom answered, thinking that the interruption had indeed been fortuitous. "Shall we go in?"

Throughout the meal, of which Rupert ate little, a feeling of tension began to build, though why the Governor had no idea. Rupert drank copiously, Tom hardly at all. And the more he drank, the more he talked: about life, literature, anything but the realities of the situation in which they were all currently involved. The Governor found himself surreptitiously drawing his watch from within his coat and examining it, wishing to heavens that Rupert would go home and sleep it off. But almost as if he were compelled to do so, Lord Rupert joined Tom in the library for port.

"Do you mind if I take off my coat?" he asked, and promptly removed it without consent.

Tom stared at him, then gave an obvious yawn. "Don't think me rude, old fellow, but I really must be making a move to bed. It's been a long day."

There was a long pause, then Rupert said quietly, "Would you like me to come with you?"

Tom answered rather stupidly, "What?"

At this Rupert flung himself out of his chair, landing on his knees at the Governor's feet. "Take me to bed with you. Please. You know it's what I want." Then, reaching up, he pulled Tom's face down and kissed him as passionately as any woman.

Even while he was thinking what he should do, part of the Governor's brain told him that to knock Rupert senseless would be to lose a good and useful ally. Yet his instinct was to throw him as far away as he possibly could. Denying this, he raised his hands and gently but firmly dislodged Rupert from his fervent embrace.

"My friend," he said, "I have a woman who means a great deal to me."

The tears which had been inevitable, now burst forth in a torrent. "I'm sorry," Rupert gasped. "I'm so sorry. It was the drink talking."

"No," answered Tom, rising from his chair and gently placing Rupert back in his, "I imagine it was your feelings which spoke. But, my dear old chap, I am not that way inclined. I am not interested in that form of sex. As I told you, I have fallen in love with a woman who is currently expecting my child."

Rupert sobbed uncontrollably. "Forgive me, please. Everything has been too much to bear recently."

"I know, I know," Tom answered soothingly. "Now, you collect yourself together, and I'll get Andrew to take you home."

"I can't apologise enough."

"Think nothing of it."

Rupert wiped his eyes with a white handkerchief. "Tom . . ."

"Yes?"

"I may as well say it, now that the truth is out. I love you. I have always loved you, right from the time we met in that stagecoach going to New York. Of course I've had other affairs; I am human after all, even though it is your idea of corruption. But know that I would do anything for you. Anything at all. You have only to ask."

Despite the memory of the kiss, which still burnt his lips with a strange and cruel sting, Tom was touched by what he had just heard.

"Thank you. I might do that one day."

Rupert's expression became earnest. "I just wish you would, Tom. I await the moment."

"Now, are you ready to leave? I really need to go to bed — alone."

"Of course." Rupert stood up, tottering slightly.

Tom rang a bell. "Tell Andrew to harness up the chaise. Lord Rupert is going home."

Robin ran his eyes over Rupert's dishevelled figure. "Yassir."

"Straight away, Robin."

"Yassir, Master Governor. Immediately."

It was too late to see Sara, Tom thought, looking at his watch. Feeling more disturbed by Rupert's advances than he cared to admit, he climbed up to the master bedroom and got into the big bed. Margaret's perfume had pervaded the bedcover, and the Governor, closing

his eyes, tried to picture her as she settled down in her small cabin for the night. He prayed then that she and Charlotte would get back to England safely, that the *Charming Nancy* would not run into any difficulties on her perilous voyage across the seas. Then he fell asleep and dreamed that he had welcomed Rupert's kisses and that the outcome of the evening had been different indeed.

CHAPTER
THIRTY-ONE

August, 1775

It was the sound of Sara's laughter that struck Tom to the heart as he approached the little house at the end of the alley. He thought that it had been a while since he had heard her laugh like that, quite wild and free and full of fun. The very noise made him want to join in, and he knocked at her door feeling more hopeful than he had for a long time.

It was answered by Calico Joel, and over his shoulder Tom could glimpse Sara sitting in her bath chair, which had been custom-built by one of the few master carpenters left in Boston. This man had had the thought of putting wheels at the side so that the occupant could move themselves around. And this was what Sara had been doing — in fact still was — as the front door opened and Tom looked inside.

She turned her head on hearing him. "Oh, Tom, look! I'm mobile. I can wheel myself about."

"Sara, how wonderful. When did the chair arrive?"

"Three days ago. I been practising."

"I'm so pleased. I shall go and pay the carpenter straight away."

Her face fell as she misunderstood. "Oh, don't go so soon. I ain't seen nothing of you."

"My darling, I'm not going now. I can stay for an hour, I promise you."

It was August, 1775, six weeks after the debacle of Bunker Hill, and Gage was now deep in conference with his fellow officers about the advisability of leaving Boston and setting up military headquarters in New York. It seemed to him to be the only proper base from which to re-establish British power in the Colonies, and most of the others agreed. However, they had decided to ask the Cabinet in London for permission to put the scheme into action. So he had written to the Earl of Dartmouth and was currently awaiting a reply.

But now he was with Sara, and she was laughing again, and the world felt a happier place for a brief while.

He took her hand and said, "How have you been, sweetheart?"

"I've been well, Sir. And the child is getting bigger. Feel it now. It's moving."

Tom put his hand on her abdomen and beneath it felt the rise and fall of an independent life. He couldn't help himself but smile with pure pleasure.

"It pleases you, doesn't it? Why, when you have other children?"

"Because this is yours and mine. We made him — or her. I hope it looks like you, not me, incidentally"

She pulled a face at him and looked round to see whether Calico Joel was listening. But the scout had gone, leaving the house as silently as ever, moving quietly as a shadow. Seeing that they were alone, Tom

leaned over and kissed her. She put her arms round his neck and kissed him in return.

"Oh Sara, I've missed you so much," the Governor said quietly.

"I hate it when you don't come to see me."

"Listen, there's a plan afoot to move headquarters to New York. If so, I shall take you with me. I want to be with you when the child is born. Whatever happens, we mustn't be separated."

Sara smiled. "And will you introduce me to your fellow officers?" Then before he could answer, said, "I wouldn't expect you to. I come from a humble background and am more than aware of it. But I'll happily go with you. What life would I have without you?"

For answer, he picked her up and carried her to the bed and lay down beside her.

"I could sleep," he said.

"Then why don't you?"

"Because you're lying next to me," he answered, and kicked off his boots.

It was as it always was between them, fiercely sweet and tender. Tom did his best not to hurt the girl but she, moving as best she could, would not allow him to hold back. So instead he plunged into a world of beauty and ecstasy, and by controlling himself as best he could, brought Sara to completion just before he came himself.

Afterwards they lay close together, staring at one another, sleeping a little, laughing as he traced the lines of her beautiful face with his forefinger.

"I love you," he said.

"What about Mrs. Gage? Did you love her?"

"I did, certainly."

"And now?"

"Despite all she did, I am still fond of her."

"What did she do, Tom?"

"Something bad which I prefer to keep to myself."

"Very good, Master."

Tom looked at her suspiciously but knew from her smile that she was teasing him.

"What shall we call the child?" she asked. "Thomas?"

"No, I have a son of that name. Besides, it may be a girl."

"So can I choose?"

"Of course you can, sweetheart."

"Then I shall call him Jasper for my father, or Jemima for my mother, if you think those names suitable."

"They are beautiful names, both of them."

"Then it is settled," said Sara, and slept in Tom Gage's arms.

Ever since he had written to London to tell them of the massacre of British troops at Bunker Hill, he had, deep within himself, felt the strong conviction that the Cabinet would take punitive measures against him. The more he thought about it the more sure Tom became. Yet he knew that his conscience was clear. That he had done his best in an ever-worsening situation. Yet he wondered now whether his reports to London had been too honest. He had told them fairly and squarely of the

dire losses his army had suffered, had urged the Cabinet to send out additional troops, and implied that the major reason for his lack of achievement in Boston was London's constant ignoring of his warnings. He had played straight with them. None the less, the Governor feared the worst.

Meanwhile, the food situation grew worse, fresh meat being exceedingly scarce and reserved for the wounded. The poor diet and the over-crowding led to disease spreading — and also to Gage's unpopularity amongst the rank and file. No man could have been more wretched or unhappy with his life than Tom was at this time. If it hadn't been for the fact of Sara and her coming child, he might seriously have considered shooting himself.

He discussed the situation with the Earl, one of the few people who remained loyal to him.

"I think my time is drawing to a close, Hugh."

"What do you mean, Sir?"

"I believe I am going to be recalled to England. They need a scapegoat to lay the blame upon, and I am the obvious target."

"But they can't do that."

"Oh yes, they can. Mark my words, when the next boat from home arrives, it will bear my orders to return."

Hugh had given Tom one of his sideways glances. "I hope you are wrong, Sir."

"Wait and see," the Governor answered with an air of finality.

402

Then, at the end of September, his worst nightmare became reality. On the 26th, HMS *Scarborough* sailed into Boston harbour with sealed orders for Gage. They were that he should return to London as promptly as possible. Opening the letter alone in his study, the Governor put his head in his hands. The axe had fallen just as he had known it would.

He felt at that moment that he had two alternatives: to get blindingly drunk or go to see Sara and hear her opinion of the matter. He chose the latter and going to the stables, put the horse that pulled the chaise into the traces. Driving through the town, realising that soon this would be the last time he would see the place, Tom felt close to tears.

Tonight the slave girl had a lovely bloom about her face. She was in the fifth month of her pregnancy and the Governor had to admit that the state became her. He thought that he had never seen her look more attractive and wondered, yet again, about the girl's ancestry. Could her grandmother have been of noble birth by any chance? A high-born creature forced into a life of prostitution in order to eat.

Staring at her, he said, "I have never seen you more beautiful."

She sighed. "Even in my wheelchair?"

"Even in that. Sweetheart, do you detest the thing?"

"Yes, I do. But Calico Joel is trying to make me walk again, an ancient cure used by the Indians. So maybe I will some day."

It was heart-rending to see her lovely face so earnest and sincere when Tom knew full well that such a thing

was not possible. Yet he had a certain faith in the Indian's powers. But now the orders from London meant that she was going to be deprived of that help, that is if she agreed to go with him to England.

"I see. But listen to me. I have been ordered back to England, and I shall be leaving in the next few days. Sara, I want you to accompany me. I will set you up in a house in London, and I can spend as much time with you as possible. You said you would go to New York but now that has all changed. Sweetheart, I am asking you to come with me and live as my mistress."

She stared at him. "Oh Tom, is what you are saying true?"

"Perfectly. I received my orders today. My time here is up."

"But how can I go with you?"

"Very easily. We shall board a ship and sail away together."

"I didn't mean that. I meant how can I leave my native land?"

Tom's highly charged emotional state suddenly exploded. "You call this place that? Your native land! What have the Colonies done for you or for your parents? You were born a slave, as was your father. Your mother became a plantation child against her will. You owe the place nothing. Nothing at all."

"But Tom, I was born in this country. I know nothing else. I am a Yankee when all is said and done."

"A Yankee, a colonist!" he repeated bitterly. "Oh, my girl, how can you be so naive?"

"Because it is true," she answered with dignity. "I love you, but I also honour my country. And because of that honour I must refuse your invitation to accompany you to London. I shall stay here and let my child be born an American."

"Oh, Sara. I'm begging you. Come with me, please."

"No, my friend. I knew that one day we would have to part, and now that day has come. I shall write to you — my writing is much better, thanks to your efforts — and tell you all about the baby. But go with you, I cannot."

The Governor turned away from her and wept bitterly, feeling that her rejection of him was personal. Then her arms came out and folded themselves round his waist.

"Oh, Sir, please don't cry. I truly want to come with you, but I just can't. Surely you understand."

With a mighty effort, Tom controlled himself, wiping his eyes and blowing his nose before turning to face her.

"Sara, I admire your loyalty but, believe me, it is false. I am offering you the chance of a lifetime but you refuse it. So you leave me with no alternative. I shall depart alone. But I will make every effort to see that you are cared for in my absence."

It was her turn to cry. "Oh, Master Governor, you are so kind and good. I cannot bear it that you are going to leave me."

"Then come with me."

She shook her head dumbly. "Don't ask it of me."

"Very well. You have made your choice. I shall come and see you once more before I go. Goodbye, Sara."

And with that he turned on his heel and walked out into the night, all feeling dying inside him.

CHAPTER
THIRTY-TWO

October, 1775

Quietly, without complaining, Gage set himself the task of packing up. All his papers were placed in white pine boxes, his personal goods in chests, his private effects in trunks. He conferred with Sir William Howe, the man who had led the forces at Bunker Hill, who was to replace him, and gave him as much instruction as he thought wise. Then, before he left, he sent for Lord Rupert Germain, who had been hiding away ever since the night when he had confessed his love. However, he need not have been afraid for Tom held out his hand as soon as Rupert entered the room.

"My dear boy, how have you been keeping?"

"Tom. Look, Sir, can we forget the last time I was here? I was drunk and spoke out of turn."

The Governor shook his head. "I don't want to forget it. Not because I share your inclinations, though I do not belittle you for having them. That is a matter entirely up to you. No, it was something you said that night that interests me."

Rupert swallowed hard. "And what was that, Sir?"

"You said you loved me and would do anything for me. Or words to that effect at least."

"Yes, it's true enough. I do care for you — very deeply — and I always will."

"Then in that case I am going to ask you to do me an enormous favour."

"Name it."

"I want you to look after my mistress when I have gone."

It was said so matter-of-factly that Rupert was quite literally winded and sat down in a nearby chair, breathing hard.

The Governor smiled, a rare thing for him at the present time. "I see I have shocked you."

"No, no. It's just that I was expecting something else."

"What?"

"I'm not sure. But certainly not that. You know I am not a ladies' man."

Tom actually laughed, though it sounded rather hollow. "I did not mean 'look after' in that sense. I meant literally. You see, the girl is a cripple."

Rupert looked horrified. "Good God, I imagined that you had fallen in love with somebody perfect. A cripple, you say."

"Yes," Tom answered somewhat irritably, "she had an accident — saving my life, for what it's worth." And he explained how Sara had jumped from her window onto a gunman whose bullet had entered her spine, damaging it irretrievably. "She believes that Calico Joel might be able to cure her. And while she has faith in that who am I to disillusion her?"

"And you say you have had a special bath chair made for her?"

"Yes, she can wheel herself around. But Rupert, she is perfect in every other respect. She is the most beautiful girl I have ever seen. She will appeal to you in that regard I feel certain."

"I can hardly wait to meet her," Rupert replied without enthusiasm.

Tom ignored it. "That can be arranged, and soon at that. But there is one other thing you need to know. She is a half-caste. You see, I fell in love with one of my slaves."

Rupert looked sick, then he said, "And I always thought you a pillar of respectability. Good God, it shows how wrong one can be."

Tom stared at him seriously. "Who are any of us to criticise the actions of others? You, of all people, should be aware of that? The most respectable person — to use one of your words — can be struck by the beauty of another and act completely out of character. I first went to Sara at a time when I thought my world was ending. And in a way it was. Since that time, I have loved her in many guises — as a father as well as a lover. Now she is to present the world with our child, and I am determined that she and the baby will prosper. I asked her to return to England with me but she refused. And do you know why?"

"No, I don't."

"Because she was born in the Colonies and says she owes them loyalty. Funnily enough, Margaret said very much the same thing to me. Can you understand it?"

"Yes, in a way."

"What do you mean?"

"When I first came out here — do you remember that Christmas, so long ago? — I was filled with enthusiasm for the place, longing to make it my home and make something of myself at the same time."

"And now?"

"Now I'm sickened by the fighting and the slaughter. But because I love you, Thomas Gage, I will stay and see your child safely into the world, and ensure that no harm comes to your woman."

"Do you promise me that?"

"I swear it," answered Rupert Germain, and laid his hand on his heart.

On the night of October 9th, the Governor paid his last visit to Sara. Earlier in the day, he and Rupert had called on her in order that she and her new protector might meet. On this occasion, she was wearing a loose-fitting gown above an overskirt of blue caught up at the sides and back. Round her neck she wore a delightful neck ruffle that Tom had bought her. The Governor, who felt his heart shattering at the sight of her, found he could hardly speak.

"Sara, this is Lord Rupert Germain. He has promised me that he will look after you when I have gone."

She had given him one of her direct glances. "How dee do, Sir. Are you sure that you wish this?"

"Of course I do, Madam. Consider me at your disposal."

"You're very kind. But I promise not to interfere with your daily life. What do you do for a livelihood, Lord Rupert?"

"Nothing. Nothing at all. I used to run a newspaper, but my views were not acceptable to the majority."

"Don't you get a little bored, Sir?"

"Sometimes I do."

"Well, we'll have to try and think of something to occupy your mind."

Rupert gave a cynical smile. "I await your comments with pleasure."

Later, after he had gone, Sara said, "Are you sure he wants to look after me?"

"I'm positive, sweetheart. Why do you ask?"

"I think he might have preferred it had I been a boy."

Tom tweaked her nose. "You're not supposed to know about such things. But take it from me, he has a good nature, and he has given me his word that he will care for you and the child. I also leave you in the hands of Calico Joel, as long as he is around that is."

Sara had sighed. "I am sad that you are going, Sir."

"Nonsense. I'll be back in the spring."

For this was the lie that everyone was pretending was the truth. That Tom's return to England was only a temporary measure and that he would return early next year to resume his old role.

"I don't think you will. I don't think I shall ever see you again."

"No," Tom answered heavily. "I don't suppose you will. It's not too late to change your mind, you know. I can still get you a passage. Oh Sara, please come."

She shook her head but said nothing. And with that gesture Tom Gage, the man who had done his best in

conditions of overwhelming difficulty, knew that he had lost her and that her homeland, America, had won.

He spent the night with her. Then in the morning he rose, dressed, went to the place where he had tethered his horse, and mounted. Sara had wheeled herself into the doorway, and Tom could see that she was crying. But he hardened his heart. He had given her every opportunity to accompany him but she had rejected him. Yet in reality this was the only way in which he could drag himself away. He wheeled his mettlesome mount.

"Goodbye, Sara."

"Goodbye, Master Governor."

"Not for much longer."

"You will always be the Governor to me," she answered simply, before vanishing into the house.

The night before he sailed, Tom dined with Hugh Percy. The Earl wore his glasses to try to hide the fact that he had wept because of the injustice that had been done to his commander. For Percy had to remain in the Colonies, which he had come to dislike, while Tom had to go and face the music alone. Earlier that day, the Governor had, in full public gaze, received his last salute as supreme commander, and Sir William Howe had been sworn in. All this in front of the men who had served with him, the Earl being one of them.

"It's a sorry state of affairs," he said eventually.

"My departure you mean?"

"Yes, Sir. I feel that the blame for everything that has happened in this benighted spot is going to be laid on your shoulders."

The ex-Governor sighed. "You're probably right. They will blame me for making all the wrong decisions."

"Wrong!" said the Earl bitterly. "What else could you have done, for God's sake? The fault lies with them for not giving clearer instructions. But they need a scapegoat, and you are going to be it, I fear."

Tom poured two glasses of port. "There's another minor problem as well."

"Sir?"

"My wife and I were not getting along too well towards the end of her stay . . ."

Hugh grimaced, knowing perfectly well that she had betrayed him.

". . . and I have to see her and try to sort things out."

And a devil of a job that's going to be, thought the Earl, with your beautiful black slave girl occupying your thoughts. But he merely smiled and said, "Oh, I am sure you will, Sir. In time."

"Well, there's no point in worrying about it. It won't improve the situation."

Hugh Percy raised his glass. "I would like to propose a toast to you, Sir. Here's health to the finest commander under whom I've served."

"Do you mean that?" asked Tom in a low voice.

"With everything I stand for."

"God bless you, Hugh."

"Stand firm, Sir. When they unleash their spleen, stand firm."

"I'll do my best," General Gage answered simply.

The next morning was a sombre occasion in Province House. Having slept a few hours, Tom got up and put on his uniform, then, refusing breakfast, said goodbye to the staff. Robin, who had seen and who knew so much, bowed before him.

"It's going to be sad being without you, Governor."

Tom smiled. "I'm not the Governor any more, Tom. That's Sir William Howe's title now."

"You'll always be Governor to me, Sir," answered the black man, echoing the words that Sara had said to him.

Andrew, smart as paint, stood before him, buttons shining. "I'll drive you to the harbour, Sir."

"No thanks, I'd rather walk. Goodbye my friend. You've been an excellent coachman."

Andrew bowed. "Thank you for giving me the opportunity, Sir." Then he bowed again, grinned half-heartedly, and turned away, wiping his eyes.

Outside the guards on duty came to the salute on seeing Tom. He returned it with a half-smile, then walked down the street, carrying his overnight bag in his hand.

As he went he looked about him, taking in every detail, knowing that this would be the last time he would ever set eyes on the place. Wooden houses stood neatly side by side, women gossiped on street corners, men went about their business — that is, if they had

any. But everywhere there was a feeling of unity, of being at one against the common enemy.

Gage turned a corner and went down Milk Street, listening to the hooves of horses clattering over cobbles, the rattle of carts and carriages, above all the constant cry of gulls. And then he saw the sea stretched like a vast blue piece of material before him, and he felt his heart leap. He must cross that autumn ocean to get back to all the problems that would face him, and there were many indeed.

Just for a moment, a crazy moment, he thought of going back, of fetching Sara and escaping with her into the open countryside and setting up as a farmer, God help him. Then he realised that there was no point, that he could never escape from all the terrible tasks that lay ahead. That he must go forward.

His brother-in-law, Stephen Kemble, was waiting with a party of others to say farewell. Gage went through the ritual, but all the time he spoke to them, his eyes scanned the small crowd that had gathered in silence to see him go.

"Well, give my regards to . . ."

But he no longer heard a word that Stephen said. For there, in the front of the group that had parted to let them through, was Sara, looking exquisite, sitting in her wheelchair like a queen, being pushed by Rupert Germain. Gage couldn't help himself. In public, and not giving a damn who saw, he waved to them.

"Goodbye," he called over the void that separated them.

"Goodbye," they called back, their voices in unison.

Tom decided, looking at them, that they made a perfect pair, Rupert's pale good looks enhancing Sara's dark loveliness. If only things were different, he thought.

The military band that had gathered at the quayside struck up "The Lilies of France", and Gage turned towards the gangplank. Then, halfway up, he wheeled round for a last look at Sara. She was waving, as was Rupert. Aware that he would never see her again, Tom blew her a kiss, then turned and walked slowly onwards.

PART THREE — MRS.GAGE

CHAPTER
THIRTY-THREE

August, 1775

She turned and walked up the gangplank, her back stiff and unyielding. Beside her she felt little Charlotte wheel round to look at her Papa, but Margaret refused to do likewise, even though she was longing to get one last glimpse of the country in which she had been born and raised. Longed, indeed, to take one final glance at the land where she had held her lover, Joseph Warren, so tightly through that hot, breathless night at Breed's Hill. But Margaret marched on unrelenting to where Captain Robertson stood waiting to greet her.

"Mrs. Gage, welcome aboard. I hope your journey will be as pleasant as possible."

"Thank you, Captain. I wonder if you would mind showing me to my cabin straight away. I feel a little unwell."

That was an expedient lie but would cover the fact that she had no intention of standing at the ship's rail and waving to those left behind.

He looked slightly startled but was too polite to comment. "Of course, Madam. If you would care to follow me."

It was a small place, little more than an oversized cupboard, Charlotte and the nursemaid sharing an equally tiny closet next door. Thankfully the Captain

and officers had their quarters close at hand, so at least they would be well protected. But none of this was in Margaret's mind as she closed the door and sat down on the bunk, feeling utterly desolate. Everything she had ever known or loved was being left behind in America. She was reaping the reward for her traitorous act in full.

Her heartbeat suddenly began to speed up and thump irregularly, frightening her somewhat. She lay flat, fighting to breath normally, wondering what was the matter with her. Then came the huge clanking as the ship weighed anchor and slowly, very slowly, she felt movement. So they were off. She sat upright, torn about going back on deck, suddenly wanting to see Tom again and give him a final wave, but her heart was beating wildly, and her spirits were too low. Margaret lay down on the bunk again and very quietly started to cry.

It was an agonising journey, the ship being shared by the wounded and maimed, victims of the terrible conflicts, to say nothing of sixty army widows and orphans. Below deck, the air was heavy with the smell of death and blood, suffocatingly so. The only relief to be had was on deck, breathing in the salt sea breezes. Yet Margaret, afraid of getting in the way, spent the time when Charlotte was with her nurse, sitting in the dining room, reading or, more frequently, staring out of the window at the vast expanse of ocean which every day increased the distance between herself and her mother country.

Burials at sea became almost a daily occurrence as the injured succumbed to their wounds. Margaret watched several, her heart wrenching as she thought of the body shooting down to the dark mysterious depths of the sea; human beings, once jolly babies, becoming food for the fishes. She wept at the first few but gradually got used to the macabre occasions and felt only a sense of wretchedness that so many had had to die in the horrible fighting over the future of the Colonies.

Eventually land was sighted, and Margaret, going on deck, was informed that it was the coast of Cornwall. Charlotte stood beside her, her face flushed with excitement.

"Is that England, Mama?"

"Yes, my dear. That was where you were born."

The child had stared, round-eyed, and for no reason Margaret's heart had started lurching again, a horrible feeling which she loathed because it made her afraid. But she had forced herself to breathe normally for the sake of her daughter and had even managed to laugh a little as the coastline drew ever nearer. But for all that, she was pleased to get back to her cabin and sit very still until the spasm passed.

The ship, which had suffered some storm damage at sea, put into Plymouth for a new mainmast and some of the walking wounded had gone ashore. Perhaps they had not realised what scarecrows they actually looked, so malnourished that their clothes flapped about them, or that their injuries would be so repellant to gaze on,

but they soon boarded the vessel again, upset by the hostile reception they had been given by the locals.

Eventually though, the ship had docked in London, sailing up the wild reaches of the Thames, and disembarkation had taken place. The wounded had been removed, bound for the hospital in Chelsea, the widows had been put ashore to fend for themselves as best they could, the orphans had been rounded up and taken to the various poorhouses. Margaret, watching the disconsolate little creatures, frightened and pale, some of them visibly shaking, had clutched Charlotte close to her and thanked God that her daughter had been born to a different strata of life.

She had decided then and there to head for Firle Place, the seat of Viscount Gage. Catching a post-chaise, she and her small entourage had been dropped at Lewes and had no alternative but to make the rest of the journey by pony and trap, the only small reward being the expression on the Viscountess's face when they had been announced and entered the room in which she sat embroidering.

"My dear!" she exclaimed breathlessly. "Oh, my dear. I knew of course that you were returning but had no idea when. How wonderful to see you."

So Tom had not told Elizabeth of his wife's guilt. Somewhat relieved, Margaret had sat down and surveyed her sister-in-law.

She was still very beautiful in the black-haired clever way that people of Jewish blood are. Elizabeth's grandfather, Rowland Gideon, had been a Portuguese Jew who had migrated to England at the end of the

seventeenth century. His son, Sampson Gideon, a financial genius of considerable note, had made a fortune in the South Sea Bubble and kept it in the crash which followed. He had married an English-woman and fathered three children, all of whom had been brought up as Christians. One of these, Elizabeth Gideon, had attracted the attention of Tom Gage's brother, not only for her great good looks but also for the dowry which she had brought to the marriage. The wedding had taken place shortly after they met, and it had, all things considered, been an extremely happy union.

Now Elizabeth gasped once more and said, "Of course you must stay with us until your plans are formulated, my dear. I shall get the guest rooms aired immediately." And she pulled a bell rope.

Having given the answering servant instructions, she sat down again.

"And how is dear Thomas? Will he be joining you, or don't you know?"

Margaret shook her head. "I can't tell you, I'm afraid. He could be out there for several more years. It depends how long the conflict takes."

Her sister-in-law raised dark eyebrows and fanned herself briefly. "You make it sound as though the colonists are ready to put up a fight. I had always considered them hideously undermanned, that is, of course, until the reports of Lexington and Concord became available in London. Did you know that the Yankees sent their account first, beating the official one by several days?"

"No, I wasn't aware of that."

"Isn't it shocking?"

But Margaret was no longer listening. In her mind she had gone back, not to those battles but to Breed's Hill, remembering how she had sat all through that hot airless night, nursing poor dead Joseph in her arms, then reburied him in the morning, putting him to lie beside the farmer in his frock.

Her eyes wandered to the landscape outside Firle Place. From where she sat, she could see great trees sweeping the lawns with pools of shadow beneath. A waterway with many kinds of fowl swimming upon it, splashed behind the gracious house. Remembering the atmosphere of Boston, where everyone lived cheek by jowl, Margaret felt that here one could draw breath in peace. It was September, 1775, and she had taken just over a month to sail home. Yet the memories she brought with her could never be forgotten.

The Viscountess was continuing to speak, and Margaret wrenched her concentration back.

"I'm sure you'll be happy here, dear girl. And just look at your little one. She seems to have settled down immediately."

They stared out of the window to where Charlotte was busy running up and down and skipping round her nursemaid, clapping her hands as she did so.

"Elizabeth, I would very much like to see my other children. Where are they at present?"

"They're all at Highmeadow, it being the vacation from school. Perhaps we should travel there in a few days and visit."

"Yes, I would like that."

The arrival of tea, carried in by countless footmen, interrupted them. But later, when Margaret had been shown to a wonderfully large room overlooking the back of the house, she flung open her window and leaned out. Before her shimmered the lake, beyond that the spreading parkland. This was paradise, a place in which one could recuperate from all the recently befallen ills. Yet she knew that a person of her nature, uprooted from her homeland, a stranger to these shores, would soon tire of such heavenly surroundings and want to be in a busier throng. She had loved her childhood home, of course, but there she had been one of the belles of New Jersey, well-connected and on every guest list. Here, she imagined, one could idle one's way to the grave. She decided that, having visited her children at Highmeadow, she would make her way to the Gage's family home in London and see what fortune the great city, of which she knew so little, might yield up at her feet.

At dinner the Viscount was charm itself but full of interminable questions about his brother, Thomas. How was he? Was he controlling the soldiers? What, in her view, should be done to bring the conflict to an end?

"The only way," said Margaret, when allowed to get a breath into the tumult, "is to send massive reinforcements to Boston. If the Government fails in this, then we will lose the war."

There was a shocked silence. "Are you serious?" asked Viscount William.

"Perfectly. The colonists are organised and tough. Further, they are inspired by love of their country. They are prepared to lay down their lives to see the nation born. A formidable task for an army to take on, wouldn't you agree?"

The Viscount absorbed what he had just heard, then said, "I suppose Tom is aware of this?"

"Oh yes, he is aware all right. He has written requesting reinforcements innumerable times, but he is given short shrift. Poor devil, I don't envy him his task."

The Viscountess cleared her throat. "My dear, we hadn't realised the affair is as critical as it is."

Margaret toyed with her spoon. "Take my word for it, the situation is terrible."

William signed to the footman who poured more wine. "And how do you like Firle Place, Margaret?"

"It's lovely, truly beautiful. I know that here I shall recover from Boston — and the journey from it — splendidly. But I've a thought to visit Park Place in the not too distant future. I know little of London as you can imagine, and I would like to learn more of it before I settle down."

William and Elizabeth exchanged a glance in which there was a certain amount of amusement.

"Of course, my dear. We had thought that you probably would. I am sure that compared with New York and Boston, London will glitter."

For some reason, Margaret found this remark fractionally irritating, but there was little she could do about it. So she just smiled and said, "I shall give you a

426

full report, of course, as soon as I have lived there a while."

But later, spending her first night for a month in a large bed in a spacious room, she found that the idea of London had got her in its grip.

"A place in which to forget everything," she whispered into the moonlight before she fell asleep.

Having spent a few days at Highmeadow, Margaret drove in the Viscount's coach towards Park Place in London, the town house of Tom Gage, bought when he had last visited the city. It had been wonderful to see her children again, but she knew as soon as she met them that the years she had spent away from them had changed the little creatures. They were polite, dutiful, made something of a fuss of her, but other than for that they were preoccupied, rapt in their own private world, totally grown away from her and treating the Viscountess as if she were their mother.

Elizabeth had given birth seven times, but each time the child had died in infancy. Therefore the pleasure of taking over the educating and bringing-up of Margaret and Thomas's progeny had been enormous. And now she had added Charlotte to the list, formally handed into her care, the Viscountess's excuse being that the country air would suit the child far better.

But Margaret had almost been relieved. The fact was that she needed to be alone in order to think. The shock of all that had happened to her in the last six months had barely started to sink in. Her betrayal of Tom, his rejection of her, her bitter-sweet love for Joseph, and

then — the cruellest cut of all — finding him dead, stripped of his clothes, on Breed's Hill. She needed, indeed she must, come to terms with all that had taken place, and there was no room for Charlotte — or indeed the others, should they have been willing to come with her — in such a tumultuous period of adjustment. With her heart thumping irregularly and her breathing barely controlled, Margaret sat in the coach heading for the legendary city.

Park Place, which she had seen briefly on her previous visit to the capital, turned out to be far finer than she remembered. Superbly situated, overlooking St. James's Palace from the second floor windows, and with Green Park a mere few paces away, Margaret went from room to room exclaiming at its stylish splendour. Then she thought of Tom, labouring in the close confines of Boston, and momentarily she was stilled, wondering what would happen to him and whether he would ever come to live in this splendid house. And, if he did, whether she would have to contend with years of icy silence like those she had endured since April. She deliberately turned her thoughts away.

At first, there was much to do, bringing the skeleton staff up to snuff and adding to their numbers. But when that was sorted out, Margaret suddenly found herself at a loose end with nothing to occupy her thoughts except memories. Determined to fight her way through them, she sat down and wrote to the Viscountess at Firle asking for a list of her friends in town and for Elizabeth's permission to call on them. When this arrived in a day or two, Margaret set off in

the small coach she had purchased, a collection of newly printed cards clasped firmly in her reticule.

She left them, as was customary, on a silver tray carried by a footman. But at one house, this golden rule was altered. She arrived at the front door at exactly the same moment as another visitor. This woman, who was of middle years and had an arresting hawkish manner, said, "Oh, my dear, you are calling on Mrs. Montagu I take it. Forgive me but I don't know your face. Are you new in town?"

"I arrived here a fortnight ago, Ma'am."

"Ah, I presume from your accent that you are from the Colonies. Do tell us about the situation there. Elizabeth will be most diverted. She is not her usual self, having so recently lost poor Edward."

The front door was opened at this point, and the formidable woman said to the footman, "Mrs. Boscawen and Mrs. . . ." She turned to Margaret.

"Gage, Margaret Gage."

"Good gracious. Are you by any chance the wife of the Governor of Massachusetts?"

"I am indeed."

"Oh, my dear, Elizabeth will be delighted to meet you." She turned to the footman. "Mrs. Boscawen and Mrs. Gage to call on Mrs. Montagu, if you please."

"Certainly, Madam. I will tell Mrs. Montagu that you are here."

After a few moments, he returned. "Will you follow me, ladies."

Hardly able to conceal her excitement that she had entered the home of Elizabeth Montagu, whose social

group was nicknamed The Blue Stockings, Margaret climbed an interesting staircase and was shown into a receiving room on the first floor.

A small woman rose to greet her visitors, a small woman of about fifty-five years with fairly unremarkable features, other than for a large nose which would have dominated her face had it not been for her eyes. For these were of an amazingly bright blue, the colour of forget-me-nots, piercingly sharp and somewhat reminiscent of Tom's. They studied Margaret with a deep and intelligent look.

"Mrs. Boscawen, how very nice to see you. And who have we here?"

"This, Ma'am, is Mrs. Gage, wife of the commander-in-chief of British forces in Boston."

"Well, well, well. So you are back in London, eh. Were you sent away for safety's sake, my dear?"

"Yes, Ma'am," Margaret lied, curtseying and dropping her gaze away from that all-seeing stare.

Mrs. Montague pealed with laughter. "Oh, say that again, do. You have such a divinely atrocious accent."

Margaret gaped at her, not quite sure how to proceed, but eventually said, "Yes, Ma'am," again, attempting to modify her tones.

Mrs. Montagu wagged a finger. "My dear, do not attempt to change the way you speak. Why, it is music to my ears to hear such a delightful drawl. If I were you, I would accentuate it when out. I assure you that you will be the centre of attention if you do. But you must excuse me. I am in poor spirits presently. My dear husband, my own sensible, plodding, kindly, generous

430

Edward has died but recently, leaving me but a pale shadow."

Margaret found herself wondering what Mrs. Montagu would be like when restored, but had not time for such deliberations for her hostess was speaking again.

"I miss him dreadfully, you know. Not that he was ever present at my meetings, preferring to sit in his study and ponder mathematical problems. Yet I miss his very absence, if you understand me."

She flashed a glance in Margaret's direction, and the Yankee saw that the great eyes were brimming with tears. The woman was as changeable as an April day and at that particular moment extremely vulnerable. Margaret felt herself warming to her.

"I know something of what you feel, Ma'am," she said. "I have lost a son recently. I understand your emotions." And I lost a lover too, she thought, in the direst circumstances possible.

"Do you?" asked Mrs. Montagu, her face brightening. "Do you really understand?"

"Absolutely."

Elizabeth was caught between weeping and laughing and decided to do both. With large fresh tears pouring down her cheeks, she simultaneously pealed with mirth.

Margaret looked at the mercurial little woman and felt that they had much in common. And if her accent amused Elizabeth, then all the better. Then a sudden memory came. A memory of her first meeting with Tom when she had laughed at his Englishness, and he had responded so light-heartedly. It had been so many years

ago that it seemed like another lifetime, yet they had been good days, very good. But Mrs. Montagu was speaking again.

"As I told you, my dear, I am still in mourning. But I am keeping up with the world for all that. I would like you to come and dine with me on Friday next. It will only be a small gathering, but my friend Sir Joshua Reynolds will be present. He is interesting, I think you will agree."

"I know little of him, Ma'am."

Mrs. Montagu turned to Mrs. Boscawen, who had been smiling serenely throughout their conversation.

"Isn't she refreshing? Where did you find her?"

"On your doorstep, my dear."

"Did you really? Fancy that. Now, Mrs. Gage, I formally invite you to attend the next meeting of The Blue Stockings."

"Why, I'd be more than delighted, Ma'am. When will that be?"

"When I decide to hold one," answered Mrs. Montagu, and wiped the tears away — though whether they were caused by sadness or mirth or a combination of the two, Margaret could not be certain.

CHAPTER
THIRTY-FOUR

September, 1775

The next morning, somewhat to Margaret's surprise, a note came from Mrs. Montagu, brought round to Park Place by a footman. In it the Blue Stocking apologised for her lack of manners on the previous day and asked if Mrs. Gage would be free to take tea with her. Margaret immediately responded in the affirmative and duly set forth that afternoon. However, just as she was about to leave the house, her heart started its irregular thumping, and she was forced to sit down for a quarter of an hour.

Used to walking round Boston, Mrs. Gage decided to go on foot and, feeling better, left the house and made her way briskly to Hill Street where Elizabeth Montagu awaited her.

"My dear Mrs. Gage, forgive my lack of courtesy. It was just that your accent amused me so much, and I felt the need to laugh. The death of my husband has cast me down low, believe me."

This was a side to the notorious Mrs. Montagu that Margaret had not expected, and she found herself staring at the little woman.

"Tell me, if you can bear to speak of it, about the passing of your little boy," Elizabeth continued.

"It was so sad because I was not with him. In fact . . ." Margaret went on in a burst of confidentiality, ". . . I have handed all my children over to my sister-in-law, Viscountess Gage, because of my husband's career."

The blue eyes became sharp. "And what of your husband? How is he?"

Margaret paused, and in that pause came sudden pangs of guilt that she should have betrayed that honest man who had tried so hard. She deliberately kept her gaze averted as she answered, "He is doing the best he can in impossible circumstances. I wouldn't have his job for a fortune."

"The talk is that he is somewhat overwhelmed."

Now Margaret did look up. "Who wouldn't be with all he has to contend with?"

The blue gaze softened. "I see that you are very fond of him, my dear. Now then, let us have tea."

The repast was brought by servants and Mrs. Montagu poured the brew. Looking at her covertly, Margaret decided that she was not as fierce as she had always believed. Indeed, the death of Elizabeth's husband had clearly shaken her badly. She wondered how Mrs. Montagu would have coped with that airless night on Breed's Hill when Joseph had lain dead in her arms. Margaret rather suspected that it would have been badly.

"About my husband," said her hostess as if unburdening herself. "He was very different from me. Altogether a serious and solid person. He never attended my soirées, you know. He preferred to read a

book or work on some problem. But he gave me absolute free rein to do as I pleased. Despite the difference in our lives, we acted in perfect harmony. Oh, I do miss him."

Margaret suddenly found herself acting entirely naturally, with no artifice or pretence. Putting down her cup, she stood up and crossed to where Mrs. Montagu was sitting. Then, crouching down, she put her arm round the other woman's shoulders and gave her a hug.

"I promise you that time heals all things," she said. "With each passing day you will recover very slightly."

Mrs. Montagu's eyes filled with tears. "Do you really think so?"

"I am certain of it," Margaret responded, taking her seat once more.

"Bless you for saying so. And bless you for comforting me. I believe you are a truly nice woman, Mrs. Gage."

"I wish I thought so too," answered Margaret softly.

The dinner party, held later that week, was nothing short of a triumph. Mrs. Gage's fine American accent together with her odd pronunciation of certain English words meant that she was the elegantly amused talk of the table. Further, she was the wife of the commander who had so disastrously ordered the troops at Concord, Lexington and Bunker Hill. In other words, her value as a guest ran high, and that night she was showered with invitations from the other people present. But it was the attitude of Sir Joshua Reynolds which most puzzled her. Fixing her with his scintillating dark eyes,

he stared at her as if he was looking into her soul. In the end, she found she could not bear such close scrutiny.

"I see you are regarding me, Sir."

"Indeed I am, Ma'am."

"And why might that be?"

"It is your very essence that intrigues me. Because you are a native of the Colonies, you lack the languid boredom of so many of your English counterparts. Why do you think I associate with the bluestockings? Because they are intelligent and can discuss things other than fashion and card play."

"I see. Have you never met anyone from the Colonies before?"

"Oh several, Madam. But none as complex as yourself."

He had given her another deep look and finally conversed with his neighbour at the table. Margaret, after thinking how very different life was in London, had turned her attention to the young man sitting on her left.

"Good evening to you, Sir."

"And good evening to you, Mrs. Gage. I was hoping you would speak to me. My name is Samuel Jenyns, son of Soame."

"How do you do, Mr. Jenyns?"

"I do a great deal better now that you are talking to me. But tell me, please, what news of your husband?"

"My husband? Why do you ask?"

"Because he is much spoken of by the beau monde."

"And what do they say of him?"

"Well, to be honest, opinion is divided. But I say that he can't be a silly Willy. After all, he married you."

She looked at him closely to see if he was deliberately insulting her, but his smile was wide and ingenuous.

"My husband is in the most difficult situation in the world," she answered with the slightest edge to her voice. "I would like to see another try to sort out the terrible state that the Colonies are in. You, for example."

"Oh, I could not do so, Ma'am. I have no military skills."

"Then it might be as well if you cease to criticise those who have."

"Touché', Mrs. Gage. I shall change the subject."

Margaret had rather deliberately turned to the man on her right. He was of a very different stamp, being small and studious, a large pincenez clasped firmly on his nose. Behind it, his eyes, pale blue and anxious, looked enormous. Margaret felt at once that he was nervous and smiled in a friendly manner. She had been introduced to him earlier but could not recall his name,

"Good evening," she said. "I am Margaret Gage."

"William Wedderburne, at your service," he responded, giving a small bow.

"Are you a close friend of Mrs. Montagu?"

"Indeed I am, Madam. I attend many meetings of The Blue Stocking Club. The people of the finest intellect foregather at such affairs."

"Indeed."

"Oh, yes," he responded enthusiastically. "Mrs. Montagu is currently in mourning, but I am certain the

437

meetings will resume soon. Tell me, Ma'am, will you be staying in town long?"

The question cut home, making Margaret realise that her future hung on a knife's edge. It was quite possible, she considered, that when Tom finally returned from the Colonies that he might well start proceedings to divorce her, and then where would she be? A lone Yankee let loose in an alien country. She tried desperately to concentrate on the conversation.

"For the time being, yes. Tell me, do you have a wife present, Sir?"

The poor fool blushed red and said, "I am not married, Madam. And you?"

"My husband is the Governor of Massachusetts and also supreme commander of the British forces in the Colonies."

"Gracious, that Gage. I had not associated the name."

"Indeed, why should you?"

"I had thought you might be one of the Sussex Gages."

"The Viscount is my brother-in-law."

Samuel Jenyns spoke up. "Mrs. Gage, I was wondering whether you might need a guide to show you the sights of London. If so, I will gladly offer my services."

William, blushing deep once more, said, "I too will be only too happy to escort you round the capital."

Margaret, looking from one earnest young face to the other, replied, "How kind of you, gentlemen."

They both gave her a gratified look, then glared at one another. And she, thinking of the youthful ages of the men in the army and of the homesteaders fighting to free their country, felt the English had much to learn about the realities of life.

After dinner, there was a game of whist, in which neither Mrs. Montagu nor Margaret joined.

"Well, my dear, did you enjoy your first encounter with my friends?" asked the hostess.

"Enormously," Margaret answered. Impulsively she put out her hand and took that of the woman sitting opposite. "It has been most kind of you to take me up like this, Mrs. Montagu."

"My pleasure entirely, Mrs. Gage. By the way, they were all very interested in you, particularly Joshua Reynolds. He whispered to me that he wanted to paint your portrait."

"Well then he shall. I would be honoured."

Mrs. Montagu's rich blue eyes — which this night had darkened to the colour of her famous Club's stockings — twinkled. "He is a dear friend but he can be a little . . . uncertain."

"What do you mean?"

"Nothing, my dear. You must judge for yourself."

And she would not be drawn further.

Going home afterwards, her reticule full of cards from people wishing her to call on them, Margaret wondered what it was about her that demanded attention. Then guessed that it was her novelty value alone that appealed, and that when that was played out she would be passed over for the next amusement.

What a strange city was London, she thought, and wondered if she would ever settle down.

"So," said Sir Joshua Reynolds, sketching her while she sat and talked to him, "you admire the works of Michelangelo and Raphael."

"I have never seen them in reality, but naturally we poor folk from the Colonies have books which we study."

"Are you being facetious, Mrs. Gage?"

"Yes, a little. I apologise."

"Please don't do so. It makes your face alter. I want to capture you just as you are."

Margaret tried to sit still, despite the thoughts running through her head. She was wondering whether Sir Joshua were married. There was no sign of a wife, but then they were in his studio where the lady was most unlikely to be present. But whether he was or not, he was quite definitely flirting with her, a fact that rather amused her. She thought of the two men who had loved her: Tom so youthful and carefree when they had first met, not weighed down as he had become with all the problems posed by her fellow countrymen; Joseph, one of those problems, yet so fresh-faced and fine, so ardent in his lovemaking, so cold and sad in death.

She must have made a little sound because Joshua said, "What's the matter?"

"Nothing. Nothing at all."

"You moved as if something had upset you. There!" He closed his sketchbook with a bang. "I have enough.

Now, when are you free to sit for me in the midst of your social hurly-burly?"

She smiled. "Next week some time, if that would suit you, Sir."

"It would suit me very well. Tell me, what are you doing this evening?"

"I had planned a quiet night at home. Why?"

"Because, Madam, if you would be willing, I would like you to accompany me to Vaux Hall Pleasure Gardens. We could travel by boat and see the lights of the place from the water. I imagine you have nothing like it in the Colonies."

"You imagine correctly."

"In that case, I await your pleasure. Will you come?"

"I would be delighted."

"Then Madam, I will call for you at seven o'clock. We can proceed to the river and hire a boat at the bankside."

"I shall be ready, Sir."

And she was, dressed very richly, her dark hair pulled back and bedecked with flowers and feathers, her face painted beautifully. Sir Joshua, however, was garbed eccentrically, wearing a great deal of red, topped by a fine wig with long curls at the back. They made a good couple, though, as they wended their way through the crowd at White Hall Stairs, Sir Joshua having hedged his bets and taken a carriage some of the way. He hired a boat with a strong oarsman, and they pulled upstream towards the celebrated pleasure gardens.

It was windy on the river, and Margaret could not help shivering a little. At once, Sir Joshua wrapped his

cloak round her, over the top of her own, and sat manfully beside her — rather closer than she wanted — challenging the elements to overcome him. But despite the cold, Margaret loved the journey, rounding the bends in the great river, seeing the lights on either bank. She thought of the great spread of water round Boston and felt then that the Colonies were as wild and savage as England was mild and gentle. Eventually, though, the lights of Vaux Hall came into view, and the boatman began to pull towards the bank.

They alighted as best they could amongst the hordes of others doing the same thing, and made their way down a walkway to an extremely unimposing entrance. Margaret felt a thrill of disappointment that anywhere should have such a dull façade, but a moment or two later could have eaten her words. For, having paid for their entrance, Joshua offered her his arm and, hastening down a dark passageway, led her out into the full blaze of the gardens, lit by a thousand lamps. Overawed, the girl from New Jersey gazed about her.

"You are impressed?" asked the painter.

"I am overwhelmed," Margaret answered. "I have never seen so many lights in one place before."

"Your words delight me, Madam. For to see you enjoying the place pleases me enormously. I am able to look at it through your eyes. Do you understand what I am saying?"

"I do perfectly."

For answer, he planted a swift kiss on her lips but so fleeting that Margaret could not have taken offence. Then he tucked her hand more securely under his arm

442

as they made their way down the Grand Walk, attracting the eyes of the passing parade.

"Why there's Sir Joshua Reynolds," whispered a woman. "But I do not know who he is with. Do you?"

They walked onward, Sir Joshua bowing to right and left to the persons who greeted him.

"You are very popular about town," Margaret commented.

"Madam, I am president of the Royal Academy, further to which I have painted the portraits of many here present. In time you will become well known too."

What was it about those words that made Margaret suddenly grow cold? she wondered.

But the great man did not notice and continued, "There's Lord George Germain. Good evening, my Lord."

At the very mention of the name Margaret's heart gave an alarming lurch, and she felt an echoing pain deep in her guts. She knew very well that Lord George, who had been at school with Tom, had developed an implacable hatred for her husband, to say nothing of his attitude to Lord Rupert. And now here she was, face to face with him. She gave a polite curtsey but said nothing.

Sir Joshua, meanwhile, was sweeping an impeccable bow before a swarthy middle-aged man, wearing a full white wig, who gave a small salute in return.

"Good evening, my friend." Lord George raised his quizzing glass. "And who have we here?"

"This, my Lord, is Mrs. Gage."

"Gage, you say? Any relation to the man in the Colonies?"

"He is my husband, Sir. I also know your brother, Lord Rupert. He and Tom are fairly close."

Lord George raised his dark brows. "Poor Rupert. I believe he has been forced to close down his newspaper. I wonder what will happen to him now."

"I imagine he will return to England," Margaret answered, trying to ignore her crazy heartbeat.

"Not the only one," said Germain. "Good evening to you, Joshua. Good evening, Ma'am." And so saying, he abruptly turned on his heel and walked away.

"I wonder what he meant by that," Margaret said thoughtfully.

"By what?"

"Not the only one. Does he know something I do not?"

"No, he was referring to yourself, my dear. You have come to join us thankfully. Now he expects his brother will as well."

"Oh, I see," Margaret answered, but she was far from convinced.

They walked to the end of the Grand Walk, laughing a little at the huge gilded statue of Aurora, which stood at the bottom. Then they crossed the Grand Cross Walk, which traversed the entire width of the pleasure gardens, and entered the South Walk, spanned by soaring triumphal arches with a distant glimpse of the ruins of Palmyra — fake of course — at the end. And suddenly Margaret seemed to see Vaux Hall for what it really was. Gone was her childish wonderment, and in

444

its place she saw peeling theatrical make-believe, tawdry fountains and tinsel statuary. She wondered how the place would look in the piercing light of a grey dawning, and shuddered away from the very idea.

"Shall we go to supper?" Sir Joshua asked, noticing nothing.

Margaret was just nodding consent but was interrupted by the ringing of a bell which meant that the firework display had started. They duly made their way and 'oohed' and 'aahed' with the rest of the crowd. Eventually, though, they reached The Grove and found their way to a supper booth shaped like an exotic temple. Thankful to have somewhere to sit, Margaret made her way within.

"Now, my dear, I am sure you would like champagne," said Sir Joshua and summoned a waiter, a rather sad character dressed in a worn-out livery, to take their order.

Margaret smiled, drawing in breath, her heart resuming its normal beat for the first time since they had met George Germain. "Yes, thank you."

"Excellent." And the painter proceeded to monopolise the proceedings; uncorking the champage himself; ordering the finest chicken and ham; returning the salad for more dressing; desiring cheesecake for dessert. Margaret, comparing it with the hardships in Boston, felt as if she were in another world entirely.

Looking round, she saw that several people were staring at their box, brilliantly lit as it was. For there were lights everywhere, even adorning the garlands of

flowers looped between the pillars, which in turn bore lamps.

"We are being greatly regarded," she said.

"Indeed, Ma'am, they are looking at your beauty," he answered gallantly.

"They are wondering who I am and what you are doing with me, no doubt."

"Then let them. For cannot a portrait painter escort his model to an evening at the Gardens."

"They are probably thinking far darker thoughts than that."

Joshua Reynolds smiled in a great flash of white teeth. "Once more, they must think what they will. They're all jealous, after all."

"You believe that?"

"Madam, I know it to be true."

The champagne was beginning to have an effect on her, for Margaret started to laugh. The first real laughter in which she had indulged since the battle of Bunker Hill. Joshua Reynolds, meanwhile, stared at her closely, regarding her with the all-seeing eye of his profession.

"That is how I want to paint you," he said softly.

Margaret looked at him. "What do you mean?"

"Like that. Laughing and gay. Yet with that strange air of hidden unhappiness which you always have."

She stopped laughing. "Do I? How perceptive of you to realise that."

"What causes it? Did your marriage fail?"

"Yes," she answered simply.

"Why?"

"I think he fell out of love with me."

"Why would any sane man do that?"

"Because of something I did."

"What?"

But that was going too far. That was a secret Margaret would never reveal. Nor would she discuss Joseph — ever. She turned away from the painter, and when she turned back she was smiling the smile she had worn earlier.

"Oh, it was just a silly little thing," she said.

CHAPTER
THIRTY-FIVE

October, 1775

Elizabeth Montagu had several people whom she regarded as friends, most of them being of long-standing and old acquaintance, but she had to admit that Margaret Gage, though a newcomer, had made the most favourable impression on her. Partly, of course, because of her generally pleasing appearance, being so darkly beautiful and strangely arresting. But the other reason was the woman's lack of affectation, her genuine concern for others, the truth of her whole personality. Yet Elizabeth sensed, having being born with a nose for secrets, that Margaret had more than her fair share of these. She also sensed that coaxing them out of her would prove impossible, and she respected Mrs. Gage for it. Yet for all this, she could not help but be curious about the woman of whom she was growing extremely fond.

Partly to please her, partly to prove to herself that the loss of her husband had not diminished her abilities, Mrs. Montagu had called a meeting of The Blue Stockings. That is to say that she had called a limited meeting, for the gentlemen of society who often attended these soirées had not been invited. This was to be a ladies-only gathering, and Elizabeth had decided that the topic of conversation would be the

situation regarding the Colonies and what action should be taken regarding them. Consequently, invitations had been issued, and those attending had dined early and hastened to Hill Street, much relieved that Mrs. Montagu had decided to continue with the club's activities.

Margaret, as an unknowing guest of honour, felt flattered to have been invited to such an august gathering of the intelligentsia, and dressed fittingly for the occasion. Wearing dark green — a colour that Tom had always liked her in — she set forth in her small coach through the early autumn evening, thinking that the nights were drawing in and that soon it would be Christmas.

She arrived to find that many of the company had already assembled and were presently socialising before the meeting proper began. Having handed her cloak to a footman, Margaret set off to find Mrs. Montagu and discovered her in conversation in the large salon.

"Ah, my dear Mrs. Gage," said Elizabeth, catching sight of her, "do come and be introduced. Ladies, I have a welcome guest. Allow me to present Mrs. Margaret Gage to you."

Three women bobbed a curtsey and then surveyed the newcomer with studied politeness.

"This is Mrs. Greene, Mrs. Carstairs and Mrs. Baldock."

Margaret, a little unsure of herself, curtseyed, then looked up. "How do you do?" she said.

"Why, I judge from your tones, Madam, that you are from the Colonies. Am I right?" asked the woman that Margaret had identified as Mrs. Baldock.

"Yes, Ma'am. I was born in New Jersey."

"Close to New York," said Mrs. Greene, as if she were informing Margaret where she had come from.

"That is correct," Mrs. Gage replied.

"Oh, I see we will have much to talk about," put in Mrs. Carstairs mildly. She was the quietest — and tallest — of the three, standing a good foot above the other two and having grey hair swept up, together with rather haphazardly applied face paint. Margaret decided that she liked her the best of the trio.

The other two were somewhat similar, both of them short and fat and with the same orange hair. Mrs. Greene eschewed any form of face paint, considering herself, no doubt, beautiful enough without. Mrs. Baldock, however, pursued fashion unsuccefully. She had false hair added to her own, the colour of which was questionable, showing the joins quite clearly. She had also a great many teeth which she flashed constantly in a totally false smile. Meanwhile her eyes, as cold and hard as any that Margaret had ever seen, weighed up the competition — as she had undoubtedly labelled Mrs. Gage — mercilessly.

Mrs. Greene spoke. "Have you been in London long, Mrs. Gage?"

"I arrived in September, Madam."

"I see."

She nodded sagely, folding her upper chin into her lower. She really was a most extraordinary shape, being quite neat about the breast but spreading outwards from the waist downwards. She was also extremely

shortsighted and peered through a lorgnette at whoever was speaking to her.

"Your first visit to England?" asked Mrs. Baldock, her cold eyes narrowing slightly.

"No. I was here a few years ago with my husband. My last daughter was born here."

"Really?" said Mrs. Carstairs faintly, and gave a slightly neighing laugh.

But Mrs. Montagu was clapping her hands. "Ladies, if you will take your seats, let us begin." There was a general shifting of direction and footmen appeared bearing extra seating. When everyone had disposed themselves, Elizabeth spoke again.

"My friends, I cannot tell you how pleased I am that we have once more gathered together. As you know, the recent death of dear Edward threw me quite out, and I believe that I would not have called this meeting so soon were it not for the presence amongst us of a great new friend of mine who has recently returned from the Colonies. I am sure that you will find her views of the utmost interest. So tonight, ladies, I thought that the ever-worsening situation should be the subject of discussion."

Mrs. Greene, who had settled her bulk in a *fauteuil*, spoke up immediately. "Well, I oppose war in every form. In my view, all the troops should be withdrawn and peace should be restored at once."

There was a silence during which Margaret felt herself growing increasingly uncomfortable.

"Hear, hear," said Mrs. Baldock. "War is an abomination fought by men and for the benefit of men.

If it was left to us women there would be no further fighting."

"The army wives and camp followers are in Boston," Margaret pointed out mildly.

This was the first time that she had addressed the general company, and there was a wave of laughter as her accent was heard publicly. She flushed, she couldn't help it, and looked down at her lap.

"How typical," said Mrs. Greene. "That the men's comforts," she stressed the word, "should be provided for them. If they had been withdrawn, I would have expected to see a swift end to the conflict."

Margaret spoke up. "It is a much more complex issue than that. You can imagine that, as a native-born Yankee, I feel very torn about the whole affair."

"What exactly do you mean?" asked a Mrs. Keppel, also present.

"I mean that the thought that my husband might be responsible for the spilling of American blood repels me. Yet at the same time, I could see that he had no course open to him but to do his duty. There are arguments for and against on both sides."

Mrs. Greene, who seemed determined to be difficult, said, "I reiterate what I said earlier. I believe that there should be no more war."

"That's all very fine," Margaret pronounced the word 'fahn' and there was another audible laugh, 'but that is a belief made in heaven."

There were several cries of "Nonsense" but who exactly the Blue Stockings were addressing was not crystal clear. Margaret steeled herself to regard them

closely and saw that there was a certain similarity amongst them. They were of an age, most of them despising the use of face paint, and all of them had a certain smug self-satisfaction which she found intensely irritating. That is all except Elizabeth Montagu, of whom Margaret had grown very fond.

At this point, Mrs. Montagu spoke up. "Ladies, please. Remember that Mrs. Gage's husband is supreme commander of the British army in Boston. She is in a position to give us first-hand knowledge of the situation. To interrupt is not in accordance with the nature of these meetings."

Mrs. Baldock, looking coldly at Margaret, said, "Then state the case fair and square, Mrs. Gage. Do."

Margaret could hear the emotion rising in her voice even though she attempted to control it. "This is the situation as I see it. The colonists have been in residence for over a hundred years and no longer feel any allegiance to Britain. They do not feel obliged to pay the taxes which are being imposed upon them. They want to be free of the yoke of the oppressor — their words not mine."

She looked at the sea of faces and wondered how any of them would have coped with holding Joseph's dead body close to her heart and burying him in the morning. Not well, she imagined.

"On the other hand," she continued, "my husband is a professional soldier. A man taught to take orders and to carry them out. He probably hates war as much as you do, Madam." Margaret looked at Mrs. Greene. "But he knows nothing else. He has been given

453

command of Boston and is doing the job to the best of his ability. With singular lack of instruction from the Cabinet, I might add. In short, ladies, the situation is as volatile as a powder keg. It is a bloody event that will shortly explode. And that is all I have to say."

There was considerable applause, and Mrs. Montagu murmured, "Well said, my dear."

"I would like to ask a question," said Mrs. Greene, crossing her ankles and giving a glimpse of extremely thin legs which looked incongruous with her bulk, "which is this. Which side are you on, Mrs. Gage?"

"I am on both," she replied unhesitatingly. "I can see the arguments of both factions."

"Ah, in the words of the Bard, 'Which is the side that I must go withal? I am with both: each army hath a hand: And in their rage, I having hold of both, they whirl asunder and dismember me . . .'"

Mrs. Greene put her head on one side, looking mighty pleased with herself, then, licking a finger, ran it over her eyebrows.

Margaret said, "An apt quotation indeed. It is King John, is it not?"

"It is indeed. The Lady Blanche's speech. Now in my view, that genius had something to say about everything. I worship Shakespeare, don't you know."

And she was off, holding forth, riddling her speech with quotations. Margaret turned to Mrs. Montagu.

"My dear, I hope I didn't let you down."

"On the contrary. You did extremely well. I think the ladies were most impressed."

"With the exception of . . ." Margaret rolled her eyes in Mrs. Greene's direction.

"Ah, well, she imagines herself to be a tremendous intellectual. Ahead of us all."

"And you have not disillusioned her?"

"Somehow I haven't the heart. If it gives her comfort to feel superior, then so be it. And now my dear, have some refreshment. You have acquitted yourself most nobly. I salute you."

With those words, Margaret felt that the evening's ordeal was over.

Sir Joshua Reynolds started her portrait, which positively leapt to life beneath the power of his brush. There was no Lady Reynolds, Margaret had discovered, and found it hard to guess his sexual needs. For though his studio often had beautiful young men in it, there was also an equal number of beautiful young women. Perhaps he whiled away his time with both, she thought. Alternatively, perhaps neither interested him. He was a puzzle, an enigma, but one whose company she relished, different as he was from any man she had ever met before.

One day, during a sitting, he raised the subject of her husband once more.

"What do you want to know about him?" she answered, gazing at him.

"Don't look at me, look towards the rose, then raise your eyes. Wait." And he left his easel and adjusted her pose back to how it had originally been. "Just what sort of man he is, that's all."

Margaret weighed her reply carefully. "He has been under a great strain recently."

"And how has it affected him?"

"He is very taken up with his work," she replied, fobbing him off, not wishing to discuss Tom or the situation this afternoon.

The artist made no further comment, merely nodding, and concentrated on the portrait which he was creating. Eventually, though, he put down his brush, and Margaret hurried towards the canvas, longing to see what he had done.

It was exquisite. He had given her a rose to hold from which she had just raised her eyes. Clad in a white gown, the deep pink of the flower stood out as something almost primitive against the material of the snowy background. Her black hair was loose, like a gypsy's, while her great dark eyes stared directly into those of the viewer. But it was the background which interested her most. It was a distant view of mountains, some with snow on their peaks, that attracted and held her attention. For it did not look like England at all but somewhere exotic and foreign. She turned to Joshua, who was cleaning his brushes.

"Have you ever visited the Colonies, Sir?"

"No, I never have."

"The background reminds me of my old home. Tell me, where is it?"

"In actual fact it is Italy. I spent some time there studying, you know. I often use it as a backdrop, but not many of my clients recognise the place."

456

He smiled at her, and Margaret saw the scar on his lip distinctly. She had been told by Mrs. Montagu herself that the painter had fallen from a horse whilst on the island of Minorca and had been permanently scarred as a result. But for all that, the man was attractive, and Margaret wondered yet again why he was not married.

Going into the changing room which led off the studio, Margaret removed the white dress in which she was being painted. And there, suddenly, she felt a wild urge to see Tom again, to put her arms round him and beg his forgiveness. She felt that she desperately needed the warmth and comfort of his physical presence.

Margaret sighed as Sir Joshua's servant helped her into her day gown. What was it she really wanted? Her dream of living the simple life with Joseph had been shattered so what was it she craved? Surely it could not be the empty existence of a belle of fashion? Yet, on the other hand, the Blue Stockings held no attraction for her. She thought of herself as London society must see her. An American curiosity, almost like a newly acquired animal in the zoo.

Fully dressed, she returned to the studio to discover Sir Joshua deep in conversation with a woman. Wondering if she was about to find out more about his private life, Margaret curtseyed.

The woman, who was tall and inclined to be bony, gave her a slightly startled stare.

"Mrs. Gage," said Sir Joshua, "I would like you to meet my sister, Frances. She keeps house for me.

"Delighted to make your acquaintance, Ma'am," said Margaret, as Frances, too, bobbed.

Sir Joshua's sister gave a fleeting smile. "Honoured, I'm sure." She had a marked Devonian accent.

So Sir Joshua's domestic arrangements were organised for him by a sibling. Margaret's curiosity about the man was yet again aroused. She held out her hand to him.

"Goodbye, Sir Joshua, until next week."

He bowed formally. "Goodbye, my dear," he said and kissed her fingers.

Elizabeth Montagu was far from well, that much was clear to see, though whether the illness was physical or mental, caused by the death of her husband, was not easy to tell. But whatever the reason, it had taken its toll on her. Her eyes were red and puffy, her cheeks highly coloured, her mouth dry and somewhat cracked about the lips.

"Oh, Elizabeth, my dear," said Margaret Gage, on being shown into her presence. "You are not looking at all yourself."

"No, sweet girl, I am not feeling it either," came the reply. "Indeed, I have been so poorly that I am thinking of going to Bath to take the waters, which do me far more good than those of Tunbridge Wells, I might add."

"London won't be the same without you," Margart answered, and really meant it. She felt she owed her entire social life to the introductions of the woman who now lay before her on a chaise, pale and unhappy.

"Will you miss me?"

"Greatly."

"Then why don't you come with me, my friend. Do you know Bath at all?"

"I went there once with Tom when we were in England on leave. And yes I could do with a break from London." She pulled a face.

Her two young admirers had fallen out with terrible results. The volatile Mr. Jenyns had challenged poor short-sighted William Wedderburne to a duel despite the fact that they had been outlawed some years previously. It had been with pistols on Hampstead Heath and, amazingly, Mr. Wedderburne had won, Samuel receiving a bullet in the arm. He was currently walking round town in a sling, swearing to get his revenge.

Mrs. Montagu gave a faint laugh. "Ah, those two young puppies. What a tangle to be sure. My dear, you should withdraw from the entire affair. Come to Bath, do."

Margaret had smiled at her. "Thank you for the invitation. I accept with pleasure. When shall we leave?"

"Would tomorrow be too soon? We can go in the afternoon and stay at an inn overnight."

"I think that sounds a splendid plan."

Margaret had gone home telling herself that she should be looking forward to a trip to Bath, a place she hardly knew at all. But instead, she had a strange presentiment lurking deep within the pit of her stomach, a presentiment that things were about to go badly wrong for her. As she began to pull things out of her clothes press for her maid to pack, she did her best

to push the feeling away. Yet somehow it not only persisted but seemed to grow worse as her thoughts turned to Boston and the plight of her benighted husband, marooned in that hostile place.

CHAPTER
THIRTY-SIX

October, 1775

As soon as she first sniffed the air of Bath, Mrs. Elizabeth Montagu described herself as feeling much recovered. Indeed, the nearer her coach drew to the legendary city of hot baths and sulphurous water, the more she braced up. Certainly by the time she and Margaret alighted at their lodging in Royal Crescent and had been shown to their quarters, neither of them were doing anything but laughing aloud and smiling.

"Do come and see my view, my dear," said Elizabeth, hurrying about her room delightedly.

Margaret, whose smaller abode was at the back of the house, across the landing, walked in and crossed to the window, looking out on the trees that were fast shedding their leaves.

"It's a truly delightful prospect," she remarked. "But how brown the leaves are. Autumn is here alas."

"You should see this view in May," Elizabeth answered her. "It is one of the most beautiful sights imaginable. Everything is blooming, and the blossom is exquisite. Promise me that you will accompany me here then."

Margaret turned to say yes, but from nowhere the horrid premonition struck her afresh. "I think that rather depends," she replied instead.

"On what?" asked Mrs. Montagu, suddenly sharp.

The words seemed to come out of Margaret's mouth of their own volition. "On when my husband returns from Boston."

"I see. Quite frankly, my dear, I had not realised that you and he were that close."

Margaret sat down on the dressing table stool. "We are not close exactly. But for all that, we are still married. If . . . when . . . he leaves Boston, I imagine my life will be very different."

"But you are a woman of intellect and position . . ."

"Oh, come now."

". . . I mean it, my dear. You have achieved status in society, and your mental capabilities speak for themselves. Why should the return of General Gage make any difference to your present modus vivendi?"

"Because he is more sober a person than I. And now, dear Elizabeth, I must finish my unpacking. Where shall we go this evening is what I need to know?"

"To the Assembly Rooms where Derrick is now Master of Ceremonies. Ah, if only you had known Beau Nash. What a character to be sure. I personally did not like him, but I admired his discipline of those attending. He was quite horrid and quite, quite wonderful."

"I would like to have met him," Margaret answered.

But Mrs. Montagu had stretched out on the bed and closed her eyes, so that the younger woman was forced to tiptoe from the room.

They dined at Lyndsey's, one of the most fashionable places in which to eat, occupying a corner table. But

462

they had hardly taken their places when a booming voice was heard summoning them.

"Mrs. Montagu, I did not realise you were in town. Come and sit with me, I beg you."

Elizabeth cast her eyes upward. "Oh Lord, if it isn't old Lady Coniston. I'm afraid we will have to join her. I do hope she won't bore you. She is quite considerably ancient and has lost most of her wits and all of her hearing."

They summoned a waiter and changed tables, sitting with the aged woman who was dining alone except for the company of a companion, who, typically, was downtrodden and hapless.

"Mrs. Montagu, you know Miss Miller." She waved a hand in the direction of the woman. "But who are you with? I do not think I know your face, my dear."

"Allow me to present Mrs. Gage to you, Lady Coniston."

"A pleasure. I do like young good-looking people about me. It helps one keep up with the times, I believe."

"A great honour to be presented to you, Lady Coniston. I hope we can become friends."

The old woman cupped her ear. "Do I detect a Yankee accent?"

"Yes, Madam. I was born in the Colonies."

"You must be quite perturbed by the situation out there. What a terrible thing for you. And not helped by that damned fool commander they've got. Can't remember his name but the man's an idiot. Lord Coniston was telling me the other night — he is my

bachelor son and a Member of the Lords, you know — that the chap has been recalled to England. A fine mess he's made of things for sure."

Margaret sat silently, wondering how best to answer. Then it occurred to her that Tom might not be the subject of the conversation at all, that the old lady's son could have been referring to any of the high command in Boston. Slightly mollified, she sat dumbly, merely giving a faint smile. Mrs. Montagu came in.

"I think it best that we drop the subject, my dear Roberta. Mrs. Gage has not come to Bath to listen to such things. She has come to forget her problems and to have some fun. And I intend to see that she does."

Was it Margaret's imagination that the name 'Mrs. Gage' had been said at full voice. And did she further fancy that Lady Coniston looked startled for a moment, before shooting her a glance and saying, "Oh. Yes, of course."

The pathetic companion spoke, her voice a wisp. "Perhaps we could all go to the theatre together. I could secure the seats."

"Yes, that would be a good idea," Lady Coniston said, clearly glad of another avenue of conversation. "Mrs. Montagu?"

"A splendid notion. Thank you Miss Miller."

It was at this juncture that the meal arrived and conversation became limited. But Margaret tasted nothing, the food turning to dust in her mouth. Had Lady Coniston really been talking about Tom? And, if so, was it true that he was going to be recalled? Margaret felt her heart go out to him, feeling certain

that if that was the case the shame would destroy him completely. She felt a deep and terrible sorrow for the man who had, after all, once been the love of her life. If she hadn't betrayed the great secret to Joseph might the whole thing have worked out differently? She sighed, feeling too exhausted even to think about it, and Mrs. Montagu caught her eye.

"I see the journey from London has fatigued you, my dear. I suggest that we go straight back when we have dined. I think that to visit the Assembly Rooms would be asking too much."

Margaret leapt at the opportunity. "In truth I am feeling a little tired. Tomorrow morning I shall be restored to my old self, I promise you."

Small talk prevailed, but eventually the meal came to an end and Mrs. Montagu rose to go, determination oozing from her small frame.

Lady Coniston laid a wrinkled old hand over that of Margaret. "Do hope I didn't say anything to upset you, Mrs. Gale."

"No, that's quite all right, my Lady. And the name is Gage, by the way."

"Gage, of course. Now where have I heard that recently?"

In the dark confines of the carriage, Elizabeth turned to Margaret, who sat in a strangely withdrawn silence.

"I warned you that she had lost her wits, my dear. You must regard what she said as the burbling of a confused old woman."

"It did not sound confused to me. She said her son told her."

Mrs. Montagu gave a snort of contempt. "That popinjay. He thinks of nothing but his cravats and his horses. I doubt that anyone would trust him with confidential information, least of all a member of the Cabinet."

In the darkness, Margaret stared at her. "Is that true?"

"Utterly. The entire family are lacking mentally, believe me. It is most unfortunate that we were obliged to sit with her. That poor wretched companion of hers is the only one who will put up with her. I shall decline their invitation to join them at the theatre." And she banged the floor with her stick to emphasise the point.

Yet despite the reassuring words, Margaret felt ill at ease. Lady Coniston had misheard her name and started to gossip about the situation in Boston. She had known something, of that much Margaret was certain. The question was, exactly what was it she had heard?

CHAPTER
THIRTY-SEVEN

October, 1775

Joseph had come back to life, for Margaret could see him distinctly. He was sitting in the kitchen of their weatherboarded home talking happily to a boy whom she knew to be their son. He was a nice child, a good-looking youngster, eager and fresh-faced, ready to take on the world as his father had been. Outside, Margaret could hear other children playing and, looking out of the window, saw that Mary, young Joseph and Elizabeth — Joseph's progeny by his first wife — were there, clearly having come to live with them. She looked round for her children but could not see them and, running upstairs, realised that they were not there but had stayed behind in England with their Aunt Elizabeth, the Viscountess. This last feeling was horrible to bear. The thought that they had chosen to remain at Firle Place rather than join their natural mother cut like a stab wound. Then she turned and saw Tom standing in the doorway, the slave girl Sara one step behind him. She knew as surely as if he had told her that the black woman was her husband's mistress.

"Get her out of my house," Margaret shouted.

Neither of them answered her, but Sara stepped forward and silently pointed at her abdomen. Staring at

it, Margaret realised with a lurch of her heart that the girl was pregnant.

"The child is mine," said Tom. And as Margaret screamed, "No. It can't be true," she woke and stared round the confines of a strange room.

Just for a moment, she thought she was with Joseph in their house in New England, then she realised that she was in Bath, that she had been dreaming a cruel dream from which she had just awoken, trembling and drenched with sweat. Shakily, Margaret stretched out an arm and poured herself some water from the carafe that stood beside her bed.

In order to drink it she had to sit upright, an action which made her feel slightly better. Arranging a pillow behind her head, Margaret stayed like that, waiting for the power of the dream to fade. It had seemed so real to her that she wondered at its meaning. Had Tom really slept with Sara and fathered a child by her? Yet its very clarity set her heart yearning for Joseph, for the life together they had never had, and, strangely, for her husband too. But most of all it made her long for her children with an ache which made the taste in her mouth turn to ash.

She heard the long case clock in the hall strike six and decided to rise and creep out of the house for a walk. Washing in cold water and dressing quickly, Margaret stole outdoors before the beau monde had even opened its eyes. Somewhat to her surprise, however, there were several people about at this early hour, most of them young men making their way to the Hot Bath. Margaret thought that they had probably not

been to bed but had gone to the bath straight from a party or card play.

Feeling a little conspicuous, she entered the Pump Room, below which the King's or Hot Bath was situated, and ordered a glass of water, watching the beaux descend to the cavernous depths below. Then she felt her attention drawn to a small figure making its way across the Pump Room, walking determinedly but with a definite limp. He looked very like one of the dream characters with whom she had so recently been involved, so much so that Margaret caught her breath. He must have heard her because he stopped and made her a small bow. "How dee do, Ma'am."

He could have been no more than four years old yet with such a pleasing countenance and bright smile that Margaret felt instantly drawn to him.

"Hello, young man. What is your name?"

"Why, Ma'am, are you a Yankee?"

"And I believe that you are a Scot."

"Aye, I am that."

"And where is your Mama?"

"Home in Edinburgh, Ma'am. I live with my grandfather in the Borders."

Having no idea where that was, Margaret continued to smile at him, entranced by his eager little face and precocious manner.

"My grandpa is a professor of medicine, and I was taken ill when I was young," the boy continued, "that's why I live with him."

"Oh, I see. And what was the nature of your illness?"

"Teething problems," the little fellow responded, immediately giving Margaret the impression that it had been something far more serious which the child had not been told about.

"So where is your guardian?"

"She's coming directly. In fact —" The boy peered over his shoulder. "— here she is now."

Margaret followed his gaze and saw a comfortable woman, looking somewhat red in the face, hurrying towards them.

"Oh Walter, there you are," she exclaimed. "I do wish you wouldn't make your way on your own. You are in my care, and there's an end to it." She flashed a look at Margaret, then dropped a small curtsey. "I do hope the boy has been no trouble, Ma'am. He will run away when I am about other business."

"I think he is delightful," said Margaret, really meaning it.

The boy bowed once more. "I must be away to the bath," he announced. "It's to help my limp, d'ye see."

"I hope very much that we will meet again."

"If you take the waters early, Ma'am, then we most assuredly will."

So saying, he made his way to the Hot Bath, ushered down the steps by his chaperone. Margaret loitered, waiting for her to return, hoping to find out more about the little chap, whose manner had so delighted her on this chilly autumn morning. Seeing the woman re-emerge, she approached her.

470

"Forgive me for not introducing myself, Ma'am. My name is Margaret Gage, and I am currently visiting Bath with Mrs. Montagu."

"And I am Mrs. Home," stated the other with a certain air of grandeur. "My husband you may have heard of. He wrote Douglas, you know."

As this meant nothing to Margaret, she merely smiled as Mrs. Home continued.

"I am so glad that Walter made a good impression on you. He is a dear child, sent to Bath for the benefit of his health. He had serious teething problems which left him lame, poor thing. Now his grandfather hopes that bathing in the Hot Bath and taking the waters might improve his position."

"How kind of you to act as his guardians."

"Not at all. Now, are you attending the Public Breakfast?"

"I don't know what that is."

"Then allow me to tell you. It is a breakfast which everybody goes to. It is accompanied by music and a great deal of noise. I can heartily recommend it."

"At what time does it begin?"

"At eight o'clock or thereabouts."

"Then I shall go back to my rooms and fetch Mrs. Montagu. I am sure she would enoy it. Tell me, will you be there?"

"I am afraid not. Walter has a reading lesson at that time. Duty calls."

"Yes, of course. Well, no doubt I shall see you round the town."

"No doubt. Good day to you, Mrs. Gage."

"Good day, Mrs. Home."

★ ★ ★

Having returned to find Mrs. Montagu somewhat distressed by her absence, Margaret soothed her down and suggested that they visit the Public Breakfast. To Elizabeth, of course, such things were well-known. But something of the air of excitement that her companion was feeling conveyed itself to the older woman and she, only a trifle reluctantly, consented to go. So, dressed very finely, both ladies sauntered forth from Royal Crescent and made their way to the Pump Room.

Inside all was splendour. The place was packed with people, all conversing at the tops of their voices, competing with the musicians who were playing like fury in the gallery above. Everybody who was anybody was present, those members of the beau monde instantly recognisable by the ease with which they achieved the ultimate in dress. Members of the other classes, however, had tried too hard and looked a little overdone as a result. There was also a third echelon of society present: the old and the sick forming a miserable queue to take a glass of the brackish water to revive their flagging spirits. Mrs. Montagu joined this, standing behind an old man who swayed so badly that he threatened to fall on her at any moment.

"My dear," she said, ducking as the ancient fellow tottered, "do go ahead and get a table. I shall join you as soon as I have partaken."

Margaret set off, managing to squeeze on the end of a table for six. Then she sat back and allowed all the noise and cheer to overwhelm her. But somehow the atmosphere failed to communicate itself. Thoughts

tortured her that across the Atlantic ocean, people were going hungry, short of food and water; that men — victims of the battles — were dying in agony, hideously maimed and suffering beyond anything that a human should have to endure. But above all these came the idea of Tom, the man she had married, shamed and shattered, making his way back to England with his career in ruins.

"You're deep in thought," said Mrs. Montagu.

"I was thinking about my husband," Margaret answered honestly.

"It seems to me, my dear, that you do little else."

"Oh, that isn't so."

"Um. Do you still hold him in high regard?"

"Of course. He has done his best in a difficult situation. I respect him for it."

"I am glad to hear it. But I fear that the majority of people in this country think otherwise."

"Well, let them," said Margaret defiantly. "They don't know the true circumstances."

"Indeed they don't. Time will tell, no doubt."

"Yes," Margaret answered slowly, "no doubt it will."

The next morning she attended the Pump Room early and again met little Walter, who, this time, ran as fast as he could with his lame leg, to meet her.

"How are you, Ma'am?"

"I'm very well. But more importantly, how are you? Do you think the treatments in this place are helping you?"

"I'm not sure," he replied seriously. "But meeting the folk here is proving excellent."

Margaret laughed aloud at his delightful mannerisms and strangely adult speech. And she was still smiling to herself long after he had disappeared to bathe and Mrs. Montagu had joined her.

"You're happy today, my dear."

"It is just little Walter. He is so amusing. He makes me miss my children though."

Elizabeth sighed. "Just as I miss my son."

Margaret stared. "I didn't know . . ."

"Yes, I called him my little Punch, for he was so happy and merry. At night when he was stripped he would roll and tumble on a blanket on the ground. I loved him so much. He was utterly adorable. But the poor little soul died of convulsions. Gracious, it was thirty years ago now, yet I can still see him as clearly as if it were yesterday."

Margaret laid her hand over Elizabeth's. "I'm so sorry."

"But your children are alive, my dear. You really should go to them."

"It's my sister-in-law, Viscountess Gage. She has been pregnant many times but has never succeeded in bringing a child to maturity. She begged me to give her my children for her to educate and I, because my home was in the Colonies, agreed. That is the reason."

"But you don't live in the Colonies now," Elizabeth answered, and there was the slightest hint of acerbity in her tone.

474

Later, after the Public Breakfast, they had entered the steamy confines of the Hot Bath, clad from head to toe in bathing dress, a large cap shaped like a mop on their heads. At Margaret's waist had been attached a little floating tray bearing a handkerchief, together with a puff box and a snuffbox, a habit in which she did not indulge but which the attendant had insisted upon. It had been on long strings so as she submerged herself up to the neck in the warm, vaporous water, it had floated upwards. It had brought a smile to her lips to see a small army of ladies, tramping round and round, trays floating in front of them, their faces set and determined. And later, somewhat red in the cheeks, being carried out to rest and sweat at home. She had gone back to Royal Crescent, but had risen soon after, dressed and gone to walk in the town where, as luck would have it, she had met young Walter and taken him to tea at Sally Lunn's Coffee House, where they feasted on buns and butter, undoing all the good of the earlier treatments.

That night they had gone to the Assembly Rooms, and Margaret had been introduced into society at its highest level. She had danced nearly every dance, watched by Elizabeth Montagu and various other older ladies, aware that she was probably the subject of gossip but not really caring. And then a memory had come back; a sharp, harsh memory that would not go away. She thought of how she and Tom Gage had danced on the night they had met. How handsome she had thought him, how fine and dashing in his red uniform.

Yet for all that she had fallen in love with someone else and betrayed the English secret to the other side. Suddenly, she felt terribly ashamed and the blood ran into her cheeks making her look flushed.

"Goodness me," she laughed up at her partner. "I must sit down. The dance is making me grow very hot."

Thankfully at that moment the final chords were played, and he bowed her to her seat.

"Thank you, Ma'am. It has been a pleasure."

"Thank you, Sir. Oh, by the way, my name is Margaret Gage."

He bowed again. "Gage," he repeated, and it seemed to her then that the whole evening was turning into a strange dream from which there would be no escape.

CHAPTER
THIRTY-EIGHT

October 11, 1775

Long after the crowd had dispersed from the quayside, Tom still remained at the ship's rail, staring at the now deserted place where earlier there had been a small throng. Though all who had seen him off — including his brother-in-law — had pretended he would return in the spring, he knew perfectly well that this was the end for him. That he had received the final recall and was now destined to spend the rest of his days in England. Standing there, alone at the rail, he thought of his arrival, of the bands playing, of taking the salute, of the reception given him at the State House. Now, while the ship waited for the tide, there was nobody left. Nothing except a stray dog picking its way disconsolately round, hoping for a scrap.

Like me, Tom thought, and banged his fist down hard, hurting himself.

He had seen Lord Rupert Germain push Sara away in her wheelchair and felt his heart receive its final blow. The mother of his child, the beautiful girl who loved him without question, was going out of his life for ever. He had known at that moment, watching them vanish slowly from view, that he would never see either of them again as long as he lived. That the two of them,

both of whom adored him in their different ways, would stay united because they had nobody else.

A strange thought went through Tom Gage's head: that they might marry and spend the rest of their days caring for his child. And on the heels of this notion came another. That over the years they might even grow close, maybe even have another baby to keep his company. That is, if Rupert could bring himself to love Sara as a man should.

He felt a touch on his arm and looking round saw that it was Thomas Flucker, the secretary of Massachusetts, also recalled to England, also destined for exile from the Colonies.

"Come on, Tom. You've stood there gazing long enough."

The ex-Governor gave a small smile. "I shall never see Boston again, my friend. Don't begrudge me my last look."

"No more shall I see it. And I say good luck. I have had enough of the cursed Colonies to last me a lifetime. Surely you have no regrets, Sir?"

"One or two."

"Well, let's drown our sorrows. The Captain has a bottle of madeira in his cabin and invites us to join him. Are you coming?"

"Yes, I'll come," Tom answered and followed Flucker below.

It was those horrible palpitations again. Margaret sat in her room in Royal Crescent and struggled for breath, gasping aloud as she did so. She had thought while she

478

was still in London, that she should consult a physician about her racing heart. But no sooner had she determined to do so than the seizures had stopped as suddenly as they had started. Indeed this was the first attack she had suffered in quite a while. Panting, Margaret staggered to the window and despite the chill of the autumn night, threw it open.

Standing there, her breathing slowly coming under control, she thought of the emptiness of her life and wished, as so many women had done before her, that she could turn back the clock. And yet, Margaret considered, would she have done things any differently? She had at that time been in love with Joseph and believed, as an American, in the rightness of his cause. Knowing him and caring for him in the way she had, she would most certainly have betrayed the secret all over again. But retribution for her act had come indeed. Joseph had died a hero's death, and she had lost the love of Tom.

Margaret stopped with a jolt. Suddenly she felt certain that Tom had sought consolation in the arms of the black slave girl, Sara. She had always suspected as much but now she knew for sure. The nights when he had driven the chaise into Boston, not wearing his uniform. He had told her that he liked to know what the population was thinking. Margaret smiled wryly, imagining to herself that he must have received a very limited viewpoint.

But when all was said and done, who could blame him? She had loved another, so why shouldn't he? Suddenly feeling drained and hopeless, Margaret

reluctantly turned back into the room and rang for her maid to help her dress for the Assembly that evening.

The ship sailed at nine o'clock that night, in the darkness. Once again, Tom went on deck and looked at the lights of Boston starting to fade.

Soon that is how I shall be, he thought. A fading memory. Someone to be forgotten.

He stared down in the dark ocean, seeing silver lights where the waves foamed about the prow. Just for a moment, he contemplated leaning over too far and letting the black waters close over his head, putting a cold end to his troubles. But being the man he was, he straightened his back and went down into his cabin, it being too chilly to remain on deck.

He lay down on his bunk, fully dressed, and wondered why he was thinking of Margaret. She was one of the many problems he would have to face when he returned to town. Yet how could he continue life with her after all that had happened? How could he carry on with a marriage in which love had died? Sighing and weary, Tom nonetheless rose up and unpacked his journal in which he wrote: "October 11th 1775. Sailed from Boston at nine o'clock. Earlier, a small crowd at the quayside included several old friends."

He dared not write anything more frank lest his diary should fall into the wrong hands.

'Made my farewells then boarded ship. Boston adieu.'

Adieu indeed. The place which had been a bustling port when he arrived now resembled a ghost town, and it had brought him nothing but heartache and misery. Battles had been fought and lost; men had been wounded, and men had died; the sands of time were running out for British imperial rule. Thomas Gage knew as surely as he knew his name that in the weary battle-torn years ahead, the colonists would fight to the death — and they would most assuredly win.

Margaret had a new evening dress, crimson velvet, a voluptuous colour, which gleamed or sulked darkly according to the light. Now, for the first time she put it on and stood looking at herself in the long mirror. Her reflection stared back at her, and Margaret studied herself unrelentingly. She saw a woman, still beautiful, but with that beauty just starting to fade. In another ten years her stunning looks would be a thing of the past. She would be nothing but a plain-faced mother. And at that moment she knew what she must do. As soon as she returned to London she must send for her brood — every one of them. The reign of her sister-in-law must be brought to an end. She had neglected them long enough. Her time as a true parent would begin.

She was quiet in the coach going to the Assembly. So much so that Elizabeth Montagu was forced to make conversation.

"You look very lovely, my dear girl. That wonderful colour truly becomes you. It was inspirational of you to choose it."

Making a great effort, Margaret patted her small hand. "While you are still in black, alas. Never mind, the time will pass quickly enough."

Elizabeth looked thoughtful. "You know, I don't mind. I respect Edward's memory and therefore the wearing of mourning clothes is no hardship to me. Oh, I did love the dear soul, and I miss him so much."

While I, considered Margaret, could think of nothing but America and how much it meant to me. Oh God, what kind of wife was I?

The Assembly was crowded as usual, but tonight, for some reason, Margaret looked at everyone with a critical eye. She saw women with over-made-up faces, grinning like apes at sweating farmers, or beaux as heavily painted as their female counterparts. She saw members of the nobility, made effete by years of inter-breeding. She saw the whole panoply of humanity, dancing and whirling and laughing over-loudly, and felt every ounce of love for her fellow creatures drain from her in a great sweep of revulsion.

Yet she, standing there in her crimson dress, caught every eye, and there was much jealous whispering behind fans and bracing up by those men certain that they were still up to the task. One of these now detached himself from the crowd and bowed before Mrs. Montagu.

"My dear Madam, we meet again. We were introduced in town by Lord Villers. I am Phillipe Texier." His accent revealed at once that he was French. He turned to Margaret. "I do not think I have had the pleasure, Madam."

482

Mrs. Montagu performed the introductions. "Mrs. Gage, may I present Monsieur Phillipe Texier to you?" Margaret curtseyed. "Monsieur Texier, this is Mrs. Margaret Gage." He bowed in a very charming, very French manner. Then said, "I am honoured," and kissed her hand.

"Have you come to Bath to take the waters?" Elizabeth asked.

"Yes, first and foremost. But secondly I am here to perform a play with Lord Villers. We shall act it in a barn. It would be delightful if you and Mrs. Gage would come and see it."

"And when is this incredible extravagance to take place?"

Monsieur Texier grinned. "In about two weeks, I believe."

"Well, if Margaret is agreeable, we shall attend."

"That will be charming. Utterly charming."

He was typical of his country; attractive, witty and with a command of English that set other nations to shame. Margaret decided that she liked him and when he offered to lead her out in a dance accepted gracefully. But even the dance seemed doomed, for the cotillion made her think of her first meeting with Tom — could it really have been nearly twenty years ago? — when he had made her laugh with his upright English accent and wonderful manners.

To try to improve her mood she drank champagne, rather a lot of it, but nothing would lift her spirits, and she felt old when Mrs. Montagu announced that it was time they left and Margaret responded, "Oh good."

Going back in the coach she was, once again, quite quiet, and it was left to Elizabeth to say, "Did you enjoy yourself, my dear?"

"Yes, of course. I'm just feeling a little out of sorts, I'm afraid."

"Oh, my sweet. And you looked so lovely in your crimson gown. I wouldn't have guessed."

Margaret smiled and changed the subject. "Tell me, what is London like at Christmas time?"

"Oh, of the greatest enjoyment. Nothing but balls and assemblies. It is enormously entertaining."

"I shall probably go to Firle and spend it with the family."

"And what will you do if your husband comes home?" Mrs. Montagu asked quietly.

Totally off her guard, the champagne loosening her tongue, Margaret answered, "I have no idea. He will probably divorce me when he does."

She felt her companion stiffen. "Really? And why should he do that, pray?"

"Because he has fallen out of love with me."

"But what could have made him do such a ridiculous thing? Did he find another woman?"

"He may have done. I don't know. But it wasn't that that made him desert me."

"Then what was it? Oh, do tell me, my dear. I am longing to know."

Suddenly Margaret felt like confiding her guilt to someone whom she regarded as a close and dear friend. "It was because I betrayed a secret," she said.

In the shadowy light of the coach's swaying interior Mrs. Montagu turned to look at her. "What do you mean exactly?" she asked.

"I told a revolutionary . . ." Her voice caught as she thought of Joseph. ". . . about the plans for Lexington and Concord. You see, I felt so torn. After all, I was born a Yankee and will remain so until the day I die. I did it for my country."

There was a stunned silence, then Mrs. Montagu said, her voice slightly clipped, "Let me get this correctly. You betrayed the English plans to the Americans?"

"Yes, if you care to put it like that."

Beside her, Margaret felt Elizabeth Montagu draw away. "But why, in heaven's name?"

"I did it for my country," Margaret repeated.

"But you betrayed your husband. Your loyalty lay with him."

"I didn't think so at the time."

How to explain to this highly intelligent little woman that a million thoughts had been at work; that at that moment she had loved Joseph equally as much as the man she had married; that the birth of America, in which he so fervently believed, had seemed of paramount importance. Just for a second, Margaret saw the situation as it must appear to a stranger — an English stranger — and recoiled.

The rest of the drive was conducted in silence, and, when they reached Royal Crescent, Mrs. Montagu bade her goodnight and then departed immediately for her bedroom. Margaret, with nothing left to do, went to

hers. But once in bed, she went through the series of events that had taken place in Boston what seemed like a hundred years earlier. Yet again she spent the night on Breed's Hill — that long, hot, airless night — holding poor Joseph's body in her arms, feeling the chill of death creep over him. Yet again she wept bitter tears, and finally Margaret slept just as the first light of day came creeping across the sky.

She woke into a silent house. Usually in the mornings she could hear the clatter of the servants preparing breakfast, the humming of Mrs. Montagu's maid as she set out the clothes that her mistress would be wearing, but today there was nothing. Total silence. Puzzled, Margaret got out of bed, pulling a night-rail over her gown. Opening the door, she spied her own maid making her way nervously upstairs.

"Bridget, where is everybody?"

The girl reached the landing and gave a small curtsey. "Mrs. Montagu has left for London with the servants, Mam."

"What?"

"I said Mrs. Montagu has gone. She rose early and was out of the house by six. She left a letter for you."

Margaret took the paper that the servant held towards her.

"My dear Mrs. Gage," she read,

"I regret to have to Inform you that I was called away early and shall not be in London for some Considerable While. I suggest you return to Town

by post-chaise. I am, dear Madam, your humble servant,

E. Montagu."

That was it! No apology and no explanation, merely this icy note. Margaret knew then that what she had confessed to on the previous evening had sealed her fate. As far as Elizabeth Montagu — still deeply mourning her husband — was concerned, Margaret was finished. She turned to the maid.

"Is it just the two of us left?"

"Yes, Mam. I've been wondering for the last hour whether to wake you and tell you."

"No, you did right to let me sleep. But now there seems little point in staying. Bridget, go to The Bear and book us two places on the flying coach. I shall hurry to the King's Bath and say goodbye to Walter."

"Yes, Mam. Shall I help you dress?"

"Yes, but we must be quick. I feel suddenly bored with Bath and can't wait to be out of the place."

Half an hour later, just before the hour of eight, she hurried to the Pump Room for the last time, forcing a glass of the warm mineral-laden water down her. This done, she looked round for Walter and saw him limping towards her, his face cherubic and smiling. Margaret bent down to him.

"Walter, I've come to say goodbye. I'm leaving Bath this morning."

"This is very sudden, Ma'am."

She told an expedient lie. "I have to return to London. I'm sorry."

Aged four, his guardian a pace or two behind him, he gave a strange little bow. "Well, adieu Madam."

"Goodbye Walter. I hope we meet again one day."

"I do hope so."

They shook hands, and Margaret said, "By the way, what is your other name? I never did discover it."

"Scott, Ma'am. I'm Walter Scott."

And with a final wave of farewell, he descended to the Hot Bath and out of her sight.

CHAPTER
THIRTY-NINE

November, 1775

Suddenly, everything had changed. Where London society had clamoured to meet her now there was nothing but closed doors. Wherever she called, wherever she went, servants informed her that the mistress of the house was absent, gone they knew not where, return date unknown. At first Margaret had thought it just a coincidence, but soon it dawned on her that she was no longer of any interest, that the story of the betrayal of her husband had swept polite company, and they had universally turned their backs on her, that she was *persona non grata*. It had been a devastating blow, and yet she could understand it. They were English; she was a Yankee. In their eyes she had acted the role of a spy for the colonists. She was finished.

The one person who received her was Sir Joshua Reynolds, sending a servant to enquire if she would give him a final sitting. Margaret, delighted that one door at least was open to her, hastily penned a note saying that she would call that very day. Then, summoning her carriage, she drove through a friendless London to the artist's studio.

The portrait, a beautiful piece of work, was up on his easel, and he was already working on it when Margaret

entered the room. Removing her hat, she went to stand by him.

"Well, Mrs. Gage, I hear that you have become a social leper," he said immediately.

"Yes, it's true. Do you know the reason?" she answered.

"Yes, I do. It seems you passed on secret information to the colonial forces."

"I wouldn't go so far as that. I merely told a friend of mine, a friend who happened to be a Yankee revolutionary, details of the British plan. That is all."

"All?" he said and turned his dark eyes on her.

"Do you consider it so very wrong, Sir Joshua?"

He put down his brush and looked at her. "What is wrong? It depends entirely on one's perspective, I believe. In the eyes of the Americans, you were, no doubt, the heroine of the hour. In the eyes of the English, you are a traitor. It is as simple as that."

"No one knew what I had done with the exception of one fine man."

"With whom, no doubt, you considered yourself in love."

Margaret stared at the painter, wondering how he could possibly have guessed.

Sir Joshua laughed drily. "I see that remark has startled you. My dear, when I paint people I see into their souls. I long ago guessed that you had a secret, my only problem was knowing exactly what it was. Now, are you going to sit for me?"

"Of course I am."

"Then if you would take your usual pose we can begin."

Margaret sat in her customary position while he worked in silence for an hour, before finally putting down his brushes. "There, it's finished."

"May I look?"

"Certainly."

The finishing touches had turned it from a fine portrait into a work of genius. She stood silently, observing, thinking that it had indeed been painted by a master.

Eventually she spoke. "Are you going to call it *Portrait of a Traitor?*"

He laughed once more. "It shall be known as *Portrait of a Woman of Secrets.*"

"I will buy it off you one day."

"Only if I am willing to sell it."

Margaret held out her hand. "Goodbye, Sir Joshua. I do not suppose that I shall see you again."

He kissed the outstretched fingers. "My door will always be open to you, Mrs. Gage. Don't forget that."

"Thank you. But I am leaving London and going to live in the country. I have been away from my children too long. I think we need each other."

Sir Joshua leaned forward and signed the portrait. "Good luck to you, my dear," he said.

"Thank you again," she said, made a curtsey, and walked from the studio to her waiting carriage.

CHAPTER
FORTY

November, 1775

It was the unhappiest day of his life, which was saying something quite considerable when one reflected on the misery he had borne of late. What had made it so terrible to bear had been the King's kindness, his gentleness. Tom had expected a royal freeze, an expression of extreme displeasure, even, perhaps, a rage. But there had been none of that. His Majesty George III had behaved like a gentleman throughout the interview, and it had hurt more, far more, than anything else could. The ex-Governor had hidden what he was feeling beneath bluff soldierly courtesy; standing to attention, giving stiff military bows, but beneath his scarlet uniform his anguish had been so keenly felt that he had had to struggle to keep the tears from his eyes in the royal presence.

He had arrived back in England on November 13th and taken a post-chaise to London, where he had spent the night with old friends, the Viscount Barrington and his wife. It had been as if he were an actor in a play, nothing seeming quite real to him, remembering lines learned long ago but almost forgotten during his time in Boston. He had sat at the dinner table and wondered if he were actually there at all, or whether the whole incident was in fact a dream. So strong had this feeling

been that he had stared uncomprehendingly when the Viscountess had spoken.

"You know about Margaret, of course."

"Margaret?" he had repeated stupidly.

Viscountess Barrington shot him a strange look. "I refer to your wife, Sir. I presume she has been in touch with you."

"Not since she left Boston, no."

"Then I've a tale to tell. And there's no need to frown, Husband. Tom needs to know what has been happening." She paused to draw breath, then continued, "Mrs. Gage caused quite a stir when she arrived in London. Got herself heavily involved with the Blue Stocking set, particularly Mrs. Montagu. As a result of that she was on every hostess's list, and Sir Joshua Reynolds even went so far as to paint her portrait."

"Good God," said Tom, genuinely surprised.

"I've never had time for those intellectual women personally. A lot of damned attitudinising in my opinion. Be that as it may, Margaret was quite the talk of the town. But recently, she and Mrs. Montagu have fallen out — about what is not clear — and now every door has closed to her. Frankly, my dear Tom, your wife has been ostracised."

He should have thought, serve the silly bitch right. But instead he felt a dull ache of sympathy, of knowing something of what she was suffering.

"And where is she now?" he asked.

Lord Barrington spoke. "I think she's gone to Firle to collect the children. I don't believe she is still in London."

Tom changed the subject. "Tomorrow I go to see His Majesty."

The Viscount looked grim. "I believe he is rather upset."

"I tried to warn them. I told them they must send huge reinforcements if they wanted to win this war. But they didn't listen. They continued on in their own sweet way, and now, mark my words, they face years of a long and bloody conflict which will probably end in defeat."

The Viscountess looked shocked. "Oh, surely not."

"Oh, surely yes. I have no wish to upset you, Madam, but I have seen the truth for myself. The colonists are tough fighters with a cause they believe in. Unless we reinforce America to the hilt, then the game is lost."

And he had said much the same thing to the King, who had looked at him with his slightly protruberant eyes and sighed.

"General Gage, I am at the mercy of my government. I cannot personally order troops to go to the Americas. You do understand that?"

"Yes, Sir, I do. But there is no other way, believe me."

George had shaken his head, his wig rustling slightly as he did so. "What a trial the Colonies are, to be sure."

"They are going to become a death trap, Sir."

George had sighed gustily. "I can only pray you are wrong, General. With all my heart I pray that."

It was a broken figure who got out of the carriage outside the house he had bought on his last visit to

494

England and slowly mounted the short flight of steps leading to the front door, which, for some strange reason, opened beneath his touch. Paying it scant attention, Tom made his way into the hall, then on into the drawing room. Every bit of furniture was covered in white dust-sheets, and he could tell that the house was empty. The silence was audible as he went into the room he had chosen for his study and sat down at the shrouded desk.

The tears came then. He wept for his wasted life, for the loss of America, for the loss of the woman with whom he had once been so in love. He felt at that moment as he had felt when the ship sailed from Boston, that there was nothing left to live for. That his life, pitiful thing that it was, might as well come to an end.

Then he heard something and raised his head from his hands. Oh how well he knew that step, quick and light; a step that told him Margaret was close by. He sat motionless and heard her come into the room, heard her indrawn breath of surprise and shock on seeing him sitting there. He turned to look at her and saw a woman in a travelling cloak, a woman much defeated by life. A woman older yet still beautiful.

Slowly Tom got to his feet and stood staring at her. And in that moment it was as if he were dying, for his whole life seemed to pass before his eyes. He was back at that Christmas Assembly, given so long ago. He was leading her out to dance, despite the disappointed comments of other young men. He had held her in his arms, the warmth and gaiety and passion of her. He

remembered the first time he had kissed her in the frozen gardens, checking that no one else was around, an old soldier's trick, and felt his heart burst into life, like a flower feeling the first of the spring sunshine.

He was back at Culloden, amongst the dying and the dismembered, feeling sick to his guts but unable to vomit because men were looking to him for a lead, for someone to look up to. He remembered picking up a starving Indian, waiting patiently to die, and bringing him back to become the great scout he was destined to be. And then he recalled something Calico Joel had said, to the effect that Margaret's betrayal was cancelled out by Tom's love for Sara.

If only that were true, he thought. But how could it be when he had loved that girl with all his heart, worshipped her beautiful body with his, planted his seed in her, given her a child? A child that would grow up a colonist and know nothing else, just like its mother before it.

And then Tom knew in a moment of great clarity that he must finally let Sara go, that he could no longer be a part of her life and that he had handed her into the care of Rupert Germain, for better or worse. He gazed at the floor lest Margaret should be able to read his thoughts.

Margaret, who had come back into the house to lock it up, could not believe her eyes when she saw Tom standing there. Just for a second, she thought it was an apparition, that he had died and she was seeing a ghost. But the smell of his skin, fresh-washed, the sound of his

breathing, were enough to tell her that this was a flesh-and-blood man who stood before her.

She longed to ask him when he had returned, for the details of his departure from that accursed town, but words stuck in her throat. Instead she just stood gazing, in silence, feeling the world stop turning and the whole of her life come up to the reckoning point.

Memories danced in then; distant memories of times long gone. She recalled her first meeting with him when he had looked so attractive in his scarlet uniform that she had picked him out in an instant. Made something of a set at him if truth be told. She remembered her wedding day — and night — almost as if they were yesterday. And then she recalled Joseph, so young and so vulnerable, such a contrast to her husband in every way.

Joseph and the country striving to be born had become almost synonymous in her mind. She had given herself to them — both of them — out of patriotism, out of love, out of need. But Joseph had died on Breed's Hill, and she had buried his body there beside that of a farmer wearing a simple country frock. Into the rich earth he had gone, and she had known then that she would never see him again except in her wild and uncontrollable dreams.

And then she thought of the rest of her days stretching out endlessly before her and suddenly knew that she needed Tom's forgiveness if she were to continue in any kind of good order.

He looked up again, and it seemed to her that there was hope in his eyes, though of what she was not

certain. Tentatively she took a step forward and held out her hand.

He stared at her for what seemed an eternity and then he did the same.

"Tom," she said, her voice a mere whisper, "forgive me, please."

He made no answer but took another step forward. She gazed at him, unable to utter another word.

And then slowly, very slowly, he took her hand in his and they both felt the past fall away as their fingers intermingled.

Historical Note

This is a work of fiction, pure and simple, based on the life of Thomas Gage, the commander-in-chief at the time of the outbreak of the American War of Independence, or Revolutionary War as it is often known. Many characters have been cut out for the sake of simplifying the story, but most of the people described actually lived and related one to the other. Obviously, others are figments of my imagination. Yet who can say what actually took place in the dark streets of Boston at that most difficult and troubled period?

Also available in ISIS Large Print:

Hester Roon

Norah Lofts

The Fleece Inn stood where the three roads joined — the roads to London, to Norwich and to the sea. Its trade was prosperous, its hospitality famous, and the host was jolly and generous.

To his servants he was cruel and menacing, and to Ellie Roon, the most menial servant at the Fleece, he was a figure of terror. Ellie was used to being bullied, but when her illegitimate daughter was born — in a rat-ridden attic of the Fleece — she decided that Hester must have a different kind of life.

And so, Hester Roon began her eventful progress in the harsh world of 18th-century England. After fleeing from the inn, and the attentions of the owner, she became involved in the London underworld. From there she found herself in a world far beyond her imaginings . . .

ISBN 978-0-7531-7734-1 (hb)
ISBN 978-0-7531-7735-8 (pb)

Royal Escape

Georgette Heyer

Dispossessed of crown and kingdom, crushed and routed at the grim Battle of Worcester, the young Charles II is forced to flee for his life. Out of the heat of battle, the outlaw King and his tiny party must journey across Cromwell's England to a Channel port and a ship bound for France and safety.

But the King, with his love of adventure, his irrepressible humour and his unmistakeable looks, is no easy man to hide . . .

ISBN 978-0-7531-7690-0 (hb)
ISBN 978-0-7531-7691-7 (pb)

Death and the Cornish Fiddler

Deryn Lake

The spring of 1765 brings a sense of recovery to the recently widowed Apothecary John Rawlings, but this does not last for long: a young child disappears in strange circumstances at the Helstone Floral (Furry) Dance, and a blind musician is never far away. Whilst this mysterious figure intrigues Rawlings, the case of the missing child alarms him: he feels he must do all in his power to attempt to rescue the young life.

Rawlings is just about to give up the child for lost when a courtesan dies one night. An examination reveals that she was smothered, and the hunt is on to find which of her lovers was responsible. Accompanied by one of them, John travels to Redruth and stumbles across a coven who practise the black arts. Recognising some of its members from the Furry Dance, he returns to Helstone, this time to find his own daughter in deadly peril . . .

ISBN 978-0-7531-7700-6 (hb)
ISBN 978-0-7531-7701-3 (pb)

Lie by Moonlight

Amanda Quick

During an investigation into a woman's death, gentleman thief turned private inquiry agent Ambrose Wells finds himself at Aldwick Castle - in the midst of chaos. The building is in flames. Men are dead. And a woman and four young girls are fleeing on horseback.

A confirmed loner, Ambrose nevertheless finds himself taking Miss Concordia Glade and her young charges under his wing. With their lives at risk, he insists they must remain in hiding until he is able to unravel the truth behind their recent imprisonment at the castle.

Concordia has never met anyone like Ambrose Wells before. He is bold, clever and inscrutable - even to the perceptive gaze of a professional teacher such as herself. He is also her only hope of protection from the unscrupulous men who are after them - powerful, shadowy figures who will stop at nothing to get what they want.

ISBN 978-0-7531-7457-9 (hb)
ISBN 978-0-7531-7458-6 (pb)